FIRE WILL FALL

OTHER NOVELS BY CAROL PLUM-UCCI

Streams of Babel

The Night My Sister Went Missing

The She

What Happened to Lani Garver

The Body of Christopher Creed

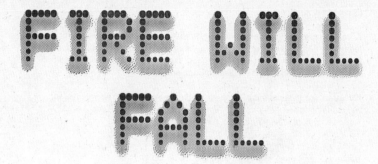

FIRE WILL FALL

Carol Plum-Ucci

HOUGHTON MIFFLIN HARCOURT

Boston   New York

To my wonderfully patient
editor, Karen Grove

Copyright © 2010 by Carol Plum-Ucci

All rights reserved. Published in the United States by Graphia, an imprint of Houghton Mifflin Harcourt Publishing Company. Originally published in hardcover in the United States by Harcourt Children's Books, an imprint of Houghton Mifflin Harcourt Publishing Company, 2010.

For information about permission to reproduce selections from this book, write to Permissions, Houghton Mifflin Harcourt Publishing Company, 215 Park Avenue South, New York, New York 10003.

Graphia and the Graphia logo are registered trademarks of Houghton Mifflin Harcourt Publishing Company.

www.hmhbooks.com

The text of this book is set in Minion.

The Library of Congress has cataloged the hardcover edition as follows:
Plum-Ucci, Carol, 1957–
Fire will fall / Carol Plum-Ucci.
p. cm.
Sequel to: Streams of Babel.
Summary: Moved to a mansion in the South Jersey Pine Barrens, four teenagers, trying to recover from being poisoned by terrorists, struggle with health issues, personal demons, and supernatural events, as operatives try to track down the terror cell.

[1. Bioterrorism—Fiction. 2. Terrorism—Fiction. 3. Communicable diseases—Fiction. 4. Spies—Fiction. 5. Interpersonal relations—Fiction. 6. Supernatural—Fiction. 7. New Jersey—Fiction.] I. Title.
PZ7.P7323Fi   2010
[Fic]—dc22   2009023854

ISBN 978-0-15-216562-8 hc
ISBN 978-0-547-55007-7 pb

Manufactured in the United States of America
DOM 10 9 8 7 6 5 4 3 2 1
4500288861

Acknowledgments

To Angela Osborne and Angela Piniera, thanks for your editorial input at times when my brain was in six pieces. I vow never to torture you again (fingers crossed behind my back). To Dr. Robyn Tiger, thank you for answering my medical questions day after day; I guess you thought those e-mails would never stop. To my husband, Rick, and my daughter Abbey, thanks for not killing me for always being off in my cave writing this book. It sure took long enough, eh?

Thanks for all!
Luv ya, Carol

ONE

SCOTT EBERMAN
FRIDAY, MAY 3, 2002
7:05 P.M.
TRINITY FALLS, NEW JERSEY

I DON'T BELIEVE IN OMENS. So when the rain fell in buckets against the living room window as I waited for our ride, I kept telling myself it wasn't a shadow of things to come; I was not leaving Trinity Falls forever. I'd be back by fall. *We were all coming back.*

The limo pulled up to the curb a minute later, and I dashed out my front door. My head was soaked two steps later. A door at the far back of the endless car opened, and a girl's hand beckoned like crazy. I dove through the door, and Rain Steckerman quickly tugged at one of my soaked sleeves so I could yank my arm out.

The driver slammed the car door, but through the glaze I noticed the door to my house was wide open and my two bags stood just inside. Nobody else was in there. This is what can happen when nine of the fifty-two pills you're taking list memory loss as a side effect.

"Let the limo driver get them!" Rain said quickly, drowning my curses. "Be rich and famous—just for this forty-five-minute drive."

I watched the driver run up the walk, grab the two swollen garbage bags, and shut the door. I don't own luggage—that's how rich I am. As for the famous part—I'm not a rock star or anything you'd want to be. I'm just a guy who lives in a small South Jersey town that found itself in a horror flick two months back.

Some unheard-of international terror cell decided our town of mostly professional, well-educated Americans would be a good place to conduct an experiment. They poisoned the water, hoping to kill every person within the five-block area off one main water vein. They only killed two, so some people like to say they failed miserably. I don't agree with that. I was half-way through paramedic training this spring when my brother and I and Rain and Cora Holman were diagnosed as "Stage Four Toxic." We never know whether we'll wake up feeling okay or like we have some butt-kicking flu. Nearly a hundred Stage Twos and Threes were diagnosed in Trinity, and even the Stage Threes responded surprisingly well to antiviral medication. Stage Four is another term for "a real challenge to cure, though doctors on four continents are trying." There is no Stage Five.

I slid my arms back into my soaked sleeves and intentionally waited until the driver got around to the trunk and popped it.

"He forgot to turn off the light." I dashed from the limo, and the rainfall drowned out the end of Rain's "Wait! My dad can take care of—"

I threw open the door, ran upstairs into the bathroom for a bath towel, and shoved it under my jacket as I took two stairs at a time down, hurrying. I reached for the living room light but stopped to survey the room before switching it off. Mom had moved us here from Las Vegas thirteen years ago, when I was six. So many kids had sat on this worn-out gray couch. We'd watched so many football games, baseball games, hockey games being won or lost here, over so many bags of Doritos and microwave popcorn. My paramedic squad had stood in the kitchen shooting the bull on so many non-busy nights. I had been in training, and my squad loved Mom's mint iced tea.

Mom's chair . . . I moved over to it, knew it still smelled like Mom because I'd stuck my nose to it a couple of times and caught my brother, Owen, doing it, too. My mom had drunk enough poisoned water to move beyond Stage Four. I banged the chair lightly with my fist instead of reaching for one last deep inhale. It's a smell you don't forget.

"Sorry!" I hollered as I raced back to the limo. The driver held the door for me again. His rain poncho didn't cover his extra-polite smile, which reminded me of a melting wax face in a horror movie.

Rain didn't look so thrilled with me now. She sidled up to Cora, whose mom died the day before mine did. Cora was wearing a sweater with a scarf around her neck, despite that it was seventy degrees outside. The limo was long, with most of the seating in one row from back to front, so Cora and Rain were facing sideways. My brother, Owen, sat sideways also, but up close to the front with his head on the backrest and his eyes shut, though I could see him shaking his head slowly back and forth over my actions.

The three of them had just been released from St. Ann's ten minutes ago. I'd gotten permission to be released earlier, having had a symptom-free day. I had come home to close up the house, get some more pictures of Mom, and pick up whatever I'd missed during our eight weeks in St. Ann's. The three of them were graduating seniors, and even though there was only two years' difference in our ages, I was eons more mature. Mom always said I was born thirty. I'm not sure the nurses would have let them come home by themselves.

The driver pulled away as I unfolded the towel, and I made certain not to give my house a last, longing look. Instead, I watched Cora while I pulled off the soaked jacket and threw the towel over my neck. She was reading get-well cards. The four of us had gotten more than fifteen thousand cards from Americans who watched the news or read *Time, Newsweek,* or *People* magazines. We tried to read all the cards and letters, but Cora was way ahead of the rest of us. She'd give us a heads-up sometimes if it was a name we all knew, like John Mayer or former vice president Al Gore or Brittany Murphy. She'd wave the card, and we'd pass it around. We got telegrams from dignitaries of over a hundred countries. All of that kept us going.

But with no remarkable improvements in our conditions yet and being moved to a more permanent locale, our foursome was getting harder to buoy. Right now, Cora was reading tensely, waiting for Rain to explode on me so she could pretend not to notice.

"Hope your little campaign of refusing help from others is worth it," Rain lectured on cue. In other words, her dad certainly would have noticed the lights being on in our house while on his way home tonight and would have turned them off and locked the door. "Now you'll wake up with the Throat from Hell tomorrow."

"Tomorrow is not important," I stated, wiping off the back of my neck and my hair with the towel. "It's always today, and today, I'm having a four-star day. Besides. Acting like an ass has therapeutic value once in a while."

Rain slowly reached out her hand, and I gave her skin. That's the good thing about Rain—she can sympathize with just about anyone. Four-star day meant it had been a symptom-free day, at least for me. I glanced at Cora again. She said nothing, but her sweater and scarf were telltale: four-star wasn't for her.

Rain moved to a little refrigerator under the TV, saying, "What's your pleasure? Coke? Diet Coke? Sprite? Or water?"

"Whatever."

"C'mon, don't be a party pooper. Club soda . . ." She made a big deal out of filling a plastic cup from a silver ice bucket and pouring Perrier over the top, though her eyes were glassy enough to reflect the little overhead light. Tears or fever? I figured tears. She seemed keyed up, like she was trying to distract herself from a horrible mood, which she'd had on a daily basis over the past three weeks. Rain was an extremist. It was always laughter or tears, with very little in between.

Still, she handed me both the cup and the bottle with both pinkies high in the air. The limo was compliments of Rain's dad, Alan Steckerman. He had been an FBI director in southern Jersey for many years, but after the 9/11 terrorist attacks last September, he moved over to the newly formed United States Intelligence Coalition, joining with agents from the FBI, the CIA, and all branches of military intelligence. There are at least two USIC supervisors in every state, and they're supposed to guard against, or in this case solve, acts of terror.

The limo is Mr. Steckerman's way of saying, "We're working

on it. In the meantime, think positive." They'd already made twelve arrests. All had been foot soldiers, but I tried to remind myself that the big guns could be caught any day.

I held up my cup, and Rain got the idea, throwing my bottle cap at Owen so he would open his eyes and raise his Coke can off his knee. Cora held up her cup, and they all looked at me. I'm supposed to be the strong one.

"Here's to the future," I said as my brain went into cliché autopilot. I knew the risks we faced better than they did. I wanted to keep it positive, but the words weren't there.

"To the future," they joined in, but their voices flickered.

I forced myself onward. "We all have mixed feelings about going out of town." Rain quietly ducked her head.

We were being taken to a place about twenty miles up the coast from Trinity Falls, a dark corner of the Pine Barrens, where the nearest house would be a half mile inland from us. The Kellerton mansion was on the historical register. New Jersey, apparently, doesn't like spending a lot of money on historic restoration of cool places, but they'll spend it for far-out health care these days. The people in the Atlantic County Historic Society offered this old mansion to "house state residents physically traumatized by an act of terror," probably realizing that it would be restored pretty fast if the state agreed.

The bottom line: Rain, Cora, Owen, and I will get to live in a beautiful mansion on fifty acres that ease up to Great Bay, like we're rich, even if we're not. The historical society wants to smooch us, not that I mind their little agenda. Everyone's got an agenda. If I feel powerless to help myself, at least I can help the little old ladies of the Atlantic County Historic Society.

Rain, on the other hand, would be farther from her friends, which meant fewer visits, and the most beautiful place in the world couldn't replace those daily gatherings—not in her mind.

I went on. "But we'll make this work. We're *all* coming out on the other side."

"Hear, hear," they cried.

"No more fights," I said, eyes firmly on Rain.

Slowly, she turned her glass to Owen and muttered, "Sorry."

"Me, too." He clinked her cup but wouldn't look her in the eyes.

I had no idea what she was apologizing for this time, or what he was forgiving her for. Between the two of them it had been a daily dropping of bombs over the past two weeks. Rain had lived kitty-corner to us for thirteen years, and they'd always been friends. At this point, she and Owen were just sick of each other.

"Listen, guys. We're going to have to readjust to more quiet, more leisure time . . ." I cleared my throat. "All I'm saying is that the more you two fight, the more wear and tear you put on yourselves. Whatever it is, either talk it out or let it drop."

Rain looked ready to explode. Finally, she kur-powed. It was about Owen again. "I just hope there's an extra TV. I don't mind that he tapes sports on *his* TV and then comes in to watch *my* TV so he doesn't miss either game. I don't mind that he takes up half my bed when I'm trying to take a nap because he's freezing and wants part of my blanket. I don't even mind that he goes from cold to hot and kicks off his smelly socks under my blanket—"

"My sweat socks do not smell," he insisted.

She ignored him. "And I don't even care that in the middle of the night, I'm kicking sweat socks out of my sheets, okay? All I want is that when our lives are upsetting me . . . I want him to understand, to . . . to be there for me."

"Rain. I am so there," he said in loud annoyance, gesturing at the roof. "What do you want me to do? Play the violin?"

"Something like that!" She sniffed.

"I don't play the violin, Katherine!" That was Rain's real name, which she hated, and nobody ever called her that. So my brother used it only to make his most worthy points.

Frankly, I sided more with my brother. Not that kicking your sweat socks off in someone else's sheets smacks of diplomacy, but I figured Rain was asking the impossible with this "be there" line. She was laying the burden on Owen to gift-wrap her peace of mind and serve it up to her. You can only give *yourself* peace of mind.

Today, peace had been hard for me to grab hold of. I had left the hospital to visit my house and put together photos of my mom and Owen and me—from back when we thought a problem was Mom doing so many *pro bono* legal cases that the electric bill was late. Now I was catching the Throat from Hell again.

I swallowed a couple of cold gulps of my club soda, and my mouth went into let-it-rip mode. "Rain. One of these days, you have to stop crying. Find your maturity. I've heard lots of girls cry . . . I've probably made some girls cry. But I feel like I've been living for the past few weeks with the Philadelphia Symphony Orchestra playing three different songs at once—"

"Leave her alone, Scott," my brother kicked in. Great. I was standing up for him, and he took up for Rain. I think this is called a circle jerk.

My brother shut his eyes. I could see his lips moving, implying that he was praying again, his usual solution to our problems. You can see how well that had been working. Cora just kept reading a get-well card like mad. Rain was sniffing, sniffing, sniffing, which is a martyr's version of crying, and even more annoying. I had heard girls say her line to me before, usually when they were crying about something. "Why can't you just *be* there for me?" It was vague—intentionally so, I'd always thought—and nothing I did qualified as "being there."

We need to find a cure—for them. We need to find the terrorists who got away—for me.

I toasted the ceiling of the limo again, the raindrops falling in pellets against it, as I fought off a screechy feeling of helplessness.

TWO

CORA HOLMAN
FRIDAY, MAY 3, 2002
7:10 P.M.
ROUTE 9

WHILE MY EYES REMAINED FOCUSED on a stack of thirty-some get-well cards, my heart was focused on the growing distance between us and St. Ann's. I could feel the tension rolling away from me with each mile that passed. I was being freed from yet another source of anxiety.

Two months back, I'd been freed from loneliness. At least three of Rain and Owen's friends had visited every day since March, and they kept implying to me, in the nicest of ways, that I was now their friend, too. I'd been a loner in high school who'd masked my social inadequacies by being a joiner. I'd been in thirteen ECs (extracurriculars), was president of none, and worked nights at Acme. This illness had had an ironic effect; it sometimes seemed like I'd paid a price with my body to break free from my solitary confinement. I didn't mind as much as the others.

My mother's death in March helped me, too, I must confess. Aleese had shown up at our door penniless when I was twelve, and my grandmother, who'd raised me, died when I was fourteen. I spent my high school years hiding the fact that my only existing relative was a morphine addict who spoke to the walls in Middle Eastern languages, something to do with her journalism job overseas. She had refused to ever let me call her "mother." She was the first victim of the water poisoning in Trinity, and I did not miss her much. I had loved sitting in the middle of Rain and Owen's crowd at St. Ann's, saying little yet never feeling unwelcome.

And yet I live with a bad memory of the place that Rain and Owen don't have. I fell into a coma my first night there in early March, and when I came out of it, a man stood beside my bed. He was reciting beautiful poetry. Yet the man came into my cubicle with some sort of dark energy, and the only way I can describe it is that it could wake a person out of a coma. Stranger still is the memory of him pulling a hypodermic needle out of his suit pocket and telling me he was going to kill me. And suddenly my ICU pod was filled with people who wrestled the man to the wall while Scott Eberman pulled tubes from me.

Mr. Steckerman made light of the whole thing later, saying they caught a violent man out in the corridors and that he was now in jail and we have nothing to worry about. I wasn't supposed to remember that he was in my room, I guess. I knew he was a member of ShadowStrike. His face and news of him were splattered on our TV screens for weeks.

Our drugs offer us as much confusion as relief, but I sense that if I speak of that man, an assassin named Richard Awali, I will bring more of his demons down on me. He's like that bogeyman in your closet when you're a child of whom you dare not speak. Because if you do, he will hear you, feed on your fear, and materialize.

I embraced the idea of a new home where any stranger coming up the road in a car could be heard a mile away. I felt glad to lose that constant exposure to strangers moving about the corridors. And yet I sympathize with Rain and Owen. It's my job to try to bring them some happiness.

"Matt Damon." I held the card up, shaking it slightly, my tradition. I had two interesting cards in my hand. "He says he wants to visit us when we're feeling up to it. He wants to make a movie about what happened in Trinity."

I passed the card to Rain, who opened it cautiously. Up until maybe two weeks ago, all the movie rights messages had thrilled her. She passed it to Scott.

"I knew about this. He called a couple of times," she said.

"You spoke to him?" Scott asked. She ought to have told us that much.

"No, the nurses did. My dad was going to call him back, but I told him not to. Not yet. I haven't . . . I just . . ." She stumbled for a thought. "I don't know if I want our lives all blasted across a movie screen. People will feel sorry for us."

Nobody argued.

"I think people who get this much attention should have won the Olympics or something," she continued. "I feel like a cheat. I don't want attention this way."

So much for Matt Damon. My second note was a trump card I had set in my lap only seconds after they started bickering. I figured I would throw it down only if the first one didn't work. It was personal.

"Jeremy Ireland." I waved the card, and I could feel all eyes open and shift to me. Not a celebrity in the traditional sense, but Jeremy was interesting enough.

"What does he say?" Rain asked.

Mission accomplished. They were all watching me. But old habits die hard, and as usual when my mother became the topic of conversation, my mind went to dull gray and my voice trembled with anxiety.

"'Dear Cora,'" I started.

Thank you for your very honest portrayal of your mother in your last e-mail. I know that was hard for you. I am still trying to piece together how the Aleese I knew became the Aleese you knew. As I said to you at the end of my visit, the accident that cost your mother her arm also cost her any ability to proceed as a photographer, and photojournalism had been her life. Before that accident, she was addicted to nothing except her own adrenaline. I do wish she hadn't abused you verbally at every turn.

I do believe you. She abused all of us at times, but she was the Queen of Hearts during the years I traveled with her. We were all mesmerized by her courage, her willingness to risk her life constantly for the betterment of humanity, and we allowed for her sharp tongue, figuring she was entitled to that indulgence. This will sound like a very strange thing for me to say, but *I am quite certain she loved you.*

My hand floated to my throat—not that I was actually thinking of crying. My mother had done little for the four-plus years she lived with me except lie on the couch, take injections, hallucinate, and try to shock me with outspoken and vulgar comments. Even after my grandmother died, I had never spiraled into reflections on whether Aleese had loved me.

Hence, my throat was tightening over what I perceived as a lie from Jeremy Ireland. I had reached out to him two weeks ago in a blast of honesty that had left me bedridden for two complete days after I sent the e-mail.

My eyes were drawn to Scott's, as his were piercing, while Rain and Owen merely looked enthralled.

He dropped his head back. "Jesus Christ, Cora. Don't do this to yourself."

The card fell limp in my lap. I'm certain he was thinking of a couple of our group therapy sessions, when I had been put to the test of talking about my mother honestly. Dr. Hollis and the three of them would sit patiently through what words I could come up with, little more than seizurelike prattle that seemed vague and disconnected. As much as I'd hated Aleese's presence, I'd dreamed of her almost nightly at St. Ann's. In her death she had become a great lecturer, invading my dreams and telling me how useless I was, and I'd hallucinated her once when we were on too strong a narcotic for joint pain. After that, I'd asked myself if I had been better off when she was alive.

Still, I'd kept Aleese's drug addiction a secret from everyone until the day she died, and now I was reading a letter like this aloud. It made sense to say I'd made some headway. But still, when my head bumped to an honest thought, it would flutter away into some invisible mist before I could form the words. It was always torture, this business of being honest about my mother. It would have been easier, I suppose, to be honest about the terrorist beside my bed. But over the years, I'd learned to find my peace in secrets, not in blurting. I sensed I might have a better chance of breaking hard habits in the remote place where we were being sent.

Scott took the card from my hand, closed it, dropped it into his own lap, and gave me a look I often enjoyed. I called it his "knowing" look, a smirk laced with some vague affection, the look that saved me from having to form words and syllables and sense. I could visualize that smirk after some atrocious nightmare and lull myself back to sleep with the image.

His bottom lip was longer than his top lip and loped lazily on one side, whether he was smiling outright or smirking like this. Toss that smile in with unflinching brown eyes, a running back's build, and endless charm and you could see why he'd been up to his ears in girls before he graduated. But he'd been miles out of my league, as well as an upperclassman. I was out of arm's reach in this limo, or he would have followed up his look with what always satisfied me—a squeeze on the back of my neck or a swat on my hair. His feet were stretched out, reaching to my ankles, and he might have tapped me there, as a way of telling me, "You don't have to say it." I lay in wait for these moments on a daily basis. Sometimes I was rewarded; sometimes I wasn't. This time I wasn't.

But Rain reached into his lap for my card. "Let us see the rest of it!"

I felt vaguely victorious that she was distracted from her problems. Yet I ached to do my thinking in private, work on being open and honest when I had my thoughts in order and my words rehearsed.

Scott merely moved the card to his far side, out of Rain's reach, his eyes shut.

"Why not?" she demanded. "She was doing fine!"

"No, she wasn't," he said.

THREE

GOD, I don't know what we need. Just bring it.

I'm usually better at stating requests to the Father & Friends, which is my term for God and Mom and my favorite saints, St. Joan and St. Stephen. I imagine them constantly watching over us. But I knew my brother was staring at me, and it's hard to think while waiting for him to bellow about how helpless I look. I wouldn't say he was exactly mad at God. You have to decide that divinity is real before you can target it with your anger.

Cora should read her personal stuff to herself first—I agreed. Her mom could make her nuts. But I didn't want Scott yanking Rain's chain. I knew what was really upsetting her tonight, and he didn't. He clumps all her upsets together, just because they look the same on the outside. She has been crying a lot lately. It can be exhausting, and that's being overly polite. After three days of it, you can want to tape her mouth shut and yank all her hair out. But I really felt bad for her tonight, due to her take on some things our favorite nurse, Haley Gibbs, told us when we were packing up our belongings.

Miss Haley was actually packing for me, because I'd just come out of a Headache from Hell at four thirty, and you feel like a ball of hot melting wax after one. I was half asleep in the chair. Cora and Rain came in to see what they could do, so Miss Haley sat them down.

"I've been elected by Dr. Godfrey to give you the speeches," she said with this huge smile that led us to believe it would all be good. She started with what we already knew. "We've found the means to level off this germ so that nobody is getting any worse. Hence, you're getting out of here. What we really want is for you to start trying to lead as normal lives as possible out at the Kellerton House. On days when you're not symptomatic, have your friends up. You'll have a two-hour window twice a day where you don't take any medication. Go out. Take walks. Go shopping. You can go anywhere you want in the car, but the nurse goes, too, if it exceeds that two hours."

"Gee, that sounds 'normal.'" Rain chuckled, though after living two months in two rooms in St. Ann's, chronically visited by doctors and research representatives from four continents, it was a leap toward normalcy.

"You don't have to wear gloves and masks anymore. You can hug your friends." Miss Haley nudged Rain. We'd actually gotten the word last week that Q3 could not be passed through the air, though they weren't sure about bodily fluids. Rain had demanded a minute-long hug from everyone who showed up.

"But keep all that to a minimum for your own sakes," Miss Haley went on. "Your resistance is low. You could seriously compromise your health with a germ that someone else's body is fighting quite well. Don't let people sneeze on you. And *don't* swap spit, and certainly *don't* swap anything more personal—not with friends or among yourselves."

Among yourselves. Even I admit that had an incestuous ring to it, and Rain didn't want to dignify it with a response.

Rain moved past it quickly. "I just want my life back. How soon until they expect us to be back to normal?" She had asked that only yesterday. And the day before and the day before. The answer was always, "Soon, we hope!"

She didn't expect the answer to be any different, I guess, and her cheerful face suddenly fell under the weight of some thought. The words "don't swap spit" kind of hung in the air. I sensed it was related. You don't usually have to wait long to hear what Rain is thinking. Out it came.

"Miss Haley. Are you . . . trying to say that what we have works sort of like an STD?"

Sexually transmitted disease. Ew. My mind doesn't twist the way Rain's does. We drank Q3 from faucets. We didn't pick it up in the back seat of a car. But Miss Haley's smile wandered around her face.

"Well, you can't think of it that way," she stumbled.

"Really? How am I supposed to think of it?" Rain's tone was edgy.

"You're supposed to think you have a *germ.* You'd be told the same thing if you had mono. Look, every major drug research company in the world is contributing to your cure. Whoever hits the jackpot will get major publicity, will rule the drug industry. Believe me, they're working day and night."

"But Miss Haley. Could we have this thing forever?" Rain asked.

The answer to that: *Yes, yes, yes.* We'd been told quite a few times: There may be no way to "cure" the germ; we might spend our lives trying to "control" the germ. It just had not been put in a sexual context before, though now that it was here, I thought, *hel-lo?*

Then I stood up. "I don't even care right now. Except, I'm afraid I *will* start caring if Rain doesn't give it a rest—"

Which got Rain started on how I can't talk about anything, and in a flash, Miss Haley was between us, pushing me toward the elevator. "You go, and let me talk to her."

Cora opted to follow me. She patted my arm while we waited for the elevator, radiating sympathy. Cora is a giant sympathy machine. She even said, "I'm sure you guys will be back to your normal lives very soon."

The way Cora talked, you would almost think this whole adventure had everything to do with us and nothing to do with her. It melted my heart usually, but now I was distracted.

Okay, so we're getting out, but we're in Convent Land, can't have sex, can't even kiss, I thought, trying the concept on for size. Nothing had really changed for any of us, except Scott, because he'd been sort of a wild man. I tried to focus on that nothing-had-changed part, but even *my* mind was going, *Five weeks? Five years? Twenty years?*

So in the limo, I was pretty upset with Miss Haley and Dr. Godfrey. Some things are better left unsaid. And I knew Rain was feeling better than me physically and if I was doing the five-weeks-five-years-twenty-years thing, then surely she was, too.

Cora had set three stacks of cards on the seat between her and me. I knew her system: One stack was "opened," the second was "unopened," and the last was "addressed to one of us instead of all four of us." Some people were nice enough to send four cards. I took a few from the "not addressed to all of us" pile. Three for me and one for Rain were right on top. I got more mail than the other three, though the reasons left me paralyzed. This first one was pretty typical.

Dear Owen,

I am fifteen and I live in Nebraska and I saw you in People mag and on the TV and Internet. I think you should be in movies. I can't believe this happened to someone hot like yourself. When you recover I will go out with you, here is my phone number—

I tossed it beside me. The first month, I got several of these a day. At first I thought, *That's nice. People are trying to make us feel better,* and every girl thought she was the only one to say that, I guess. But I was the only one of us who got a steady stream on this theme. They had started driving me batty, but especially right now. I dropped the other two addressed to me on top of it and picked from the "unopened/addressed to all of us" pile.

Dear Cora, Rain, Owen and Scott:

Then came the rhyming part. If we read all the Hallmark rhymes, we would never get to the bottom of our mail.

I hope they catch all the guys who did this to you. No lethal injections. They deserve to be hung. On television.

I laid that one aside, too. Quickly. If I saw a card that mentioned "the guys who did this" I almost always closed it really fast and forced my brain somewhere else. Rain and Cora and I decided we did better to think of ourselves as merely "under the weather" as opposed to "victimized." Because sometimes I would start thinking of "those guys" and something like a violent earthquake would start, though it was inside me. I'm supposed to be the guy who can put myself in anyone's shoes, including a terrorist's. I'd like to keep it that way.

Rain, Miss Talk It Out, couldn't stand her silent self any longer. Out her comment flew, like one of those squirrels that gets in your walls and shoots out from under the bed in the middle of the night, hissing at you.

"What was the point in Miss Haley saying all of that? What a bummer."

Hiss, scratch, hiss, hiss.

"All of what?" Scott murmured without opening his eyes.

"Ohhh . . ." she said snidely. "She basically said we're in the Clap Club. The Gonorrhea Guild. Why was I so dumb for so many years? Now I'll have no memories. I'm one of those girls who had, like, two sexual thoughts in high school. One sophomore year, and one junior year."

I smiled. She was probably exaggerating, but not by much.

Scott probably smiled on the inside. "Keep it that way."

"I think I was just getting around to my senior year thought when Danny Hall broke up with me. I was always thinking, 'I'll just . . . think of it after that next big game.' When you're on four sports that win like crazy, that doesn't leave you much time. Now it'll be like telling myself, 'Don't think of an elephant.' What do you think of?"

"Are you thinking of getting laid tomorrow?" Scott asked drowsily.

"*Ew.*"

"Next week?"

"What, do I look like Jeanine?"

"Jeanine the Machine," Scott droned, trying to smile, but he didn't quite make it.

"You're missing the point," Rain said.

"No, we're not. Nobody is missing any point. Except maybe Cora . . ." Scott opened one eye to gaze at Little Miss Reading Mail Like Crazy. To Cora, chickens don't lay eggs. She ignored him nicely. "Live in the now, Rain."

I agreed. "You've got your life. Worry about the rest later."

I was glad Cora was sitting between us. I was suspicious Rain had wanted to hit me a few times recently, and her energy wafted into my space, making me pull farther back into the corner.

"This is exactly what I'm talking about," she said, doing that sniffing thing again.

Just. Shut. Up. I shut my eyes to fake asleep, but that didn't silence her.

"Why is it lately that you can't feel bad about something at the same time I feel bad about it? When I'm up, you're down. When I'm down, all you can do is make really glib statements like 'you've got your life.' Why can't you ever be on my wavelength?"

Because whatever your opinion is, you suck up all the oxygen in the room. There's nothing left to say and no air left to say it with.

"Well?" she kept going.

"I don't think that *is* glib, Rain," I argued, then stammered over what I'd planned to say next. It was that I went around all the time thinking of things that we had to be thankful for. I'd gotten the idea from my Young Life leader, Dan Hadley. Young Life is a church youth group that meets on Wednesdays. I'd been spiraling the day Dan came to visit me at St. Ann's. Dan had survived three bouts of leukemia as a kid.

He suggested, "When you get like this, thank God for everything you can think of that's good. Even things you might never have noticed otherwise, like that bird that just flew by your window. You'll feel your energy shift. You won't be so consumed by those negative what-ifs."

To my amazement, it honestly worked . . . most of the time. It had since become a habit. But when I had tried to share this with Scott, I was accused of being "religious," like that's some sin. And Rain just wasn't there yet, wasn't thinking of God in any terms except that he had allowed her senior year to be train-wrecked.

In the past week, when Rain couldn't get what she wanted out of me, she resorted to twisting the knife. "You never talk horny. Sometimes I think you're gay."

My eyes snapped open. Last November, Rain had called me from this party, all crying, saying Jeanine had single-handedly finished off a bottle of Boone's Farm wine in fifteen minutes and had now been in the backyard "on her knees" for going on half an hour. In our neck of the woods, "on your knees" does not mean throwing up. Jeanine is one of those people who should not ever drink. So, I drove over there and pulled her away from these guys by the hair. Rain and I took her to Wawa for a cappuccino and an in-your-face fest. Some people went around school afterward saying I was gay. Sometimes I feel there is this "charming" idea in our "charming" American culture that there are no plain and simple good guys out there. If you don't line up in the backyard for the Jeanine show, it's because you're gay.

Scott came to life, and I had to admire him for handling this so well. He used to get angry all the time. Now he couldn't afford to. He had an aneurysm in his head that could blow under too much stress.

He simply said, "Rain. Stop calling names. Stop torturing my brother. I can get you a shrink tomorrow if you want to talk about this, but the fact is . . . nobody in this car wants to talk about it. If you can't button it up, go sit in the front."

He laid his head back, letting out a long breath of pent-up energy. He obviously had something on his mind, and this was all a big distraction.

My brother can be intense. Even his jokes have a kind of backhanded feel to them. But any subject change had to be a good one. "What's up, bro?"

FOUR

SCOTT EBERMAN
FRIDAY, MAY 3, 2002
7:22 P.M.
ROUTE 9

"I NEED ... A JOB," I said.

Rain picked up her yearbook and stared at a page. Her friends had gotten everyone in the class of around six hundred kids to sign it, and the rule was, "You can't put 'get well soon.' You have to be original." Every page was literally covered with pen scrawl.

"You mean . . . a paycheck?" she asked impatiently, obviously still steaming. "You don't need money, not until you get better."

I ignored the limitations of her vision. "How can I talk your dad into letting me work for USIC? Whatever it is they're doing, I bet it's not all that hard. Making phone calls . . . checking up on leads about where those guys are hiding . . ."

She let the book drop down and stared at me, torn between her natural sympathy and her desire to get even for my pushing the pause button on her sore subject of we-may-never-have-sex, ever. Her tone wasn't spiteful. "In all the years my dad was in the FBI, I never, ever heard him spill one work-related secret. How likely do you think it is that he's going to spill USIC secrets about terrorists to you?"

That was putting it bluntly. "Thanks for your help and support."

Score: Even. She broke into a smile. "Meagan Monahan wrote, 'Thanks for always being the designated driver. When you come back, the whole hockey team is taking you out and being *your* designated driver!' Dang. Why did I waste all of high school being the designated driver?"

"Must be nice to have nothing to think about except high school." I shouldn't have said it, but blurting had replaced yelling in my life by necessity.

I was reminded of one strange miracle: Having already had one aneurysm removed from my heart while another lived on in my head, I had fewer of our weird headaches than the other three. I believe the reason is that I'd found ways to be a fighter. I was proactive in the medication we were being given, and even did online research on drug cocktails that might better restore us to our former selves. But I had gone about as far as I could with all of that. A cocktail was being designed, but wouldn't be ready until September—or that was the first promised date from any of the research teams.

I shut my eyes and lay my head back. I had not been in a limo before, ever. My girlfriend of the hour around my senior prom, Sandy Copeland, was the daughter of the fire chief. The two of us and Ronnie Dobbins and his date thought it would be a riot to go on the back of the fire truck. We were not the most elegant folks to arrive, but we'd been the loudest. So, the limo was cool. Under the circumstances. But while I tried to pretend we were rich, I'm not a great pretender.

The car turned, finally. I lowered the window a couple of inches, just to smell the reality. Branches swished against the car, flinging raindrops onto my face. *My god, this is out in the sticks,* my head echoed, and with each passing minute I felt a little more sorry for Rain. I had been out here once recently with Mr. Steckerman on a four-star day, but the drive itself was now gone from me. Meds.

Finally, the road opened up very wide, and beyond it was a pile of black boxes that reached up to the treetops, with little orange dots in the windows suggesting candles, though this was modern times and you had to infer they were the plug-in types of candles. It looked like a small city of candlelit windows in some sort of castle. It was to be home for god knows how long. Or how short.

FIVE

I LAY ON MY BED looking for the hundredth time at the cover of *People* magazine, the one from March featuring the four Trinity Falls victims. I imagine a lot of other kids stare at this picture, too. The reason? You look at them and think, "Could they *really* have this illness?"

You read this gag-inspiring list of autoimmune symptoms they live with, and you have to flip back to the cover again—and back and forth from the pictures to the writing. Their hair is so shiny. Their skin isn't dinged up. They don't naturally have a drop of ugly in them. But the universe has been known to play cruel jokes on people like that, and they stand as evidence.

There does appear to be something kind of wrong—but it's hard to pinpoint. You have to look closely. They're kind of pale and have what looks like a slight bruising at the corners of their mouths and around their eyes. You'd almost think it was shadows. Then, there's some sort of translucent or fluorescent factor to their skin that you can't help staring at. It's not gross. If you're a sci-fi head, you'd say they look a little radioactive. If you're a goth, you might say they look like pretty vampires. It almost looks like a strength instead of a weakness, but that's only if you're using imagination.

Reality is that they live like early AIDS patients who haven't hit the throes of it yet, only no magazine has had the audacity to make a comparison between their Q3 and the AIDS virus. Their drug protocol is very similar, and yet it's politically correct to hope that the Trinity Four, as they're called, will be cured relatively quickly. Q3 is a cruel virus, allowing them to feel normal on lots of days. But as soon as they get their hopes up that they're improving, they get flu symptoms and slamming headaches. I've got the inside scoop on them. For a number of reasons, the Trinity Four is personal to me.

I laid the magazine down on my chest, feeling sleep coming on. I was almost asleep, because I'm pretty regulated. I lie down at 10:00 and almost never see my digital clock hit 10:05. Tonight, I heard Shahzad Hamdani's keypad clattering from across the hall in my mom's old room. Hamdani is not regulated at all—up, down, up, down, all night, since there hasn't been a need for a schedule. In Pakistan, you're allowed to quit school after eighth grade, so Hamdani hasn't seen the inside of the Halls of Knowledge in three years, except for his first day of school in America, when he met me. Our hacking escapades got us in trouble immediately, and hence it was also his last day. He says that even in Karachi he did his best hacking and v-spying between two in the morning and sunrise. He generally knows to be quiet between 10:00 and 10:05, but once I'm out, I'm not an evil prick about his noise.

"Hel-lo?" I hollered across the hall to him. "My five minutes, please? Do I ask for a lot in this thing we call our life?"

"*Yerklun un stivach,*" he mumbled, or some such thing, which could mean anything from "one more minute" to "bite me" in one of the twenty or so languages he can converse in, not including dialects. It's a gift. He jokes that he was born crying in three languages.

I fought my compulsive desire to blast him, stuffed the magazine under my pillow where it belonged, and headed across the hall. The clincher wasn't *what* he was saying but the fact that he wasn't speaking English. Hamdani only forgets what language he's in when he's totally absorbed.

He was now staring into the glow of his screen, his light off. His profile glowed blue, and his fist was pushed up against his mouth as he thought. His hand flopped down on the mouse, and he drummed his fingers on top.

I reached for the switch and turned on the overhead, which only caused him to flinch and lean closer to the screen. "*Yerklun un stivach...*"

"English, dude. You're in America."

"Sorry. I am wondering if I should send to USIC this dead-dog article."

"I thought our interest was dead people." I scanned the wall in front of him, where my mother used to have a mirror. It's just a bare wall now, except that Hamdani has taped up hard copies of eight or nine recent news stories from MSNBC, most of them only a few paragraphs long. "Six Die as Mystery Illness Grips Cruise Line." "Food Poisoning Suspected in 11 Deaths at Mardi Gras." "Dengue Fever Claims 9 in Nepal Hotel

District." "Mystery Disease in Tripura Claims 14 on British Military Base."

He finds the stories buried in worldwide news about dirty politicians, crimes, forest fires . . . He hard copies any that might be the work of a terror cell looking to kill fifty or so people without attracting attention to itself. He then sends them to Hodji Montu, a USIC agent we're tight with.

I studied the picture of the skeleton in the middle of a dusty road. "What's so great about a dog corpse?"

He reads Spanish easily and pointed to a line of text under the picture. "Outskirts of Mexico City. Several locals are hysterical. They say the dog fell down in the road sick, and several hours later, this is what it looked like."

He enlarged the picture two hundred percent, and even in black-and-white I could see the bones lay in some sort of gloppy mound with a few hairs sticking out.

"Um . . . *ew?*" I plopped down beside him on my mom's bed—now his bed—yawning. "You know that's bullshit. Bodies don't deteriorate that fast. Aren't Mexican locals given to smoking homegrown marijuana?"

"They say it is the fourth such incident in as many days. They contacted a photographer from a Mexico City newspaper, who came for this one and photographed the deterioration." He spun up a PDF page that had been off the screen and pointed to a similar picture, only in this one you could still see it had been a dog. Had a tail, had some hair, but some internal organs were already showing.

"This was shot at hour two." He pointed.

Fat chance I would escape my usual nightmares tonight.

The recurring one was my favorite: My mom reaches out to me through prison bars, crying, *"Tyler, you rat, how could you?"*

"Why can't you find your weird stories at ten in the morning? How did you even capture this swill?"

"I surfed," he said. *Duh.*

I said that the Trinity Four are personal to me. The first reason is that as self-proclaimed v-spies, Hamdani and I look for members of ShadowStrike online. We follow them into chat rooms and try to script their chatter, and we give it to USIC. But they're not easy to find, and in the five weeks we've lived and worked here together, our search engines have coughed up *nada.* After ShadowStrike members were arrested in March for the Trinity Falls water poisoning, it seems that all chatter from extremists anywhere on the planet suddenly stifled itself. You'd think ShadowStrike was defunct, if you were an impatient type. But we know more operatives are out there, including two dangerous officers—one a scientist and the other a trained assassin—who escaped Trinity Falls by the hairs on their asses. OmarLoggi and VaporStrike were two log-ins we hunted constantly.

Our favorite game in the world is trying to find them online. But in the barren wasteland of online intelligence lately, Hamdani succumbs to surfing the news. ShadowStrike specializes in designer germs, hence Hamdani's charming collection of suspected Weapons of Mass Destruction on the wall.

"Don't be a smart-ass," I begged him. "It's late. How in the hell did you bump into dead dogs in your search for potential terror attacks?"

He slumped back in the chair, watching the edge of the keypad, blinking. It's the first clue I had that "I surfed" might have been a stalling tactic and not smart-assery.

His gaze turned to me with those big Pakistani browns, and he said, "I decided I would surf for the germ 'tularemia.'"

Ah. This is *really* personal. My eyes flew to the photo of the bones and glob pile, then looked down at my hand on the back of his chair. I knew how many scabbies were on that one hand, because I'd counted them a dozen times. Thirty-nine: four between my fingers, one under my pinkie fingernail, eleven on my fingers, thirteen on the back of my hand, and ten on my palm. The rest of our bodies were decorated, too. We have a little more in common with the Trinity Four than that we'd love to see the same guys caught. We had been struck, too, in a different way, though they have no idea.

"Obviously, this would be a far more stringent mutation of tularemia than what you and I were attacked with," he said.

"They're *sure* it's tularemia?"

"So they say."

"Who's *they?*" I wished I'd paid attention in Spanish class so I could read it myself.

He rolled the mouse around again until the other picture came clear. "In Mexico, they still get away with 'authorities say' over something like this. They are not panic stricken about emerging infectious diseases and terrorists like the Americans."

I wondered if "authorities' would be the Mexican government or American Intelligence.

"Maybe USIC already knows about the dead dog," I said. "But send it to Hodji anyway. Tularemia. That's gotta be ShadowStrike."

In the past two weeks, I could actually forget that Hamdani and I are infected with a strain of tularemia. The first day we were released from Beth Israel Hospital, I took down all the mirrors in the house or covered them with a towel. I am so used to looking at Shahzad's face that I forget to notice the hundred dots covering it, and I can't see my own face. We look more like chickenpox victims than tularemics, because we were struck with a waterborne mutation of the original that's about twelve times as potent in what it does to skin tissue. But our hundreds of bumpy dots haven't itched or burned in about ten days. They're just crusty. We have to sit on a pillow and toss around a lot while sleeping, but you can actually fail to remember for minutes at a time.

He printed out the first page but hesitated after opening an e-mail to Hodji Montu. Hodji rarely responds to anything we send to him with more than a grunt or rolled eyes on his daily visits to check in on us and make sure we're behaving. He's the closest thing we've got to a father figure between the two of us. We're not supposed to be v-spying. We're underage. And we're supposed to be recovering from our brush with death.

"Authorities found tularemia in tissue cells, according to this," Hamdani said. "But it is another mutation, apparently far stronger than what Catalyst had when he scratched us in the face."

"USIC has grown men who sit around all day and surf for people and animals turning up dead," I reminded him. "I'm sure they know about it."

"So, then, let us give them something they don't know . . ." he mused, and I took it more as a prayer to his Allah than a comment to me. He surfed again, this time for "dead dogs," "Mexico," and "April 2002."

I met Hamdani on a Thursday in early March when he showed up as a new student in my school, which he was supposed to start attending like a regular student. He'd just arrived from Pakistan. I've been an expert hacker for going on three years, and I can detect my own likeness with just a few lines of idle chitchat. That night, I captured his screen at this Internet café where USIC had set him up as a v-spy, scripting the chatter of a ShadowStrike guy seated twenty terminals away. I figured out what he was up to in a minute and a half. The next day I invited myself to the party by giving USIC track 'n' translate programs (TNTs) that they couldn't refuse. Hamdani and I captured phone and Internet chatter like crazy from my house on Friday, and I got some idea that it would be an adrenaline rush to see the terrorists we'd been scripting.

We went to a ShadowStrike recruitment party near Trinity Falls Saturday and pretended to be recruits. But we were acting too nervous and got skunked out by the leaders. Fortunately, Hodji had followed us and had the place raided —hence a lot of arrests were made. Catalyst was one of two recruiters there, though he never even got handcuffed. He took six USIC bullets in the head but managed to scratch us first.

The Trinity Four, as we call Rain, Scott, Owen, and Cora, know of Hamdani only as the Kid. That's his USIC nickname, which was alluded to in a *Newsweek* article in January. Hodji has been down to see them at St. Ann's. He gives us updates on them, and once or twice he has told them stories about serving as a bodyguard to the Kid in Pakistan while the Kid scripted chatter of dangerous extremists who were seated three terminals away in his uncle's Internet café.

The Trinity Four think he's now working from Nigeria or something. They have no idea I even exist.

Hodji would joke to us, "You'd think I was telling them

about Peter Pan." He said it took their minds off their symptoms, hearing about a guy their age who could script chatter with the best of v-spies. They were told that the Kid had worked on Trinity Falls, but not that he and his new best friend took a hit while acting stupid down there.

Hamdani and I are USIC's biggest kept secret at the moment. We can't step outside. If one person saw us, they would think they had hallucinated. If two people saw us, it would create a national panic within about nine hours. Welcome to 2002.

"So, what's your take?" I asked. "You think ShadowStrike is in Mexico, injecting dogs with a newer mutation of tularemia to see what happens to them?"

We scanned his Google returns. "Nothing in the news, but . . ." He clicked on the International Organization for Animal Rights news page, where "Tulum Couple Charged with Killing Stray Dogs" was the headline. Not exactly something you'd come up with while surfing for strains of known WMDs. Whatever we find is usually by thin threads.

"Look at this." He breathed in awe. It was in English. I dove in.

"'A Tulum couple was arrested yesterday after neighboring farmers discovered a shed filled with animal remains. A scorching odor had plagued the area for days, according to local police, who questioned Alvarez and Maria Vincente, suspecting the source was on their farm. Though the couple denied any knowledge of the odor, police discovered the corpses in a grain silo.

"'At least one corpse was smoking and 'making a strange crackling noise,' while others were fully deteriorated, an officer said. It is not known why the Vincentes killed the animals or what method was used. Due to the mysterious disintegration factor, the corpses are being examined by the Centers for Disease Control in Atlanta.'"

We exhaled in frustration. Hamdani stated the obvious: "If the CDC has been contacted, USIC knows."

Our game is to find what they *don't* know.

"But you think these might be tied to the dog corpse found in the road, which 'authorities say' was infected with some new strain of tularemia," I laid out.

He shrugged. "That was near Mexico City, and these dog corpses are across the country, near Cancún . . ."

I pulled up a chair behind him and stuck my pillow under my butt. I had grabbed it off my bed without even thinking. I figured the hard chair would keep me awake while he opened his favorite new search engine. He had designed it, and it searched only chat rooms and chatter in twenty-some languages. I saw him plug in "Vincente," "dogs," "Mexico," "Tulum," a/o "Mexico City." But I had seen him do stuff like this many times in the last five weeks. I needed to get to sleep. I put my chin on his shoulder, thinking this might annoy him enough to hurry it along and give me my measly five minutes.

However, many minutes later, he was shaking me awake. "Will you please get your scabs off my scabs and look at this?"

I blinked.

ALERT: OmarLoggi is Online: www.tijuanaprime.com/chat/hodgpog-hall/%853.18.05%/ Enter 9:59 pm

I raised my head slowly. "My god . . ."

Hamdani hacked into the chat room as an invisible guest. The chatter was just disappearing, but he hit CTRL-C and managed to capture it into Notepad and translate. It was only a few lines.

> **OmarLoggi:** I had a runner go to pay the Vincentes' bail. I thought it would be a thousand pesos, but the Tulum judge wanted upwards of nine thousand. We smelled the CDC immediately and left them to rot in the can. He knows nothing, and his wife knows less. They cannot hurt us.

We went off like an explosion, flying out of the chairs, whooping . . . I landed standing in the middle of the bed.

"Your face is bleeding," Hamdani noted, sitting down quickly again. "Go! Script it!"

I flew across the hall to my own room, to my four terminals that I never shut down, in case of something like this. I ripped the towel off my favorite monitor—the towel kept the light down—and plopped my sorry butt into the chair too fast. I hardly felt it.

"Boys! What are you doing? The neighbors will hear!" Miss Alexa, our USIC live-in nurse, shouted up the stairs. That would be a bad thing. We kept the curtains drawn. I was supposed to be living somewhere else, and the house was supposed to be rented to an elderly couple while my mom sat in federal prison.

I didn't bother answering Miss Alexa. *OmarLoggi is online.* Ho ho. Omar is a former professor of marine biology in Hamburg who designed the germ that infected Trinity Falls. Vapor-Strike is not a scientist but an officer of some sort. He's a trained assassin.

There wasn't a lot more chatter to catch. Omar was talking

to a log-in named Pasco, not familiar to me, so I dog-leashed him to track later. Hamdani got the IP address of where Omar was chattering from. He came in my room to do the translation of their last two exchanges before they exited. He whipped the towel off the terminal next to me.

"Sit on that towel!" I warned him. I don't like the possibility of sitting my butt pustules where his butt pustules have been, if you'll pardon me. He calls me on my obsessive-compulsive behavior daily, but now he looked peaceful and gratified.

"You need me to translate?" he asked.

"Yes, but don't toy with me," I said. "What's going on?"

Hamdani's smile is forever with his eyes and not his mouth. It keeps his face from breaking open like mine just had.

He said, "Omar is in Cancún."

Well, well. We'd been placing bets for weeks. Sydney, Australia. Beijing, China. The Polynesian Islands. Pakistan. Omar's whereabouts was huge. Cancún boiled my blood, because it is a beautiful Mexican place where people slurp margaritas on the beach and get twenty-buck massages and snorkel.

I moved my chair down so he could move his toweled ass into place. He can identify the language pretty quickly if I can't, and then we have translation programs to do most of the work. After that we have to fill in with whatever English words are missing so USIC can understand it. The initial translation is usually clunky, but I let him fill in:

Pasco: What were their last calculations before the arrest?
OmarLoggi: The dog died in two minutes and twenty-nine seconds and deteriorated in three hours and fifty minutes. This is a vast improvement over our trials in Mexico City.

Pasco: May I share this with our friends in Colony Two?

"Whoa . . . whoa . . ." I think I said it first. Trinity Falls had been known as Colony One. This was the first mention of any new colonies.

Miss Alexa was now behind us. Because USIC employs her, we didn't bother sending her away from our soon-to-be-classified secrets. "Boys. You know what Hodji has told you over and over again."

"We're not boys," I snapped. Or if we are, maybe USIC ought to consider hiring boys. "In the world of computers, boys are the men and men are—"

"Yadda yadda, young men. You're supposed to be using your computers to play chess and download e-books. To fully recover, you need sleep." She marched her girth out while Hamdani translated the last line.

OmarLoggi: Tell no one in Colony Two yet. I want to kill my monkeys first. Their circulatory components mirror humans more closely than dogs.

Exits followed. The top of my head broke into a sweat, and Hamdani said nothing. As happy as we used to get in March, back when we were capturing chatter like crazy, I had forgotten there were moments like this. When you get excited over some ShadowStrike chatter, there's obviously some puke factor attached. *There's a Colony Two. Omar's got some disgusting new mutation of what had gotten us that is powerful enough to take apart a dog in four hours.*

I tried to focus on the good: *Omar had just used an Internet café server in Cancún.* Hamdani put it all in an e-mail to Hodji and simply wrote, This is an anonymous tip from a friend. He attached the script and hit SEND.

Because of our ages, we're not allowed to work for any American Intelligence agencies. We got a nurse because it was the least American Intelligence could do after we kicked butt capturing chatter and helped save more people from dying in Trinity Falls. The New York squad had scoured its policy manuals to figure out some way to help the two of us, whom they owed, without creating a paper trail that spoke of "encouraging minors to v-spy on American soil." Their pages on "hired nurses" lacked a demand for reasons on the receipts. It was a glitch in the red tape that worked in our favor, and they went with it, though we would have done better with a secretary.

Still, we send USIC articles and our versions of alerts all the time, and with such thin covers that only an asshole would not know it was us. We don't get paid. That's the bite-me part.

Miss Alexa returned and began wiping the bleeding pustule on my face with a hot washcloth. Nurses are very motherly. I kind of like it, since my mother had never been the motherly type. Miss Alexa wiped the back of my neck, clucking about our ages. It was weird, finding out shit that USIC would probably only figure out weeks later if it weren't for us, and having some kindly nurse wiping my face down and telling me to go to bed.

I didn't question my life. I have to admit, pustules and all, it was better than it had been, back when I was staring at blackboards and having my hundred-and-two-pound body pummeled in gym class.

SIX

CORA HOLMAN
SATURDAY, MAY 4, 2002
7:30 A.M.
KELLERTON HOUSE

THE MORNING SUN poured in through the endlessly tall windows, and I was sucked from bed like a dreamer. I stared out the window facing east. Glimpses of sea blue shone through the pine trees. A barrier island lay on the other side of Great Bay, but I couldn't think of which one, and the mist hid the horizon. The north window revealed more lawn and forest, both very still.

Before I realized what I was doing, I had scanned the woods, the bramble between trees, looking for the forms or even shadows of strangers. I forced myself to stop the paranoia and to simply bask a moment in the silence, something I hadn't heard in a couple of months. I reached for the sweater I had hung on the bedpost last night.

Descending the sweeping staircase, I studied the faces in the Civil War portraits. The bearded officers were dressed with lots of officer brocade on their shoulders, and I went through a mental exercise that I find myself doing every time I look at a picture of a man. I imagine the face on a real-live body, and the mouth is uttering, "Cora, I'm your father."

I'm a slightly diluted image of my mother. I have no idea what my father looks like. As I've gazed at myself lately, I've felt like I'm teetering on a genetic fence. My father's invisible contributions to me could be anything from Swiss to South American.

I felt a hand on my shoulder and turned. Mrs. Starn, head of the historical society, stood beside me. We'd met her last night.

"You're up early," I said.

She was already dressed. "At my age, you don't sleep more than five hours on any given night." She had mentioned last night being in her late eighties, and her white bun and frail frame attested to it, though she still had a lot of bounce in her step. She had also mentioned staying here last night, though she didn't live here. She'd said something about furniture men coming early today to bring a new couch for the TV room.

I followed her through the double doors of the parlor, taking in again the huge fireplace, the massive drapes over tall windows, and the face of a stern woman in the portrait above the couch. She had dark hair like mine and ramrod-straight posture, the kind I'd been accused once in a while of having. I remembered from last night her having the type of gaze that follows you around the room.

This woman's eyes in the portrait didn't twinkle like the men's had. We watched each other. I had some idea of the discomforts that had cost her the light in her eyes.

"That's Patience Kellerton," Mrs. Starn said. "The matriarch. Mother of thirteen children, though she'd lost several at the time this portrait was painted."

I stared at the picture, memories stirring.

"When I was in fifth grade, my class took a field trip here for the house and grounds history tour," I said. I remembered that portrait. "Mrs. Kellerton's eyes follow you all around the room. That got a lot of kids asking questions about the Kellerton children, the ghost stories."

Mrs. Starn smiled and cleared her throat. "I wondered how much time would pass before one of you four asked about those morbid tales."

I pooh-poohed the subject. "I didn't even remember them until this morning. We've got too much reality haunting us. If any of us saw a ghost, we would laugh . . . tell it to go find someone who scared easily."

"I'm a historian, and hence, I like accuracy. So many students asked about the six dead Kellerton children on field trips here that the tour guides were equipped with answers. The first is, 'To lose that many offspring in the eighteen hundreds, when you'd given birth to thirteen, was unfortunate but not highly unusual.'"

"All six had epilepsy?" I asked. Details like this were just out of reach lately, but I remembered something about seizures.

"Diabetes, we now think. Obviously it was something genetic, something that struck around puberty, as all six children passed away between the ages of thirteen and seventeen, having enjoyed perfect health as children."

"Poor Mrs. Kellerton," I said, staring at the portrait. I could understand why she didn't have any sparkle in those trailing eyes. "It *is* kind of coincidental that we would end up here . . . Perfect health as children, then something threatening strikes in our teenage years . . ."

Mrs. Starn laughed uneasily. "That has been duly noted lately at board meetings. It is a coincidence, something no one thought of until after the grant came through—and after we realized we'd only be getting the four of you and not the Level Threes as well. But I made sure to keep any talk of strange spiritual influences as a sidebar. Mrs. Kellerton ran the glass foundry after Captain Kellerton was killed in the Civil War, then the sawmill. My comment to my board was well taken: 'Let's not get carried away.'"

I liked her levelheadedness; I'd always had an easier time talking to adults than to people my own age. I hunted around for my feelings on the subject of a spiritual realm, which were confused.

"Sometimes lately I sense my mother around me, which is not a good feeling. We didn't have a great relationship. She was . . ." I put my hand to my throat, my compulsive gesture when talking about Aleese in our therapy sessions. ". . . she died a drug addict. But sensing my mother—that's different from walking around in a place like this and expecting to see one of the dead Kellerton children. Perhaps it's that my mother is personal to me. Spooky stories are impersonal. Something like that . . ."

"I definitely believe in contact with the dead, though not in the silly way that locals love to ramble about," Mrs. Starn said, which made my head turn. "Parents and loved ones go off to higher places and see things from a higher perspective. They can definitely help us out."

"Mm . . . yes," I stumbled, not wanting to announce that most often, I felt my mother was laughing at me. Our therapist,

Dr. Hollis, believed it was our drug protocol. I'd been the only one to hallucinate on one of our early painkillers toward the end of March, and it had been of Aleese standing beside my bed, laughing at me in a taunting way. It turned out to be a nurse who had awakened me from a dream of Aleese. Our drug had been changed immediately, however, and I hadn't seen Aleese since. I simply sensed her.

Mrs. Starn put a reassuring hand on my arm, gazing into my eyes. I suppose the wisdom of her years took over. "Maybe your mother has something wonderful to share, if you just relax and give her a chance."

I highly doubted that.

"As for Mrs. Kellerton, perhaps she wants to be part of the restoration of your health, as she could not do as much for her own children."

I smiled. I liked that idea. It was hard to talk about my mother—or to look into the dark, wandering eyes of Mrs. Kellerton, which resembled my mother's in their sharpness. But it wasn't hard to look into Mrs. Starn's eyes and take in almost ninety years of wisdom.

Mrs. Starn went back to putting fresh flowers in a vase on top of the piano, and I walked aimlessly through the antique-filled rooms downstairs. Drifting back up the stairs, I found myself standing at Scott's closed door. I didn't hear him moving, and I forced myself to go and get dressed. I felt off center, pulled in many directions, and like I might find peace in this house by walking into it, like you'd walk into a hot spot in the road on a summer's night.

SEVEN

HODJI MONTU dropped in on Shahzad and me in the morning. In Pakistan, the two of them had been really tight. V-spy and bodyguard.

Since Shahzad came to live on American soil, his relationship with Hodji is tricky. Hodji can't acknowledge what we do, or he could lose his job.

I've noted to Hamdani many times how funny it is that he got both a bodyguard and money while living in Pakistan, but here in America, he's unprotected and working for free. But I don't think there's a line of reasoning in the Pakistani culture to capture the essence of "what the fuck." He refuses to complain.

Hodji clomped his cowboy boots on my mom's hardwood floors and came into the dining room, where we were eating this concoction Nurse Alexa makes for us, which is scrambled eggs with blotches of spinach in it. Our tongues are healing. We try not to discuss the sorry state of our food choices.

"I got word last night from an anonymous source that Omar is alive and well and hanging out in Mexico," he said innocently.

"Anonymous sources are quite wonderful, yes," Shahzad noted.

Hodji sat down at the head of the table and forced himself to look at each of us. He is as good a liar as Intelligence could create for working undercover, but we know him very well, so it's obvious that he forces himself to look at us. Nobody would *want* to look at us. He craned his neck back to see into the kitchen and listen for Nurse Alexa pattering about. The kitchen was silent. She retreats to her room behind the pantry sometimes and closes the door to read a novel.

He watched Shahzad pick at his eggs.

His face brightened. "You guys want to live somewhere else for a while? Are you up for a little change of scene?"

I raised my hand as an enthusiastic *yes.* "I keep waiting for this place to get spray-painted, despite the rumor of some elderly couple living here. The news stations *had* to report our address when my mom was arrested for spying. They just *had* to come out here and shoot footage of our house. I'm surprised we haven't found a few crosses burning on the lawn already."

"What means this burning of crosses?" Hamdani asked.

Pakistanis. I ignored him. "I don't expect the graciousness of our neighbors to last much longer. Where to?"

Not that you could call any element of being poisoned fun, but I had thought it might come close to fun to live with the victims of the Trinity Falls water poisoning instead of in my Long Island house. In fact, Hodji had gotten us kind of excited early in March to go to this place on Great Bay near New Gretna to live with the Trinity Four.

But a week later, Hodji got nervous. The only people outside of USIC who knew our status as v-spies were in jail. They were either ShadowStrike members or recruits who had been arrested at the same raid where Hamdani and I got discovered and scratched in the face. But despite high security, there were ways to get word out of prison, and Hodji was growing more and more concerned about ShadowStrike members who were not in jail discovering us. And he was also concerned that our presence at the Kellerton House might jeopardize the safety of the Trinity Four.

"I'm not sure of the 'where' yet," he said. "But I'll get on it this afternoon. If ShadowStrike had any idea who you are, they might come after you. I do need to go out of town for three days, and it won't be the last time."

He shifted nervously in his seat, avoiding Shahzad's eyes. Hodji had gone away several times, and Shahzad got separation anxiety each time.

"Where are you going?" he asked.

"Can't say."

Shahzad took off in Punjabi, which is his tendency when he gets upset. I only understood the words "Cancún" and "Mexico" and sensed his total frustration that Hodji was probably going to help look for Omar. And despite that we had fed him the intelligence about where Omar was, he would not confirm his plans.

"Stop picking," Hodji interrupted, knocking one of Shahzad's hands away from his cheek. Hamdani likes to pick his scabs when he's thinking. "And stop focusing on what you don't get instead of what you do. I've got a meeting with the squad in New York today. I've got a great plan of protection in mind, just in case those idiots eventually try to do more harm to my two most trusted, uh, v-spies-oops-I-mean-friends. That is, if your senses of humor are still working."

My sense of humor only malfunctioned for about half of each day. Hamdani never had any, so the remark was directed at me.

"I'm not sure USIC will go for it. But I would like to propose faking your deaths. If you had new identities, I could go back to work and quit worrying about you all the time. So. How would you feel about, uh, dying in some staged accident? Becoming two other guys?"

Hamdani watched patiently for more information, as if this were a perfectly normal conversation.

I finally decided, well, screw him if he can't see the humor. "Do we get to be carried out of here in body bags? You won't let anyone accidentally embalm us, right?"

Hodji said, "We would drive you to the morgue, get death certificates, the whole schmear. We can even drug you with chloroform—maybe. We've done worse in Intelligence to set a realistic stage. We can have a 'funeral.' Of course, we'll tell your uncle Ahmer in Pakistan, Shahzad, and have him come back for a 'funeral' so it would look good in the newspaper. I trust him with my life."

"Will USIC go for this?" Hamdani made a face like Hodji had warts on his cheeks.

Hodji shrugged uneasily, repeating his doubts. "The Witness Protection Program doesn't do minors without parents. You're setting yet another precedent. And wherever it is, it would have to be somewhere you can stay out of sight for weeks—months, if necessary. Our country is in a state of national panic right now over acts of terror. Considering the two of you look like a radioactive rain shower dropped on you, you'll have the media chasing you five minutes after you're seen in public. It would have to be someplace where you can heal in private. A farm or something. Maybe in Kansas or Oklahoma, say. I'll check our contacts—if USIC agrees to this. Tyler, we would have to tell your mother in jail that you actually died. That's . . . horrendous, as far as I'm concerned. USIC might say the same."

"I'm only a minor for another eight months. If I were eighteen, would it be so iffy?" I asked.

"Intelligence has been known to lie about causes of death for the sake of national security, even to family members," he said. "But yes, it's iffy. A minor is a minor, whether he's got eight months to go or ten years to go. God forbid the truth should come out—"

"She's earned it," I said, though I felt the bottom fall out of me. Turning in my own mother for spying for the North Koreans made me feel like a hero when I was looking at Shahzad and Hodji but like fungus-infested roadkill in the middle of every night. "She stole my high school years from me. She was so embarrassing, I couldn't even make friends," I went on, mostly for my own sanity. No one could understand the feeling. I could have lived with having a hooker for a mother. *Walk a mile in my shoes,* I had told my shrink at Beth Israel.

I wandered away from them, up to my bedroom. Ever since eighth grade, when I found out about my mom, it was the only room in the house that felt like I belonged in it. I'm a pretty ridiculous information head—I like keeping information just because. In ninth grade I was on lithium for obsessive-compulsive disorder after my mom got a load of all my CDs and how obsessed I'd gotten over cataloging and cleaning them. She forced me to the doctor's office, but it's hard to trust a woman who is a big fat liar. I went off the medication after a month or so. I enjoy collecting facts about people and still can't see the big deal in that part of it.

I had five shelves of CDs, the length of the room, probably containing every online *People* magazine article ever printed, every NatGeo, Yahoo!, and MSNBC article on every person ever featured, and that's for starters. I have a corkboard that runs the length of the wall, and almost every centimeter is covered with people news I've read. Mostly right now, it's covered with pictures of Cora Holman.

I use two bedroom doors turned up on their sides as desktops, and they meet in the corner. On them I have four towers, four flat-screens, four printers capable of varying tricks, and six extra hard drives, also full of information. I'm also a cord-cover freak. In all of that hardware, you would be hard-pressed to find a loose cord.

My bed was in the middle of all this . . . unmade today. So it looks to me like some rabid goose flew in here and took a dump right in the middle of the room. That's what has bugged me worse than anything about being sick. When your inability to clean gets to be a problem, you know that terrorists have managed to climb very far up your ass.

Hodji and Shahzad had followed me up. I hadn't let too many people in here over the years, because the complex nature of Being Tyler was too weird on most people's eyeballs.

"The first time I was in this room, back in March, I thought all these CDs were music," Hodji said, and I detected a note of concern. Only about forty of them were music. "Did they get you back on lithium?"

That's the obsessive-compulsive-disorder drug. The doctors nixed it because I'm taking so much other shit right now to reduce the f/x of ulceroglandular tularemia. Decision: They would fix my head after fixing my body.

I was pretty proud of myself for standing in the middle of my room and not cussing out the bed for being unmade. I felt something more powerful than my compulsiveness, despite that my compulsiveness went over the top lately.

I didn't answer. At least not directly. "Got a great idea. You want Shahzad and me to 'die' and have nobody question it? Let's burn down the house."

I glanced at the two of them, their jaws floating and their eyes scanning this info tank of CDs, which could have served the New York Public Library extremely well. I guess the two of them knew me well enough not to focus on the loss to mankind. Considering my compulsions, this was major ground breaking.

"...dangerous..." Hodji was remarking. "...don't want to take out the whole neighborhood...kerosene fire would burn fast and dramatically but not hotly...not as dangerous." Blah blah.

I was looking at my CDs, reading the side jackets. I had science dudes, then history dudes, then criminal dudes, then detective dudes, then various writer and novelist dudes whom I'd never had time to read, then philosophers and musicians and movie stars.

"Do you know where all your mom's money is?" Hodji was asking. "It would probably be a good idea to get it all out of the house sometime soon, no matter what we do about your—"

Hamdani and I are surviving here on cash payments that my mom had hidden all over the damn place. If you deposit money you earned as a spy, it could send the IRS into epileptic seizures. I knew most of the hiding places by v-spying on her. Over a hundred thousand in cash and precious metals—gold, silver, and platinum coins—were buried behind the fireplace, behind the stove, under the floorboards where Shahzad now slept, yadda yadda.

"Why?" I turned, ignoring his slight flinch, which could still happen if either Shahzad or I turned our faces to him without warning and his thoughts had been on something else. "I don't want it."

I gazed at my CDs again. I think at last count it was eleven hundred and eight.

"So, pick a night when there's no wind," I told him. "But make it a second-story fire. Shahzad and I can hole up on the first floor to get taken out on stretchers, right? I really want to do the body-bag part. That sounds like a rip."

They said nothing about my bad pun, and I attacked the damn bed to make it before the sight of it gave me a hole in my head.

EIGHT

**SCOTT EBERMAN
SATURDAY, MAY 4, 2002
9:30 A.M.
HIS BEDROOM**

Rain's prediction that I would get the Throat from Hell was dead on. I glanced at my watch. 9:31. I'd slept the clock around, but I shut my eyes again, trying to enjoy the fact that for the first time in two months, I had slept on a mattress that wasn't wrapped in a rubber sheet.

I opened my eyes minutes later as I suddenly smelled Cora. One side effect of our antiretroviral meds is an overly keen sense of smell. It could be annoying, as not all smells are good. Cora has a distinctive smell, some combination of talcum powder and carnations, and it was wafting in from the corridor. She was standing out there, god knows why, but she'd done that at St. Ann's sometimes—just stood outside the door until I smelled her and told her to come in.

If any of a hundred girls smelled that way, I'd have admitted it could drive me nuts. But Cora's got that virginal, never-been-kissed, honor-student way about her, and even I have a conscience. I'd been with my share of girls, but any innocence they'd had was either gone long before they got to me, or they seriously wanted it gone. You don't cuss in front of a statue of the Blessed Mother, and you don't smell Cora Holman and think bad thoughts. Especially if you're a germ fest and it would be pointless anyway.

I didn't want to force my throat into speaking. I finally picked up a paperback on vitamins for AIDS patients I'd been planning to read last night before crashing, and I threw it at the door. Her face appeared a moment later, wide-eyed and blushing.

Rain and Owen and I just barged in on each other with a knock. Sometimes Cora's shyness was adorable; other times it was annoying. We didn't always have the energy to lead her around by the nose. I gestured her in.

"Can I get you anything?" she asked.

I fumbled for a slushy our new live-in nurse, Marg, had left for me an hour ago, but by now it was warm and watery, and the orange juice burned on the way down.

"Do you want a refill?" she asked quickly. "Regular water?"

I shook my head, thinking my eyeballs would blow out. I patted the bed, not exactly wanting company, but Cora was more like the family pet than a person, insofar as she wasn't as noisy. She handed me the TV remote and sat at the edge of the bed where it had lain. The *Montel Williams Show* was on the muted screen, somehow making me think of idle time I didn't want. I looked at Cora instead.

She was a little like one of the portrait people who had stared from the walls of the stairwell when I stumbled up here last night. A woman in eighteenth-century garb now stared at me from a portrait between the two windows. Cora wasn't dressed like her, but she wasn't dressed like us either. Our hospital rooms at St. Ann's had been littered with jeans, cutoffs, gym trunks, sweatpants. I think Cora owned one pair of jeans. Right now, she was wearing black shorts, a black top that matched, and a really thin gold chain around her neck with a locket that I knew contained a picture of her grandmother. Her hair, the same color as a Hershey bar, was pulled tight in some knotty thing at the back of her neck, like she took all the time in the world to fix herself up. Well, she had the time. We each had our little coping mechanisms. Hers was being impeccable.

I pointed to her and held up four fingers.

"Yes, four-star. I went out for about twenty minutes and looked all around this property. There's a pond, there." She pointed out the south window. I could only see treetops and a blue sky. "The old outbuildings are, well, starting to fall down, because they haven't been restored and are a hundred and fifty years old at least. Great Bay is on the eastern side, but you can't see the barrier islands right now. Too misty. When you're up to it, you have to let me show you about."

She sounded casual, but hope rang through it. I let a fact seep back in that both strengthened and alarmed me: Cora got flustered when I was symptomatic. It made me want to get up, though I'd have to face my boredom once I did.

"I took some pictures," she continued. "And Mrs. Starn showed me a darkroom down in the basement. It's the old-fashioned kind, the kind I suppose Aleese used to develop her war photos. I learned how to develop film the old-fashioned way at school, and I'm going to develop these. Mrs. Starn said the photo historian will bring me some chemicals this morning."

She must have gotten up at seven to accomplish all this. I

felt outdone and tried to sit up. She was suddenly on her knees beside me, helping me wedge the pillows around. I forced myself to speak and ignore the razorblades.

"Be careful of those chemicals."

"I will. I have gloves."

"Wear a mask."

"Oh."

"Ask Marg for one." I grimaced without meaning to.

"I'll go find her . . ." She backed away on her knees and stood guiltily, like she had caused my pain.

I made some annoyed, choppy motion with my hand that was meant as some version of "Relax, will you?" But she took it wrong.

". . . and I'll bring you a new slushy!" And she bolted out the door again.

I threw back the blanket and sat on the side of the bed. I could have stayed in bed all day and nursed my sore throat, but I wouldn't be the worse for having gotten up. Our immune systems actually still worked. But it was like a car running on three pistons. This symptom would go away in a couple of days like it had the last few times—whether I stayed horizontal or faced my life.

NINE

I APPROACH THE BATHROOM and turn on the light switch, only to find Tyler sitting on the toilet seat with his mouth open and his eyes staring at me. Except only the whites of his eyes show. With his skin condition it appears most horrific, and I am not amused by his grin when he hears me gasp.

"Did I blink when you turned on the light?" he asks. "It's important that you don't blink, or it will ruin everything. I am so stoked to play dead."

"You do not blink," I tell him.

"You gotta winkie-tink?" He stands. He has not been using the toilet—just sitting in the dark, awaiting my arrival so as to alarm me.

"Where you have been?" I ask. "You get quiet after Hodji leaves."

"I cleaned the toilet and shower. Now I'm practicing being dead."

I roll my eyes, not at all sure that Hodji should have told Tyler of this plan yet, despite that it involves us so personally. I have had years of experience with American Intelligence, and I do not think USIC will go for it. It is too radical, reflecting Hodji's fear for our security. He is "too emotionally involved," and as their policies do not acknowledge help from minors, there can be no help for minors, USIC will say. If an anonymous source turns out to be a minor, that is not their problem.

And besides, I have more pressing news to report. "I just found Omar online again today. He was at an Internet café in Tijuana. He either has a plane . . . or a patch on his computer."

"Tijuana? That's a border town. Oh shit. Are you thinking what I'm thinking?"

"That he is in Mexico because he is planning to cross over?" I spell it out. "I thought of it first thing last night, but I had also hoped perhaps he was looking for a country in which to practice a new designer germ without attracting attention to himself."

"He could have done that in Ethiopia," Tyler points out. "Or the Sudan, or fucking Greenland . . ."

I finish and turn to wash my hands, shaking my head at the challenges. "I don't believe USIC has agents in Tijuana. Their base south of the border is Mexico City, and I would imagine that having received that e-mail from us, they sent whomever they had there to look for him in Cancún. Perhaps he is not even in Tijuana but drawing off its server. Perhaps he is in Europe. The agents will be angry if I sent them to Cancún for nothing."

"The agents don't know you sent that tip," Tyler says and starts to pee. He can't withhold a hooting laugh. Obviously, they did know. They just have to pretend they don't know for the sake of their policies. Regardless of a source's age, they are not going to send a script like our gift of last night into the shredder and pretend they didn't receive it.

"Relax. You're not responsible for how they interpret the info that you so graciously send." Tyler continues. "Who was Omar talking to, and what did he say?"

"He was talking to VaporStrike," I say, which will be news to him. This is the first resurrection of VaporStrike online since he and Omar escaped Trinity Falls together.

I think Tyler will be very impressed by this, but he doesn't stop to think of it, in light of his other question: "Did they discuss their new germ that can turn a corpse into a skeleton in four hours or less?"

"Indirectly. He said, 'Fire will fall upon Colony Two.'"

I hear Tyler stop peeing, midstream. My troubles with ShadowStrike and the Trinity Falls water poisoning started with online chatter I captured in November of last year. It was this: "Waters will run red in Colony One."

Tyler mutters curses and follows with what I believe will be the next Question of Our Lives. "Where in hell is Colony Two?"

It seemed that the place was already known by both men, and they did not name it outright. But, anyway, Tyler would not assume the answers would be so easy. The question is rhetorical.

He flushes and then begins his washing ritual, which is quite involved, using very hot water and his own prescription soap bar each time, with suds rising to his elbows. It is disturbing to watch the scalding water run over his pustules, and I turn and face out into the hallway.

He finally brushes past me, and I know he is rushing to my terminal to see this chatter. He cannot understand it, as I have not yet translated it. I sit, saying, "They were having an argument. About the location of Colony Two. Omar does not like it."

"Why not?"

"He wants to strike a group of engineers on convention," I say, copying and pasting. "Aeronautical engineers. Aero companies make weapons for military use as well as the planes which transport them."

"So, their thought this time is to do damage to a weapons manufacturer," he says. "What are we expecting? Aero executives to croak in their hotel beds and turn into puddles of bone and large intestine before their wives and kids even realize they're dead?"

I ignore his sarcasm and consider the logic. "Perhaps this is one of those conventions for executives only, and the families will not be struck."

Tyler cannot endure the wait. "How difficult can this be to trace? How many aerospace engineering companies are there that create arms *and* are having a convention?"

"I have only begun to check on that. But it appears that of American companies inventing parts as well as, say, missiles, there are well over five hundred. Most participate in an annual convention."

The translation appears on the screen, however tattered from lack of synonymous terms. I create what I perceive to be proper English where there is none, and he reads behind me.

OmarLoggi: I have studied the weapons made by this aero firm and am just about ready to give a go-ahead. We could take out all their executives and throw the peons remaining into a tailspin. They will have to shut down. They will feel they have been visited by the devil himself

> when the coroner arrives to declare as dead the piles of
> bones and cartilage and seepage.
>
> **VaporStrike:** May I be so quick as to tell the others, then,
> "Fire will fall in Colony Two"?
>
> **OmarLoggi:** Don't be hasty. I have reservations.
>
> **VaporStrike:** We cannot strike this firm at its offices, because
> of its security. The convention facility is perfect. With
> your new vinegar, the victims only have to indulge once.

Tyler looks down at his arms, which he is compulsive enough never to scratch or pick at. "We should consider ourselves lucky. He's probably been working with tularemia for about thirty years. He's probably just now ironing out all the kinks. What if we'd been struck by that strain?"

Americans love to ask "What if?" Instead of answering, I create more text.

> **VaporStrike:** The troops are in place.
>
> **OmarLoggi:** Tell them to calm down. We have to be
> extremely careful.
>
> **VaporStrike:** It is not as risky as you are thinking. They will
> look for us to strike in Britain, Spain . . . Ethiopia.

Tyler steps backward, saying, "Whoa. Guess it's an American hit. But we already knew that, eh?"

"Say where, you devils," I mutter at the screen. At times I have felt my muttering has brought me luck.

> **VaporStrike:** Speak to me of your reservation.
>
> **OmarLoggi:** It is bad luck to keep striking the young.

"Jeezus." Tyler shudders. "I suppose '*keep* striking' is a reference to almost killing four teenagers last time."

ShadowStrike obviously kept up with the news concerning their almost-successes. Yet it is upsetting to hear them make reference directly to the Trinity Four, whom we helped save. I try to wait patiently for more chatter to appear.

> **VaporStrike:** You are referencing the fact that there is an amusement park directly across the street from the target.

Tyler points to this line on the screen, chuckles evilly, and says, "*Bingo.*"

I can barely enjoy the fact that we just cut our search down to one-tenth of what it would have been. Tyler always manages to state horrific things more easily than I do, and I had to listen to him thinking aloud.

"It's one thing to imagine full-grown adults melting like the witch in the *Wizard of Oz*. It's another thing to think of it happening to kids. What, do they come off the slide at the water park and simply start to smoke like—"

"Will you please show more respect?" I ask patiently.

"It's gross. I can't help it."

> **Omar:** The industrialized world will find your choice most offensive, my friend. We have to think of how we could be viewed—if we want further backing and further political support from others.
>
> **VaporStrike:** As we will never trumpet our success like some organizations do, how will anyone prove, or even be aware, that it was us?

Omar: Our major backers will know, although I have just spoken with Chancellor. He is like-minded to you.

"Who is Chancellor?" I ask, banking the code name in the front of my mind. It is new to us. My fingers itch to send this to Hodji.

"Obviously someone holding the purse strings," Tyler says.

VaporStrike: They are all like-minded to us. We would not change critical plans if we were endangering puppies, would we?

Omar: Your meaning?

VaporStrike: These are the children of dogs.

Omar: I see.

VaporStrike: I am not completely inhuman. I am not saying to intentionally strike many men's offspring. I am saying let's not alter our course for what we realize is certainly not a tragic loss, even if much of the world is deceived into thinking it is.

I note their exits and try not to absorb their philosophies into my brain. It will only give me a useless asthma attack. I focus on how happy I am to see that we have more to puzzle over. We can eliminate many convention centers as the potential hit site by focusing on those that are in close proximity to an amusement park. I ask Tyler the best way to do this. It seems there is no easy method. He will download lists of amusement parks and we will begin the daunting task of comparing their addresses to those of nearby convention centers and engineering firms using them as hosts. I perceive it may be a long and boring day.

TEN

SCOTT EBERMAN
SATURDAY, MAY 4, 2002
10:15 A.M.
DINING ROOM

CORA'S SLUSHY NEVER ARRIVED. Not like her. When I came out of the shower, swallowing razorblades, I could hear Alan overhead with what sounded like Mike Tiger. I thought as I got dressed of going up and starting my nagging saga for a job. But they were moving furniture or something. And I couldn't talk very well. So I put it off.

Owen had started taking the stairs down slowly. I caught up to him, laying a hand on his neck. Clammy.

"That new elevator is calling my name, bro," he said. "Got rust in my hip joints again. And I didn't get any sleep. I kept having that dream from hell."

We had decided last night that the elevator would be used only if we broke a leg. We didn't have any exercise programs due to the blood thinners we were taking, which in our case could turn a serious bruise into a fatality. We all hoped to swim in Great Bay over the summer, but that was a month away at least. The best exercise we might get some days was walking up and down these stairs.

I nudged him to continue his tale, but with hesitation. He had a few recurring doozies in the nightmare department. They all had to do with fires.

"I'm running down an avenue in some huge city, and all the skyscrapers are on fire. These explosions keep going off. They're bombs. They're, like . . . bright orange."

"Maybe you're having a dream about fireworks and are just missing the point," I joked.

"Not funny. And I think it's New York. Because as I'm running, the streets come together in points. Times Square . . . Herald Square . . . I thought once I got out here, I'd quit having that stupid nightmare. I had it, like, ten times at St. Ann's. I wake up still smelling smoke. Do I smell like smoke to you?"

I let my eyebrows rise and drop, but I didn't bother sticking my nose up to him. "It's the antiretroviral. Throws off your sense of smell."

He stuck his nose to the crook of his elbow and sniffed anyway. After a couple of blinks and a silence that seemed pregnant with eerie suggestions, he just started his one-step-at-a-time descent again.

"We're all dreaming weird stuff," I pointed out. "Even Rain, Miss Zero Imagination."

He said nothing. It really bothered me. We were at an impasse lately. We used silence to bridge gaps where we couldn't agree on a subject. He believed in things I simply couldn't visualize—religious stuff, like an end to this world.

"Owen. If you're thinking some major, huge apocalypse is coming and you're dreaming about the shit, that's only a metaphor for what you've already been through. It's like a guy who's been hit by a car thinking he could get hit by a train. Normal thought. But not realistic."

He reached the bottom and rested his back with his hands on his knees. It reminded me of football, of when he hit the sideline after a long stint on the field. He would stand like this and huff every time. Only now, there was no equipment. He was basically skin and bones and a thin layer of muscle. He could still perspire, though. He wiped sweat off his forehead, then smelled the palm of his hand this time.

"Smoke," he said. "Honest to god—"

"Go wash your hands," I said with all the patience I could muster. "Don't be a dork. Your religious fire-and-brimstone philosophy is backing up into your meds."

"My what?" He straightened and scratched his head. Breaking fevers bring out all sorts of stuff, and his scalp itched so badly at times that he'd buzzed his hair. You could see little scratches and blotches of heat rash under his blond nubs. "I don't even know what a 'brimstone' is, okay? What is it, like, the clay stuff the Egyptians smeared around to make their walls? All I know is what I dream and what I smell. Don't pick on me."

"Sorry," I muttered glibly. He could be totally defensive. If you're going to believe in an apocalypse, you have to be.

"I miss Mom. I need a Mom hug." He sighed. Mom listened to everything Owen ever had to say and never laughed at him. I felt unequipped, totally, to stand in for her.

But I reached my arms around him for what turned out to be a no-good hug. I was uptight, and not because he was a sweaty mess from walking downstairs while doing battle with the Q3 in his hip joints. Nothing bodily grosses me out. It's because I had this fuckin' thought: *What if I smell smoke?* Before I could think, I was holding my breath while I tried to hug him like Mom used to. I even laid this big kiss on his cheek like he used to get from her. But he swung away, looking about as gratified as a kid who's craving ice cream and gets a mouthful of lima beans.

Cora was standing at the head of the table when we entered the dining room, and the reason she never brought me my slushy stood beside her. The guy was tall, had a couple of inches on me at six-one.

"This is Mr. Calloway, whom I was telling you about," she said as we walked in, then turned to Owen. "He's with the historical society. He's going to refresh me on black-and-white photo development in a minute."

"Henry. Please." The man put out his hand to shake, and when I threw back my hands and pointed to my neck, he understood nicely enough. "Perhaps we should practice Far Eastern traditions around here, to avoid contagion." He bowed at us, which made Owen grin distractedly.

"You and I have already met," Henry said to him, picking up a file folder off the table. "I was at your last Thanksgiving Day football game."

"Trinity versus Mainland? Really?" Owen sank down in a chair I pulled out for him and shook out a sore leg. Football. That would get him thinking normally for a while.

"Yes. I saw your first interception and didn't think anything could top that."

My brother actually laughed. His second interception was more dramatic—at least it looked that way from the sidelines. He got some height that came out of nowhere. In the *Atlantic*

City Press photo, Jim Grimes, Mainland's running back, was all but eating Owen's ass when he intercepted.

"Did I meet you that day?" Owen asked in confusion.

"Not exactly." He opened the file and handed my brother a fairly big photo. I looked. Owen's number 72 took up the whole frame as he was run into the sidelines. Obviously, Henry had shot the photo a split second before getting smacked in the face by him and the Mainland player.

Owen smiled big. It was a nice move, bringing that picture. "Are you . . . all right?"

"Fine, fine. I was a track star in college. Despite that I'm turning thirty soon, I can still be fast when I'm about to be creamed."

"Wow. May I have this?"

"Absolutely."

I meandered into the kitchen to find Marg. I pointed at my throat as she was getting ready to turn on the blender full of oranges and ice cubes. She had our charts on clipboards on the walls already, and I looked at them while she blended. On top was the monthly calendar, obviously sent by St. Ann's. There was a green X for every headache. My brother's had twice as many as the rest of us—nothing new to me but ominous to look at. I grabbed a wet paper towel for Owen's sweaty hands. Marg put a glass in my grip and spun me toward the door, or away from the charts is probably more accurate.

Owen sat staring at a muffin in front of him, but he and Henry were talking about the game still as he let me wipe down his palms and fingers.

"You got sisters and brothers in Mainland?" Owen asked.

"No. My family's from Massachusetts. But I'd just started a

new job and two of my bosses had kids at Mainland. So I went with them."

I debated over whether to do battle with a muffin myself and decided against it, sending more slushy down my throat. It felt good.

"Where do you work?" Owen asked.

"Astor College. While I'm working on my doctorate in Philly, I'm on a genetic research team here and teach two classes. Photography is just a hobby."

I had the glass to my mouth and almost spit back into it. Cora looked at me and dropped her eyes quickly. Astor College was where one of the terrorists who poisoned Trinity Falls's water had been a visiting professor. Omar Loggi had snowed the college with false credentials, and his buddies tried to recruit students to be in ShadowStrike.

Henry cleared his throat awkwardly. "I know the place leaves a bad taste in your mouths. But Astor College is a huge, diverse place. It serves all kinds of people and has changed all its policies about visiting professors. It's back on the same path of excellence it's been on since 1900. Maybe I can redeem the place in your eyes."

"Maybe." Owen shrugged, casting a glance at Cora. "Cora and I, we don't much like to think about those guys."

Marg appeared with a surgical mask and handed it to Cora. Then Cora and Henry left for the basement, each carrying a box. I waited until they had gone downstairs and then went into the front hall. I stood looking up the stairs, listening for sounds of Alan and Mike. I knew they would become babbling idiots, talking about the weather, if I came anywhere near them. *Damn, I need a job.*

I'm a gut-instinct guy. And even though my mind wasn't working clearly, I could see images—strange things I'd seen on the house tour last night—and I suddenly knew how to get closer and hear them. Instead of going up, I silently followed Cora and Henry into the darkness of the basement.

ELEVEN

OWEN EBERMAN
SATURDAY, MAY 4, 2002
10:30 A.M.
DINING ROOM

I ATE A MUFFIN and drank my glass of orange juice after Scott drifted away, and I felt kind of relieved when his energy left the room. I love my brother for sure, but he's like a cyclone coming past you, and this was supposed to be the first peaceful morning I'd experienced in months.

I heard this bell *ding*, and when I looked out the dining room door, this real-live goat was standing square in the middle of the porch, staring in through the screen door. I had to shake my head to make certain I wasn't seeing stuff. I called Marg, and she came from the kitchen, drying her hands on a towel.

I pointed to the goat staring in, shaking its head and making its bell go *ding, ding*.

"There are two of them right now, though there used to be six," she said. "They belong to the property. There was so much to show you last night . . . out of sight, out of mind. It'll become one of your jobs to feed them. I just don't want them in the house."

I got this huge smile—barnyard animals do that to me—and I walked out there with a bran muffin. I'd heard goats will eat anything.

He was small, the kind with the tall horns and the goatee. He kept going *"Baa-AA-Baa,"* even after I sat down on the step. He ate pieces of muffin out of my hand but would stop after each bite, all *"Baa-AA-Baa."*

"Where's your buddy?" I asked him, looking all around. No other goat was in sight.

"Baa-AA-Baa."

We'd had a golden retriever, Champ, who finally died a couple of years back at fourteen. I always talked to Champ about my problems and felt certain he understood, and even if he didn't, I could get a load off without being laughed at by my friends, lectured by my brother, or touched affectionately by my mom. Back then, I'd wanted my mom to quit hugging on me. These days, I realized how crazy that had been. I scratched the goat behind its smooth ears.

"Can we talk?" I asked. "I gather you're not going to tell anyone my dark secrets."

"Baa-AA-Baa."

"Because everyone else would refuse to shut up about how I am some psycho-loon. I don't think it's such a gigantic sin to wish that this world would end soon."

"Baa-AA-Baa."

"Did you hear Scott ragging on about my fires-and-bombs dreams?"

"Baa-AA-aa-Baa-baa."

74

"What is it with people telling me what *my* dreams mean and don't mean? I could see if people were telling me about *their* dreams."

"*Baa-AA-Baa.*"

"They think that me and my dreams are inconvenient. But that is untrue, my man. I guess most people have this secret wish to die in a nice, safe, and comfortable bed. I don't get it. Whether I get blown up, beheaded on the Internet, or die in a bed, I don't really care. I'll do you one better: Since we're all going where we're going, I would rather die in a great story than a mediocre one. Apocalyptic dreams are *not* inconvenient. They're just a reminder that this disgusting and violent world will end, and something you could actually deal with is coming—"

"Dude, that is morbid. You want to be beheaded on the Internet? I'm calling Dr. Hollis."

I don't have to see Rain. I can smell her. She smells like strawberry shampoo, and she's got so much hair that you can't miss it. She was standing maybe two feet behind me in her bare, silent feet.

"That's not what I said, and I was not talking to you," I snapped over my shoulder.

"I know. You're talking to a goat." Her tone seemed more annoyed than appalled.

But to make sure no lecture was coming, I said, "I don't want to talk about it."

"Can I just sit with you?"

It's a free country. She sat down beside me on the step, scratched the goat behind the ears, and finally announced, "Marg said not to let the Professor in the house. He tries to come in, she says."

The Professor? I buried a grin. "What's the other one's name?"

"Sheep."

"Are you serious?"

She didn't laugh with me. She was fighting off my death-and-destruction monologue, which would be a kick in the stomach if you're so grounded in this world that you can't visualize the next. I knew Rain like I knew my face in the mirror. Here's her gig: She wants to fall in love, get married, have three kids, and be a gym teacher. Fine. But the truth is, if her kids were grown and her husband was bald and paunchy and she'd taught gym for twenty years and it looked like there was very little left except to get decrepit and croak, my dreams would be interesting to her. I'd be one of the few things left that wasn't boring. It's a convenience thing. She'll drive an SUV for twenty years and *then* think about what could be ultimately true.

And yet I couldn't resist picking up a piece of her hair and running it between my nose and mouth. That strong smell of shampoo . . . everything about Rain was strong and real. She could bring me down to earth. *You're a kick in the stomach, that's what you are, Owen. Just . . . be nice.*

I let go of her hair and flopped my hand onto her back. She quit petting the Professor, who strutted off—muffin gone, conversation over. I rubbed up and down her spine, which inspired her to lean forward, rest her head on my knee, and wrap her arms under her legs.

"Sorry," I said. "My weird dreams, they bend my head around . . ."

She didn't answer right away, which meant either that she

was devising a way to play shrink and talk me out of wanting to see the end of this world, or I had freaked her out beyond words. When she finally spoke up, she didn't seem all that freaked out. "Unfortunately, I dreamed about elephants all bloody night."

"Elephants . . ." I remembered her saying in the limo that Miss Haley's comments about forced abstinence were like telling us, "Don't think of an elephant." It makes you think of elephants.

I said, "Dude, don't let Miss Haley open Pandora's box on you. You were, like, a completely hormonally repressed athlete before she said it. Remain that way."

"Do not say 'hormones' to me right now."

"A perfectly nonsexual creature."

"Do *not* say 'sex.' I don't think you get it. I think I discovered the most frustrating thing in the world this morning. It's called 'the half hour between the time that you wake up and the time that you get up.' In half an hour, I made out with Danny Hall twenty times."

I sighed. Back to earth. "Guys call it the Dreaded Fifteen— it's fifteen minutes if you're a guy. You're supposed to put your feet on the floor as soon as you realize your eyes are open if you're on a team that made the playoffs. It keeps your game tension good if you resist all temptations to think about girls during the Dreaded Fifteen."

Rain might be calling Dr. Hollis on me, but I was going to call Miss Haley on her and yell, *Your speeches have train-wrecked a perfectly upstanding girl. Why did you have to go there?* I hoped that would be the end of it, but it turned out Rain was just getting started.

"Remember when you guys brought that anatomically correct blow-up doll into the locker room for Dempsey on his birthday last year?"

My mind was a blank, but I pushed her head off my knee. I'm only human, too.

"Dempsey had asked out fifteen girls who all said no. Remember? Some of the guys thought that would make a funny birthday present. Dobbins threw it into the gym when the coach came out of his office to see what the ruckus was. And all the cheerleaders were screaming in horror ..."

Blow-Up Beatrix Buxom Bunz came clear in my mind, with, like, nine guys dancing the seizure salsa with her in the locker room. One side of my mouth slid up, then the other.

"I almost got benched with those idiots. I told the coach I never touched the thing ... for some reason, he believed me."

"I wonder why?" Her sarcasm blew out in a sigh. "Anyway. I was online just now on my new laptop. I thought it might take away my urge to think about 'elephants' if I tried to find, like, Blow-Up Bernie Big-Beef Bronco—"

I turned to stare, and she turned as if something caught her attention at the far end of the porch, so I was staring into her hair. Was she messing with me? I figured she was, but I couldn't resist it. I bit.

"We would have a major problem with any anatomically correct blow-up doll."

"I'm having a problem *now*."

"A different type of problem. You have to blow up Beatrix with a hair dryer. Every time I heard your hair dryer turn on ... I would wonder if that was my cue to leave the floor quickly."

She put her forehead on her knees so I still couldn't see her face, but I heard this "Hah, hah, hah, hah" while her shoulders shook. I thought of something else.

"God forbid you jump on and blow a hole in the dude . . . You'd be all *pssssssssssst,* down the stairs, out the front door, over the treetops . . ."

". . . halfway back to Trinity Falls in my . . . my red negligee attire. Hey. Maybe I wouldn't need my car out here after all."

The bronchitis part of Q3 started making us wheeze and cough after we'd cracked up enough. But I was on a roll. "Big-Beef Bernie probably wouldn't do much for you—unless he was uploaded with a voice box and five thousand different sayings. Things like, 'I understand how you feel.' 'I love how you put that. Say it again.'"

She usually punched my arm when my teasing struck close to her sore spots, but she just sat up, looked me dead in the eye, and got this huge victory grin on her face. *Okay, so she'd made me laugh.* My blow-up dreams had been neutralized by blow-up dolls. So, maybe they were just nightmares, and my brother was right, and this world can make you laugh sometimes, too. *Score one, Rain.*

But there was a slight problem here. I'd often thought if I lived long enough, I wanted to be a minister. And yet I'd spent half my life in a locker room. My sense of humor was under siege. I couldn't prevent myself from laughing at stuff like Blow-Up Beatrix Buxom Bunz. I was thinking about how I could have more self-discipline when this ice pick jabbed through my temple and left my stomach sick. This is how my Headaches from Hell often started—with a stabbing pain like an ice pick being twisted in my head for about four hours. *Not again. Not so soon.*

"On a different subject . . ." Rain's voice cut through. "I stole a tape for you from Cora's box in her closet. It's one her mom and Jeremy Ireland taped back in the 1980s. I know how much you love that woman."

"Thanks," I muttered, not wanting to let on to Rain that she'd worked so hard to make me laugh and right away some pain was bumming me again. I forced my mouth into auto-pilot. "It's our big secret that I think Aleese Holman is one of the coolest women of modern times. You can't tell Cora and Scott that I forgave her for the drug habit. Cora would hurl. Truth is, lots of eccentric people do weird stuff . . ."

"Anyway. You can watch it. I left it in the VHS for you."

I had thought the ice-pick pain was subsiding, but as the Professor walked around in the grass, the clangs from his bell started sending smaller tremors to follow the jab. All our headaches could be classified as strange, but this one was even stranger, coming on within a day of my last one, and so close to a meal that you'd almost think Marg had poisoned me.

TWELVE

SCOTT EBERMAN
SATURDAY, MAY 4, 2002
10:30 A.M.
BASEMENT

I FUMBLED DOWN TO THE BASEMENT, remembering the place as I'd seen it in a flashlight beam on last night's house tour. It had at one time been servants' quarters, and a fireplace sat in the center of the big room you entered at the foot of the stairs. There were no lights, Mrs. Starn had said, except for two outlets added thirty years ago in the photo historian's darkroom. But in the beam of the flashlight, I had seen this metal ornament over the mantel. I asked Mrs. Starn what that was, and she said it was a speaking tube that Mrs. Kellerton had used to summon servants without clanging bells or hollering.

I stood in the center of the big room, hearing Cora's muffled voice from down the hall. They had the darkroom door shut.

What I'd seen last night was buried under the fog of drugs and moving-day stress. I never miss a trick, but lately I relied on my instincts more than my memory. Something had interested me on the third floor, and I'd spent a long time looking at the same metal ornaments on the walls in all four bedrooms that were on the third floor. They looked like old-fashioned speaking tubes of some sort. Three of them had been filled in with concrete, meaning you couldn't hear through them. One of them had just been a hole.

I stared at the metal ornament above the mantel until my eyes got used to the gloom, helped by a little light coming from a basement window in a far-off corner. I could make out that metal thing and could even see the blackened hole in it. I had a one-in-four chance.

I could hear something, surely, though it wasn't voices. It sounded like something dragging, far off, maybe in another third-floor room.

My luck tended to swing like a pendulum. I had been one of four people in Trinity Falls who drank enough poisoned water to end up in a place like this. We were four out of a population of eleven thousand. That would make us very, very unlucky. But any time I've had bad luck in life, I've noticed I've had good luck in some other way that could be as charming as my bad luck was alarming.

". . . wished the floors creaked just a little." Alan's voice.

"Dang. We should build our new offices out of these beams."

"Nah. I'd prefer to hear someone creeping up on me. Especially with my dear friend Scott wandering around. Get a couple of keys made for this room. He wouldn't break a lock, though if we ever left it open, he might feel privileged . . ."

I backed slowly up to a rocker that I spotted as my eyes became accustomed, and I sat in it, just as content as a porch dweller at the age of ninety. The voices weren't quite perfect.

And they weren't so loud that Cora could hear it from behind that closed door when she was talking, and not so soft that I had to stick my ear right up to it. I rocked back and forth slowly.

Tiger's voice started this time. "So, guess what Hodji Montu picked up last night?"

"A woman? I hear he's going through an ugly divorce."

"He got lucky, let's say, but not that kind of luck. He found Omar."

"Sweet Jesus. So soon?" Alan said, and a moan followed.

"Omar's in Mexico."

"How'd Hodji get that?"

"It's classified. Some source to the New York squad, and I don't ask. But Hodji is leaving for there this afternoon with a few of those agents, and they'll meet up with some border people. They're going to try to lure Omar in. And where he is, you know VaporStrike is one step either ahead or behind."

"Jeezus, Mike. I hoped we might have a year off."

"Would have been nice. But apparently the cell is quite anxious to show off its new designer germs. They're planning to strike an aeronautical engineering convention."

"Any clue where?" Alan asked.

"Not yet. But I just got an update from Imperial while I was pulling in here. Latest simply says it's across the street from an amusement park. The amusement park would get hit, too."

"You really think the target is in America?" he asked.

"With Omar surfacing in Mexico, I think the writing's on the wall."

I flinched at the sharp sound of their footsteps. Maybe Alan went to the window, but the syllables I couldn't hear, I could piece together.

"I think logic would dictate that the target site is not only American, but it's very close to here, to Trinity Falls, to New York—'Home Base,' as those devils used to say."

"I thought we had decided that dogs don't return to their vomit," Mike said, "though obviously, Imperial wouldn't have called me on my cell phone if he didn't feel the same way."

"In this case, we would think that their next strike would be Spain or Egypt or somewhere utterly surprising. Except for one thing. Omar's lab. We found one lab near Trinity Falls but decided it was either a decoy or a small satellite lab. We found traces of the Q3 virus in it, but it was little more than a closet at Astor College, and it couldn't have contained the type of equipment it would take to cultivate strains of biochemical weapons. Since our CDC sources believe that Q3 had to be cultivated near the strike site, the real lab could possibly still be functional. They may want to get to it."

My skin crawled from my forehead to my ankles. *They may be near here . . . or coming here.*

Alan went on. "I think they'd rather risk coming to their old lab than trying to move it, trying to move whatever molds and mildews and platelet blasters they're cultivating."

"Disgusting," Mike said.

"But logical."

"So we're looking for convention centers near here that are planning to house an aeronautical engineering convention. Do we have to wait for a lot of stats and printouts from headquarters? Or can we start looking into what logic would dictate?"

"What do you mean?" Alan asked.

"Summer's comin'. South Jersey's got three cities with a convention center right across from an amusement pier. If we find one having an aero convention sometime soon, can we start combing those cities for look-alikes to our photos on file?"

"I'm thinking we should wait for the stats. What's the likelihood it would be—" Alan said something that was probably a few cities, but he dragged a chair across the floor at the same time. I'd think it through later.

Mike Tiger said thoughtfully, "You could be dead-on. There are a lot of convention facilities in this state, but their business drops to nothing in the summer unless they're by the ocean. Still, I can't blame you for not wanting to tie up a lot of funds and agents on a whim."

"What happened to the Kid?" Alan asked. "Is our chatter-chasing guru functioning yet? I hope the New York squad had the good sense to transport him to Nigeria, or somewhere he can actually go back to work. Ironic, isn't it? He can work for the Americans so long as he's not on American soil?"

Mike laughed, though he didn't sound amused. "It's crazy. I can surely understand USIC's rules about not hiring minors. But I heard Hodji Montu say once that half the intelligence the Kid's dad sold us before he died actually came from the Kid. He's been at this from Pakistan since he was about ten years old. But I don't think they were able to move him out of the country. I understand he is extremely ill, though it's all very hush-hush. I highly doubt he's capable of tracking Omar, but maybe Washington has other v-spies. You want to wait for them before looking into—"

The chair skidded back a little and drowned their voices, and I heard footsteps moving away. Their voices turned silent. Meeting adjourned until later, obviously.

The Kid is extremely ill. That took some of the jollies out of me right away. Roger O'Hare had mentioned his bad asthma several times, but I thought the Kid had come to America to get rid of it. And is "extremely ill" a phrase you would use to describe chronic asthma? Something sounded amiss, and my paramedic alarm bell rang in frustration, like when my ambulance squad got a call and we couldn't find the house right away. However, asking would probably be useless. We had asked Roger for an e-mail address for the Kid once we got our laptop gifts, saying we wanted to write him thank-you notes. Roger had said he would pass on our thanks, and no address was provided.

The rest of this info was mind-boggling, and I let it roll through my head like water over a dry sponge. A potential terror attack nearby ... not across some ocean. I felt guilty feeling so happy about that. But then, if the dudes were going to make trouble, it ought to be near to me, where maybe I could get my foot into it somehow. I forced away thoughts of the Kid and sat there rocking contentedly and chuckling, ignoring my sore throat and feeling all the luck I'd experienced in life come rushing back to even the score a little.

I glanced down the hall at Cora's darkroom door, hearing Henry's voice and realizing some of the challenges here. I fumbled in my pocket for the pile of tissues I always carried around lately, balled them up, and stuck them hard into the little hole in the speaking tube. It barely showed in the dark, and I hoped it would keep other people from hearing anything. They didn't need to hear USIC-anything, not while Cora was so busy trying to ignore all of that, trying so hard to be normal.

Jeezus. I couldn't even remember what normal was ...

THIRTEEN

**CORA HOLMAN
SATURDAY, MAY 4, 2002
11:45 A.M.
THE POND**

I FELT ALEESE DRIFTING THROUGH ME during my darkroom lesson. After forty-five minutes of feeling like her ghost was laughing at my meager talents in the blackness, I was more than glad to head back upstairs. Fortunately, in my darkroom class at school, I had been a sponge, and Henry offered more praise and encouragement than instruction.

He and I walked around the grounds, and he also gave me some great pointers on how to frame a shot. We took priceless pictures of a goat with a bell around its neck—a perfect subject. He wanted to *baa* at us more than move around. Henry mentioned there being two of them, and I hoped to see the other as we walked down a trail that ended at the pretty pond. Seeing the water, I raised my camera to my face.

"You can always block the shot better in the darkroom, but try to block it as well as you can from the start . . . from now," he said.

His camera was digital, whereas I still loved film. We took the same shot of the pond, and he was able to show me his in the viewfinder. His was far better, I gathered, as he had focused with the pond in the middle, whereas in mine it had been at the bottom of the frame.

"Stand there . . ." He moved ahead of me, turned, and took a shot of me holding my camera with one hand, a stray branch in the other. He showed it to me.

"See? And if you're shooting people, you want their eyes as much in the center as possible."

I blushed, looking at the image. For all intents and purposes, it was a really great shot. A puffy white cloud had dimmed the sky moments ago, which made the light in the surroundings slightly foreboding. I looked wide-eyed and yet focused, as someone walking through an enchanted forest might. My dark eyes were at the very center of the frame and would pull an onlooker's eyes to them. I would say the picture spoke volumes about my being slightly anxious and slightly shy.

"You're a good subject," he said, nudging me playfully. "Come on. You want to shoot some water? Water always involves catching the light correctly."

I looked up at the numerous cotton puffs above us, thinking we would get a variety of lighting opportunities at the pond just by showing up. I halted when we got to the break in the trees.

Rain was sitting Indian-style on a large flat rock that hung over the water's edge, with her back to us. She was leaning off to the side, her head on one hand. Then I saw the tissue in her grip and figured she might be crying.

"Maybe I should leave you for now," Henry said, probably sensing my mood shift.

I waved in thanks and went slowly toward Rain, feeling my insides sway. I had not gotten Henry's phone number or made any further plans with him. I could get Mrs. Starn to put me in contact later.

I sat down slowly beside her while she blew her nose in a tissue she'd obviously used far too many times. I reached in my pocket for the stash Scott replenished daily in our jackets as part of his staying-busy routine. I handed her another.

"Thanks. I'm trying to keep my crying out of everyone's earshot. I know it's getting on all your nerves."

"Not mine," I lied, putting an arm around her shoulder. I had been very sympathetic to her crying at first, but into the second week of it, even I had felt drained. I didn't expect to have much to offer her in the way of comfort. "What's wrong?"

"Owen has another HH." Headache from Hell.

"Already?" I flinched. He'd never had one two days in a row. The rest of us could go as many as five days.

"I broke my ass making up some story about looking up dirty Internet purchases, which made him laugh and all. He was doing great. Then . . . he got up very suddenly and left. He's in his room with the curtains drawn and the lights off. We know what that means." She wiped tears around on her face, not bothering with the soggy tissue. "I'm just starting to wonder if we've been given false hopes."

"By whom?"

"By the doctors and nurses at St. Ann's. They were always so cheerful. And what with the cards, and telegrams from royals, and calls from Hollywood, yadda yadda. It was a big, old mess, but sometimes I could feel . . ."

"Euphoric?"

"Yeah, with all that attention. Who wouldn't?"

"I loved the flowers," I said. The whole lobby at St. Ann's had been wall-to-wall flowers for several weeks.

"But we're down to maybe six cards a day. Dr. Godfrey is only coming up here twice a week, and those happy nurses are gone. They've been replaced by a nurse who's cheerful enough, but she's a hospice specialist. She's got death on the brain."

"What do you mean?"

"I had to listen to her speech early this morning about how we should fully understand things. Like if something goes wrong here—somebody spirals, has a terrible fall, catches something deadly, and starts to crash and bleed out—there will be no more exploratory diagnostics for a while. It would only give info that they couldn't do anything about. They're not doing any invasive surgeries until we improve. We would hemorrhage."

I didn't know what to say. I rubbed her back a little as the wind blew up a gust. "Well, don't panic about Owen" was all I could think of. "We all learned back at St. Ann's not to panic. It's a lesson I'd like to carry through life."

The wind rose through the trees and hissed a little. The leaves were still budding. She stayed silent, so I tried a change of subject.

"What dirty Internet purchases?"

Her smile spread a little finally, then she turned and bobbed me lightly on the nose with one knuckle. "You don't want to know."

All three of them assumed they had to hush their trash talk

when I came into a room. Often, I entered to find any combination of them, and the talk would suddenly cease. It bothered me. I didn't mind hearing *anything*. It's just that when it came my turn to contribute, I couldn't think of a thing to say.

"You're still wigging out over Miss Haley," I guessed.

"You're not?"

I crinkled my nose, trying to remember how Dr. Hollis had taught me to tell the truth. Children of drug addicts are notoriously bad at truth telling. He'd told me to inhale slowly and release the truth on the exhale.

"I just . . . put it on the back burner. It's no tragic loss. My last conquest? I think dinosaurs were still roaming around Trinity Falls."

"Who?" she asked, suddenly interested.

Three breaths, and on the exhale: "Danny Daggett. Seventh grade closet game."

"Oh . . . damn!" Her horror echoed through the trees as it rightfully should have. I giggled. "How'd you get stuck with him?"

"Luck of the draw."

"Ole rooster legs. He *still* looks like he's nine—"

"To answer your question, I'm not troubled by my losses. But would you mind, please, not sharing that with the boys?"

"Why? They don't care."

I cared. I was growing more comfortable with them every day, and sometimes I could even forget the canyons that had separated them from me in high school. But most of that was because I always tried to pass myself off as mysterious rather than naive. What I just told Rain would truly blow my cover, I decided.

Rain continued to gripe. "And I would love to know how Scott goes around acting so cool, when his past is so much about being Joe Romance. Did you know that in December of freshman year, he was the girls' pinup in the Slut of the Month Club?"

My eyes flew to her. "What's that?"

"Slut of the Month Club. It was some gag going on inside Sarah Shoemaker's softball locker, but anyone on the team could vote on the guy. And there's some truth in all jokes. Someone had scrawled across his chest in the picture, 'Beware of Mr. Bag 'n' Bolt.'"

I covered my smile with my hand.

She kept laughing, throwing in a cough now and again, but it was good to hear. I had missed hearing her laugh as much lately. And yet, it was becoming plain that most of our laughter had to do with the past, while our future was a dark and very serious matter.

"Do you think we've seen the end of terror attacks?" she asked uneasily. I sensed her quandary. Surely, we wouldn't want anyone else to be in our shoes, but we hated feeling so freakishly alone.

I just went with the truth. "Only some of those men were arrested. There's more of them out there. But maybe they'll lie dormant for years."

"I wish I'd been attacked by a serial killer instead of those guys." She folded her hands in her lap, restlessly letting her left fingers bend back her right, and then the opposite. "That way, I would have had a chance at scratching someone's eyes out."

I understood her feeling. Nonetheless . . . "You wouldn't want to wake up and see a terrorist at your bedside," I said.

She watched me, her fingers relaxing. The only people to bring up my having been attacked in the ICU by a Shadow-Strike assassin were Dr. Hollis and Mr. Steckerman. And it was a vague, brief mention each time. I was supposed to bring up "whatever I remembered and wanted to discuss," as Dr. Hollis had put it.

I went on, "They're more like demons. Oma always used to say she suspected that the devil personified would be very well spoken and wear an expensive suit."

"You . . . thought you were finally meeting your dad," she stumbled.

"Please. Don't tell Scott I remember this," I begged her.

She nodded, shifting around uncomfortably. "It would be cool if he knew you remembered him saving your life."

"I wouldn't forget that. He almost killed himself trying. I just haven't said anything because . . . it gets him all hyped up to talk your dad into a USIC job so he could go find those guys. I don't want . . ." I trailed off, feeling selfish, but Rain finished my sentence.

"What? You don't want to wake up to find one beside your bed again, if he comes looking for Scott and gets lost in the dark?"

I laughed uncomfortably. It definitely sounded stupid.

"I don't think that's so dumb. I mean, if he's helping USIC, that makes him a target. Though the part about waking up to see another one, that's a lot of what-ifs all strung together," Rain said.

"Still, I'm paranoid."

"You have reason to be." She rubbed my knee and assured me flatly, "Scott will never get a USIC job. USIC policies are etched in blood. Intelligence will take some clerks at eighteen, but he's in bad health. They simply won't have it . . . unless he recovers, and then we won't be living with him, and you've got nothing to worry about. Maybe Marg will give Scott medical things to do. Maybe he can draw our blood and do the chart thing . . ."

She was done crying, it seemed, but I felt uneasy over all this speak about Scott becoming a target. I don't know which bothered me more—him becoming a potential target or me having been one for reasons never made clear. I supposed I had been the easiest hit; I'd been in a coma, utterly helpless.

I suggested we go back to the house, as it had been a while since we'd taken any pills, and we were sure to be due for something. But that was the small reason covering what could become a big compulsion if I let it. I was finding my peaceful spot on the property, and it happened to be wherever Scott Eberman was. It had been like that at St. Ann's, too. He'd go down to help out in the phone station in the ER, and our ward became an anxious place. He'd come back to the ward, and I would relax.

I was not relaxed now. I found myself drawn back to the house—back to where he was. As I stood up and glanced across the pond, I was met with a pair of eyes. They peered between a six-inch space in the bramble of vines and leaves between three trees. I froze, watching, trying to be reasonable, wondering if I were hallucinating again. But I decided I definitely was swapping gazes with someone . . . or something . . .

"Rain?"

When I sensed her looking up at me, I could neither move nor explain. She peered across the water, too.

"What do you see?" she asked.

My hand rose to my throat, but the scream wouldn't come. I waited for the person to blink. I told myself that if it didn't blink, it was surely a hallucination.

"What is it?" she demanded, nudging my leg hard. It spun my gaze, and when I found the small hole in the bramble again, no one was there.

I pointed and said, "Someone was back there—staring at us."

She stood up slowly. "It's probably one of those damn photographers."

We'd been warned about straggling journalists at St. Ann's. They'd been told not to come here, not to photograph us. I'd rather it be a snooping photographer than a hallucination . . . or someone in ShadowStrike.

Rain moved forward, squinting slightly. "I didn't see anything, but I believe you. I'm gonna kick some butt."

"No, you're not . . ." I grabbed her arm.

But she actually stood on the rock and shouted. "Hey, pervert! I got an STD from a WMD! Why don't you come over here and catch it?"

"Don't," I whispered, my hair standing. "It could be some local drunk who got lost walking home last night."

She jumped down off the rock and followed the sandy beach around toward the other side of the pond, and I followed. Where it ended, we picked up the trail that led around to the other side.

"Please." I took her arm, planting my feet.

"I hate being afraid of things. I really hate that worse than anything . . ." She pulled away and kept going. I could suddenly see why she was a great sports player, and why her father was reluctant to let her have her car out here. She had a reckless streak. Someone could punch her and knock her down, or she could spiral into a bad mood while driving and crash the car into a tree.

But no one was behind the bramble. There *was* a trail back there, though I hadn't heard any sneaker tread running or any twigs cracking. *Aleese? Mrs. Kellerton?*

"Let's just go back to the house," I said.

"Whatever." Rain took my arm and walked beside me. I resisted the urge to look back. I resisted the urge to run, too, though my instincts told me to get inside to safety.

FOURTEEN

SHAHZAD HAMDANI
SATURDAY, MAY 4, 2002
NOON
HIS BEDROOM

I HAVE ASKED TYLER to surf for "tularemia" again and see if he comes up with any more suspicious deaths. But he lacks my experience in looking past horrific news for what information bits might be helpful. He grows distracted easily. He copes by reading Cora Holman's blog for the umpteenth time.

He finally comes away from his own terminals and into my room only when he hears the rooster crowing from my dog-leash program. We see that VaporStrike is online, but he idles, waiting for someone else.

Tyler spouts impatiently, "Cora hasn't written in her blog in a couple of days. Think she's okay?"

"I can find out from Hodji . . . if you wish. He told you not to get obsessed. We did our best to save them. Now we don't need heartbreak if one of them doesn't make it. We have to think of us, he says."

"Yeah, but . . . we're geeks and totally boring," he complains.

Even now, I do not understand his obsession with Cora Holman. I am prone to the other, as we do not see many yellow-haired women in Pakistan, and I find her so interesting to gaze at pictorially. As well, I shook Miss Rain's hand once, and her charm and charisma ran up my arm like electricity. Miss Cora had been too ill to meet me.

"Maybe we are not so boring these days," I say as Omar logs on. "Though I am confused. They should not be meeting so soon."

Omar and VaporStrike exchange in Spanish, with which I am familiar, and we can almost translate aloud.

OmarLoggi: I have only one location left before I will become recognizable in one of these cafés. What on earth is it?

VaporStrike: I have been on the phone with Chancellor. I think you will be unhappy with him, though he is quite pleased with himself. He said to tell you he created ten thousand milligrams of FireFall. With one milligram, he was able to kill your remaining three monkeys.

Tyler adds quickly, "At least they haven't killed any people. Yet. Can I throw up anyway? I like monkeys."

I am more taken by this player, Chancellor, who must be a fellow scientist as well as a financial backer. So far, Omar is the only scientist we have ever known of in ShadowStrike. Hodji will be pleased with us when we send this.

OmarLoggi: You idiots. What of the monkey corpses? How do you plan to dispose of them? Didn't your mother teach you never to play with fire? I wish you had waited until I could cross over and come to you.

"*Whoa!*" Our voices clatter with more exclamations, and I bang my fists victoriously on the desk. Tyler makes the victory dance in the middle of my bed. *Cross over and come to you.*

He puts truths together aloud. "VaporStrike is in America. How the fuck did he get back in? Did he swim?"

"He is with this Chancellor person . . ." I watch carefully, thinking he will spill his whereabouts. He does, but in such an indirect way it only creates more frustration.

> **VaporStrike:** I took care of the corpse disposal.
> **OmarLoggi:** I can't wait to hear.
> **VaporStrike:** I double bagged all three. Two I buried by the water's edge. However, it created an odor that permeates many miles. For the other, I decided to contact you to see what you wanted me to do.

"They're near water," Tyler murmurs. "Lake? River? Ocean? C'mon . . ."

> **OmarLoggi:** Keep to your job, my little assassin, and let me keep to mine. I told you this fire will cook a man from the inside out. Do you think it will not eat through garbage bags? Where is your mind?
> **VaporStrike:** What's done is done. Chancellor is not concerned. He said if anyone finds the remains and is stupid enough to handle them much, we will have another test subject. There. It has started.

OmarLoggi: Do you really think a babe in arms like Chancellor will force my hand? Don't let him play with fire again. You need to put the remaining corpse inside a steel drum. Do not bury it. The ground will smoke orange. You need to find a dumpster where the trash men are coming tomorrow.

VaporStrike: All of this nonsense I will do for you. In return, I expect you will give a go-ahead on Colony Two. The germ is fully operative.

They idle long. I search the chatter for any details of where VaporStrike may be. I wonder if my word "water" is a bad translation. VaporStrike has used the word *marea,* and the normal word for water is *agua. Marea* is more often associated with coasts and *tides.*

I explain this to Tyler, who gets a jolt of revelation that causes him to clamp on to my scabby shoulder. "Lab monkeys? Don't you have to have a *lab?* Didn't Roger tell us while we were in Beth Israel that they hadn't found Omar's local Trinity Falls lab after the raid? Aren't there all sorts of barrier islands down that way?"

I will look on a map directly, but chatter appears.

OmarLoggi: Do not pressure me. If you want to assassinate, go find me some v-spies instead of killing my lab monkeys.

He exits, and Tyler makes some "bring it on" banter, reminding me of the USIC agents' belief that he had a death wish and suicidal tendencies. That was all before he turned in his mother as a spy, which seemed to calm him somewhat. I think now he has only a reckless streak, which could also get us killed if we are not careful.

He settles down finally and asks, "So . . . you're thinking that VaporStrike is on an island in New Jersey?" Before I can answer, he makes a stinging point. "*We're* on an island, buddy. *Long* Island. New York is not that far away. And Long Island *was* the home-away-from-home for VaporStrike back in March, back when he was using the Trinitron Internet café to launch his dirty secrets."

When I was brought here from Pakistan, it was to v-spy on VaporStrike and other operatives from inside Trinitron, where I could use the café's intranet system to quickly cache their screens and translate. VaporStrike and others had launched their experiment on Trinity Falls from less than a mile from here. They scattered to the winds or were captured down at Trinity.

I shake my head, trying to sort out the confusing issues. If they are using the Jersey lab, VaporStrike would not travel three hours to his former jurisdiction simply to get rid of a deadly, telling steel drum. Unless, of course, he can't find week-end trash collection in New Jersey but he can in New York. Still, New York is huge, and VaporStrike would be stupid to return to a place where police and USIC agents have photos of him and would recognize him instantly. I do not feel unsafe, despite Omar's encouragement to have us found. I feel more concerned about what else—or who else—might wind up suffering some hideous death before USIC can catch the lot of them.

FIFTEEN

I FELT LIKE A VAMPIRE who'd had his first red meal. If intelligence were blood, I would have grown fangs after my eavesdropping session in the basement. I parked myself on the parlor couch facing the hallway, waiting for Mike and Alan to either sneak off to their third-floor hangout and talk some more or take a cell phone call, of which I could hear one end. *Jersey cities with convention centers right across from amusement piers.* I played eenie-meenie-minie-moe with Wildwood, Asbury Park, and Griffith's Landing. My problem was that, like most New Jersey natives, I could name the barrier islands in order from north to south, but I couldn't tell you what cities on the mainland were behind each one. I had no idea which barrier isles lay in front of me, but Omar's main lab is somewhere within driving distance of the strike. I didn't know whether to laugh or be stunned.

I pretended to read, though it was like pretending to sleep when burglars are in the house. Finally, Mike Tiger left in his car, heading back to Manhattan for some meeting, and the goodbye comments let me know he'd either be spending the night with his family in North Jersey or he wouldn't be back until late tonight. Alan went to the kitchen to talk to Marg. I could hear his car keys rattling in his hand, which meant he was leaving, too. *Damn.*

Cora and Rain came back from a walk outside, huffing and looking not thrilled about something. Rain went for the sound of her dad's voice, and Cora came in to me, finding her smile.

"You're still up," she said.

I was working on my second slushy and was starting to feel okay to talk.

"You're winded," I noted.

She didn't answer, though I knew well the way her eyes darted when she got nervous about something.

"You meet up with the Jersey Devil out there?" I swallowed a gulp of slushy orange. "You shouldn't be running. Not on all these blood thinners."

She rolled her eyes. "I wish I could say I was running to get this winded. We were walking quickly. It's . . . Jersey Devilish. I really don't think you want to hear."

I moved my feet to make room for her, and she sat on the couch, but not like she usually sits when I'm around—like she's ready to jump up again. She sank down on the cushions, laid her head on the backrest, and shut her eyes with a huge exhale.

I watched her from between my knees, not sure I was up for the usual Cora games—i.e., trying to drag information out of her. I went back to my pretend reading, my ears ready to hear Alan's cell phone ring. He was responding to something Rain must have been whispering. I couldn't hear a damn word of it.

Time to play the game. I toed Cora in the leg. "What happened?"

"Nothing."

"Right." I toed her in the ribs, in a tickle spot, which made her squirm sideways and almost smile. Then I crossed my ankles on top of her so she couldn't get away until she confessed. I had pinned her down like this once at St. Ann's, just to torture her, when I was reading on the couch in the lounge. I'd actually spent very little time with the three of them at the hospital. I knew everyone in the place and did everything from answer phones in the ER to clean the break room when I felt good. That day, I hadn't been feeling good, and misery loves company. She got so jumpy from being held down that the game was over in about thirty seconds.

I figured I could squirt an answer out of her by trying it again. She merely dropped a hand onto my sweat sock and lay there with her eyes shut.

Alan's voice rose so slightly that I figured only my tuned-in ears would catch it. "Cora shouldn't be afraid of that—"

"Don't talk to her now," Rain whispered. "Not while . . ." and I could hear no more.

Cora was sitting under Mrs. Kellerton's portrait—the one that looked at you no matter where in the room you were. She opened her eyes and kinked her neck so that for a moment she was looking at the portrait upside down. I was four feet to the left and five feet under the woman, and I still felt those eyes were watching me. I always wondered how painters did that.

Cora dropped her head again and started talking in the calmest of monotones. "I had the best time with Henry. You have to get to know him. He's an excellent photographer. He's going to give me copies of his prints so that I can try to get the same shot, same lighting . . . He reminded me of everything I forgot about developing old-fashioned film."

Obviously there was some big secret going on, and Henry Calloway was the diversionary topic. *Whatever.* A part of me wanted to leap up and hear what Rain and Alan were whispering about, but Cora was absently picking lint off my sock, and it kept me grounded. She rarely touched me. I had touched her a lot—a swat on the head on my way past, a nudge with my foot in therapy sessions, which could get her to spill some secret if she halfway decided she was going to anyway. I'm a touchy-feely guy. She's a kind, sensitive, sympathetic ice cube.

"Tell me about him."

"Okay . . . He helped Mrs. Starn and the historical society write the grant to convert this place. He knows a lot about grants from being a professor. His department only gave him a five-hundred-dollar budget for research last year because it was his first year, and he drew another ten thousand in government grant money. He wants to exhume one of the bodies of the Kellerton children to prove they had diabetes."

She turned to me at that point, knowing that exhuming bodies would be of interest to me. She glanced up at the portrait again, but this time with a slight grin that looked excited.

"Because Mrs. Kellerton kept such accurate records of all their symptoms, he says he can publish a report on an herb called pitasara that she sent for from India, which seemed to help. Mrs. Kellerton wrote that she felt it kept her youngest two children alive for an extra two years."

"So . . . this pitasara could be helpful to diabetic patients with an intolerance to synthetic insulin."

"Correct. If he can prove it was diabetes."

Interesting. Totally. I wondered if Henry would let me read his research to pass some time, maybe help him out a bit. I almost said as much, but something stirred up my gut instincts—maybe stirred them up for the second time, and the first time I had been too distracted by Owen and by the memory of the speaking tube down in the basement.

"Be careful," I said instead.

"Of what?"

"Of Mr. Almost Professor. For one, you're contagious."

I pulled my feet off of her and put my eyes back on the page.

"And what else?" she asked. She put her hand on my knee and leaned closer, sounding deeply concerned. Something had spooked her outside.

"He's hot for you," I said, lest she think it was something worse.

She froze and then laughed. "What on earth would make you think a thing like that?"

I read a few lines before thinking of how my gut instincts could be explained. Maybe they couldn't. "He's a guy . . . you're not."

"I've had teachers younger than he is," she argued.

"So?" I didn't look up, so I could keep my straight face. I felt it was important.

"So, that's absurd!"

Not unless he's gay. Cora never had any big brothers to give her the lines on how guys think. She was a beautiful young girl. He was—

"He's a physicist." She giggled. "And on the board of this place. Surely he understands the situation with our health."

"Cora. Guys on death row get swooning girls in droves. And have you checked out Owen's fan mail? I think half of our fifteen thousand cards were from teenage girls who told him he was hot and offered their phone numbers. It doesn't matter, okay? A guy is a guy, and he's one."

"Well, you and Owen don't think of us like that," she argued.

"Well, we're extraordinary," I lied.

I kept reading, though the words weren't going in. I was suddenly aware of her warm hand on my knee. She opened her mouth to raise some other worthless argument, but my knee and I bolted away from her and her hand before I could hit the phase of thinking about where girls' hands had been known to travel. I felt her watching my back, her incomplete sentence dangling in the air. *Lesson: I can touch you, but you can't touch me.* I wasn't looking to be fair—only to get by.

Alan now mumbled to Rain in the dining room. I moved toward the door, yawning and stretching, my instincts telling me not to look too interested when I got in their line of vision.

They were coming out into the foyer together, and Alan was saying, "They're allowed to stare. It's a free country. They're just not allowed to shoot photos."

"You're *sure* it was a journalist?" Rain asked him.

"I'll go take a look around, but if it wasn't, it was some local. Rain, you have been in every magazine and newspaper in the country. I think it's perfectly normal that some locals are going to get overly curious . . . to want to see you without exactly wanting to meet you."

"But you're *sure?*" she asked again.

He took her by the hands and cast me a wary glance. He decided to continue. "What members of ShadowStrike remain at large have zero interest in the four of you. They simply don't think in the terms you're suggesting. It's nothing personal and never was, though I know that's hard for you to comprehend."

We saw terrorists in our sleep after Cora was attacked in the ICU. Nobody at St. Ann's gave us pills, tried to inject us, or fooled with an IV bag unless I'd known them personally for at least two years. Alan watched Rain, and I sensed his anxiety over what she would most surely ask next. Certain things he could never answer well.

"What about what happened in the ICU to . . ." Rain stopped short of Cora's name. Mr. Steckerman took Rain by the hand and led her out to the porch, and I followed.

He came up with his usual answer. "That was the weirdest move in the halls of terror that American Intelligence has ever seen. You have to think of this in the same terms as a bombing in an Israeli marketplace. Terrorists don't typically enter hospitals to finish off victims that they only managed to maim. It's not about that."

He had answered like this over and over, each time with equal patience, as if he'd never answered the question before. Dr. Hollis had told him something about the value of repetition in curing trauma. Problem: Rain could be equally repetitive.

"So, why did they do it this time?" she asked again.

"Because they were still close by. Because they thought it would be easy. But we were right there. It wasn't easy, was it? The guy who made the attempt on Cora's life is in jail forever, and they won't try it again."

"So . . . where are they now?"

Yesterday, his answer might have been "Barcelona or somewhere. Don't worry about it." Today I knew that would be a lie. I studied the tops of the trees, waiting with interest to hear how he would answer. Alan's generally not a liar, in spite of the secrecy of his job.

"Can I just say that we know where they are?"

Her eyes flew to him. Mine, too.

"*They're* the ones being watched. Not you."

Great answer. Still, he shifted the subject just a little more to drive her farther from that fear. "But I would appreciate it if you didn't wander around the woods by yourself for a while, just until we're sure that all the journalists are following our requests. You don't want to see a picture of yourself on the cover of some supermarket rag, of a private moment with your friends, right?"

She laughed finally. It wasn't loud. "If I find somebody, can I kick some butt?"

"No, you may not."

He hadn't laughed yet, but she threw her arms around him anyway. "I just get turned around sometimes. Like when I'm with Cora. She's still a little jumpy. Daddy, when can I have my car out here?"

"Soon, I hope," he said evasively, but I knew he was afraid of her taking off, coming back late, and missing a dose of something while she was with friends from Trinity. I was afraid of her driving while getting into a crying jag and deciding it would be best to drive off a bridge or smack a tree. "As for Cora, give her time in the fresh air. For both of you, I assume you'll go to sleep from here on in without me sitting between your beds and reading the newspaper."

She had to think about it for a minute, and didn't bother unwrapping herself from him. "That behavior was for St. Ann's. Out here, we're good."

He unlaced her arms to look at her. "That's good, too. Because you know the deal. I can come out here every day. I'm still a dad. But I can't live out here. I can't even be out here more than I'm home. I *am* a target, which doesn't put my life in any more danger than it ever has. But that's one of the reasons I agreed to send you out here. It's not good for you to be around me all the time. Not this spring or summer."

Rain had been hearing her dad was a target since she was a little girl, so that part didn't hit her terribly hard. She looked over at the trees and back at her feet.

"I think I'll go look at the bay until lunch is ready. Mrs. Starn said that by noon the mist is usually burned off and you can see the islands. And besides. There aren't as many trees over there." Her laugh was driven by some courage. "Wanna come, Cora?"

Cora had silently come up behind me, and when I turned, she was watching the woods. It seemed her biggest problem was going to be fear of spooks—that and how she followed me around like a puppy dog when I let it happen.

I took her by the arm and urged her toward Rain. "Go," I said.

But she stiffened. "I'd like to, but I've got this blog, and it's getting all these hits, and I should post something for people to read."

She turned back inside, and if I didn't know her well, I would have said that it wasn't an excuse. Rain followed her but reappeared a moment later with a pair of field glasses I'd seen on one of the shelves in the parlor. She took off toward the beach.

"I'll go check the woods," Alan said.

"Can I come? See how USIC guys search a property?" I asked with a plastic smile.

"Believe me, it's about as boring as watching paint dry," he said. "Welcome to real life, which is not the world of *Law and Order*. Besides, I wish you'd keep an eye on Rain. She's restless. I don't want her to get an idea that a swim in May would solve everything."

Rain was an excuse, too. He didn't want me anywhere near his job. Between him and Cora, I felt abused by endless bullshit, and I went to find Rain just because Owen was still coming out of his Headache from Hell, and if I had to hear him imply one more time that the next life would be cooler than this one, I'd get a headache myself.

When I reached her, Rain was already sitting on the sandy beach, looking through a pair of ancient field glasses that I'd seen on one of the shelves in the parlor.

"Those things really work?" I asked.

"Perfectly," she mumbled, "if you don't jerk them around too quickly."

She studied the mist, and I doubt she could see through it with the field glasses, because she finally dropped them with a sigh.

"It feels good to face into the sun," she said as I sat down beside her, bored out of my tree. My mind diverted to medical intrigue.

"Sun produces vitamin D, which we desperately need. S'probably why it feels good."

"Maybe I'll come to this side of the house more often," she said. "The woods are creepy."

"We shouldn't come out here without sunblock," I told her, and she grabbed my hand and dragged it into her lap absently.

"Your mind just won't stop working, will it? You can't get out of medic mode."

"If there were some other mode, like counterintelligence mode, I would get into that."

She had no response other than the one she'd always given, so she changed the subject, raising the glasses again. "Islands are still misty. What's on the other side?"

She was asking which barrier island lay directly across the bay. You could now see the houses, whitewashed in sun. It was a warm day, one of the July-come-early days my mom always had loved. We get a few in May. Rain and I both had on T-shirts, and we weren't cold. I'd have felt fine in shorts. The bay was a strip of blue, but it was deceiving, we'd been told last night. The houses we were looking at were about six miles across the bay, though they looked like two.

"Brigantine?" I guessed.

"Nah. We're farther north than that. It's bigger. There's a city over there."

"How do you know?" I asked, as the visibility was only about two blocks in, and all that lined the horizon were houses.

"Because Daddy said that's one reason why he's afraid to let me have my car keys out here. He said 'the city' on the other side would be too tempting, and I'd end up on road trips when I should be resting up. God, I can't wait to get my real life back."

She watched through the breeze while I beat one fist on the sand, indenting a small, smooth hole to ward off feelings of panic, of missing the bustle of St. Ann's, and remembering something my mother had once said about retirement funds. She'd never had one, and I used to harp on her about that.

"I don't ever want to retire," Mom had said. "I've seen too many people look forward to it, and with six months of nothing to do, they drop dead. I call it death by inertia. That's not the way I want to go."

She had gone the way she wanted to—the way I wanted to, but in another seventy years at least. I wasn't sure Alan—or the nurses and doctors at St. Ann's—really understood the concept of death by inertia. Americans are so into leisure time. They bank their lives on getting twenty years of it, and come retirement, a lot of them do drop dead. *I could drop dead this summer . . .*

Rain spoke up. And if there are ever times when I believe in Owen's God, it's at a moment like this, when I could panic or get depressed, and some great distraction appears out of the blue.

Or in this case, it was out of the white *onto* the blue. The mist had been clearing little by little since I looked out the window this morning. It had been cottony white over the bay then, and now it was more blue than white. And with a long gust of wind, it cleared enough that I could see what city lay on the other side. I knew it was Griffith's Landing, because of the giant Ferris wheel that suddenly materialized. That Ferris wheel was on half the brochures about the Jersey Shore. I think my game of eenie-meenie-minie-moe between Asbury Park, Griffith's Landing, or Wildwood had just ended. If we were just behind Griffith's Landing, that might put Asbury Park too far to the north and Wildwood too far to the south to be within driving distance of a lab near Astor College.

"Oh god, I wish I was there," Rain said, watching the huge

wheel through the field glasses. "Can you see that? It's going around. It's the weekend. The Icon Pier has the best roller coasters anywhere."

My body went a little rigid as my head got full of ideas. Fortunately, I'm pretty good at multitasking, so I continued on in my calm tone. "It's probably a good thing you're not there, Rain. A roller coaster could give you a hemorrhage."

"Oh, shut up." She dropped the field glasses into my lap and stood up. "Do you have to be such a downer?"

"Sorry, but—"

"Oh, you and Daddy. I can't sit here and look at the Icon Pier. I'm going to go look in the spooky woods again. If I find a journalist, at least I'll have an excuse to kick some ass."

She stalked off, and I hoped she was kidding.

I raised the field glasses and watched the cars flowing down Ocean Boulevard into Griffith. The boulevard juts northward toward our property, making the piece I saw only about a mile off. I didn't have a clear view, but enough that I could catch a glimpse of a black Taurus and know what I was seeing. Alan had just said he was going back to Trinity Falls. If I saw his Taurus on the causeway into Griffith, I could take it as a nod that Alan, too, was thinking it could be the next Zone of the Unthinkable.

I didn't see his car, not after watching for a full fifteen minutes. But I'm not easily put off. I figured, *well, if he's not there, then he can't run into me there.*

My car was out in the back of the former visitors' parking lot, where I'd left it four days ago when I followed Alan out here to look the place over. Having learned of the limo from Alan while here, I rode back with him. I could have a look around Griffith, and I could even take Rain, though it would probably torture her more than help her. I decided I shouldn't remind her that I have a car until I was ready for her to start nagging me every ten seconds to go somewhere.

I spun around as a camera clicked, but it was only Cora, taking a shot of the water.

"Thought you had a blog to write before lunch," I said.

She said something like, "I can't think of anything to say. Everyone will be reading it."

It sounded like a perfect reason to be out here again so fast. I walked back to the path between the trees, spun around, and caught her watching me, disappointment all over her face. I felt flattered but defensive—probably more defensive. I pretended this was all about her being scared, which was probably part of it, but not all.

"Cora, I'd make a terrible bodyguard," I said. "The only thing I can shoot is a hypo."

"What do you mean?" she asked, suddenly flipping her lens focus this way and that.

"I mean, you're using me like a bulletproof vest. I can't make the terrorists go away. You have to do it yourself. You have to get rid of your own paranoia."

With that she seemed annoyed. Annoyance on Cora equals jerking her chin to the water and finding it oh-so-interesting.

"Say it," I said.

"Say what?"

"Whatever it is that's bothering you. Come on. I'm not a dentist, either, and prying things out of you gets annoying."

"Okay, then, so . . . don't be a dentist. Or a bodyguard. Just be a friend." The twisting of the focus on her camera lens turned into some sort of mild spasm.

What came out of my mouth sounded like laughter, but I hoped she didn't take it personally. Ronnie Dobbins and I decided one night last year that we could be friends with women but not with girls, and there's a difference between women and girls that has nothing to do at all with children. As Ronnie summed it up, "A girl is any female between the ages of seventeen and twenty-five who could spin heads on the beach. A woman is any other female. We can be friendly with women, but not with girls."

We both had protective feelings toward our moms, talked to them about anything, were nice to all their friends. I had women friends on my ambulance squad. He could lay a mother lode of personal problems on this one female professor he had who was fiftyish. I really couldn't argue with him.

"Let's face it," he'd said. "We're scuzwads. We're dogs."

I'd broken up with many girls who said they wanted to stay friends, but we never did for long. I joked about it, but people say there's seriousness in all jokes, and this one joke had come out of me in a glurt that night Ronnie and I were cruising: "I can be friends with any girl . . . if I'm banging her, too."

I just had no clue what to say to Cora. Out came, "What do we do first? Play Barbies?"

She laughed, Goddess of Manners that she was, then turned to the water, still fooling with her focus wheel. The camera was becoming more like a third arm, something that gave her power, I decided. She would never have tried to lure me closer without having all the dials on the lens to spaz over. I wasn't a champ at being friends with girls, but she wasn't a champ at being friends with anyone. It was a ballsy statement for her.

"You really want to be my friend?" I asked.

She turned sideways and nodded, staring at my sneakers.

"Really?"

"Yes."

"You have to pass the test. I don't let just anyone be my friend."

She took a step backwards, like my bloody-hell thoughts about sex and girls were seeping out of my brain and sending bad images into her head. She'd trusted me before this. I didn't want that to change.

I asked quickly, "Can you come with me in my car after we eat, take pictures of what I tell you to, not ask any questions, and keep it a secret from Rain and Owen?"

SIXTEEN

TYLER PING
SATURDAY, MAY 4, 2002
1:10 P.M.
SHAHZAD'S BEDROOM

HAMDANI HAD BEEN QUIET AT LUNCH, but he could get quiet and moody whenever Hodji was leaving town, and I let him toy with his food without harassing him. I wondered if he had more thoughts about how to confirm that VaporStrike was in New Jersey, but I didn't ask.

After heading back upstairs, he fell asleep on his bed, and I went to my room and surfed for tularemia again, hoping to find another dead animal. I got nothing. I tried various searches on dead animals that could disintegrate in a matter of hours, but it's hard to know how to word that in a surf sentence.

Hamdani's asthmatic snores called out to me, and I went to his room and sat down quietly at his terminal. I was all too aware of how he was less mentally screwed up lately than I was, and how I had come to rely on him to do all our dirty work. Hamdani had leashed Omar and VaporStrike, but at the moment the screen blinked sleepily:

OmarLoggi is not online. VaporStrike is not online.

I got a twitch to surf with Dog Leash for Omar's former log-in, back when he poisoned the water in Trinity Falls and we were chasing him around in the days just before the raid.

I typed "Omar0324" and clicked on "leash." Five minutes passed. This program searches through every server personally hosting chat software between here and Tokyo, looking for that log-in. After another minute or two of listening to Hamdani cut logs, I suddenly thought I was dreaming, too, as this popped up:

ALERT: Omar0324 is Online: www.tijuanaprime.com/chat/ hodgpog-hall/%853.18.05%/ Enter11:07am

Dumbwad, Jeezus. Omar was arrogant enough to think we would never look for his old ID, believing he wouldn't have the nerve to use it. I clicked on the link, glancing at Hamdani. I wouldn't wake him up until I had proven that my worth to USIC was as good as his. They were conversing in some strange language that my program recognized as Nobiin, some minor language of Egypt. I ran it through our translator and came up with rough English of

Omar0324: Tried all the Dr. Scholl's products and none of them is adequate for this job.
HotKeys: Have you tried a physician?

HotKeys. This log-in was brand new. I wondered quickly if the "hot" referred to some germ involved in the creation of Fire-Fall, making the new guy a scientist, or if the "keys" referred to a keypad, making him a computer specialist. Hodji had predicted that Omar might try to gain more control over his online communications with a professional who could increase security and also counterspy.

> **Omar0324:** See a doctor in this tired and dusty neighborhood? I would as soon approach a witch doctor. At least I would not get further infected from unclean utensils in that case.
>
> **HotKeys:** It is only an infected bunion. You could get an antibiotic.
>
> **Omar0324:** I will ask Pasco to help out if it doesn't clear up. How is your work going? Did you find me any answers yet?

Pasco. They had all sorts of new friends, it seemed. Pasco, possibly a doctor, and HotKeys, a probable computer geek, from this session, and Chancellor, the independently wealthy scientist from the last. Even though none of this spelled out any certainties, Hodji would love this stuff. I wished he would hurry up, finish with his meeting, and call. And I wished hellfire upon Omar and his infected goddamn bunion. The guy works tirelessly to poison hundreds of people while looking for an antibiotic for his stink-foot.

> **HotKeys:** I am working on your answers. I will catch you some v-spies if you have any. Your hundred thousand euros will be well spent—that much I can assure you.

With that, I shook Hamdani to wake up. I couldn't help it. ShadowStrike was obviously paying some guy a hundred thousand euros to try to expose us, and USIC wasn't paying us shit to expose ShadowStrike. Hamdani was almost immediately standing, staring over my shoulder while gulping oxygen into his chest. Finally, he wheezed asthmatically.

"I should have stayed in Pakistan where I was paid well and remained in adequate health," he croaked. "Allah must be angry with me about something."

"Nah. Allah just wanted you to meet me," I joked, though my insides were so blazing over this payment information that I was ready to put my face through the wall.

> HotKeys: Chancellor asked me to pass on a message to you concerning his swans.

"Shit, I was expecting more monkeys or something akin to them," I said. "What does a swan have to do with—"

Hamdani's hand landed on my shoulder, and he said almost as soon as it appeared, "'Swans' would be a code word. Let us translate carefully."

> Omar0324: Hurry. I must leave here soon.
>
> HotKeys: He says their health has been restored and they are ready for the lake. He says he bolstered gray swan's food to see if it matters.
>
> Omar0324: You mean #16 food. He may die of food tampering, but I am anxious to see if he endures.

A minute passed like an eternity before Hamdani plopped onto the bed. I watched him hold his stomach and wipe spit off his bottom lip. I was glad I had woken him up. This turned into what I call a "butt-muscle moment," where you can either totally squeeze or totally shit.

"Send it to Hodji," he said. "Tell him it appears that Shadow-Strike is holding hostages and is experimenting on them with designer germs and drugs. Perhaps he already knows. Perhaps we need to forgive him for going to Mexico."

It was my first experience with code words, but Hamdani had been doing this for years. I watched him, amazed. And ready to hurl. Sometimes there's nothing to do but turn, type, and hit SEND.

SEVENTEEN

OWEN EBERMAN
SATURDAY, MAY 4, 2002
1:30 P.M.
PORCH

After big headaches, we have these things we've come to call aftershocks, which I was having lots of. They're like your headache, only they're gone thirty seconds later, and you can get them every twenty minutes or so. I didn't eat any lunch except what Marg forced me to, and I got it down by taking it to the porch and sharing half with the nanny goat. The Professor was nowhere to be seen.

Sheep was a grin. She was bigger and wider and fatter than the Professor, and her *baa* was lower and louder, more like "*Fww-ay.*" The goats reminded me of Rain and me. The loud, dominating female forces the unobtrusive male to look for quiet places to hide out. Sheep was happy to share my cheese-burger and some thoughts.

"You weren't around this morning to hear me tell your boyfriend that I want a meaningful life."

"*Fww-ay.*"

"It used to bother my mom a lot when parents said, 'Raising my kids is the most important job in the world.'"

"*Fww-ay.*"

"She said they were being unwise. We had a neighborhood full of parents where the mom stayed home and gave up everything to raise the kids. Lots of those kids were teenagers when we moved in, so we can see what happened. It didn't make them vice president or Gandhi or the inventor of a cancer cure."

"*Fww-ay.*"

"They just grew up, gave up everything, and threw their lives into *their* kids. It's kind of like the mayflies, ya know?"

"*Fww-ay.*"

"What fun is that?"

"*Fww-ay.*"

"Anyway. If you knew Rain, you would understand why I never, ever allowed her to get into my thoughts during the Dreaded Fifteen. I could so easily fall in love with her, even though I hate her sometimes. I think that's *why* I hate her sometimes."

"*Fww-ay.*"

"She wants that normal life so bad. She could so suck me dry . . . oops, bad pun. And it's the weirdest, because I would love to find out if I'm supposed to be, like, a Gandhi. Or a Nelson Mandela. I want to do something before I die that's so outstanding that my great-great-grandkids will know I was there for them. That's what *I* call meaningful living. She wants to be chairman of the PTA. And yet I'm always secretly looking at her like she's stronger than me. What is up? Is there something *wrong* with me? I mean, beyond the obvious?"

I took off my baseball cap and rubbed my itchy nubs.

"*Baa-AA-baa.*" The Professor came strutting around from the side of the house. His bell went *ding, ding.* Sheep's bell didn't *ding*, I realized. Sheep backed down from me, told him "*Fww-ay*," and proceeded to ram him in the side. She didn't want him near me, and he shied away.

"I totally understand, buddy. These women are rough."

I went into the TV room to watch Aleese Holman, a woman, perhaps, but at least not a typical one. She reminded me more of my mom. They were both do-gooders, though Aleese also happened to have an enormous streak of ballsy. Okay, if it was too arrogant to think of becoming a Mandela or a Gandhi, maybe I could become some guy version of Aleese Holman and try to prove that war is wrong. There was a recliner on the far end of this posh new couch, and I pushed the button and said "*Ahhhh*" as I went back.

Rain must have crashed out on her bed upstairs, and I celebrated my aloneness by kissing the remote. I hit PLAY, and a couple of lines showed up on the screen: "June 1984: In Which Aleese Talks about American Soil."

As the footage rolled, you could tell by a close-up of her profile that Aleese was in her early twenties. That's only about six years older than Cora is now, so it was easy to see the likenesses and the differences. She and Cora had the same color hair and almost the same features, but Cora is pretty stunning, and her mother was very muscular around the neck and shoulders, with her wavy hair cropped off short so she wouldn't have to take care of it. But she had that same porcelain skin that could blush rosy pink, and Aleese was blushing.

She was sitting with her knees up, and a baby rested on her knees.

I recognized the voice from behind the camera as a younger Jeremy Ireland, and he said in his thick British, "Tell us what you're doing with a baby, Aleese."

"I'm delivering him to a family . . ." She rubbed her nose into the baby's belly. "I am! I am! I'm delivering you! Dang. I love babies . . ."

I thought, *Eeek. No wonder Cora's scared to watch her mom's tapes.* Cora mentioned once in group therapy how she felt scared that she would find on the tapes drunken escapades, barroom brawls, and maybe even sex acts between what good things her mother had done. I didn't think she would be happy watching her mother coo over some baby. Aleese had passed Cora off at birth and went twelve years without trying to even see her. I was only slightly more confused than I was nauseated.

"Yes, we all know Aleese loves babies," Jeremy said, to make things worse. "I've got four minutes of tape left for your VJ—"

Aleese turned toward the camera and faced the baby toward it. It looked like a newborn, blinking at nothing and everything. It was darker—black or Hispanic or Arab.

Aleese said, "Okay. This is . . . Baby X. He was born in Atlantic City Medical Center." She bounced him once and grinned. "There was this time in high school—the first time I ever got arrested for making my opinions known—when I protested the abortion clinic on New York Avenue in Atlantic City . . ."

She was blushing again. "*Why* did I protest an abortion clinic? I . . . because. That's why. I'm not religious. I'm not planning on having any kids myself, at least not for the next ten years. 'Because' is a good enough reason, right? This is America. I'm allowed to protest if I want."

"Stop being defensive and tell about the baby," Jeremy interrupted.

She had to bounce him and coo a couple of times. *Cora should definitely never see this one.* I almost fast-forwarded, but Aleese started talking again.

"So, I met this pregnant fourteen-year-old six months ago when I was in the clinic in Atlantic City getting my whenever-I'm-home-and-it's-free checkup. So, this girl started confiding to me that she was going to terminate, which was making her really sad. So, I made her a deal. I said if she wanted to have the baby but couldn't raise it, I would take the baby. Not to keep the baby, but to put it up for adoption. Mom paid for the lawyer. Mom actually wanted the baby but did the right thing and decided it needed a daddy, too. Mom wanted ten kids. She's only got me, and I ain't no picnic. For the record."

"Mom" would be Cora's Oma, who had raised her. I wondered why Oma decided to raise Cora if Aleese didn't want her, after not keeping this baby. Maybe because Cora was Aleese's flesh and blood, but there were so many unanswered questions about Cora's life that I wondered sometimes how Cora could stand being Cora.

"So, today, this baby is going to his new family. The only thing I wanted was the opportunity to deliver him, play with him for an hour or two."

"And how do you feel about what you've done?" Jeremy asked.

She looked at him weirdly, blushing again. "Don't make me into a hero. The girl was the hero. *In my opinion.* Christ, why is it, in America, we always have to say *in my opinion*? One nation

... under God, *in my opinion* ... Think there's room for *in my opinion* at the top of a penny?"

"I think it's *In God We Trust* that's on the penny," Jeremy said impatiently.

"In God We Trust, in my opinion ..."

"Look. I want to keep this for my VJ of you. I don't want three minutes of cooing, I want three minutes of Aleese."

She flipped him the bird, which made me flinch—it was like she was flipping it at me. "I wanna keep this baby. I wanna keep you, I wanna keep you!" She nuzzled her nose into the baby's stomach.

"You ..." I almost said "bitch" for Cora's sake.

Jeremy gave a respectful pause before asking, "So, why don't you keep him? You'd make a great mother."

"Nah, I'm not staying. This baby belongs in America. Don't you? Don't you!"

"Aleese ..." Jeremy's next question was a thought provoker. "For someone who loves this country so much, you spend very little time in it. You're twenty-four, and since you were twenty, you spent two weeks here six months ago, and two weeks now, this time merely to keep a promise to a pregnant teenager and deliver a baby to a couple you've never met. If you love the place as much as you say, why not be here to enjoy it?"

VJ ... I decided the term meant "video journal," and this was a rhythm of theirs. Jeremy would act like an interviewer, pose questions, and tape what she did or said. I sensed the importance of it, though Aleese was laughing at the moment, her head up, away from the baby, while she searched the ceiling for answers.

She shrugged, laughing a little. "Most people are in America to enjoy America. The rest of us ... we make it possible for others to enjoy America. My job? I prowl the badlands, the out-lands, and bring back photos that will keep Americans grateful ... and protective, and ... cognizant of their good luck in this world. It's no place for a baby. This child should have an American life. He's a symbol."

"A symbol of what?"

"Gardens ... is what I'm thinking of at the moment. I don't know why I love American gardens so much. The Swiss and the Germans are better at gardens. But this baby needs to go about in a stroller designed by JCPenney and learn to walk thinking that the world is rooms filled with giant, colorful Lego toys. The first day of kindergarten, his parents should walk him down the street to the local public school, where he'll learn from big alphabet letters and math worksheets with cartoon foxes and bears cheering him on. He needs to ride bikes and have a locker and learn to play football, soccer, and street hockey. He needs to wake up on Christmas mornings to a Walkman and a golden retriever puppy and a mountain bike. He needs to see all the Disney movies the first week they come out. He needs a dad and a mom. He needs to start each school day saying the Pledge of Allegiance ... *in my opinion.*"

She laughed, but I didn't. Aleese Holman talked kind of like she wrote. It was like an endless poem that she could spit out while cooing and joking around. It was an unusual talent, and I could see why Jeremy liked doing this.

She added, "Most people are lucky enough to get to play in America, to put the bread on the table in freedom and live off the fat of the land. The rest of us? We have other shoes to fill. We're the photographers, the journalists, the soldiers, the Peace Corps workers, the artists, the chroniclers of disaster ... We bring back perspective. We bring back the less pleasant truths. We, um, foster gratitude. We allow others to play while we do the hard stuff."

She struck the electric chord I was looking for. Scott and Cora and Rain and I obviously hadn't been sent to any badlands. We were no longer "normal people from Trinity Falls," but the rest was unclear. I could sit here and pray for people, because I'd heard of other people in St. Ann's doing that—people who wanted to do some good but were too sick to move about. I could be nice to Rain, because she was high maintenance. But I thought of Scott wanting to go to work for USIC, to actually catch those guys. I thought of what the Kid did, giving up his teenage years so that he could help intelligence agencies find cold-blooded killers.

I felt entirely useless as more truth crawled all over me: I was nothing like Aleese Holman. I was *nothing* like Joan of Arc. I wasn't even close to the Kid. I was Owen Eberman, decent athlete, decent student, and otherwise couch potato, who just happened to drink the wrong water at the wrong time.

I asked Dan recently about this thing he'd referred to as "a calling," because I'd kind of wanted one—sort of like Joan of Arc or St. Stephen. When you think you might die, it's time to put it all out there and get arrogant. What have you got to lose? Hadley said the apostles asked Jesus questions, toward the end of his life, about where they were going and what they'd be doing. His answer, in plain English: "If I told you the whole thing now, you'd lose your minds."

I finally drifted off to sleep, watching sand on the TV and not caring. Sand was like my life. Something was going on behind the scenes, but I wasn't privy to it. It was like the mist of my dreams, which I drifted into in the afternoon quiet while Rain was asleep and Cora and Scott were off on a road trip. Figures floated around in shadows behind the mist. But no one came out of it. No voices spoke to me.

EIGHTEEN

CORA HOLMAN
SATURDAY, MAY 4, 2002
1:30 P.M.
GRIFFITH'S LANDING BOARDWALK

SCOTT WANTED ME TO SHOOT A PICTURE of a
burning building while we were standing in a crowd of people.
He kept pointing insistently at the smoky flames and red brick
structure, but I wasn't tall enough and could only capture the
backs of men and women in the crowd, even when standing on
my toes. Finally, the crowd broke a little, people moving left and
right, and I raised the camera to my face. The lens had been jostled, and all was a blur. I quickly readjusted the focus, and as the
image came clear, I was staring straight into my dead mother's
face. Her black eyes and smile took up the lens.

"You can't escape me. Dead does not mean gone."

I jerked the thing from my eyes, expecting to see her standing two feet in front of me. But it was only the crowd again. I
tried screaming, but it came out like hissing, and as I turned to
flee, a seat belt jerked me into place. I was staring out the window from the passenger seat. The sun was out.

"You okay?" Scott asked.

I put a hand to my banging heart, still hearing the reverb of my yell. I could have startled him enough to drive off the road. We were just turning off Route 9 onto the Griffith's Landing causeway.

He jostled my head a little and said, "It's only a dream," in a mothering way.

"I've been having the most atrocious nightmares about my mother lately," I confessed dizzily.

His hand left me. "I'd say, 'You can come get in my bed,' but I don't think that would work out very well."

He was trying to make me laugh, and as usual, he got his wish. But the smile faded away again as I stared into the camera in my lap and it stared back. I tended to think of it as a life form sometimes. In another dream, it started to pulsate in my hands like a giant heart. I loved the thing, but only when I could forget that it had been to so many places, had seen so many atrocities, and recorded all of humanity's heartaches that Jeremy told me of. It's like I hadn't totally taken possession of it. Half of this camera still belonged to Aleese. Half of it *was part of* Aleese.

"I sent Jeremy Ireland an e-mail after I couldn't think of much to say in my blog, and I asked him to please persist in finding out what he can about my father," I said. "I'm sure Aleese just . . . got stuck in my mind after I sent it."

The narrow highway was kind of pretty, with marshes and bay streams on either side, and a small city on the horizon ahead. I could see a tall Ferris wheel looming over the buildings, and we passed a sign that read "Griffith's Landing: 6 miles." I had fond memories of Oma bringing me and some friends here for the rides when I was twelve.

Scott turned to glance at me a few times. My heart should have slowed down, but one of our meds listed heart palpitations as a side effect, and I seemed to be more susceptible to side effects than the other three.

"Ya know, if you tell your bad dreams, they tend to fade away faster."

"Did they teach you that in paramedic school?" I yawned.

"Nope. Learned it from Mom."

The differences between his mother and mine lit the car with an inflamed discomfort. For me, at least. He grabbed my hand out of my lap and did this acupressure maneuver in the center of my palm, applying pressure with his thumb, which sent some sort of white energy up my arm and throughout my body. It had a calming effect, and he'd done it to me several times at St. Ann's when he'd been in hearing distance of one of my nightmares.

I blurted out the dream, mostly because I needed to give payback for my calm.

He flinched when I got to the part of Aleese being seen in the lens but not in the real crowd. "Cora, your nightmares are really vivid. Maybe you should think of becoming a writer."

At the moment, I was an editor, per se, of our journals, but that was it. I kept them on my hard drive, planning to weave them all together someday for our memories. "I've no idea what I want to be. Right now, I guess I'm just glad *to* be."

"Wish I felt that, uh, content," he said, and dropped his hand back onto the steering wheel in frustration. I had kept my word by not asking him why we were coming to Griffith's Landing. I thought of ways to ask him but sensed he wouldn't like it. And he wasn't done with the other subject yet.

"I'd say it's pretty normal to have nightmares like that when you've had a mother like yours. A wild boar would have made a better parent."

As usual, his loyalty cut my anxiety in half.

"Some wild animals devour their young," he went on. "But they're not drug addicts living on Social Security and relying on their children to pick up after them . . ."

One memory suddenly came clear that I hadn't mentioned before. I'd been afraid of its implications. But Scott liked when I confessed things, and I was suddenly basking in the white energy of relaxation.

I went for it. "A lot of times when I would come home after school, I would see the checkbook out on the dining room table. Aleese paid the bills when I was in school. Always. I never saw her write out a check. But we never got a shutoff notice. And after she died and I looked through all the records, I also saw that she never spent on drugs any of the money that Oma had left to her or me. She used her Social Security to get her morphine."

His hand moved back to the top of the steering wheel. I took it that he was stunned that I would defend her. I wondered if I should have.

"I think . . ."—I stumbled with the frightening part—". . . she may have been drug free every day until late afternoon."

"Oh. She only got high when she sensed it was time for *you* to come home."

"That's right."

"The awful, terrible, unendurable Cora Holman. Your presence would make anybody want to shoot up, darlin'. It's all your fault that your mother was a pig," he said.

I laughed at how ludicrous it sounded. But the truth was equally ludicrous: Aleese could never bear my presence.

"I think if I could just find my father, I would stop being haunted by my mother."

"Haunted?" He turned to gaze at me. "Am I supposed to pull over here? Find out if you need some more therapy?"

Responses like this were why I didn't bare my soul frequently and easily. My thoughts aroused the suspicions of stable people.

"I meant that I would stop *dreaming* about her," I said quickly, though I wasn't so sure that was true. I felt haunted.

With his one arm still on the top of the wheel, he jerked to the right, having driven into the double line. He squirmed in the seat, though I didn't get the feeling it was over the concept of being haunted. Scott could not dwell for long on a thought about a spiritual realm.

Sure enough, he said after a long silence, "I've never had any desire to find my father. Owen hasn't either. However, we had a great mom. I can't discourage you, though I'm a frank and honest guy. And if you don't mind my saying so, there were probably a thousand journalists' bars your mother passed through in her travels across the continents, and I doubt she was very, um, demure."

He meant that Aleese was probably not very picky about her lovers. I had no reason to believe otherwise.

"A shadow in a bar could have left an indent on the spare pillow when she woke up in the a.m., all hung-over." He didn't look at me.

I was under no delusions there. "I just know that when I

think about my father, I feel a great deal of peace," I said. "I think I'll find a more permanent peace if I can find him."

"So then . . . go for it." He put his hand on my knee and squeezed. Hands on, hands off, hands on. Scott Eberman amazed me with how easily he could reach out and touch. I knew he had been up to his neck in girls in high school, and his touching girls probably came as naturally as breathing.

I gazed down at the camera balanced on my knees beside his hand, and the lens picked up fat rays of summer sun and delivered some version of Morse code into my face. It reminded me of giggles. *Aleese is giggling at my lack of experience.*

I grasped for an outside thought, something not to do with dead mothers and sickness and medications and side effects. Professor Calloway's face came clear—*Henry's* face. Trying to remember to call him Henry was like calling a teacher by a first name. Henry was not what I'd call a handsome man. For one, being twenty-nine years old almost defies the thought. And his features were too delicate—not rugged like Scott's or Owen's or the other boys in school that girls went the most gaga for. But I had been so comfortable with him. Being outdoors and taking photos was the first time in months I had been able to forget, for nearly a whole hour, that I was even sick. My time with him had passed with barely a hint of my usual anxiety. I would crush on Scott Eberman until I died and hadn't meant to make a comparison. But I suddenly became aware of one . . . that I had talked so easily with Henry, and everything I said to Scott came hard, like I had to blowtorch my words and present them as gold.

Scott's mind reading could drive me crazy at times, but at the moment it was downright freaky.

"Do me a favor," he said. "Don't show Mr. Professor anything we shoot today."

"Why not?"

He pinched his lips together, then let air shoot out in a blast of anxiety. "You promised me you wouldn't ask questions."

So I had. Maybe his mind reading wasn't so freaky this time; I realized I had crossed my legs when he had had his hand on my knee, which pulled it slightly out of his reach. And my anxiety built as I sensed his own filling the car. He was so fixated on getting a USIC job. This was somehow related, I just knew it. I shut my eyes, only to see myself in the ICU, a strange man standing over me who I'd thought was Jeremy Ireland. *"I am sent by Omar. You don't know him, but he knows you well. He made you ill. And now, you are about to be sacrificed. Are you afraid of dying? I hope not."*

"Just . . . assure me we're not going to run into any of *them*," I felt the need to say.

"Nah. Don't worry about it."

I tried not to worry, in spite of him sending me glances.

"When is *he* coming over again?" He smiled in a teasing way that made me certain it was to get rid of the tension in the car.

"Henry? Tomorrow, maybe." I hoped.

"Be. Careful."

"Don't start being ridiculous again," I begged. "Don't ruin my fun."

"I've been around the block a hundred times, and right now, even I can get confused about my feelings. You're not the only one who has weird dreams. Last night I dreamed I was doing the nasty with Nurse Marg."

I giggled, laying my forehead into my hand. I managed, "She's a lot prettier than some of the nurses at St. Ann's."

"She's got to be thirty-five," he said.

I got his point.

"But my dreams are not half as confused as some of the things I think when I'm awake." He rambled on. "I was elected the family elder when I was about five years old. Mom and Owen ... they were the kids. Don't get me wrong. I loved my mom. Dearly. But she thought the saints were going to drop down and pay the electric bill if she went around doing good deeds. I was doing dishes by the time I was five years old. I've done my own laundry since I was eight. Not that I mind. I'd say I was cut out for responsibility, but . . ."

"But sometimes you feel overwhelmed," I guessed.

"Overwhelmed, yeah. Confused, yeah."

"By us?" I meant by Owen, Rain, and me. I tried constantly to be low maintenance for him. Of course he would be overwhelmed, but with his never having hinted at it before, I didn't know what to make of it. It was kind of like hearing that Santa Claus is confused by trains.

I squiggled sideways in the seat belt, laying my cheek on the backrest, watching him. I put my hand out and touched his shoulder, thinking, perhaps, I could send my sympathies through him for healing, sort of like his acupressure being healing to me. It seemed better for me when I was touching him, as opposed to when he was touching me.

He pinched his lips like he was hiding a grin. It finally cracked on his face in a full-blown smile.

"Cora Holman, you are so easy to manipulate."

My hand froze, then I pulled it away. He kept laughing. "Do you see how I just got you to feel sorry for me?"

I sat up. "You manipulated me? How?"

"Everything I just told you was true. But you're so naive. You're a setup waiting to happen. Listen to me. Men can be liars, but generally they're not. They just arrange the facts any way that serves them. If I want a girl's sympathy, I know how to arrange things to get it. I'm withholding from you that my mother was named Attorney of the Year twice in the state of New Jersey by a legal ethics committee. I'm not telling you how many times she hugged me in thanks, how many candles she lit for me in church when she knew I was out bagging babes left and right, drinking shots on a Saturday night, trying to forget all the decent colleges I'd been accepted to that we simply couldn't afford. I've always worked hard, but my mother was a saint. God gave me to her for one reason only. She deserved a break."

I turned and sat straight again, cursing Aleese's winking camera for putting me up to a bad joke. "Why are you telling me this?"

"I don't know," he said. "I don't need a reason for everything. Maybe I'm sensing life is nowhere near done with you, Cora Holman. You're going to pass through this. When you come out on the other side, there will be men and jobs and people . . . and pirates."

"All I want to do is go to Astor College and get a condo in Trinity Falls."

"There's pirates everywhere. Watch out for yourself."

"Where are *you* going to be after we get out of here?" I asked. I hadn't meant to sound so attached. But I suddenly had trouble envisioning my life when he wasn't within calling distance, if ever I got into trouble. He got that smile on his face and cracked up all over again. He had gotten me to say that—in his mind.

I sighed, embarrassed. "Could we . . . just talk about normal things?"

"Oh! You mean when you bring up trite subjects and I pretend I'm really interested?" He was laughing, not tensely. I had no answer. "Fine. Just one more thing. Don't trust any man until you're around twenty-five."

"How can you know that? You're not even twenty."

"Darlin' . . ." He jerked the wheel, and the car pulled into a parking space. I hadn't even noticed, but we were right under a Ferris wheel and had driven several side streets to get here. ". . . it ain't the years. It's the mileage."

We walked to the boardwalk ramp, and I could see several dozen high school girls ahead, along with either mothers or coaches or something. I could hear cheers in the background and wondered if this was a cheerleading convention. I felt dizzy from the conversation, dizzy and disoriented. I put the camera to my face with more gut reaction than thought.

"Catch the structure . . . the front entrance . . . and anyone who looks, um, out of place," Scott said.

"And . . . what qualifies as out of place?" I asked.

He just walked backwards across the boardwalk, his eyes darting all over the building—up, down, side to side.

I took a full roll of the Griffith's Landing Convention Center, catching a few pairs of men who stopped and stared at the building and conversed. I tried to ignore those who stopped to study the cheerleaders. Still, since I had no idea what I was looking for, I had no idea if I was doing a good job. I only knew that the pictures were clear.

"Let's go into the amusement park," Scott said. "Just . . . shoot with your instincts."

"My instincts," I repeated. I was never inclined to think about my instincts one way or the other. "You forgot your sunglasses," I noticed.

"I didn't forget them. I'm eliminating anything that's making me blind to something," he said. "I want to see . . . everything."

But without his mirrored glasses, I could see the weakness in his eyes, the feeling of having to guess and suggest pictures of what would probably not mean anything to anyone.

He said flatly, "It's hard to even find your instincts in this medicinal mess that's coursing through us. We'll do our best."

I actually enjoyed shooting the amusement park. The carousel and the little children on the duckie ride were similar to things I liked to photograph in Trinity Falls. They were happy and scenic, and I couldn't wait to develop the film and see if I had captured the immortality in a child's face when a brightly colored horse takes him up and down and into imaginary places.

I didn't even feel left out shooting the bigger rides in the back. There were high school kids my age back there. Catching their faces on the roller coasters gave me flashbacks of when life had been happy. The summer after seventh grade, two years before Oma died, had been my last trip to an amusement park. And photographing it now seemed to be making up for things I missed in high school.

Scott's words, "*shoot with your instincts,*" propelled me

through the entrance of the indoor water park, along with some "shoving" from my mother's annoying ghost, which now seemed to wail around me. Scott got us in with his paramedic ID card, saying at the entrance that he had business with the first aid office. The young teenager in charge simply let us through. I took picture after picture, not frantically, but very attentively. *Water, water, water . . . splashing, falling, loud, musical water, water, water . . .*

I looked up as I changed rolls to see Scott watching me.

"Is this what you call my instincts?" I asked.

He sucked in a breath and thought long before exhaling. "My instincts are so clouded right now, it's like they're drunk. It could be . . . reminding us of all the water we drank last winter."

I shot picture after picture, but after he said that, I felt my spine tingling, as if I were being watched. Aleese lurked in some far-off corner. But as we left the park, she was everywhere, still. I expected to see her in the upper windows of the convention center when I shot it. Behind the glass of a drugstore, watching us. Down at the water's edge.

Then it happened, something so similar to the dream that I almost dropped the camera. As we returned to the boardwalk, I changed to the wide-angle lens that would capture the entire width of the boardwalk. When I looked through the viewfinder, at least a dozen of the hundred or so strollers were staring right at us. One here . . . one there . . . Adjusting the focus made the sets of eyes more frightening, more fixating, like Mrs. Kellerton's intense gaze was coming at me from a dozen places.

I shot only one picture before lowering the camera to look at all these stares. A woman smiled and came across the boardwalk to us.

"Are you . . . two of the Trinity Falls victims?" she asked nicely.

People magazine. I hadn't thought of it, and obviously, Scott hadn't either. We'd been in all the big national magazines, but we'd been on the cover of *People*. We had famous faces.

Scott had placed his hands tightly on my shoulders, maybe because he'd noticed all the stares, too. And now, he dug his fingers in defensively but lied in a nice enough voice. "Sorry. But you're not the first person today to ask us that. We must look like them or something."

"Well, whew, in that case," the woman said. "I wouldn't want to be them right now. My son goes to Pinelands. He says there's a kitty going around on whether they'll live or die, poor things. Your coloring, though. That's probably what did it. You look like you're wearing too much sunblock for May. Otherwise, sorry for the confusion."

And she turned away with a smile. I let myself lean back against Scott's chest this time, and a laugh roared out of me. I don't know why.

He mumbled a few curses as his arms crossed in front of me for comfort. "Why am I not surprised? Don't repeat that to Owen or Rain, please. And I think we should go."

I didn't want to look into any more stares, but I couldn't help it. At least four were men. And they didn't look curious. They looked—

Don't be a wuss. My mother's voice banged through me. Or maybe it was simply a stunning, deep-seated reaction to the woman. Maybe I was discovering my angry side. I raised the camera to my face and snapped a photo of a man staring at us while opening up his cell phone. He turned and walked quickly away down the boardwalk. I turned the camera to a second glaring man, and he did the same. Some people were staring out of curiosity, but a total of six men scrambled away from the view of my lens, like cockroaches scrambling away from the light. I had my motor drive on, which had given me pictures of each from the front or the side.

For once, Scott wasn't noticing his surroundings. So enthused about my picture taking at first, he was now walking two steps in front of me, inhaling, exhaling, staring at the boards, trying to blow the woman's opinion of us-as-myth out into the sea. He finally grabbed me by the bottom of my shirt and pulled me along impatiently. I said nothing to him about what I had just captured on film. I couldn't make sense of it.

NINETEEN

SHAHZAD HAMDANI
SATURDAY, MAY 4, 2002
3:10 P.M.
DINING ROOM

HODJI CAME BACK AFTER HIS MEETING to say what I had suspected: USIC rejected the plan to fake our deaths. However, they would work on a plan to move us to a different locale, he reported. But as we did not qualify for the Witness Protection Program, they would have to find loopholes in USIC rules and regulations, which could take a week or more.

Tyler wanders off in a foul mood, but I stay with Hodji to bring up "swans" and "food #16" and whether any Americans had been reported missing in Mexico who might be hostages. While we worked together in Pakistan, Hodji had talked to me at liberty so that I could chase online any concept that fell into my brain. Here he is worried about USIC's rules of violating national security and losing his job. USIC is so huge a concept in America, and it was only background noise to our intense partnership in Pakistan.

Instead of answering my questions, he gets up out of his dining room chair and moves Tyler's out of the way. Tyler had flung it backwards to make his moody escape, and the sound of it still rings in my ears. Hodji reaches my chair and merely drops his arms around my shoulders and rubs my hair. I am not comfortable laying my head on his paunch. My village is given to kisses but not hugs between men.

He speaks before I can tell him to remove himself. "Aw, relax. Let me hug you for once. I have nothing else to offer you. I am a small man in a huge, overwhelming organization called the government."

I unravel his spider arms from me anyway. "Maybe you should tell them you choose your freedom and dignity over their payments to you."

"Don't needle me, please. I need every dollar I can get right now. Alicia is divorcing me."

I look up into his tense face. Hodji's wife, whom I have never met, has been married to him for seventeen years. He has never spoken ill of her, but the fact that he has spent much more time with me than with her speaks loudly of uncomfortable situations. Hodji also has a son, Twain. I wonder what will become of this boy my age, whom I have never met, if his parents divorce. Women petitioning for divorce is almost unheard of in my little corner of Pakistan.

"What of Twain?" I ask.

"He . . . found out about you, finally. After all these years . . ."

"He knows my name?"

"No. His mom hired a private detective who followed us the day back in March when I took you down to see Ground Zero.

I knew I was being tailed, but I thought it was USIC and standard policy. Headquarters is entitled to tail us, tap our phones, or polygraph us any time they want, to make sure we haven't flipped. Alicia thought I was out cheating..." He laughed sadly. "Anyway, Twain found out I'd been entertaining a kid his age all these years, and he sides with his mother. I guess you could say he's jealous, and with good reason. The divorce is not about you—don't worry. It's about me. It's about my job, my dedication to ... god knows what, all of a sudden. But you'll have to take it on faith that I can't answer your questions."

"Even though I give to you the answers that raise the more questions?" I ask. Then, seeing his tortured look, I mutter, "Sorry."

I am trying to feel sorry about him and Mrs. Montu and Twain, but I am familiar with what phone calls and e-mails he got over the years. Perhaps they did not complain of him being gone for months to be with me, but they do not honor him either. They want to know what they will get out of him. "We have to replace the car." "We have to join the country club so Twain can swim on the good team. When is your next bonus?" "Why didn't you call last night to find out how Twain did on his history test? Maybe you don't care." *Maybe we had a roomful of subversives in Uncle's Internet café, all armed, and I was scripting up to three terminals at once.* He works to keep the world safe, but it is not enough unless it has to do directly with them.

I say as much to him in the most polite terminology I can find. He swallows hard and looks for his own words.

"You just have to accept it," he finally says. "They're normal. We're not."

"You are extraordinary. They just don't see it."

"Well. Extraordinary is not grounds for divorce. Or if it is, here they call it 'mental cruelty,' 'desertion,' and 'verbal abuse.'"

I am stunned. "What bad thing did you say to Mrs. Montu?"

"Nothing. Er, I don't know. I haven't seen the divorce complaint. Perhaps not saying enough is verbal abuse. At any rate, she wants to marry somebody else. I'm not going to stand in her way."

I have led a sheltered life insofar as men with women are concerned, but I do not miss the implication of this.

"Will you countersue for this cheating?"

He rubs my hair absently, staring as if to see past my eyes and into my spirit. "Don't you think I've got enough fights going on right now? My wise Egyptian mother used to advise, 'Pick your battles.'"

"You will miss your boy," I say.

"I've *always* missed my boy. Things happen so quickly. I don't know when he reached an age where he was bitter toward me instead of looking forward to my being at home. Last year, I guess. When he was a freshman, he would still be staring out the living room window, watching and waiting as I pulled up in the car after three months in Pakistan with you and your dad and Ahmer."

I feel as if I have done something awful. As if, when my parents died last September, I took another boy's father and kept him for myself. Hodji must sense that I feel this way because he speaks quickly.

He says, "Thank you for being unselfish you. Thank you for

everything you do for me, for my country. If you did it for my country, you did it for my family."

But I am uncomfortable with the words. I did many things for my father before he died, relative to his own life as a v-spy for the Americans. He never said thank you, and I never listened for it. My family left me in Pakistan for three years when they came to America. I was to help Uncle Ahmer with the Internet café he had owned with my father. I only saw them for three weeks of the year when they would come home to visit me. I missed my father dreadfully but did not think to complain. For a son to do the best for his father, it is not something I was raised ever to question.

But I am driven further into unhappiness as Hodji leaves. He will be gone three days; he will not have news on where we are going for at least a week, and there is nothing for us to do but wait.

Tyler has grown restless, perhaps tired of these four walls, which remind him of his mother. I follow up the stairs, where he is blustering that the place even smells like her still. I suppose it is normal for a house to smell like its inhabitant for a while after she leaves, though I don't smell anything except ammonia and the overwhelming rubber of many surgical gloves. Nurse Alexa lets Tyler use what cleaning supplies he wishes, if he uses the gloves and mask to protect his skin and lungs. I think he is imagining the smell of his mother.

"There's so much dust in this room, it's, like, taking form," he complains, standing atop his desk with his dusting gloves on. Then he asks me not to penetrate his door frame and bring the dust from his mother's room into his room. "I'm seeing spooks in the dust."

He has just dusted yesterday after having admitted as much. His obsessive-compulsive disorder, which had been noticeable but tolerable, seems to have taken on a life of its own, what with this bad news.

"Tyler, do come down off that desk and be of help to me," I plead. "We need to ID these three new log-ins: Chancellor, Pasco, and HotKeys. They either have hostages or mysterious, unwilling participants in their experiments. And we need to know where VaporStrike went with his rotting monkey corpse in the steel drum. Earlier you were concerned he might be near us. Does that no longer worry you?"

"Why should I care? *Why?*" He rests his forehead on one of his many wall-length shelves. "Go find them if you're so pure at heart. If I can't have money, I want a little appreciation. Doing something for nothing is, to me, like trying to run your car with no gas." He picks up the dust cloth again and rubs hard at some disk cases he's taken out. "To hell with USIC."

I try, "Instead of thinking of yourself, think of a hostage being injected with toxins against his will."

"Do not guilt me." He says it with enough emphasis that I know I have guilted him. "Why couldn't Hodji get USIC to agree to burn down my house?"

I say with a shrug, "They think that it is cruel to any mother, even yours, and too radical a lie. Don't worry. Hodji will think of something else."

"Wish he wasn't traveling." He seems devoted to personally dusting all six sides of every disk case in that row. "I can see how much we matter. You and I are way down on USIC's list of priorities—why? Probably because the intelligence we're feeding them is far more interesting."

"We do not know that Hodji is going to Mexico," I reply, though I suspect he is, obviously.

"Don't you understand?" Tyler says through clenched teeth. "I *wanted* to be dead. I want to start over! This house has stuck out like a sore thumb ever since my mom was arrested. Everyone in this town knows she lived here. And while I'm here, I feel like I'm sore, too. Call it a psychological tick. But Hodji's ideas were important to me. Now? I'm just Tyler-the-Screw Ping."

Angrily, he sweeps every CD off the top shelf, and hundreds of cases hit the floor, the bed, the wall. I hear Nurse Alexa shouting up the stairs for what happened.

"We dropped some CDs. Do not worry," I shout down to her.

"There's one thing USIC needs to think about that they refuse to think about," he says.

"What is that?"

"The . . . psychological end of being this messed up. They think it's none of their business. They think that's a doctor's business. That's the problem with this country. Everybody's a goddamn specialist. And I don't think any doctor is going to write me a prescription slip for a new identity. They would say a new identity is none of *their* business. Can somebody from that dumb, way-huge, massive bureaucracy of Intelligence use some intelligence? Please?"

Nurse Alexa has not believed my tone, as she appears behind me, winded from climbing the stairs. Silently, she begins picking up CDs, having taken note of Tyler's fury. One good thing: Tyler has taped each case shut with a small piece of clear tape, I notice, trying not to roll my eyes.

"My uncle would say that . . . that you cannot run away from trouble. You have to fight the trouble where you are, or it will follow you," I say, suddenly hearing roosters crow behind me. I mutter, "Omar is online."

Tyler looks torn; he wants to jump down. But he remains on the desk. "How many times have I been beaten up in school? I never quit going," he says. "But this is different. I came to this country with a fake name, a fake passport, and a fake identity shoved straight up my ass. Now I want something of my own choosing. What is it about USIC that they can't, uh, *get involved* with that?"

TWENTY

**CORA HOLMAN
SATURDAY, MAY 4, 2002
3:25 P.M.
LIBRARY**

"SCOTT, we just can't get involved with that. We can't share classified material with outsiders, even if they just want to help. Not even you," Mr. Steckerman was saying to him in the parlor. I was in the next room, the library, trying to add something to my blog. But as usual, I imagined the hundreds of eyes reading it and drew a blank after only a few lines about being out of the hospital. I watched the double doors that separated the two rooms but knew Scott would feel betrayed if I simply closed them. His voice rose.

"You know what, Alan? When you tell me there's nothing you can do, you don't have to look so . . . so proud about it. What do you have to be proud about, when you're telling me you're just a . . . a helpless little fish in a huge pool?"

"I'm not meaning to look proud, Scott."

"You're right. Actually, you don't look proud. You look . . . pitiful. Pitifully small."

"I am, I suppose."

I flinched, deleting a line of my blog that came out clunky. Mr. Steckerman was getting the better of Scott by going along with him. But it was maddening, even from the next room. Marg had opened the windows, and I could hear the wind rustle through the trees from my comfy seat on the couch. I tried to ignore them as I stared into my screen and forced myself to retype the line.

"So small you can't even make a petty decision?"

"Scott, for you to help us, we would have to reveal classified material, and do you know how tight national security is right now? Tighter than it's been since World War II. Now tell me where the two of you went this afternoon. It's important."

Scott laughed triumphantly. "We were abducted by aliens."

"Not funny."

"Who's laughing? You reap what you sow."

Scott had seen Mr. Steckerman's car parked outside as we drove up, and almost as an afterthought had asked me to leave the rolls of film in one of the outbuildings. He distracted the man while I hid the film under an antique carriage missing a wheel. They were having a fairly heated conversation when I came in. Mr. Steckerman wanted to know where we had been. We had said we went to the CVS, but we had no bag, no purchase. I had made a fast exit into this room while he and Scott argued about why Scott couldn't work for USIC.

"All I can say is that I got a phone call from one of my agents who said he saw your car parked somewhere. And I want you to confirm that," Mr. Steckerman said.

"We were on Mars."

"Great. Were you also in Griffith's Landing?"

Scott thought long and hard, I guess, because the rubber tread of his sneaker clomped a few times. "No."

"Scott, don't lie to me," Mr. Steckerman pleaded sternly. "Listen. The four of you need to check with me before you leave the property from here on in."

"Why?"

"It has to do with, er, *People* and the other magazines you've been in," Mr. Steckerman stammered. I'd have almost sworn he was omitting something that was making him nervous. "When Godfrey gave you permission to go out in the car, he wasn't thinking—and I wasn't thinking—that you are very recognizable. People can be cruel. And if not cruel, invasive and—"

"I think we can handle it," Scott said with genuine calm, though with his next line I thought he was being defiant. "I'll take it under advisement. Thanks, Alan."

"No, you will listen to me and do what I'm telling you!" I heard a sound like a rolled-up newspaper being slapped down on a table. He went on in annoyance. "After all we've done for you kids, you should not be acting like this."

"I don't want anyone doing anything for *me*," Scott said, equally loud. "I want to do something for *somebody*. Okay? Something important. Why is that so hard to understand?"

I found myself drawn into the room, thinking I could defuse this somehow. I could feel Scott's pride, along with his lack of usefulness, filling the air with toxic energy. And Mr. Steckerman was so red in the face I wondered about his health as well. I found myself moving toward Scott.

"You don't understand the pressure we are under!" Mr. Steckerman yelled.

"What about pressure do I not understand, Alan?"

"Cora, give me the film you brought out of the car."

I flinched in surprise.

"When the two of you pulled up, you had a fistful of film in your hand, Cora," he persisted. "When you came in the door, the rolls were gone. What did you do with them? I want to know what you were photographing and why it is that one of my agents thought he saw you in Griffith's Landing. What in hell would make you go there today?"

Why would he want my film? I looked at Scott in confusion, my privacy threatened and violated. I thought of the men scrambling away from my lens when I raised the camera to my face. I knew it meant something . . . people not wanting to be photographed . . . but the big picture eluded me. I'd relied on Scott all day to know the meanings of things, and at the moment he only knew the meaning of getting what he wanted.

"Hel-*lo*. It's the closest place to get to the beach and boards," Scott said. "If you didn't want us there, you should have said something. If you're going to keep so many little secrets, I'd say there's a natural consequence to your actions."

Mr. Steckerman's voice rose above his. "Do not condescend to me. Cora, give me the film."

"I . . . it wasn't film," I heard myself stammer as I moved close to Scott. He brought his arm around me protectively. "It was just . . . We're allowed to sneak junk food once in a while, aren't we?"

"Where is the packaging?"

"I . . . threw it outside."

"You littered? You're sick as a dog, and you can still remember to put on a necklace that matches your shirt and shorts! Please don't insult my intelligence."

This was worse than having a principal in your face. It took everything I had to say the right thing. "If you want Scott to answer anything, then you'll find a way to get him a job. It will help him. Sitting around isn't making him well."

Scott snickered with his lips closed, which made his shoulders shake, and I stood very straight, in spite of Mr. Steckerman's impatience.

"Look!" he hollered again. "I'm a man pulled in many directions, and you kids are acting very ungrateful. You think we have no problems, because you're sick and we're well. You've never felt this from a parent's perspective! I've just had to tell my daughter she can't have her car out here, and her driver's license is now invalid until she's more emotionally stable. She took off, and right now, I don't know where she is."

I let out a little gasp. That news must have hit Rain hard. A breeze blew in from the window, and I realized that storm clouds were coming. I wondered if I should go look for her.

Scott had refused to ever talk about his symptoms when they came upon him, but I could see that our road trip and lengthy walk in the warm sun had been too much on him. His face was red and he was shiny with sweat. He rubbed the bridge of his nose, which he often did to massage away the start of one of our headaches. He only smiled slightly when he answered.

"Welcome to my nightmare, Alan." He moved toward the stairs, toward his room. Mr. Steckerman turned to me with a look like he was considering taking me by the throat.

"Are you going to tell me anything?"

I swallowed, my heart in Scott Eberman's pocket. "No."

He started to turn, and my guilt exploded. "But I'll help you find Rain."

He muttered, "She'll probably come back, but I don't want to risk her being out there in a storm. Owen took off straight ahead. I'll go east, you go west."

He didn't sound angry anymore. I wondered how he could juggle so many situations.

TWENTY-ONE

I SEE A GATHERING DARKNESS outside the bedroom window as tall clouds roll. A thunderstorm is rising, which means we will shut down the computers. Tyler does not trust surge protectors. Hodji has called, saying he is on a plane that is delayed on the runway, and I can call him anytime. But he is waiting for a change of heart in Twain about this never wanting to see him again and anxiously awaits his boy's call. He promised that nothing but his son calling and wanting to talk would keep him from answering his call waiting.

Tyler is sitting in my chair, clicking the mouse many times. He is no longer pouting and cleaning. I am happy that while he gets very uncouth and angry, he bounces back quickly.

I caution him to be careful to do only untraceable activity, as HotKeys is being paid much to trace v-spies. But Tyler is excited to discover if VaporStrike's server is merely a patch also.

As a groan of thunder resounds in the sky, we hear a *cockle-doo-dle-doo*. I stand behind him, watching as he grabs the mouse.

ALERT: Omar0324 is Online: www.lessismore.com/chat/blue-fishbay/%917.18.63%/ Enter5:59pm

VaporStrike logs on a minute later. With just a few clicks, we detect that Omar comes off a server in Tijuana, and Vapor-Strike is visiting a chat room from what appears to be a server in Manhattan. Quickly, Tyler opens a program he just finished that identifies IP addresses, and he copies and pastes the address into the search engine. "No such IP address exists" came as the results.

"See?" Tyler said. "He's . . . somewhere with tides. Is it an island? Can I be selfish and hope it's not ours?"

"No, you cannot be selfish," I say, thinking of our earlier conversation when we were trying to decide if VaporStrike was on a New Jersey barrier island or if he had returned to his home away from home: here. "If he is not near our tides, he's near *theirs.*"

Tyler stays silent, understanding my meaning of "theirs" to be the Trinity Four. We feel like something akin to guardian angels, an inspiration that came from my father, I felt. A way of life that was jeopardized when Trinity Falls was assaulted. He'd had many ways to describe the small towns of America. "There is a graciousness," he'd often said, "an innocence . . . a step between regular earth and heaven in those heartlands." It's not that we undervalue ourselves. To the contrary. I would prefer VaporStrike was close to us. I know Tyler does, too.

"These guys are getting too slick, too paranoid about potentially being watched. They're gonna give me a headache."

"Obviously they suspect they have v-spies," I note.

"I think they suspect everything and know nothing," Tyler muses. "They can't know about us. How could they know about us?"

Nurse Alexa calls upstairs in a loud voice that makes me flinch, saying that our dinner is prepared and to hurry, that she wants to see us eating before she goes on her Saturday visit to her sister's. We eat early on Saturdays so Miss Alexa can eat with her sister.

"Actually, I already *have* a headache," Tyler mutters in annoyance.

He returns to the chat screen as I shout down for her that we promise to be right down, and she should go. She will not like this, but she looks forward to these Saturday visits, as she cannot be with us 24/7. I hear the front door slam after a grumble about how promises must be kept.

Both men are logged in but idling. I assume they wait for HotKeys. Another rumble of thunder makes Tyler flip vulgar sign language up at the sky.

Finally, they make an exchange, all in Punjabi, which I know, so I translate out loud and cut and paste during their pauses.

VaporStrike: Your antics with the swans are not amusing to our backers.

Omar0324: MY antics? It was your idea to toy with one of the swans' food.

VaporStrike: I am not your mother.

Omar0324: You nag like her.

VaporStrike: Don't tamper with their food. It is cruel. Cruelty to animals.

Omar0324: I am not a silly American who thinks animals need rights.

"What are they talking about?" Tyler pushes me in the soreness of my shoulder. He is taking this literally.

I am not. "They are arguing over the people they are . . . holding or applying drugs to. VaporStrike is saying that too much tampering with their doses is cruel, but he is being ironic. He actually thinks it's very funny."

"I can't understand how you can get all of that," he says in amazement.

Years of practice. Coded sentences make slightly less sense than regular communication, regardless of how hard the sender tries to be clever.

VaporStrike: I am passing on messages to you from Chancellor. Whisper down the row. Let us hope I get this right: The swans have wandered a bit. He wants to put up an electrical fence. Let one of them take a spark or two.

I try to think of what this could mean, but thinking too hard can do no good, either. "They're using codes inside translations in disappearing chatter . . ." I breathe. "These must be highly guarded secrets."

"What does it mean?" Tyler asks.

I am knowledgeable only in linguistics and the languages of the computer. Hodji is best at discerning codes.

"He wants to keep the swans from getting away?" Tyler persists.

I shake my head. "Take a spark or two. Spark . . . Fire? FireFall?"

I don't want to say it, but he cannot resist. "Tell me he's not going to give that shit to a human . . ."

> **Omar0324:** Remind Chancellor that if he outright kills a
> swan it will be counterproductive.

Tyler pushes my hand away from picking a scab. I do not understand how Chancellor plans to expose a human being to FireFall without it killing him—not if one milligram killed three monkeys. By spraying aerosol in the room with the hostage? By brushing it against his skin only?

> **Omar0324:** And tell Chancellor to be careful of the snakes
> regardless of what he decides. They are indigenous to
> that area.

"Snakes would be law enforcement," I whisper, though I cannot figure out why I am whispering. Tyler wants me to skin his palm, though it is obvious.

> **VaporStrike:** He is well aware of the snakes. You make too
> much of them. They come out of the water this time of
> year.
> **Omar0324:** Colony Two is a snake pit. I do not think he
> appreciates, as he has never been bitten.

"*Bingo,*" Tyler admits. "A shitty *bingo* . . . Chancellor and his hostages are near Colony Two. What the fuck. We should have gotten it through online news if people were reported missing down there."

I remind him, "Whores and prostitutes are often not missed for days after a serial killer murders them. This Colony Two would have to be near Atlantic City. Where there's gambling, there is prostitution, and maybe ShadowStrike has seized several prostitutes for experiments—"

> **Omar0324:** In fact, I would like very much for you to get
> your own neck out of there quickly.

Our surprised yells bounce off the walls, and Tyler cackles, rejoicing freely, forgetting our feelings of protection toward the Trinity Four. "I'm thinking of Hodji. If his flight is no longer delayed, he is on his way to Mexico. It's like he took a sucker punch. Left the action to—"

"It's not funny when you consider who delivered the punch." I feel not only guilty but unprotected. I am once again haunted by a web post left by Omar, just after his escape in March, on a web board for parents of asthmatic children. It was as if he wanted me, known only to him as the Kid, to find it. *We will strike and, unlike others you choose to call "terrorists," you will never be sure it is us. . . . You will never know quite where we are, who we are, and where we will turn up next.*

Perhaps I have v-spied for so long that my instincts exceed my knowledge accurately. The following appears after an arrogant period of idling:

> **VaporStrike:** Did I suggest to you that I was in the snake pit?
> Your inferences concerning my intelligence alarm me.

> **Omar0324:** I told you to dispose of the monkey corpses personally. I'm assuming you didn't hire a delivery service.
>
> **VaporStrike:** The brethren have steel drums in their possession for the WMD. I had one of them deliver the remains to me on the Parkway.

In all my years gathering online intelligence, I know Hodji's saying to be true: "When it rains, it pours." We have learned so much in two sessions that my brain does not feel equipped to process more. But I am forced to. It becomes very personal:

> **Omar0324:** Where will you dispose of it?
>
> **VaporStrike:** I remember from March that the dumpster behind Trinitron gets a Wednesday/Sunday pickup.

Trinitron, the Internet café, his former haunt. I had been brought from Pakistan in March to capture and translate his chatter there. He had scattered to the winds after the raid. I remained and am still living a mile away. Now, he is coming back.

Tyler is stunned to silence for once, and I pull out my cell phone, dial Hodji, and hear his busy clicks. He had said the only reasons he would not take my calls were if he was taking off, or if he was talking to Twain. I assumed he had taken off by now.

Tyler realizes and suddenly does not find Hodji and his flight to Mexico so funny.

"Sonofabitch," he explodes. "Tell me he's got that ungrateful brat of his on the phone whom I would love to switch lives with. It's a long flight. He could play dad for hours—"

I think to text, but I have only recently learned how to do it, and I find hitting the buttons two and three times annoying. I send Hodji an e-mail, thinking he would have heard my calling clicks and check all communications immediately. Perhaps he can read while he is listening. In the e-mail I simply say:

> *VS in NJ today... HERE tonight... 1 mile from HERE.*
> *VS has Fire. 911911911. Check script.*

"You forgot to tell him that Chancellor has prisoners and he's injecting shit into them and wanting to expose them to the Real Deal," Tyler says.

"I suggested almost as much when he was here, and he refused to comment."

"Ungrateful little henpecked morons," Tyler notes of the New York squad, but I do not want to get sidetracked into complaints.

"I do not think this is Hodji's fault," I say. "He works for a huge agency."

"So who am I supposed to be mad at?" Tyler persists.

I do not know and only recite a truth, not meaning to make him angrier. "In a big agency, there is no one to assume blame."

"Tell that to my sorry ass when it gets separated from my head and they show it on the Internet. I'm done with Big Agency." He leaves the room again. He perceives he has won something. I feel I will have won something only if I don't stop to look for someone to blame. Blaming, in a government with its many rules, is like swinging at shadows.

But he reappears again moments later. The sad truth is that we cannot resist what we do, given what we know. It would be as much folly as a lifeguard refusing to save a drowning person because he has been fired from beach patrol duty.

I put all the chatter into a script for Hodji with no note or signature. I do not encrypt it, believing he will check his e-mail quickly. But as I hit SEND, images fill my head of him acknowledging his son's complaints for hours which, in this country, would be considered the honorable thing to do.

HotKeys joins Omar and VaporStrike suddenly, and I watch with impatience as their hellos contain jokes about foot fungus. Then

> **Omar0324:** Be quick with what you have to say. I cannot remain here much longer.
>
> **HotKeys:** I am tweaking programs to help catch your v-spies. In the interim, the only way we can think to verify whether or not USIC is onto us is to post people at various locations that might attract USIC attention.
>
> **Omar0324:** Such as the convention center.
>
> **HotKeys:** And the amusement pier across the street. They have photos of some of the better-known USIC agents. None were seen. But you will never believe who was.
>
> **Omar0324:** Don't dawdle. I'm running out of time.
>
> **HotKeys:** Two of the Trinity Falls victims.
>
> **Omar0324:** The teenagers???
>
> **HotKeys:** Two. Pasco recognized them from the cover of People.
>
> **Omar0324:** What in hell were they doing at the site? I thought they were too sick to leave their hospice.
>
> **HotKeys:** Apparently the peace and quiet is suiting them already. They were taking photos in front of the convention center.

A long pause follows, in which both Tyler and I sit frozen. We would understand that these men would devour *People* magazine as well as *Time* and *Newsweek* in order to fully congratulate themselves, but it still strikes us like gunshots smoking out of the screen to hear them refer directly to the Trinity Four.

I shoot off another e-mail to Hodji:

> *2 of Trinity 4 wandered into Colony 2. C2 very near to C1. New log-in Pasco spotted them.*

I hit SEND, in spite of feeling that perhaps the extremists are wrong and they saw others who resembled them. I nudge Tyler. "Go to your room and see if any of the Trinity Four possesses an e-mail address yet." I have read in *People* and heard from Hodji that the CEO of Dell has sent them each a laptop along with hopes for a speedy recovery. Perhaps they have started to use e-mail again.

I call Hodji again, and his line still rings busy.

Their chatter has gone into more exchanges.

Omar0324: You must be mistaken. Or perhaps they visited the amusement rides. They are teenagers, and some days their health is possibly sufficient for this.

HotKeys: I have considered that. It just took his mind apart to see them standing there. He said he recognized the boy first—the older of the two—and then the dark-haired girl you found so strikingly beautiful that day you saw her sleeping in the hospital. He thinks the girl snapped a picture of him.

I send Hodji more mail:

> *Scott and Cora seen in C2.*

I hear Tyler's keys clattering to see if he can drum up an e-mail address.

> **Omar0324:** He's a moron. I suppose he was flitting about without a hat or glasses even.
> **HotKeys:** That's fine coming from a man who condones experiments on swans. Do not panic. It is possible they were simply taking a stroll and shooting pictures.
> **Omar0324:** Of the convention center. Our convention center.
> **VaporStrike:** I said, do not panic. I tend to think HotKeys is right. What are the alternatives? That USIC told teenagers their secrets?
> **Omar0324:** Impossible, the way Americans protect their young.
> **VaporStrike:** And these are sick teenagers. Would USIC send them to Colony Two to do their dirty work?
> **Omar0324:** Thank you, my friend. You speak wisdom. I will dwell on this tonight, when sleep eludes me as usual, and see if I can think up some other explanation. Maybe Chancellor will have one . . .

I have not found Chancellor online yet with this motley crew, and I quickly dog-leash HotKeys, hoping they will meet up in some other chat room.

I finish the script after they log off and send it to Hodji, though I accompany it with one final message:

> *Cora and Scott are not in danger.*

My conscience is burdened, and I feel I should not disrupt his chance to make amends with his son if I can help it.

I remember that I am supposed to patch my own IP address so that it does not register to our server, where the billing address will be this house. I feel more general anxiety than a feeling of being unsafe. However, I wish USIC had sent us a secretary instead of a nurse to ease their consciences. Miss Alexa has a fire-arms license, which makes us feel safe and secure, except there is the problem that she cannot be here all the time. There are trips to the grocery and the CVS, and visits to family and friends, which any nurse would want in order to keep her sanity.

When I mentioned this hole in the protection to Hodji, he had wanted to come over and be with us during those hours. However, he was very busy with other tasks, and he also made the sad mistake of saying "I'll try to baby-sit you guys" to Tyler, whose response indicated that such terminology has a negative connotation in English. He said that "Hodji could baby-sit his own ass," and he would hot-wire the house with bombs and sub-terfuge to protect us. I do not believe Tyler would be so stupid as to hot-wire his own house, and I have not seen him engage in any activities involving wires. Only cleaning supplies.

But the fact that the hole in the protection plan had never actually been addressed led me to open my control panel to install a patch on our IP address and hide our location, just to be safe.

I am halfway into the task when Tyler hollers to me. "Cora added a few lines to her blog, and there's now a guest registry."

I go in to him, feeling a greater urgency to contact the girl, though I have no idea what to say. I sit on the edge of Tyler's bed. He sits in the chair, and I look at her beautiful picture, taken by some nurse at St. Ann's. She is sitting up on her bed, in a black tank shirt and lounge pants, making what Americans call the peace sign at the camera.

Tyler leans sideways, clutching his chest. "Be still, my heart."

"Hush." Under her photo is some language about leaving the hospital yesterday, but she does not mention where she has gone. I sense this is wise. She started the blog several days ago, and already she has had two thousand visitors. It will be a popular web page.

"Send her a message through the registry. She was in there just today. Maybe she will be back soon," I say. Then, "Get up and let me write it."

He pulls up his other desk chair for me to sit in. He does not like others to sit their bottoms where his bottom will sit. He has his own chair in the dining room also. I am happy that, at least, he does not argue with me about who should write this note.

Dear Miss Cora,

I start, and decide to keep it straight to the point, like my usual e-mails to USIC.

> *Were you in a certain city today shooting pictures of a convention center and an amusement pier? If so, which city? It is important, and hence, you must let me know your movements. Yours most sincerely, The Kid*

When I met Miss Rain and Owen, Roger would not let me identify myself as the Kid. I took up Scott Eberman's hand in the ICU and told him all about myself, but he was in a drug-induced coma and heard none of it. And I feel I am violating some sacred boundary by contacting Cora. Hodji would not like it, but Hodji is busy speaking with some other boy.

"Do you think this will frighten her?" I ask. I do not want to intrude upon what peace and quiet the State of New Jersey is trying to secure for them.

"We need to know. Just send it."

I hit SEND and wait and wait. Obviously she is not online, and I have no idea when she will come back. I wonder if anyone, among the people we are trying to help, has time for us.

TWENTY-TWO

WHEN I HAD NOT HEARD THE SOUNDS of Mr. Steckerman's calling for at least fifteen minutes, I realized I was far from the house. With the black clouds forming above the trees, I turned back in the direction I'd come from, hoping to find the main trail again. I scanned the tall trunks and tumbling summer bramble on both sides, though I had a feeling Rain had not come this far.

I looked for eyes in the bramble like I had seen earlier today and felt thousands of pairs watching me. But my mind was in such a state of confusion about Aleese, my father, and terrorists that I knew better than to play into it too strongly. I only spun once, and seeing nothing but woods, I started calling.

"Rain? Rain!" My camera, which had become a security blanket of sorts, was back at the house, and I gripped at the pit of my stomach where it would have hung. I wasn't sure where I was ... couldn't see the main trail forming anywhere in front of me.

Aleese is enjoying this, my weary brain noted, and I even spoke to ward off feelings of helplessness. "If you're going to show up, do something constructive and don't be a pig. Show me out of here."

Then I felt silly. I sat down on a log to gather some strength and try not to be negative. Somehow, I was still four-star, even after the hells of seeing terrorists with my own eyes and being so possessed as to take pictures of them. It helped me to consider that maybe this lengthy list of medications we were on was actually working. Dr. Godfrey had explained to us that the same protocol in different bodies would produce slightly different results. I suffered with the most side effects, but that was not nearly so bad as to be knocked down with low white-cell counts and the chronic headaches that poor Owen dealt with.

I was merely exhausted. I started to wonder if my weary bones would carry me back. I saw something red flash and gasped. Just a blotch, which disappeared behind some bramble, but it sent me slowly to my feet.

I listened for the goats. One of them had been *baa*-ing when I left the house, but it sounded off to the left and I had gone right. I thought if I could hear it, I could find my way back.

But the woods were deadly still. Something flashed again to my right, this time looking more orange. Orange . . . a color worn by hunters . . . Might someone think I was a deer and shoot?

"Hello?" I yelled and repeated it after a lengthy silence.

This time a normal voice hollered. "Cora?"

Henry Calloway. *Miracles. Thank you, Aleese, for once.*

He appeared out of the brush just ahead of me in a rusty red Astor College sweatshirt—the school's colors being red and white. Still, my knees were Jell-O.

He ran up and put an arm around me to stop my swaying. He pointed ahead. "That's the main trail I came down. It's harder to see in the summer when everything's alive."

"Whew," I huffed. "I was starting to think—"

"You were lost? Look, let me give you a present." He handed me a cell phone. "This is my personal cell. The college also gives me one, so I have two. Please. Don't ever come out here again without it. If you use it only for emergencies, I won't get charged a thing."

He pulled out a second phone, dialed the first, and once it rang, he hung up. "Now you have my number in your 'calls missed' box. Use it anytime you wish."

I thanked him, staring at the little phone in wonder. A dozen of the richer students in schools had had cell phones last year.

I jumped out of my skin as the phone rumbled in my palm.

"Answer it," he said. "Just pull it open."

I managed to pry it apart and put it to my ear. "Yes?"

"Henry, did you find Rain?" It was Marg.

"No. Not yet. Marg, this is Cora."

"Then I suppose Henry found you."

"He did. Here . . ." I handed the phone to him and continued to lean into his tall form in relief. He guided us down the path while laughing pleasantly, telling Marg the phone was now mine and it was the least he could do.

"It might rain before we get back to the house. She might come in drenched. Maybe you should run a hot bath or something."

When the phone was back in my grip, he said, "Tomorrow I'll come back here after I do some work in the morning, and

I'll take you on a tour of the trails if you're up for it. They're not difficult to follow. In fact, I'm going to spray the trees with blue paint. As long as you can follow the blue circles on the trunks, you'll know you're not lost."

"Thank you," I said. "For everything."

"I'm happy to help." We walked along the main trail in silence, him moving at a slow enough pace to keep me from getting winded again. I was not uncomfortable in the silence. I spoke merely to try to recover the escape-from-reality feeling I'd had with him last time.

"Mrs. Starn . . . she said you have a cabin out this way?"

"Yes. It actually belongs to the college, and, generally, more experienced researchers get them. But after I came up with the ten thousand in research grants, I think they looked at me a little more carefully." His laugh was uncomfortable, laced with humility. I liked it.

"Are you . . . going to study the body of the one Kellerton children there after you exhume it?"

He squeezed my shoulder as if to say, *No bad thoughts allowed.* "Great heavens, no. I'll do that in the medical center's forensics or pathology lab with two dozen or so curious researchers looking on. I have to handle that one carefully, as it ought to bring some good press. Good press brings more research funds."

"Sounds so exciting."

"Right now, I'm actually helping a friend with his research, allowing him to use my cabin. He's in the geology department, interested in tsunamis—tidal waves. He believes one struck New Jersey sometime in the past thousand years."

I ceased to lean on him, devouring this news with interest.

"You seem to have the most interesting life," I said. "I could just get lost in the stories you tell."

"Then I'll be sure to bring you plenty more. I'd love to invite you to visit the cabin. I'll find out if I can. The problem would be my partner's soil samples. They're being tested under various laboratory conditions. Do you know what spores are?"

I had heard the word. "Something in the air?"

"Actually, spores come from plants and soil. But they're not good for the lungs, and even I wear a mask around his samples." He proceeded to tell me how there were limestone tracings in all two hundred of his friend's soil samples, which had been taken from as far north as Sussex County, as far south as Cape May, and as far west as Cherry Hill. Limestone tracings indicate that the soil has been underwater, he explained, and the amount of limestone can reveal how long ago the submergence was.

"My associate keeps coming up with less than a thousand years," he said, "which is indicative of extreme trauma to the area."

"Wow. A tidal wave in the Atlantic?"

He went on about their theory, all the while comforting me over the impossibility of it happening again in our lifetime. No stress, just interesting imagery. It made the walk go quickly, and we were actually about two hundred feet from the house when Marg came out in running pants and shoes.

"I'll leave you in good hands and call tomorrow," he promised me.

As he turned to leave, Marg said, "Mr. Steckerman spotted Owen and Rain down on the flat rock by the pond. She had stopped crying, he said, and he didn't want to interrupt a conversation that *wasn't* making her cry by barging in as a visual reminder of what *had* made her cry."

"Smart thinking," I said.

"I'm going to tell them to come in, and then try to get a jog in before it rains."

I looked at the darkening sky. "You might have to make it a sprint." She looked like the athletic sort.

"Will you be okay until I get back? Are you symptomatic?" She laid the back of her hand to my face.

"No. I was coming a little unglued before Henry came to my rescue." I sighed. "I guess you could say I'm not a woods person."

I watched her jog off in the opposite direction from Henry, then I watched him walk down the trail as far as I could see before I turned to the house . . . back to my sickness, my thoughts of Aleese, talk of USIC and medication, and everything that weighed so heavily on my shoulders.

TWENTY-THREE

SHAHZAD HAMDANI
SATURDAY, MAY 4, 2002
3:42 P.M.
UPSTAIRS

I AM GOOD AT THE WAITING GAME, but my sense of urgency to hear from Miss Cora makes me impatient. I sit in Tyler's extra desk chair watching him swat at the corners of his ceiling with a long-stick feather duster when I hear the rooster crowing from my room.

I wander across the hall to my terminal. It seems too soon for Omar, but I remember HotKeys is trying to catch v-spies, which might be too tempting for him to stay away. It is Omar, and as only twenty-some minutes have passed, I feel he has simply left one Internet café and walked a quarter mile to another. He is off of a new server.

A few minutes later Tyler follows me and sits on the bed.

"Can't these guys get a life?" Tyler asks. "They're worse than we are. Haven't they heard of cell phones?"

"The charges leave too many trails, too much evidence," I remind him, reading a few lines that I know Tyler will not like.

"You really don't want to know what Omar and VaporStrike are saying to one another."

"So long as they're not on Long Island and they're not bothering the Trinity Four, I really don't care," he says.

They are using several of the Egyptian languages, and I have scripted them so far as saying HotKeys has a Ph.D. in computer science, and there is a repeated mention that ShadowStrike has paid him a hundred thousand euros to find their v-spies.

Tyler notes this time, "That kinda puts a price on our heads. Doesn't it?"

That many euros is equivalent to even more dollars. We both believe that all information we have provided to Hodji since Omar turned up in Mexico has been exclusive to us.

"Shall we send USIC a bill for the same amount?" he asks, as I knew he would.

"It is a fat chance you will have of redeeming those funds, and now, stifle your fat complaints," I say. They are chatting again.

Omar0324: Where is HotKeys? Taking a sauna?
VaporStrike: He is running his little programs. Have patience.
Omar0324: He had better be as smart as you promised, because he is surely not swift. I am walking about on an infected foot. You must tell him I don't like his constant wasting of my time.

Tyler aligns himself behind me, sees my script, and says something idiotic like, "Bring it on." I am back to the live chat and I copy and paste, trying to include all the little missing words in English, but my brain is distracted with Miss Cora and much fog. I want a blast from my inhaler, which increases my heart rate and, often, the blood flow to my head. But I left it downstairs and I don't want Tyler to leave right now. I simply plod on.

> **VaporStrike:** I think this time you will be pleased. His program to catch v-spies is quite involved. I do not understand computer language but have seen the program as an RTF. It is two hundred text pages long.

"We need to get our hands on that," I say.
Tyler laughs. "Dream on."

> **Omar0324:** It's about time he did something useful. What has he found?
> **VaporStrike:** It appears he picked up a v-spy on your other log-in, OmarLoggi.
> **Omar0324:** Impossible.
> **VaporStrike:** God knows how USIC collects their persistent v-spies. With the delivery of great riches, I suppose.

Tyler's disgusted laugh sounds like a trumpet blast. I lean instinctively away from the terminal.

> **Omar0324:** If that new log-in is unsafe, how can this old one possibly be safe? It is the very one I used in Colony One. Is he insane?
> **VaporStrike:** USIC has a saying: Dogs do not return to their vomit. Such would apply to log-ins as well, but he wants to be certain.

"We're not USIC," Tyler notes. "We think dogs sometimes *do* return to their vomit."

It suddenly occurs to me what I am forgetting. I had started to put a patch on the IP address at this terminal when Tyler called me in to help locate an e-mail address for Miss Cora. It entered my head as having been done. I try to remember if I actually finished it. I do not think so. But suddenly, I have no memory. HotKeys could be reading our IP address, and I raise the situation to Tyler.

"Oh . . . shit," he confirms, his hand landing on my pock-infested shoulder with a bang. "Exit. Now!"

As I put my fingers back to the keys, he pulls me back with a change of mind. "No, don't touch anything. Those homespun detection programs read activity, not presence—"

"But we created a trail of activity to find them! It is too late."

Our fingers wag helplessly on invisible keypads. We don't know what to do.

Omar0324: We are being watched?

VaporStrike: HotKeys does not believe we are being watched, but he will know more soon.

Omar0324: I would have kept my comments to harmless gossip. I would have encrypted it in some language of the Congo.

VaporStrike: HotKeys really is not expecting anything.

"Stupid," Tyler says anxiously. "If we're stupid, they're stupider. Right?"

I cannot answer. The game of computer chase has always

been full of snags and blunders, as technology changes constantly, and without faces and bodily presences, human nature is inclined to taking many more risks. Whether we are blundering worse than they are, I cannot decide. But blundering is something I have accepted of myself in the past. However, I have never been caught so badly as this might turn out. And never without Hodji just a phone call away. We finally see, at the top of the screen,

> HotKeys has entered the chat.
>
> **HotKeys:** I had better be smart because I am not swift? Is that what you said?
>
> **Omar0324:** My friend, if you are going to play God in your omnipresence, you must play Him in your forgiveness as well.
>
> **HotKeys:** Your heinous gossip is forgiven. I am a tolerant man. I cannot be in a chat while I am watching a chat. I can, however, watch you and those who are watching you at the same time.
>
> **Omar0324:** You have picked up a v-spy?
>
> **HotKeys:** On this log-in, yes.

Tyler curses more, which I am very tired of hearing. It does not help.

I find myself whispering. "Maybe he can detect the activity but not trace it."

"Maybe he wears bloomers to bed and sucks his thumb," Tyler replies.

Omar logs off and is gone. He is afraid to say anything, I sense, and I wonder if VaporStrike will share that fear and abruptly depart also. I see a tiny number at the bottom of the screen change. "Number of guests: 4" now drops to "3." With VaporStrike and HotKeys remaining as visible log-ins, the third party is us.

As VaporStrike and HotKeys idle, I grab the mouse and click EXIT. The number will now change to "2."

Tyler grumbles that it is too late as we head swiftly back to his room, where his hard-drive technology allows us to watch without being numbered. I want to see how savvy these men are. Very few people are even aware of that little number, and those who see it suspect it is a floating chat manager patrolling for profanity. They are speaking in English, which may mean they are too panicked to endure the small complications of their translation programs. Unfortunately, my fear is thrown right into my face.

HotKeys: He just logged off, the idiot. Do you see a little line, "Number of guests: 2" somewhere at the bottom of the window? It just changed from "3."

VaporStrike: That was a v-spy? Often those numbers don't match up.

HotKeys: If he had left it alone, we might have assumed it was a chat manager—which is not even a person. It is a roaming computer program, checking for keywords in English which are considered profane.

VaporStrike: How do you know it wasn't such a program?

HotKeys: Because, my electronically challenged friend . . . he logged off as soon as I said there was a v-spy.

VaporStrike: Too ironic, yes. Should we exit?

HotKeys: He is gone. No one is watching us now.

Tyler nudges me but does not brag about our current invisibility to these men, his computers having been patched out years ago.

VaporStrike is idling, but I sense precisely what he is doing. He is trying to remember today's scripts to see what was revealed to us.

VaporStrike: They cannot know about the swans.
HotKeys: Guess again. USIC's computer labs are impossible to penetrate, but I hacked a few of their laptops.
VaporStrike: I knew you would be worth your fee. Where is Omar when I need a witness? How did you do that?
HotKeys: Don't weary me with your silly questions.

Tyler exclaims in horror, "How *did* he hack a USIC laptop?"

"How did you find their cell phone numbers and hack into their calls in March?" I say to him, just to shut up his chronic speaking. There are always ways. USIC warns against laptops, but guys out in the field like Hodji sometimes have no choice.

Like Hodji. The air in the room turns dense as I think of the many e-mails I have sent him today. I tell myself that there are a hundred USIC agents in New York and New Jersey, and they could not be talking about him. But my sudden wheezing fit makes what comes on to the screen seem in slow motion, as if I am in a dream where I cannot run from monsters.

HotKeys: Here is what I just pulled from one laptop. Are you ready?
VaporStrike: I am.
HotKeys: Are you sure?

VaporStrike: Do not dawdle as if you are a small child.
HotKeys: The unread e-mails read as follows:

> *VS in NJ today . . . HERE tonight . . . 1 mile from HERE.*
> *VS has Fire. 911911911. Check script. 2 of Trinity 4 wan-*
> *dered into Colony 2 . . . C2 very near to C1. New log-in*
> *Pasco spotted them . . . Scott and Cora seen in C2 . . .*
> *Cora and Scott are not in danger.*

It falls out onto the screen in its entirety, in English, so that it takes over the room. I am seeing in double, then in sixes.

VaporStrike: The v-spy used the word "HERE"? To describe
    my whereabouts?
HotKeys: You had better run for cover. Run for your life.
VaporStrike: My friend, you do not know me well yet. At
    times when most men run, it is not yet time to run. HERE?
    Find me an address and allow me to make good use of
    myself, being that I'm IN TOWN.

Abruptly, HotKeys exits, which could mean he is off to do his bidding, or perhaps he has been kicked off somehow. I doubt it is that second thing.

"I'm dreaming this," Tyler breathes. "He can't find us."

But he can. It could take ten minutes or all night, depending on how good a hacker he is. I wish so deeply for Nurse Alexa to return that I am afraid I will scream. As for Hodji, I try his busy phone again and wish to leave one more message, telling him he has no right to hear his son's bitter complaints at a time like this.

But his devotion to his ungrateful son is the least of his current frailties, I realize. He does not have wings, and even if I could tell him of this final twist, he would only suffer because of it, because there is no way he could get to us quickly.

"We need to find Roger O'Hare," I say. "We need to find another USIC agent. Maybe Miss Susan from my Trinitron days . . ."

Tyler stares at me as if I have two noses. "Give me another option. I don't actually like chasing down people to beg them to take information that could cost us our asses, especially when they refuse to thank us."

I have to agree with this. There is always my uncle Ahmer in Pakistan, who would at this time be opening his Internet café for the start of business. He is quick to serve but would have no better chance of reaching Hodji than we would.

"Let's call the police," Tyler suggests.

We look at each other, covered in these hideous, purple speckles that would defy explanation inside a police officer's realm of comprehension.

He laughs, which makes me feel better, and decides, "Nah, let's wait it out. Hodji can't stay on the phone forever with his kid. VaporStrike can't find us that fast."

TWENTY-FOUR

**OWEN EBERMAN
SATURDAY, MAY 4, 2002
3:45 P.M.
THE POND**

I CHASED RAIN down to this little pond after her dad gave her the bad news. The water was pretty, a serene place even though the clouds overhead were dark. I sat beside her on this flat rock that jutted out over the water. It wasn't raining yet, so I let her cry it out using my jeans as a tear catcher until they were soaked through in one spot. She had made me laugh earlier today, so it was my turn. But I was having aftershocks and couldn't think of anything.

"Where are the goats?" I finally settled on.

She blew her nose into a snotty tissue she found in her cut-offs. "I came out here and fed them when you were out of it. Now? I dunno."

She stayed slumped, studying the wet spot she'd left on my thigh from crying. She finally noted with a sniff, "You're sitting Indian-style."

Not where I wanted this conversation to go. I could never sit Indian-style in high school. Too muscle-bound.

"Well, don't look," I told her.

"That doesn't bother you?"

I sighed, wishing I were a comedian, that I could just peel off the joke I couldn't think of that would make her laugh. "No."

She stared into my eyes incredulously. "You know what? Sometimes I think you don't care whether you live or die."

Yah, yah, yah. She wanted answers to everything, and she wanted them to be what she wanted to hear. I wondered how she'd respond to my sudden thought: *I care whether I live or die. But I care more about* how *I live and* how *I die.* I don't know why out-there thoughts hit me more often than the other three—except that I'd spent a lot more time than they'd ever done thinking about the meaning of life. I was born thinking of the meaning of life, Mom said. I'd talk to her about how fulfilled she'd always felt, basically existing as a charity lawyer, while everyone in town was out making big bucks and trekking on down to Disney with their kids every year. We decided she was happier. One Saturday sophomore year we were talking like that. She reached over, tousled my hair, and said, *"Owen, if ever anything goes wrong, you remember I said it: You got enough oil in your lamp."* I wished a lot lately that I'd asked her what that meant.

Rain didn't like my silence. "Listen to me! If you ever die, I'll kill you."

Okay, so she wouldn't like my intense answers. I could manipulate her into feeling better. "Well. I always feel better when *you* quit crying."

She patted my leg, going around the tear spot with her

finger. She was thinking of something, and it wasn't what it does to a guy when a girl runs her finger in circles on his thigh. Or maybe she did know. After a long silence, she scooted over the top of my leg and wiggled her butt in between my ankles and my body so that I quickly straightened my legs. She tossed one leg on either side of me and put her arms around my neck. We looked like some seesaw contraption.

I knew she was going to kiss me next, and I put my hand over her mouth. She was trying to explain herself, but I just pressed my palm onto her blather and started talking myself.

"Rain, don't even go there. There's twenty-five good reasons not to go there."

Her eyebrows shot up when I didn't move my hand, and I got on with it.

"First, you're using me. You're upset about your car. And you really want Danny Hall, and I can't do anything about that, but I don't like thinking of myself as the red ribbon. You know how I've always hated red . . ." She rolled her eyes and made noise, but I clamped down and kept going.

"Second, Miss Haley was making some sense, whether we want to admit to it or not. I'm in worse health than you are. If you swapped spit with me, you would be getting the short end of the stick. I probably have more germs, and you could catch them. That's not a fair deal. Third . . ."

She was trying to chew on my palm, her lips doing some "screw you, let me talk!" thing, but if the only girl I'd been really good friends with throughout life was going into attack mode, I had a right to say my piece. This thing was not going to happen.

"Third, if you got pregnant, it could kill you. Fourth, if you ever die, *I'll* kill *you*. Fifth . . ."

I let go, because she found the fleshy part of my hand to bite into. She said, "What do you take me for? You think I was after the whole schmear?"

She meant she just wanted to kiss and make out, risk the passing of germs Miss Haley had warned about. I would love to say the thought gave me shudders, like kissing your sister would. It had been easier to keep Rain in the category of sister when I was distracted by three sports and a school full of others. "Remember our deal from eighth grade? We would never go out?"

Her right eyebrow kinked like it did whenever she got annoyed. "We said people who go out also break up and don't speak to each other, and we didn't want to ruin the convenience of living kitty-cornered to each other. It was about T-shirts and socks! What does that matter now—"

"I never borrowed your T-shirts," I stalled. "You borrowed *my* T-shirts—"

"You've still got half my Wigwams. I've bought, like, ninety pair over the years. You've bought six. Yet you've got half that didn't wear out, and I've got half. Don't make out like you got the short end of the stick."

"You stole my toothbrush."

"That was *my* toothbrush. My spare. You stole it from me first. I needed it back."

"What are we arguing about?" I drummed my fingers on her back.

"Elephants."

Sex. She was going to beat the tar out of the subject, and I was defenseless. "Right. You were saying you weren't after the whole schmear."

"Of course not. When did you decide I resemble a ho?"

I flinched warily and let air escape between my clenched teeth. "Never. But somehow I'm having trouble imagining you choosing a jumping-off point. You've been in a reckless mood for three weeks."

I should not have said it. It was half a yes, which was not what I meant to imply. The hardness of this rock was killing my hip joints and wearing out my back, and I'd just had two aftershocks on the way out here. But I was watching her, watching her lips moving in until her nose bumped mine, in awe of how much it would take to turn a seventeen-year-old guy into a no-can-do. I wasn't there yet, no matter how much pain I was in.

But it had always been some crazy comedy hour with me and Rain. We'd had a couple of moments of temptation in the past. We almost broke down one night on my living room couch freshman year—we'd gotten really close. And then she just started cracking up, and neither of us could stop laughing, and I don't even know why. We ended up in a fight about who laughed first and didn't talk for a week. The other time was out back of a house at a party in the fall, and she said, "Um . . . you got a booger."

This time, her lips made a slow touchdown, and there she paused, probably imagining the thousand germs that would pass as soon as she pressed harder. It drove me mad. It's like every Dreaded Fifteen I'd intentionally left her out of backed up on me—kind of like I always knew it would. I wrapped my arms around her back, and all I had to do was push her toward me with one finger. Then

"Fww-ay."

Rain's eyelashes almost got tangled with mine as we stared

at each other. She turned in amazement as Sheep jumped up on the rock beside us.

"*Fww-ay. Fww-ay. Fww-ay.*"

Rain stared Sheep in the lips and asked incredulously, "Can't you go find something to do?"

"*Fww-ay. Fww-ay. Fww-ay.*"

I said, "Translated from goat speak, I think that means 'get a room.'"

Rain slumped with a sigh. "Do you believe in the devil?" she asked.

"*Fww-ay. Fww-ay. Fww-ay.*" Sheep was more vocal than the Professor.

I had to confess, "I believe in signs. I think . . . that is a bad sign. Rain, I love you, girl. But if we were meant to be together, it would have happened a long time before now—"

"*Damn* it!" She unwrapped herself without my having to ask. I stood up slowly and stumbled down onto the little sandy beach. She jumped down beside me and kicked sand at Sheep, who backed away about ten feet but kept up with the noise.

We tried to ignore it, though as we walked along slowly toward the house, the goat followed, raising a ruckus, like, every fifteen seconds.

"All right, fine. But there's something you should know. You can ask Jeanine how many times I've said this, and she'll tell you a hundred. I have always said that I would date all sorts of guys. But when it came time to get married, I was after you."

I had never heard her say that before, and yet it's like I was hearing it for the hundredth time somehow. No news flash. I probably felt the same way. I settled on, "I'm flattered. But how can you think that far ahead?"

"Because I'm not ditsy. I know exactly what I want in life."

She was either saying I was ditsy or admitting to a number of people from school finding her ditsy. I was too confused to be sure. As we walked along, she took my silence to be something other than a third aftershock, which I was trying to hide.

"You're *flattered*? That's *all* you have to say to me? Ride the reality train, Charlie Brown! I've been up to my earlobes in boys since . . . it mattered. I'm just persnickety, that's all. Don't accuse me of throwing myself at you in some fit of desperation—"

The aftershock passed in a long exhale, and I think she got the message this time, stopping with me and laying a hand on my shoulder. "Aw, Bubba," she muttered, her favorite words of sympathy to me over the years. And she shushed at the noisy goat.

I finally straightened up and started walking again. "I'm not accusing you of anything, Rain. It's just that your timing is atrocious."

"Actually, it's not. I think I'm running out of time. I'll take what I can get."

I knew where she was going with this, but I hadn't heard the spin she put on it. She said, "One afternoon in March the nurse let me go down to Godfrey's office when you were bad off. She said I could ask if they would override his no-morphine role in the case of your headaches. He was on the phone with that guy Frank from the CDC. I overheard him say, 'I'm going to do my best to save them all, Frank. But from my experiences with autoimmune diseases this ferocious? Statistically speaking, we'll end up losing one.'"

Sheep shut up for a moment. The breeze wasn't even blowing, and the silence made the impact she wanted. *She thinks I'm the statistic waiting to happen.* True, I would probably be voted least-likely-to-make-it by Godfrey, by anybody with eyes to see with, but I still had some fight left in me—just not for the same reasons the rest of them did. I was not so in love with this world that I totally wanted to stay in it when my mom was someplace better, when all my favorite saints lived up there, the ones I prayed to so often that I felt they were friends.

"If it's any consolation to you," I said, mustering all my pride until it buzzed around in my ears, "I have no plans of dying a victim, of withering away in a bed, at least not unless I do something halfway cool with my life. If I just withered, I would feel like I never lived."

"Well, then, you better start thinking about the future a little more. And I don't mean with me. Thanks for the wake-up call."

"Rain, you've got a lot of years to adventure-ize before you think about settling down."

"Yeah, I know. Just take it under advisement: I got my pride, and if you snooze, you lose. You just snoozed."

She always thought about things faster than I did. And between aftershocks and the goat—

"Will you shut up?" I demanded, turning and facing Sheep, but she just got louder.

"Maybe there's something wrong with her," Rain suggested. She moved toward Sheep, who started back toward the pond, and she followed. I really needed to crash on that comfy couch in front of the TV. But maybe the Professor had gotten tangled up somewhere and this was a call for help. I followed them.

"It's gonna thunder . . . why are we following a goat?" Rain asked after fifty paces.

Only because Sheep seemed to know where she was going. She took us down the path on the other side of the pond and stopped and turned to us, *baa*-ing her fool head off.

Rain grabbed my hand and stood, looking all around. "This is the place where Cora thought she saw eyes this morning."

"Whose eyes?" I had missed something.

"Well, if we knew, I wouldn't be pissing myself right now. Daddy swore it was only a journalist. But it could have been some local drunk. I didn't see anything—"

"So, maybe it was nobody. And a local drunk wouldn't upset a goat," I told her, and moved to where Sheep had planted herself. There was something in the underbrush that looked like bramble, only with white stripes in it. I realized it was a skeleton.

"What is that smell?" Rain whispered.

It smelled scorchy. I wasn't sure it was coming off the pile of bones. That could have been here for days. In fact, I was sure it wasn't coming from the bones. It smelled electrical.

I shook my head as Rain moved ahead of me. I said, "Dead animal. Champ used to get all excited about dead animals. He liked to roll on them."

"*Ew.*"

"But I didn't think goats were like that. And the smell—"

Rain reached down toward the bramble. "It's gooey," she muttered nervously and added, "What the hell . . ."

She picked something up out of the pile of goo and held it up. It was a red ribbon with a bell on it. She had picked the ribbon up by scooping inside the loop with her pinkie finger. The ribbon broke apart, and when the bell hit the ground it made the *ding, ding* we had heard on the Professor that morning.

I stood rooted in confusion. Could there have been a third

goat that died a month ago? I didn't have time to think, because Rain screeched at the top of her lungs, "Sco-ooooooo-ttt!" She wanted my brother on some terrified instinctive level.

"What's wrong?" I demanded.

"It's burning my finger! It hurts, it hurts . . ."

The last thing in the world I felt like doing was running, but I ran and pulled her along to get ice on what looked to me, by stray glances, like a third-degree burn in the making.

TWENTY-FIVE

CORA HOLMAN
SATURDAY, MAY 4, 2002
4:15 P.M.
HER BEDROOM

I SPENT A FEW MINUTES LYING ON MY BED trying again to think of what I could write in my blog. I finally opened my laptop and watched while Windows loaded. Hard footsteps resounded on the stairs. The familiar sound of Rain's crying followed, and Scott's door went flying open. I quickly cast the laptop aside to run and get her out of his room. He had an HH brewing that probably wouldn't peak for a while, but she was the last thing he needed.

I didn't make it in time. Before I even passed through the doorway, I heard his objections. "Shut *up* and back *out*—"

"I'm sorry . . . I am, but," Rain babbled, and she hiccupped when I tried to pull her out gently by the shoulder.

"Whatever it is, find Marg," Scott groaned. "I'm not the staff of St. Ann's—"

"Marg isn't down there. My dad's car is gone," Rain said,

planting her feet and shaking my hand off. "I think I got bit by a snake."

After taking a couple of seconds for it to sink in, Scott shot up so he was sitting. He groaned, holding his head. "*Shhh.* Whisper. Don't panic." He moved the palms of his hands from his temples to in front of his eyes. "Hit the light switch."

I lit the small lamp by his bed, which illuminated the room with a dull orange glow, but he kept his hands over his eyes for a minute while he questioned her.

"Where?"

"Out by the other side of the pond. We saw this pile of glurpy stuff and I think a snake must have jumped out of it before I—"

"*Shhh!*" He shook his head and continued after a few moments of silence. "*Where?* Toe? Heel? Your face?"

"My pinkie."

He swallowed. "D'you remember to keep the wound lower than your heart?"

"Yeah."

"D'you remember not to run?"

She only hiccupped in response, and Owen was out of breath.

Scott took his hands from his face, and he flinched with pain. Our headaches peaked slowly. In another two hours, he could not have done this. He gestured with his fingers and she put her hand in his palm. He blinked at it.

"I don't see any fang punctures," he noted as I crept up and looked over her shoulder. Owen eased himself down on the bed, still huffing.

"It was in an animal carcass," Owen said. "It was a dead goat, some other goat—"

"Well, carcasses can attract snakes," Scott said. "Where's Marg? She's got that triage drawer in the kitchen—"

I kept my voice at a whisper as I said, "She wanted to go jogging before the rain started. She's a runner. She should be back in half an—"

"Great timing. Where's Alan?"

"Car's gone," Rain said.

Scott let out a weak laugh and forced himself to his feet and out into the corridor. We all followed him down the stairs as he grumbled the whole way. "What good is having a nurse if she's dumb enough to take off while nobody else is here? She's done, she's fired. Jesus Christ. And USIC is so busy creaming itself over its goddamn important secrets that it can't say when it's coming and going . . . You know what? Fine. Let Alan find out via the Easter Bunny his daughter got bit by a snake. We're not calling him."

We got down into the kitchen and Scott pointed to the stool, which Rain sat on, and he opened Marg's triage drawer, which we were introduced to on the house tour.

He blinked at the wound again, looking genuinely confused at her red pinkie, swollen right where her fingerprint would be. "I don't see a puncture. Looks like a burn."

"It was in some sort of dead animal," Rain said, her face red and streaky, but she seemed more in control now. "If I didn't know better, I'd swear it was the Professor. I felt this searing pain when I pulled up a bell by the red ribbon."

"Obviously, it's not *that* goat." Scott rubbed the bridge of his nose and forced his eyes open wider. "Well. Could be a baby water moccasin got in there. Wounds would be like pinheads, and it would swell." He searched the drawer and came out with what looked like a pencil with a sloped razor on the end. He pulled wrapping off it with his teeth and blew the paper toward the sink. He talked with the blunt end between his teeth while donning two sets of gloves, one on top of the other. "Problem: If we can't see a puncture wound, I gotta create one. Then we'll pump whatever the hell it is out with the snake kit."

"Will it hurt?" Rain asked.

"Just the razor. Everything hurts less when you remain calm."

I backed toward the kitchen door on instinct. A nurse I would never be. Scott pulled her finger over the sink and said to me, "Call Dr. Godfrey and see if I can give her antivenin. Tell him I said Marg's fired."

I went into the parlor and dialed the number on the house phone from the speed dial. I got Dr. Godfrey's pager, and while waiting for him to call back, I stood at the window watching for our nurse. It was drizzling, though no downpour had struck. I tried not to let my mind wander to the portrait of Mrs. Kellerton, but somehow she consumed the room with her dark eyes. I felt her energy combine with my mother's when I was in here, in some way that was disturbing. I could have used some feelings of comfort, but they were not forthcoming in the silences that bulged in here.

From the kitchen Rain made threatening blasts, though it wasn't supposed to be painful. "I'm gonna hurl . . . I'm gonna kill that nurse . . ." and Scott kept telling Rain to pipe down before he smacked her, until I wanted to dive under the couch. USIC agents had been here all day, and I wondered why she hadn't jogged then.

Dr. Godfrey called back after five minutes, and I gave him

the news quickly. He spoke without too much alarm. "She kept the wound low, and Scott's using an extraction kit."

"Correct," I said. "He wants to know if he can give her antivenin."

"Just one unit for now," he said. "It won't compromise your protocol, but there are side effects, and she doesn't need any more of those. He probably knows this, but tell him St. Ann's treats fifty water moccasin bites a year. Nobody's keeled over from one in half a century. Tell him to draw some blood and to give her the antivenin right away. Where's Marg?"

I didn't feel comfortable repeating Scott's edicts about having her fired. I was about to say she was jogging when I caught sight of her out the window. She was far off, pacing back and forth between two trees over by the path that led to the pond, and appeared to be talking on a cell phone in spite of the drizzle. Feeling doubly annoyed now, I went toward the front door to hail her but decided to give Scott the news first. I shouted in Dr. Godfrey's instructions rather than see the procedure in progress.

"*Shhh!*" Scott said back. "Stop yelling."

His headache. This was a fiasco, but we were managing, working together.

"I'll be there in twenty minutes," the doctor said. "Get her lying down as soon as you can."

I watched in confusion as Marg started jogging again in the middle of the lawn, and when she came in the front door, she was out of breath.

Somehow, I told her what happened. She moved quickly into the kitchen. I followed to see Rain with her cheek on Owen's chest, her eyelids drooping while she huffed. Marg threw off her jacket, tossed it on the counter, and whipped a pair of surgery gloves out of the drawer, but she was a little late.

The look Scott gave her as he pulled his gloves off and dropped them in the wastebasket could have frozen God. His eyes flew to each of us, then back to her.

"Are you stupid?" he asked. "Alan was here most of the day. Couldn't you do your jogging then?"

She muttered an apology and moved toward Rain, looking with concern at the butterfly bandage already applied. She never mentioned taking a cell phone call that delayed her return and, watching water drip from her hair, I couldn't help it—I moved over to Scott, cupped my hand to his ear, and whispered that she'd been outside jabbering on the phone. He watched her, not too pleased.

"Tell me again how this happened," Marg asked Rain.

Rain told her about the dead animal, the bell, the searing pain, and something went slightly wrong on Marg's face, though I wouldn't have noticed if I weren't fixated on her already. I'd say it was not enough emotion, not enough surprise. You'd almost believe she knew half the story already. Something definitely was "off" here, as Scott used to say about times when his gut instincts didn't match the facts. I supposed I was being too paranoid, my episode in the ICU making me look at people critically. Anyone could get a call on a cell phone while jogging.

Scott didn't feel that merciful. He held up a tube of blood and stuck it right in her eyes, like maybe she was too stupid to know what it was.

"Here's a blood sample. She's had antivenin . . ."

"You gave her *antivenin?*" Marg asked, her eyes suddenly going wide.

"Um, *yeah.*" He spoke slowly with exaggerated patience. "It won't interfere with our protocol. Godfrey just said to. Is there something wrong with that?"

"I just . . . am wondering if it was a snakebite."

I flinched and jumped back as he suddenly flung her backwards by the arm and held her against the refrigerator. Her shoulders striking created a *bang* as things toppled inside. He looked crazed.

"Listen to me, if you want to keep this job more than five minutes. We see terrorists in our *sleep.* And I don't know you from Adam, it suddenly occurs to me. Who hired you? USIC or the State of New Jersey? You picked a strange time to be among the missing. What were you doing outside on a cell phone? What's the big secret? Were you talking to some buddies staying in Griffith's Landing?"

I thought perhaps he was going overboard, until I watched her jaw bob before she replied. "I . . . was talking to my mother."

"Oh, really? Call her back. I want to talk to her."

Marg swallowed. She was lying. I knew it. Scott did, too.

He breathed, "You're surrounded by kids with dead mothers. You lie about your mother to us, you can burn in hell—"

"Scott, get ahold of yourself." Her voice was soothing, and she raised her hands in the air but didn't try to touch him. "I'm . . . fine. USIC hired me. You can ask Alan."

"Alan and I are not exactly speaking right now." He gripped her arm tighter. "Why are you questioning a stupid shot of antivenin? Would you be happy if one of us died of a snakebite?"

"Look . . ." She reached slowly toward her jacket. "I'm getting out my cell phone. I left you the number on a big note beside your bed. But here it is again."

He didn't move. None of us had been on the lookout for notes, with Rain's finger frightening us. I felt confused. Scott didn't look confused. "Phone number? That's great. Fine, fat, fucking lot of good that's going to do if you're two miles up the road, Alan's gone, and somebody keels over here!"

"I'm dialing Alan," she said, still calm somehow. "You talk to him until you're comfortable with who I am. You *need* to be comfortable with that in order to recover—"

"Well, I'm not!" He let go of her finally, ignoring the phone she held out to him. I didn't know what to think. I sucked myself closer to the door frame, and he stood over me, hurling orders. "I've got a Headache from Hell. Don't try to come near me. Don't come within five feet of any of these kids, and don't try to feed them anything until I see Mike Tiger by my bedside, on his knees, begging me to believe him that you're okay."

"Calm down, Scott. You *have* to eat in two hours—"

"Well, that doesn't give you much time to dig him out of what dirty little secrets he's amusing himself with to haul his ass back here."

"Fine, *shh-shh*." She tried a soothing tone again while moving slowly toward Rain. "But I have to look at her wound..."

His opinion was contagious, and Owen's arms went tighter around Rain as he glared.

"Rain, give me your hand." Scott went back to her, mumbling in disgust. "Trust me."

She put her hand out, and Scott held on to her wrist as Marg undid the butterfly bandage and studied the wound. They stood between Rain and the sink, which gave me a view I didn't exactly want, but I could see he'd cut a path half the length of her pinkie with the razorblade, and I wondered how she'd managed to keep from screaming her head off, what with all the crying she did over the slightest thing.

"There shouldn't be any infection," Marg finally said, gently pressing the butterfly back in place. "Nice job."

"We do what we can," Scott muttered, and then pushed past me, his hands to his temples.

We left the kitchen and followed him back up the stairs but didn't try to intrude as he shut the door, and we heard him drop onto the mattress with a groan. Rain went toward her room, and when I told her Dr. Godfrey was coming and to lie down, Owen went with her. I promised them that if I heard our suspicious nurse coming up the stairs, I would wake them up, though truthfully, I figured Scott was as paranoid as I was. *Still, better safe than sorry,* I reminded myself.

TWENTY-SIX

CORA HOLMAN
SATURDAY, MAY 4, 2002
4:45 P.M.
HER BEDROOM

I TRIED TO SETTLE INTO MY JOURNAL, a task devoid of anxiety. It had not been a peaceful first day in our new surroundings. The only nonstressful thing that happened had been meeting Henry.

The computer had booted while I had been downstairs, and I took it into my lap, suddenly wondering if my journal would be any less stressful than everything else, as my plans were to turn my journal into a blog. *So many people reading my words.* I'd never written journals when Aleese was alive. I seemed unable to face my life, to tell truths even to myself. Some of my journal entries at St. Ann's had been chances to see how honest I could be without shocking myself. It was kind of fun, and I definitely reached some milestones.

Writing was a form of healing to me, but realizing that other people would read what I wrote brought me back to my own shyness, something I didn't want to mix with my writing. I figured I could write a second journal and simply not post it.

But I went to my e-mail to see if anyone had signed my guest book. I already had four messages just since Scott had argued with Mr. Steckerman. Three were from people I didn't know, and they offered encouragement and heartfelt prayers and support. I stared at the one marked "urgent" before clicking, hoping it was not what the CEO of Dell had spoken of over the phone to me when he had called to say he was sending us each a laptop.

"Reach out to others, but be prepared for a few nuts and kooks," he had said.

I wondered if this was one. My heart sped up as I read the brief message.

> *Were you in a certain city today shooting pictures of a convention center and an amusement pier? If so, which city? It is important, and hence, you must let me know your movements. Yours most sincerely, The Kid*

The signature registered, but the message lit me like a bad circuit, and I sat there frozen, my chest crackling sparks as I read it twice. I felt naked, which didn't help the impression of thousands of eyes watching me all day, regardless of where I was. Staring at the signature, I tried to think of some way it could be a kook. The e-mail address to which I was supposed to reply was printed below the name: hodjimontu22@gmail.com. I knew Hodji Montu, though he was one of the New York USIC agents and hadn't been around nearly as much as the New Jersey ones. Roger O'Hare had told me once that he was the Kid's protector.

I copied and pasted the address into a new e-mail, still suspicious of a hoax, but what else could I do? Not reply, when it might be him? I listened for some miraculous movement from Scott's room, but he didn't stir.

I did take pictures at a convention center today.

I typed slowly. Scott could more easily make a decision. I tested the waters.

Why do you need to know? Cora

I hit SEND and received another message from a well-wisher, which I read without much ability to concentrate. I felt thankful that it was only five lines long. By the time I finished I had already received a reply from hodjimontu22, a fact that amazed me.

> *Please tell me what city you were in today and what you were doing. You must trust me. While you were in St. Ann's you maintained your affection for a very old and balding stuffed rabbit named Baba, about which Roger O'Hare used to tease you. K.*

Baba was a favorite stuffed toy from my childhood that I resurrected from the closet shelf to sleep with on the night Aleese died. Only Mr. O'Hare would have known about the teasing. I had still been in a private ICU pod when he would come in and have lengthy conversations with Baba, using a high-pitched voice for Baba and a low voice for himself.

Intrigued, I carried the laptop into the hall. Still, I swallowed a mouthful of saliva guiltily as I turned Scott's doorknob, forced myself to enter the blackness, and closed it behind me. I had no idea if he would scream at me to leave.

The curtains were drawn tightly. The room was impossible to see into, save the closest things to me, lit in a glow from the laptop. The long drapes had been pulled from the hooks that usually held them back. I moved silently, with my arm in front of me, until I could feel a bedpost. I could hear him breathing, but with a couple of groans that let me know he was awake.

"Can I get you anything?" I whispered.

It took him a while to answer. "A gun."

I felt horribly selfish and more stupid. I ought to be able to make a decision by myself, but I didn't have all the facts. I brought the laptop silently to his side, hoping he would recognize its glow and realize this was something important. If he was to the point where the headache spiked, he would want to do little more than flail out to slap it shut and eliminate the light. But it might not spike for an hour or more.

"What . . ." he grumbled impatiently.

"I got an e-mail from the Kid," I whispered.

He said nothing.

"He wants to know if we were taking pictures at a convention center today."

After a moment, he sat up again, not bothering, as I surely would have, to press both palms firmly against his temples again. "Never a dull moment."

"Do you want me to leave?"

"Give."

I slid the laptop in front of him. In the glow of the screen I could see him grimacing, trying to read the e-mail. He put his hands over his eyes, saying, "There were earlier ones?"

I guessed he got that from the context. I took the laptop and read in hushed whispers the Kid's first e-mail and my reply.

I knew better than to touch him, but my heart sputtered as he cursed. He finally came back around to it. "So . . . should you answer him, in other words . . ."

"Correct."

He leaned backwards, rolling his neck around slowly. "Yeah, answer him."

I took the laptop and moved quickly toward the door.

"Stay," he said in a normal voice.

I made my way back to a chair at the foot of the bed and sunk cautiously into it, glad for a place close to him even if his pain made me crazy. I began

Scott and I were in Griffith's Landing.

I began a new e-mail. Feeling the urge to add more, I typed,

I hope we haven't caused you any trouble. Cora

Another e-mail appeared.

No trouble. Please tell us why you were there and retrace your steps for us. K.

I read the e-mail in a whisper, hoping it would distract Scott rather than prolong his agony. I could retrace our steps, but it would be up to Scott to say why we were there. I still had no clue.

"Tell him..." Scott lay back. My eyes had grown accustomed to the dark, and I could see the wastebasket on his stomach as he lay back again. "Tell him I overheard Alan Steckerman and Mike Tiger talking about a hit on a convention center across from an amusement park in New Jersey. I went with ... what was most logical."

After a long minute, a reply said,

> *How in hell do you overhear a USIC conversation? Anything you'd like to teach the Kid and me? Luv, Tyler*

A smile bloomed on my face. The Kid had a friend with him. Tyler. You could tell the "voices" apart, even in e-mail.

"The Kid's friend wants to know how you overhear a USIC conversation," I whispered. After a moment, he said, "Tell them I said, 'Don't ask.'"

I put my part in.

> *We shot photos of the convention center, then an amusement pier, and the water park that's in the back. On the boardwalk people kept staring at us. I think it might have been due to People magazine, but I got scared. We left. As to how you overhear a USIC conversation, Scott says, "Don't ask."*

I saw I had already received another message as I hit SEND. It was the same e-mail address, only this one said,

P.S. I am in love with you, Cora Holman. Tyler

I flinched, wondering again if this were a hoax, a bunch of high schoolers who had read about the Kid in *Newsweek* and were being cruel. They wouldn't know about Baba; however, I felt watched all over again. Another e-mail dropped quickly into the box.

This one said,

> *Miss Cora, do not be offended by Tyler's frankness. He means only the utmost of respect for you, though he is American schooled and very fresh. We think you and Miss Rain are our princesses. Please forgive. K.*

A bigger smile bloomed on my face. I suddenly felt incredibly important, or at least to be in the virtual presence of incredible importance. It was a better rush than meeting a movie star, more like meeting Peter Pan. I thought of the Kid every several days or so. The fact that he thought of us was something I had never considered. Within a few seconds, a new e-mail appeared.

> *Miss Cora, thank you for your info. We are grateful. We would like to see your pictures. However, please do not return to Griffith's Landing in the future. You are unaccustomed to so much attention, but your faces are very well known, and you could easily be recognized by people whom you would wish to avoid. K.*

I thought of the men scattering as I shot their photos on the boardwalk and wondered about Scott's remark to Marg about the idea of her being outside to talk on her cell phone . . . "*Were you talking to some buddies staying in Griffith's Landing?*" I wondered at all the deep, dark places his imagination must be traveling, which probably brought on his headache. Maybe he'd guessed the truth too late—maybe we'd managed to walk straight into a horde of ShadowStrike operatives. The Kid's e-mail made it seem like they were around here in swarms. I thought of Richard Awali, my would-be assasin, and wanted desperately to get out of this dark room . . . out of New Jersey.

I jumped a foot when the door opened slowly. It was Mr. Tiger. He closed the door quietly, moved past me with a pat on my hand, and stood beside Scott's bed. The glow of my screen was the only light in the room, but I could see Mr. Tiger looking down at him for a minute before deciding that he was awake.

"I understand I'm supposed to get down on my knees," he said in an almost whisper.

"Mike. What the fuck kind of nurse did you guys—"

"*Shhh, shhh* . . . don't wear yourself out fretting. That was *our* mistake today. We got an emergency call and forgot she was out jogging. She didn't want to bust us, but we were the stupid ones, Alan and me. It won't happen again, buddy. We're working on getting more help, but they gotta pass our clearances—"

Scott managed some sarcasm. "Must have been a hell of an emergency."

"Yeah. But you guys should not have suffered. Godfrey's here, looking at Rain now. There's nothing for you to worry about. She's a good nurse. Honest. And she passed a polygraph."

Scott shifted around on the mattress, and I felt uncomfortable with the answer myself. Weren't polygraphs passed by both the innocent and the treacherously guilty? People who were trained to lie? I tried to tell myself I was being silly, but what had happened to me in the ICU of St. Ann's had not been silliness.

"What are you guys doing?" Mike turned to me. I lowered the lid on my computer, waiting to hear how Scott would answer, and he was still in I'm-not-telling-you-anything mode.

"She's writing in her blog and keeping me company. Tell Godfrey to come in here when he's done with Rain."

"Sure," Mike said. "Again, we're sorry."

After he left, Scott didn't give me any commentary on his thoughts about Marg. I supposed he didn't want to think about it now. He asked, "They answer?"

I looked at my box. "About five times."

He cursed. "Wish I could rouse myself for the party."

"Hopefully, there will be many more," I whispered. "They're funny. They're brilliant."

He drew air through his teeth but managed to say, "Remember our conversation in the car about manipulating?"

"Sure."

"Watch me manipulate the whole lot of them."

I could hear Dr. Godfrey's footsteps as they came toward us, and he opened and closed the door as quietly as Mr. Tiger had done. By "lot," I supposed Scott meant both USIC and the medics.

"How's Rain?" Scott ran his heel up and down the sheet to cut the pain. "Truth, please."

The doctor whispered. "We're still not sure what it is—bee sting, snakebite . . . You did all the right stuff. We had Owen lead

Mike and me back to the site, and there's nothing back there but bramble, honest to god."

Scott thought for a minute. "Owen wouldn't make that up. He's not delusional."

"I know. Maybe he remembered the wrong spot, though he swears . . . At any rate, I'm taking her blood back to see if anything strange turns up in it, but I wouldn't worry about that. Just worry if she starts showing signs of overload on her liver. That antivenin can do bad things to the wrong liver, and hers is already working double-time due to a couple of her medications."

Liver damage? Just what we needed to hear. I could not imagine this day containing any more anxiety. But Scott let out a long sigh, took the doctor by the arm, and whispered, "I want you to do something for me. Go down in my file. Get the DNR form. I need to sign it."

DNR. *Do not resuscitate.*

Dr. Godfrey took all his vitals, reading with a penlight. "Your temperature's ninety-nine, and you have low blood pressure. That's not raising huge alarms, Scott."

Scott made some swiping motion at his head and discussed the aneurysm in his head in medical terms that I didn't understand, except that it really hurt. I was sure he wasn't lying about that much, and Dr. Godfrey must have been sure, too. He stood stroking his chin with his hand. "I don't think you kids ought to be allowed to sign those DNR forms. You're too young. Yet I'm only the physician, and far be it from me to question the State of—"

"Walk a mile in my shoes," Scott mumbled.

"I'll make you a deal. You know how I feel about morphine and you kids. It's a mask, and with an, um, illness this new, we need to know everything. But you've had a lousy day, son. I'll get you some morphine . . . if you won't sign that form."

"Bring me the form *and* the morphine, and I'll decide," he said.

"You don't get both, not from me." He left the room.

Scott groaned again, and it was impossible to listen to. Fortunately, I saw another e-mail from hodjimontu22. As I clicked on it, Scott managed to say, "Marg was a great lay in that dream last night. What came over me?"

It was a courageous comment. I exploded with laughter that squirted out my nose in an effort to stay hushed, and I opened the first e-mail to be no less entertained.

> *So, answer my question, Princess Numero Uno. How do you overhear a USIC conversation? We'd have our best chance by sticking our heads down the nearest toilet with a straw in one ear. Tyler*

I replied,

> *I didn't overhear it. Scott did. He wants to work for USIC.*

A reply came seconds later.

> *Pfwaaa.*

I ought to leave Tyler alone, but I was entranced. Before Dr. Godfrey could come back with Scott's wishes and I could get to see precisely how he was manipulating the doctor, we exchanged a series of rapid-fire e-mails.

ME: *You guys work for USIC. Can't you put in a good word for him?*

TYLER: *We do NOT work FOR USIC. We bestow on them our most generous favors, and they show us no gratitude.*

ME: *Then . . . do you suggest that we give our photos taken in Griffith's Landing to Alan Steckerman, or should we not?*

TYLER: *Let me ask the boss. He's in the other room doing bad things on his PC.*

TYLER: *Kid says to please e-mail the photos to us immediately.*

ME: *Unfortunately, they were taken with film.*

TYLER: *Film???? What the fuck is that?*

ME: *Ha. Sorry.*

TYLER: *Do you have a scanner?*

ME: *Not yet. I can get one tomorrow.*

With that, Dr. Godfrey came back carrying a clipboard. He left the door open this time, so it was not so hard to see him from the light in the hall. He held a hypodermic needle up with one hand, the clipboard with the other, and said, "I suppose one could say I'm caught in a loophole, but I feel like I have my head in a noose."

After a moment, Scott took the clipboard and the pen that was on it, and I heard scrawling. My heart lurched. We hadn't discussed the DNR form at all, except to hear that it might be wise to sign if we "felt death coming on" and really wanted to go, as no surgeries would be performed unless our blood vessels had strengthened. I knew Scott felt bad, and like he said today in his manipulation speech, people generally don't lie. But I wondered in confusion where the line of truth was.

Dr. Godfrey let the clipboard sit on the bed while he studied Scott with his hands on his hips. Tyler was taking his time replying, so the room was deadly silent. He finally swept the clipboard up and moved toward the door. But he turned around and came back with a sigh when Scott groaned again.

He said, "Okay, I guess I'm a softy. Roll over."

So, Scott had manipulated a morphine shot out of him, but he could have gotten that without signing that dreadful form. So I was clueless as to all the fuss.

This time, a lengthier e-mail came. It had that more dignified, less comical tone to it, and I noticed it was signed by the Kid and not Tyler.

> *Miss Cora, I do not have much time to talk as I am detained by pressing issues at my terminal. Unfortunately, you cannot see us nor meet us nor know where we are. But you can e-mail the photos as soon as you get your scanner. We thank you for your help. As for telling the Jersey or New York squads what you have found before showing us, I must be honest in saying that USIC has left us in an unsafe and compromised situation, and our trust in them is severely breached. We would not*

be the best advisors on whom you should trust. Best of luck with your overhearing. And welcome to the Show. We think of you every hour and hope someday for the privilege of looking upon you in person and hearing your beautiful voices. Be strong. Our friendship is with you always. K.

After that, I did not dare answer, but I felt torn between embracing the laptop to get a second blast of their courage or leaving it on the bed for Scott to read and fleeing the room. *"Welcome to the Show."* I felt Aleese laugh all over the place.

Scott moaned, but it sounded like a moan of relief, like maybe the morphine was working. I walked to his side, clutching the laptop. Between his blinks, I could see the whites of his eyes.

"How are you now?" I whispered.

"Cut the pain in half." He sat up slowly, and I sat beside him on the bed. "Half is not great. Half is . . . better. I wanted to be alert and sane enough to e-mail them."

"Unfortunately, they're gone for now. Party's over. But you can read it all. It's a bit disturbing."

He muttered a few more bad words and said, "It's payback time from God . . . for going to too many parties in high school." He read through all the exchanges twice, saying nothing until the second time through. Then he let out a groan that sounded like he'd been saving it up.

"USIC betrayed their trust . . ." he mumbled. "Betcha it's got to do with their ages. Some red-tape clusterfuck over not being allowed to take intelligence from minors . . . *'And therefore we have no budget to assist minors . . .'*"

He lay back slowly, obviously in pain in spite of the morphine. I could sense the situation upsetting him and tried to draw him away from it.

"Why all the fuss with the DNR form?" I hissed. "You didn't have to sign it to get the drug."

He pushed against his eyes with his fingertips and said, "The DNR form was how I got him to loosen up about the morphine."

I understood.

"As for actually signing it? I agree with him . . . You guys aren't old enough. But I am. There's only one thought that's kept me putting one foot in front of the other. That's wanting to catch the guys who killed our moms and did this to us. If I can't do that here? I'll wait for them in hell."

"How can you be so crude?" I whispered, angry at what could almost be taken as suicidal thoughts, and for his seeming ignorance of the bigger issue. Aleese poured through me, laughing as usual, muttering that it was about time I got angry. *"Say it!"* she screamed.

"What about—" I couldn't.

"What about Owen?" he asked.

I nodded, feeling my eyes well up, supposing Owen was important also.

"Truth? I'm starting to think Owen won't make it through this. He's deteriorating too quickly. Takes him an entire minute to walk down a flight of stairs. I haven't watched him go up yet. I'm too scared."

I stayed silent, thankful for the blackness, thankful for this gift I had of being able to cry without spazzing and making noises. But he reached up, found my face, and brushed a tear away. I heard him suck it off his thumb.

"There. You can tell Miss Haley we swapped body fluids," he said.

"Not funny." I waited an eternity for him to wipe more away or rub my hair or . . . anything. But he only tugged a strand affectionately, which made me sniff loudly.

"You'd be fine without me, Cora Holman. You'll be amazed at how fine you'll be."

There was something about the tenses he mixed that made it sound half prophetic. Aleese badgered me, *"Go, girlie. Frost him. Don't look back."* Or maybe it was something inside me that suddenly realized how exhausted I was making myself by chronically thinking that I was so weak, so needy, so stuck on seeing Scott Eberman as a legend. I didn't know why a selfish thought should hit me at a time like this. Maybe it was a defense mechanism.

But I snapped my laptop completely shut, straightened my posture, and stood up. I said, "While you're busy dying, I'll be out here writing my blog for the Americans who love us. Call me if you need anything."

He said nothing. I left.

TWENTY-SEVEN

OWEN EBERMAN
SATURDAY, MAY 4, 2002
7:05 P.M.
RAIN'S BEDROOM

WE ACTUALLY ATE THE FOOD Marg served us for dinner, having been convinced by Mr. Tiger that the mistake was theirs and not hers. But we ate in Rain's bedroom. Rain wasn't supposed to get up, and after the running and the trips up the stairs after her injury, my hips were done for the day.

Cora ate with us. She picked at her food and looked so distracted and tense that I wanted to go check on my brother. Before I could get up the energy to hobble down there, a voice called, "Anybody home?"

"Dempsey!" Rain's fork dropped and bounced eagerly on the bed.

John Dempsey, one of our best buddies, came through the door. Rain crawled to the edge of the bed, got up on her knees, and gave him a huge hug.

"I hear you got bit by a water moccasin," Dempsey said,

rocking her sideways. "Touché. That means you can join in with all us guys who love freshwater fishing. I've been bit twice."

He kept patting her back, waiting for her to let go, but she didn't.

"Rain," he finally said. "It's only been two days."

He and maybe six other friends from school had been at St. Ann's to see us the night before we were released. I'd been laid up and missed it.

"Yeah, but I was afraid it might be longer."

"We told you we wouldn't do that to you. Dobbins, Tannis, and Jeanine are downstairs getting a house tour from your nurse." He checked out Rain's butterfly and laid a kiss on it. "The antivenin isn't too bad. Starts making you seasick about four hours after you take it."

"I feel great. I'm not sure I needed it," she said, turning her pinkie this way and that. "You should have seen Scott. He's gonna be a surgeon somehow, someday, I'm telling you. He opened up the wound and used a venom extractor to suck everything out. I thought it was going to suck my finger off. It still burns, but he must have gotten it all or I'd be dead. Right?"

"You'd be really sick," Dempsey said. "Godfrey says you're cool?"

"He's taking my blood back to St. Ann's to see if he can decide if it was a snake or a bee or something else. He says in the meantime, I have to stay lying down. I'm on observation for liver damage, but . . . forget about that. No bummers. I'm so happy to see you guys."

Dempsey went around to the far side of the bed and got a hug from Cora. Bob Dobbins, Tannis Halib, and Jeanine

Fitzpatrick came in next. Bob and Tannis played football with me. Jeanine had been Rain's co-captain on field hockey. Dobbins was carrying a grocery bag.

"S'up?" I said, knocking knuckles with him. "What's in the bag?"

"Party goods. We were going to see if you guys were copasetic to party in the woods. But we'll be okay in here."

Our friends were good sports. Dobbins tossed a bag of Fritos, which were Rain's favorite, into the middle of the bed, then pretzels, which were my favorite, and stuck a Mountain Dew in her hand and a Dr Pepper in mine. They were our favorite sodas. We weren't supposed to be having any of this stuff, but you gotta live a little. Thank god we had big beds. Cora moved over to Rain's chair, having decided to open her laptop, and the six of us piled on.

"Where's Scott?" Dempsey asked.

"He's down," I said. "Down" meant anything that prevented one of us from getting out of bed. We didn't discuss symptoms too much with our friends and tried to keep things upbeat when they were around. Dempsey just accepted it. He got up and leaned down beside Cora, put his chin on her shoulder, and said, "What are you doing? Studying for a test?"

We still had some homework to do so we could graduate, but it was a breeze, and we had most of three months' work done by the end of March.

"I started a blog, and people keep signing the guest book. It's pretty amazing." She turned the screen and showed them the messages left by people from all over, her pretty smile making Dempsey stare into the side of her head.

He'd had a crush on almost every girl in school over the years, but he kept returning to Cora. None of us had ever really noticed Cora, and to that he always responded that he liked "going it alone sometimes."

Cora was almost as aloof to Jon now as she had been for years, though she was always polite. She pretended he wasn't there. I decided to help her out a little before she had to put a stop to it herself. "Did you hear about the speech Nurse Haley gave us the night before we left?"

"My mom told me, yeah," Jon said quizzically, returning to the bed. "Sounds complicated. Let's see. We can touch you, but we can't stick our fingers in your mouths when we got cuts on our hands. You can catch it by swapping spit—they think, but they're not sure."

Nobody laughed, waiting tensely for Rain's take on this. Whatever Rain joked about, everyone would joke about. But she was rammy and probably still frustrated about what never came down between her and me at the pond, and her finger burned. She would not tell about the pond to this crew—yet. They'd take a while to believe it.

"Nurses are so outspoken. They'll talk about anything. She says we're in the Gonorrhea Guild. It'll work like an STD, honest to god."

Dobbins shook his head. "That is so not right. There's no justice in the universe. How do the president of the 'No' Girls and the only guy who never misses a Young Life meeting get in a mess like this?"

"What's the 'No' Girls?" Rain's head went up.

I'd never told her this one. It's strictly locker-room speak. Dobbins grinned helplessly as Tannis and Jon and I laughed into our laps.

"Rain, it means that when it came time to decide who we

were all taking to the junior prom, we had to pull straws to see who was going to get stuck with you," Dobbins said.

Rain and I could have been voted Least Likely to Catch an STD in school.

"Now I have to sit around here and wish I had been you." She nudged Jeanine.

I shushed everyone after laughs exploded. There are no secrets in this group. Jeanine drinks and has random sex, but she's remorseful on Monday and apologizes and explains herself and asks for forgiveness, which sounds like heaping more dumb behavior onto dumb behavior, but she gets away with it somehow. It's hard to cut up about somebody who's vulnerable and crying in your face. Twice she had "gone on a ride" with a few guys in the music crowd (we call them Head Bangers in our school) who kind of hate us, and she'd have us threatening to kick their butts by the end of school on Monday.

Jeanine is adorable, and in a very pseudo-sexy way. She's a tall, lean athlete, all strappy muscle and bone, always with the same unkempt ponytail, no makeup, and you never see her without her varsity jacket. Zero cleavage. You just can't imagine her doing this stuff.

"Oh, no. You don't wish you were me." She giggled, gripping her long ponytail nervously. "Something terrible happened a few weeks back. Are you ready for information overload?"

We said no, but that didn't stop her.

"I was shopping for my prom dress with my mom. And this other lady came in with her daughter. No names, okay? And my mom got in these silent giggle fits, and she exploded once we got back out in the mall. She said, 'Did you see that woman in there? When we were your age, she used to pull trains.'"

"Whoa . . ." I tried to quiet Dempsey and Tannis as their sides split.

Cora's bare feet were crossed on the bed, driving Dempsey mad. "Cora. You know what a pulled train is? It's when there's plural guys and a singular girl—"

"Don't taint her." Dobbins tossed a Dorito at his head. "Will you not be satisfied until her mind is just as scummed over as yours? Continue, Jeanine. Don't listen, Cora."

Cora's smiling face turned bright red, and I often thought the comments about her naiveté bothered her more than the unedited remarks that flew between us all.

Jeanine's voice got lower, and heads went in. "I was all 'Mom! How could you tell me a thing like that, and how can you even remember it?' She said, 'Certain things people never forget. So take it under advisement if you're ever thinking of creating a sex scandal.' Well, she didn't know I'd already taken a few stupid pills. So as I see it, I have to go live somewhere else as an adult. I have to marry someone from out of town."

"Maybe you'll have sons," Dempsey said. "That'd make for fewer trips to the mall. At any rate, I'll marry you, Jeanine!"

"You would marry anybody," she noted, and turned to the rest of us. "So, you see, Rain? Don't ever wish you were me, unless you want to be in the mall with your kids someday with moms suddenly crawling out of the woodwork, guffawing into their handbags. Would you want your daughter standing there, all 'Mom. Why's everyone staring at you?'"

Rain pinched her lips to keep a grin from forming, but I was glad to see it coming out her eyes.

"Remember all the abstinence speeches Mr. Hypocrite used to give us?" she asked. She was talking about my brother, who gave *her* plenty of abstinence speeches last year—while he threatened to sic a hooker on me if I didn't decide to Do It before graduation. "Scott tried to explain to me before going to sleep last night that I have five boyfriends. Right here."

She held up her fingers and wagged them. Jeanine tried to smack them down while her mouth made some horrified O shape that didn't last too long. She laughed spasmodically into her knee.

"What are you staring at *me* for?" Dempsey demanded of Rain.

"Because you get turned down so often. It must be, um, frustrating."

"I know nothing about my five girlfriends. Even if I did, I don't own a manual to loan you. And boys and girls are very different. In case you never noticed."

"This conversation grows gravely inappropriate," Dobbins said, studying the side of his soda can. For once, it wasn't me asking Rain to shut up.

She ignored him, as I could have predicted, rambling on about Miss Haley's speech opening Pandora's box. "Adrianna LoPresti, our illustrious field hockey co-captain who would say *anything* . . . she says if you're going to make a date with your five boyfriends, you need a 'trigger' and so to surf the Internet for dirty pictures. The problem? Dirty pictures do nothing for me except gross me out."

"All right . . . enough," Dobbins said over the cackles dripping from the ceiling. He wanted to be a teacher. I figured he would be a good one because of how he could take control of situations. He talked on in total seriousness until everyone was listening. "Rain, the nurse said you got hurt near what you thought was an animal carcass? Tell me about this, as I might have some interesting fodder that would shed some light."

"It *was* an animal carcass," she insisted, swapping glances with me. "Or it was a pile of animal bones all caught in bramble. Very strange."

"Because when we were driving up here, I couldn't figure out how to turn off Ronnie's police radio, so I was listening to it."

Ronnie Dobbins was Scott's good friend, and he had just been accepted into the training program for state troopers in December. He had one of those endlessly babbling police CB radios in his bedroom, and I wasn't surprised he had one in his car, too. He'd obviously loaned his car to Bob tonight.

"Did you know there were weird animal remains found in Griffith's Landing this afternoon?"

I sat up and listened, and everyone must have seen or sensed it, because the room got very silent.

"Like . . . goats?" Rain tore a marshmallow pack open and plopped one in her mouth. "It was definitely a goat. There's two other goats on this property, and they have bells on red ribbons around their necks. I started to feel the pain right after I lifted a red ribbon with a bell attached to it. It had been, like, imbedded in all this goo and bones in the bramble. I touched it with my pinkie."

He pinched his lips, slowly shaking his head. "Your nurse didn't say what kind of animal you found. What they found in Griffith's Landing were dead monkeys."

"Monkeys?" Rain looked totally lost. I figured it wasn't related, but the group's interest was piqued because you don't hear of monkeys in these parts unless they're in the Philadelphia zoo.

"Yeah. *Monkeys.*" He spun his index finger in the air. "These guys were blathering, so it wasn't all so easy to hear, but I know they found two dead monkeys and said some strange stuff about the corpses."

Dobbins went on. "In a nutshell, the cops found these two piles of bones buried under the boardwalk in Griffith's Landing around three fifteen, having followed some stench that covered half the island. The CDC was at the scene. Your dad's name got mentioned, Rain. He was there."

With that, Cora's head shot up, and she stared at Dobbins, too. Rain looked even more confused. "Daddy had run off for some emergency just before I got hurt. Mr. Tiger said tonight that with the emergency, they forgot to tell Marg and just took off. *Monkeys?* He's leaving us unattended due to dead *monkeys?* I mean, monkeys, dead or alive, are weird in these parts. But they've got nothing to do with his job. I don't get it. And come to think of it, he hasn't come back yet. When Scott blew a fuse at the nurse, Dad sent Mr. Tiger back here to soothe him down. I guess my dad and Scott had a fight. I'm, like, forced into this bed rest that I don't want or need, and Dad's over in Griffith's with animal bones?"

I didn't get it either. Dobbins chewed a Dorito and swallowed, shrugging. "According to all this chatter, the CDC had to collect the remains in a steel drum, something about how the remains ate through three plastic garbage bags, and they were afraid of somebody getting burned."

"Burned by *what?*" Rain asked, her face screwed up into a total confusion fest.

"I don't know," he said. "What hurt you?"

The question hovered unanswered. Finally Rain said to me,

"Bubba, do you remember that we smelled something kind of scorchy? I totally forgot about that. It smelled like an electrical fire . . . something around there did."

I remembered but was distracted by other notable facts. "I couldn't find the spot again when I took Mr. Tiger out there. I swore I had the right spot. Mr. Tiger took a soil sample, just to be Mr. Polite-as-Always, because it looked like it had been dug out recently. But I couldn't smell anything at that point. Look . . ." I scratched my itchy head with impatience. "What happened to us was confusing enough. I'm sure it had nothing to do with whatever the hell is going on in Griffith's Landing. Let's find a more pleasing subject. You guys did not smell it. It was sickening."

"What's up, Cora?" Dempsey finally couldn't resist grabbing her foot, and he rocked it back and forth. I honestly don't think she noticed. She was staring wide-eyed at her screen. She didn't answer right away, but I'd warned all our friends about long pauses between when you ask Cora a question and when you might get your answer. They just watched her patiently.

"Um . . . excuse me." She finally got up and walked into the corridor—almost floated, more like she was in a trance than that she had to go to the bathroom. I followed, concerned. Marg had just come up the stairs, and she and Cora met at my brother's closed door. I recognized what Marg had under her other arm by the red plastic casing. It was a morphine drip. At St. Ann's word filtered down to us that morphine drips were a last resort for the four of us, and it meant things were really bad. I stood numbly, watching her listen on her cell phone with the other hand.

"You can't go in there right now," Marg said to Cora, lifting the cell phone away from her mouth. Cora's face turned bright red and, faster than Marg, she stood between her and the door. "Cora, let me in there. He needs me."

"Then ... I want to go in with you."

Marg sighed. "How, oh how, can I redeem myself? Mike Tiger was here, I've got my security clearance papers from USIC down in my bedroom, if you want to see them. Now move out of the way. I've got Dr. Godfrey on the phone, who just sent this drip up from St. Ann's at my request. Want to talk to him? Here."

She shoved the cell phone out to Cora, who listened for a few minutes. I pulled Rain's bedroom door shut to keep this bad news from spreading as I watched Marg enter my brother's room. She left the door open a crack.

"I'm sorry, I'm sorry ..." Cora said kind of quietly into the cell phone. "I ... just came into the corridor because I had to ask Scott a question, and the nurse is saying I can't see him and she's about to hook him up to something ... I, yes, I believe you about her. I just ... Why can't I see him?"

I tiptoed past her and actually stuck my head into my brother's room. I could hear him talking to Marg, which meant he was alert. But his whispers gunned, stop-start, stop-start, like he was in excruciating pain. He didn't sound angry with her anymore, which was one good thing.

Cora came in, handed the cell phone back to Marg, brushed my hand, and ended up gripping my finger so tight I thought she was going to break it. "Hey," I whispered right in her ear, "remember our motto. Don't panic. He's been in a coma. We've seen him worse."

I took her back out in the corridor, but as we waited for

Marg, I tried everything possible to hook into a distracting thought.

"You were upset when you came out here. What's wrong with you?" I asked, but she only muttered, "I needed to talk to him." She looked a little nuts, so I didn't bug her.

Marg finally came out, pulling off latex gloves and dropping them into her apron pocket. "It's just a lot of pain, that's all we know. The shot of morphine Dr. Godfrey gave him didn't help for long. I finally won the morphine war with him tonight. He might be the emerging infectious disease specialist, but I'm the hospice specialist, and there's no reason under the sun for your brother to have to endure that kind of pain. Now he'll sleep."

The nurse was growing on me, though Cora's grip on my finger told otherwise in her case. I allowed for more paranoia from her because she was the one who was attacked at St. Ann's. She was back to breaking my finger again, her eyes moving back and forth from Scott's door to Marg in some sort of anxious confusion. I used my breaking finger like a leash to lure Cora back toward Rain's room.

"What's up with you? Spill," I said, extracting my hand and shaking her by the shoulders a little. Sometimes that got her mouth working in group therapy.

But she just pushed past me, went back into the room, picked up her laptop, and stared at it. Her nervous energy sort of filled up the room, and conversations that had been going on kind of pizzled down until everyone was staring at her.

She finally let fly. "I, um, I need advice."

Dempsey moved over beside her, lay his chin back on her shoulder, and looked at the screen in confusion.

"Cora Holman asks for advice," he said. "Sounds like the Twilight Zone."

"I do need help. I'll have to explain some things. And if you wouldn't mind not touching me, please, that would make it easier." Her fingers trembled as she rubbed her forehead nervously. Dempsey returned to the bed. Nobody laughed.

"I've been helping Scott with something. But he can't tell me what to do next. Tonight, I got an e-mail from the Kid. And a friend he apparently lives with. We did a lot of joking back and forth at first—"

"*The* Kid? The intelligence Kid?" Rain said, rising off her pillows. I went around behind Cora so I could see her screen. Tannis and Dobbins followed.

"I'm sure they didn't wish for me to show this to anyone. But the last e-mails were not so funny, and without Scott, I—I'm at a loss. I don't know what to do with them."

She showed us a couple of e-mails from a guy named Tyler who sounded sharp and funny. He was discouraging my brother from getting a USIC job.

"Here's the one from the Kid that started upsetting me." She opened a longer e-mail and pointed to some lines in the middle and read them out loud. *"I must be honest in saying that USIC has left us in an unsafe and compromised situation, and our trust in them is severely breached. We would not be the best advisors on whom you should trust."*

"Trust with what?" Rain asked.

"Some . . . some pictures Scott and I took today in Griffith's Landing." Cora sat with her elbow beside her keypad, twisting a piece of hair. Her fingers still shook.

"You guys were in Griffith's Landing?" Rain asked.

Cora didn't answer directly. "It's complicated. Scott had me, um, doing something for him. I wasn't sure why I was doing it or what it all meant. And I don't want to say. I think it's for Scott to say."

"I'm not confused," Dempsey joked, and nobody laughed this time either.

She brought up another e-mail that looked like just a bunch of jumbled letters that went on and on for pages. Except at the very top was a note in English: *"Get this to Hodji quickly! No one else!"*

"Hodji is the agent from New York City who was in to visit us a couple of times in the very beginning," Rain said. I remembered him. He didn't stay around as long as the other agents. Roger O'Hare had said that Hodji's job in Pakistan had become almost exclusively to serve as bodyguard to the Kid. Now the Kid had been moved elsewhere. We were figuring South Africa or somewhere. Nobody had mentioned whether Hodji followed.

"Anyway . . ." Cora held out both hands, helplessly. "Do we have any idea how I can get this to Hodji Montu without telling anyone else in USIC?"

I didn't understand why that would be necessary. "Why would they send something to you and tell you to get it to Hodji?"

"You're asking why they couldn't give it to Hodji themselves," she said for me. She flipped back to the first e-mail and put her finger to an earlier line. *"Miss Cora, I do not have much time to talk as I am detained by pressing issues at my terminal."*

"I think, maybe, they were in some sort of trouble," Cora

said. "I mean . . . they were funny. They were goofing around, and yet so together. I'd imagine they have nerves of steel from all they do and could goof around in tense situations—"

"Cora, you gotta give this to my dad," Rain said.

Cora shook her head back and forth.

"He can get it to Hodji easily, wherever he is."

When Cora didn't stop shaking her head, Rain said, "'Trust no one' does not mean don't trust the guys in USIC."

"*I must be honest in saying that USIC has left us in an unsafe and compromised situation, and our trust in them is severely breached,*" Cora quoted them again, and when Rain opened her mouth to argue, she started shaking her head harder. "I knew this could start an argument. That's why I've been sitting here for ten minutes trying to decide—I would probably trust USIC anyway, except for Scott. Their policies are so etched in stone that they can watch him go on a morphine drip and say it's not their department. He doesn't just want a job. He *needs* a job. It would make him better . . . At any rate, I'm looking to do this the way the Kid asked . . ."

"You could call the New York office and ask to have Hodji call you back. He probably would get the message," Rain said, but I could sense the tension in her voice, sense her blood starting to boil. She had a very tight relationship with her dad, probably from losing her mom at age three. Other friends in our crowd griped about their parents chronically, but she never went there. I understood it from having been raised with only a mom. If the tables were turned, and Cora were telling me she didn't trust my mother, my blood would boil, too.

Cora sat pretty rigid while typing, probably surfing for the

USIC homepage. But with her being so hypersensitive to other people's moods, I doubt she missed that Rain was seething.

Rain didn't bother holding on to it. "Cora, maybe my dad knows something that Scott doesn't, okay? Like how stressful it is chasing down dangerous men who'd like to kill you. How can that be good for a sick person?"

Kind of acridly, Cora said, "I don't know."

"And you and I talked about this yesterday. You were the one all scared he could attract a Richard Awali to this place, remember? Do you want to wake up in the night and find one standing over your bed with revenge on his mind? Whatever it is the guy tried to inject you with, it's probably a lot more potent now, what with the two more months they've had to play with it—"

"Rain." I knocked her arm to shut her up. She had a point, but Cora wasn't up for it. Her jaw chattered, and I doubted it was all chills.

"Your dad told you, told us all, quite frankly that terrorists would have no further reason to bother us," Cora said. "Do you really believe that? Are you certain that what you saw out in the woods today is unrelated to what's going on in Griffith's Landing?"

"If Daddy thought it was related, he would have come flying back here," she said.

"Your father thinks you were bit by a snake. That's the assumption we were going on when Marg called him. And that may be because someone removed the corpse—somebody not USIC. We really *don't* know who around here we can trust. Do we?" I'd never seen Cora stand up for herself before, and it was icy.

Jeanine broke the silence. "Hey! Maybe it was Mrs. Kellerton who moved the skeleton. Some guy on my street was camping out here ten years ago. He heard a splash, and when he turned, she was standing on top of the water. Just staring and staring, her eyes like orange hell . . ."

Though we loved that sort of thing a year ago, the speech did little more than irritate us. Rain stared until some annoyed laugh flew out of her mouth. She reached for the laptop and said, "We're showing my dad."

I had thought Cora was merely playing with her keypad, but I heard a double click, just as Rain grabbed it. And she said, "I just hit a 'delete all' in my mailbox."

"Great." Rain mumbled and stood up. "I'm telling him everything you said. And I'm waiting for him on the porch. Screw this bed-rest thing. Let's all go. I need fresh air. He's like a dad to you, Cora. Or he would be, if you would chill out. Untrustworthy? That's rich. Wait until he finds out you just erased something probably important to national security."

I let Dobbins and Tannis go with her. Cora stayed seated and didn't look like she was all so four-star.

"So much for asking for help," Dempsey said, meaning it as a joke, and somehow she managed to laugh between sniffs.

I took the laptop from her, putting it on Rain's bed, and offered her a hand up. "Cora, I appreciate you taking up for my brother. No matter how I feel about it personally."

She gripped the sleeve of Jon's jacket, staring out the window to the pond. It gave even more depth to her commitment to Scott. She was committed to him doing something that personally terrified her.

TWENTY-EIGHT

CORA HOLMAN
SATURDAY, MAY 4, 2002
8:00 P.M.
PORCH

ALEESE'S IMAGINED PROMPTS were growing maddening. I imagined she had prompted me to say the first unkind words of my life to Scott, and now he was bad off enough to need a morphine drip. If those were to be my last words to him, I could not endure it. And I had imagined her congratulating me afterward and prompting me to ask for advice on finding Hodji. And that had turned out so badly.

I cursed her in my heart as I followed Owen down the stairs and took the arm Jon Dempsey offered me. I let the words actually form on my lips and fall out into the huffing breaths. And I heard the closest thing to an audible voice since that hallucination in St. Ann's: *"You don't have to sound like me. I just want you to learn from me."* My mother as teacher. Too strange a concept to dwell on.

Below us, Rain opened the front door, and my heart leaped

as red flashers filled the hall. I thought it might be an ambulance transport for Scott. Maybe Marg had decided a morphine drip wasn't good enough. But hurrying down, I saw it was a squad car. Mr. Steckerman got out of the passenger side, and Marg came out to meet him. They talked on the porch, and with the car's engine it was hard to hear as we huddled in the doorway, wondering if it was okay for us to come out.

". . . were up there together in Mike Tiger's car, and that's when he got the call to come to New York ASAP," Mr. Steckerman was saying. He looked none too thrilled. "How's Scott?"

"He's on a morphine drip," Marg said, and I watched Mr. Steckerman try to hide a flinch.

He sank down on the stairs, holding his head. Rain ushered us outside, and we moved fairly quietly. I'd never seen him break form before, and it made us move quietly around to the front of him and stare. Was he this upset about Scott? I knew he was capable of it, but he had just returned here in a Griffith's Landing police car.

"Where's Mr. Tiger?" Rain approached her dad, though the rest of us stood back. She sat beside him on the step and put an arm around him when he didn't answer right away.

"He had to go back to New York for an emergency meeting. The officer was good enough to bring me . . ." He suddenly remembered to wave at the policeman, who stepped back into his car and drove away again.

"What kind of an emergency meeting?" Rain asked, patting his hair sympathetically.

He mumbled something calming, and I think everyone was so relieved to realize this was not an ambulance for Scott that they missed the fact that he looked distracted and anxious.

Rain glared at me and said in all her frankness, "Daddy, do you know any way to get in touch with Mr. Montu? Cora has something to tell him."

Diplomatic of her, I supposed, swallowing my guilt. He gave me an absent glance, and I sensed he took her to mean I had a thank-you note for one of his gifts to us or that he had left something in my hospital room that I wanted to return.

"Whatever it is, you should just hold on to it for now," he said. "Mr. Montu was in a pretty bad car accident about an hour and a half ago. He's in the Nassau County Medical Center on Long Island."

Rain stared. "What happened? I thought you guys could drive a hundred and twenty and not lose control—"

"He was trying to save the lives of two boys," he said.

The woods sucked me backwards, and I heard through some long tunnel the gasps of people turning to me. Dempsey was right there and kept me from tumbling sideways.

"It can't be them," Jon mumbled. But I knew otherwise. I moved to Mr. Steckerman, my knees giving way just as I got to him and slamming the concrete, probably bringing me the types of bruises Marg loathed.

"Go for it," Aleese said. *"You've got rights. The right to know."* I wondered if she had pushed me.

He was saying something to Rain about "the Kid and his hacker friend" and a house fire and smoke inhalation, and he didn't have further details yet.

"Mr. Steckerman," I heard myself say. "Is it USIC's fault that they're dead?"

I hadn't time to cry or think about anything except that he could get very angry at me. I don't know what leap he took to suspect I was asking a logical or innocent question. Maybe Aleese hit on a subject that already consumed him. He nodded, slowly at first, and then emphatically.

"Yes," he swallowed. "Yes. It was our fault."

I knelt, frozen, the air so still that the crickets were deafening. My hand found the back of Mr. Steckerman's neck, which I rubbed in numb sympathy, but my eyes shot to Rain, who stared at me, dumbfounded.

TWENTY-NINE

CORA HOLMAN
SATURDAY, MAY 4, 2002
9:00 P.M.
HER BEDROOM

WE'RE NOT ALLOWED TO SLEEP with our doors locked. Mr. Steckerman turned my knob at nine o'clock, nine thirty, and ten, having gotten wise to the fact that I had information for Mr. Montu. He kept asking in his kindest voice what it was and wouldn't I please share it with him. I wondered if Aleese had been off badgering him, as she had been strangely silent after I came into my room. But he looked completely sane—tired, but more sane than I felt.

I merely gripped my laptop, staring off into space, feeling like I was falling off a cliff. Around ten, an e-mail dropped into my box, and I all but lunged for it, thinking maybe Tyler or the Kid had sent one last thing that had wandered through cyberspace before arriving. It was from Jeremy Ireland, and I saw in the subject line, "Re: Thanks for Further Help." I had titled my e-mail of this afternoon as that, just before Scott and I drove over to Griffith's Landing.

*Cora, I have been agonizing over the situation with your
father since I left you in St. Ann's and you'd asked if I
were he. I do know something about your father, which
I definitely do not want to share. However, I don't feel it
is my place to keep it from you.*

I rubbed my eyes wearily, thinking that if Aleese had chosen
to take a few hours off from harassing me, I couldn't escape her
anyway. My e-mails concerned her.

*While visiting you in St. Ann's and watching your mum's
video war journals with you, I noticed the dreaded one
in the box marked Iran-Iraq War, January 1986. You will
find some answers there. I would prefer not to be the
bearer of bad news in this case, and perhaps you will
understand by watching.*

I stared out my window. Off in the distance I could see the
pond glowing in the moonlight. It looked as lonely as I felt. I
wished I were still surrounded by people instead of wondering,
alone and horrified, if my mother had slept with Iraqi president
Saddam Hussein. Knowing nothing of her romantic past, I wondered if she hadn't been the type to sleep with important people
to get interviews and information. Nothing seemed impossible,
and I couldn't imagine what other name associated with the Iran-
Iraq War would make Jeremy so tightlipped and anxious. I was
not exactly familiar with the names of Iraqi officials.

But Saddam Hussein had been on the news a lot lately, as
there was much talk about whether America would declare war
on Iraq. One news station reported he had allegedly tiled an
image of President George Bush Senior onto the floor of a hotel

used frequently by his dignitaries, so that they would walk on his face all day. He was among the most hated men in America.

I could remember no other Iraqi names . . . or any Iranian ones. *Aleese, Aleese . . . what on earth did you do? Who am I?*

I simply knew I could not look at that tape—not now.

But I was drawn to the box, which now sat on the floor of my closet behind my row of summer shoes. I picked numbly through it, found the tape marked IRAN-IRAQ WAR, JANUARY 1986, and stared at it. I don't know what I expected, perhaps that it would grow fangs and bite me in the face.

Mr. Steckerman knocked at my door once more, this time with the house phone. He held it out to me.

"Hodji Montu," he said.

I lay the tape on top, and my thoughts of Aleese momentarily dissolved. I must have said hello.

"Hey, kid. Long time no see." Mr. Montu sounded raspy, like he'd either lost his voice or had a stuffy head, or both.

Mr. Steckerman walked out again and shut the door. I heard his footsteps on the stairs going down, meaning he wasn't eavesdropping, which fed my guilt.

"Mr. Montu . . . are you all right?"

"Car crash. I was racing from the airport to try to get to the house where my boys were. Guess you heard I didn't get there in time."

"I heard there was an explosion or something."

"Freak accident. The Kid's friend Tyler had what we call a pong bomb in his closet. He either lit it or it got too close to the heater and somehow caught fire."

"A pong bomb." I dropped down on the bed and leaned back on my pillows.

"Yeah ... size of a Ping-Pong ball. For a while, people could get them online ... thought they were like a cherry bomb. They're actually about ten times more powerful. Explosion went off upstairs. Fortunately, I was on one of those infamous delayed flights everyone's been squawking about since 9/11. We were still on the runway when their nurse put an emergency call through to the captain of our flight. Said the house was on fire ... she saw it coming back from dinner. By the time I got to the house, the firemen, the cops, even the TV crews were there, and I freaked when I saw the TV crews. Last thing anyone needed. I hit a telephone pole, and the airbags didn't inflate. Took the steering wheel in the face."

That explained his clogged voice.

"The boys ... what?" I asked, unsure if I wanted to hear this. "They couldn't get out?"

"No. They weren't in the best of health."

"What do you mean?" I sat up slowly.

He stayed silent, his breathing growing labored until he coughed and gasped. I had known that the Kid suffered from asthma. Roger O'Hare had told us that.

"Please tell me," I said.

"James Imperial is going to release the whole truth to the media anyway. The fire chief made some comments to the TV crew there about seeing a bunch of prescription drugs on the kitchen counter and maybe sick people being there, so there's no stopping it. Back when you guys were first admitted to St. Ann's, the Kid and Tyler had a run-in with some members of ShadowStrike. One guy scratched them in the face with the tularemia virus under his nails. That's another weapon of mass destruction—WMD. It infected them."

I almost dropped the phone. *"You're serious?"*

"Very. I'm just trying to brace you for it because you'll see it all over the news soon anyway. It probably won't be pretty. Tyler's mom was a spy for the North Koreans and she was recently jailed, so this will be the second time that house will be front and center in the news."

I'd remembered that news broadcast, how Rain and Scott had carried on that all spies ought to be given a lethal injection. To have a parent who was a spy had to be the most embarrassing of scandals these days.

"I'm telling you big secrets right now. It will be out in a couple of days," Hodji said, as I must have gasped. "Shahzad's family died, for all intents and purposes, in the Trade Center disaster, and Tyler's mother was always a single parent. In the interests of national security we had to keep their infection a secret, so we managed to get them a USIC nurse, and she agreed on her own to, let's say, 'get custody' of Tyler, but it was a big, convoluted mess. Growing bigger."

"But . . ." I stumbled for my thought before it struck me. "They should have been here with us! Why weren't they?"

"Some things they were doing were really dangerous. We didn't have the authority to stop them. We didn't have any further authority to help them. We didn't want to bring that sort of danger down on your house."

My guilt overwhelmed my gratitude, turning my insides sludgy. I pictured Richard Awali, hypodermic glistening between him and me . . . I had a momentary flashback, how he'd intentionally pushed the thing up to my face so I would look at it. A new dimension to my horror show emerged. Suddenly Aleese showed up, floating right over the top of my head. *"Don't go there. Stay focused. Ask the question."*

"Well . . . why are you calling it a freak accident? How do you know the dangerous men didn't come and do this?"

"It has to do with Tyler. One of our v-spies in Washington did some quick work . . . found out that he had ordered a pong bomb online six months ago. We have the receipt; we have some chatter he posted on one of his hacker web boards. It said something about a kid in school who always picked on him, and about the pong bomb. He wrote, 'I only wanted to blow up Bruno's *Cliffs Notes* and his hard copies downloaded off antiplagiarism.com. I didn't want to blow his face off, so the pong bomb is resting in peace on my closet shelf . . .' Something like that." He laughed a little, sadly. "Tyler was a funny guy."

Then he coughed loudly, I was certain to cover crying. I wanted Aleese to actually materialize so I could throw the phone at her. *Why is she always leading me the wrong way? She so needs me to know they didn't die as heroes. I have to get off this medication.*

He collected himself fairly quickly. "Uh, Alan says you have something to tell me."

"I was e-mailing with them around five o'clock," I said stiffly. *"USIC has left us in an unsafe and compromised situation, and our trust in them is severely breached—"*

"How did you find them?" he asked.

"They found us."

"I told them not to do that," he said. "For what purposes?"

I didn't exactly answer. I said, "They sent me a long, long document that had been encrypted somehow, and they said to get it to you quickly."

"Can you e-mail it to me?"

"The Kid said not to trust anyone but you with the

document. When it looked like it was going to fall into Mr. Steckerman's hands, I deleted it from my hard drive."

"Did you save a hard copy?"

"Of course." I hopped off the bed and went to my printer. I knew the remote print function had worked while Rain was threatening to give it to her father. I had heard it clicking and spitting out pages from the other side of the wall.

"Good girl. Now listen. You have to give that hard copy to Alan. He'll fax it to New York. But don't worry about anyone understanding it. Somebody will have to type all those codes back in verbatim, then they can e-mail it to me. I've got the only copy of Shahzad's encryption program. Nobody can read it but me, but if it will make you feel better, tell Alan I said it's classified, Level Four. He's Level Three. He wouldn't dare keep a copy—"

"Shahzad."

"That was his name." Before Mr. Montu's voice could crack much more, he hurried on. "That was the only e-mail he sent?"

"No, there were a dozen others, all today, but we were, you know . . . just joking around. There's nothing in them."

"Save them for when I get there. I'm coming to you as soon as I can get out of here."

"There were also some pictures that Scott and I took . . . in Griffith's Landing," I confessed. "Mr. Steckerman asked for them."

"What in hell were you guys doing there?"

I clenched my teeth together, praying for Scott to wake up, get better, and take control.

"Cora, you need to show them to Mike and Alan if you think it's anything relevant," he said. "Alan's a good man, and he's not exactly in the path of my wrath right now."

But he's in the path of Scott's wrath, I thought.

"You also have bad feelings about some of the agents?" I asked.

"I don't want to get into a blame game, but I actually resigned an hour ago," he said.

I threw my head back on the pillow, feeling the swamp of isolation grow around me in the echo of unanswered questions. Like, if Tyler and Shahzad died in an accident, why did USIC feel responsible? Was it like Scott said? Should they have had round-the-clock protection, even if it was from themselves in their bad health? Had some giant paperwork mess prevented it? Was Hodji lying about the pong bomb? And was it really a murder?

"But you're coming," I said, repeating his words. "Down here, to us, to me."

"In lieu of my boys, I'll have you guys. USIC will allow me that much, I'm sure."

He sounded worn out, and I felt the same. I all but staggered downstairs to find Mr. Steckerman sitting on the bottom step, staring into space. I handed him the phone with one hand and the encrypted document in the other.

"He says to fax this to New York," I said. "He said to tell you it's classified, Level Four."

He grabbed the twenty or so pages and stared at me, seeing that it was unreadable. I started back up, and he fell in beside me, saying, "Cora, we'll talk in the morning. We have to."

I thought about the pictures and sighed. Scott picked the greatest time to be of no help.

"We'll talk in the morning," I said, enough defensiveness rising in my voice to startle even me. "So long as you don't . . . crowd me."

He stopped, and I kept going. Aleese was laughing her side off.

THIRTY

OWEN EBERMAN
SATURDAY, MAY 4, 2002
10:05 P.M.
TV ROOM

OUR FRIENDS LEFT PRETTY QUICK after Rain's dad made that announcement about the Kid. We turned on her little TV. After watching a rerun of one of the funniest *Seinfeld* episodes ever recorded with neither of us cracking a laugh, I asked how her finger was.

"Fine," she said absently, and we started a conversation that made no sense, like, going in every direction at once.

"I'm concerned about my dad," she said. "I've never seen him look so bad."

"I want to go check on my brother. Marg's asleep on a cot outside the door. She won't let me past."

"Dude, our friends came out here tonight to find that I can't go outside and even sit at a bonfire. Then, they watched Cora and me get in an argument, and then they had to hear that two kids died. It's not going to be long. They're going to stop coming. We're a total bummer. Us. Happy and Smiley."

"Cora was sure acting weird tonight, wasn't she? If my brother were up and about, I'd ask him first thing if her medication is blitzkrieg-ing her personality. He'd know what to do."

"Am I a weak person, Owen? Because those two dead kids are surely making me feel like it. Like everything I did in school was just not good enough, like I should have been working undercover for my dad or something strange and Nancy Drew—ish like that."

Good. Feel it. I felt it. Though, if I were being realistic, I should not expect her to want to play superhero. I suppose not everybody was cut out for it. "You're normal. Or, you just want to be normal."

"What's the difference between normal and mediocre?" She turned to me.

Ah. The question I'd asked myself on and off for years. I suppose if you are born to be normal, then normal is outstanding. I was not normal. Beyond that, I didn't have much chance to pause and reflect. Rain grabbed the remote and turned up the volume.

". . . home of alleged North Korean spy Cynthia Lu Ping finds itself newsworthy again tonight as a mysterious explosion and fire took the life of her son, Tyler, and a friend, Shahzad Hamdani. Cynthia Ping was arrested in March for allegedly selling secrets to the North Koreans. Tyler Ping and Hamdani were in the residence when the bomb exploded around five fifteen. They died of smoke inhalation and were pronounced dead at the scene."

Their school ID photos flashed up. They looked like juvenile delinquent hoods, and I stared long at the image of Shahzad Hamdani, as I now had a face to go with the Kid's name.

"Nobody looks good in those photos," Rain said angrily. "Couldn't they find some cute family photos?"

It got worse. "Police are investigating the possibility of a suicide pact between the two youths. Ping spent five days in the psychiatry unit of Beth Israel Medical Center in March, just before his mother was arrested, though the reasons remain confidential. Hamdani arrived from Pakistan in March and had been living with Ping after his aunt, a middle school principal, asked him to leave her home, where he had been residing, due to disrespect for authority. Apparently, both boys quit Island Trees high school in March, and drugs were found in the home."

We watched in horror as the news changed to a plane crash near Midway Airport in Chicago, and Rain screamed with her hand over her mouth.

"That's it?" she cried. "That can't be all they have to say! Daddy!"

She went stumbling out of the room, me trailing behind her. Her dad hadn't gone home yet. We found him sitting on the bottom step of the stairs like he was waiting for something or someone.

When she recited the horrible newscast, he said, "USIC has not spoken on the subject yet. That's entirely the police, firemen, and local media putting things together."

"Will USIC announce them as heroes?" Rain asked. "They ought to get, like, the Purple Heart or something."

"Yes, they ought to be named Agents of the Year," he said. I noticed for the first time how much gray hair Mr. Steckerman had. When all of this started, it had only been gray at the temples. In two months, the gray had taken over most of his head. "But they probably won't. I'm just hoping James Imperial will come clean and say *all* that USIC knows about them, not just that they were WMD victims. Nothing about them needs to remain classified now that they're dead—that's my humble opinion. I've got a suggestion for you. Why don't you guys watch movies on VHS until all of this passes? I know that broadcast seems grossly unfair, but Hodji told us to accept it. Before putting together a statement, USIC will sift through all it can say and all that would not violate national security. It could be a day or two, and because Tyler's mother is now infamous, it'll be more of the same on TV in the meantime. Just don't look at it."

He only wanted Rain to be as normal as possible. He didn't want her to have to look at something that would upset normal people. But the unfairness of this was astonishing. At a loss for words, I was suddenly ready to end this day quickly. We simply turned to go upstairs to sleep. Rain said nothing. Neither of us had any energy.

THIRTY-ONE

Marg had slept outside Scott's door on a cot, and when I awoke around seven, the cot was already folded and pushed off to the side of the corridor. I stood with my ear against his door, my hand on the knob for about five minutes, but I was afraid to turn it and find the bed empty. His seemingly prophetic words, *You'd be fine without me,* still buzzed in my ears, though I knew we would be told immediately if he started to crash and bleed out. That was terminology which I'd only learned via overhearing the medics at St. Ann's, and I found it crude beyond comprehension. However, an ambulance might have pulled up here in the night, and with our non-creaking stairs, they might have been able to transport him out of here while I was in the throes of my strange, deep dreams.

Finally, I heard him clear his throat, and I sank into the wall, my hand flying to my eyes in relief. A groan of pain followed, and I finally wrenched myself away.

I sat alone in the dining room. Rain and Owen were still sleeping. I heard Marg on the phone with Dr. Godfrey.

"... because it's gone on so long. Their headaches generally last four hours or so, and the nosebleed concerns me greatly. Should I force a transport on him?" She went on after a pause. "He says he'll know if it bursts, and the only thing he cares about is that his brother isn't standing right there."

Nosebleed . . . Our mothers died with nosebleeds. The teaspoon clattered against the cup as I forced myself to stir my tea.

Marg served me breakfast and tried to make pleasant small talk, which let me know Dr. Godfrey's response must have been to respect Scott's wishes and leave him be. After a few bites of fruit and whatever pills Marg dropped in front of me, I simply forced my legs into action—simple, everyday actions of making my bed, brushing my teeth, picking out a necklace that went with the neckline of my T-shirt, unboxing my books and putting them on the empty shelf. It felt meaningless but sane. I decided I ought to begin to develop the film I had taken in Griffith's Landing.

Mr. Steckerman arrived by seven thirty and was talking to Marg quietly in the dining room as I passed by to go outside. And when I returned from our hiding place with the film and flipped on the red lights down in the old photo lab, I heard Mr. Tiger's car engine purring beside the house. It was difficult to concentrate.

I didn't know what I would say to Mr. Steckerman and tried not to worry about it. I focused on improving my technique, and the finished product of picture number one met with my satisfaction after only three prints. And after only developing two images of the Griffith's Landing Convention Center, I found myself gazing through negatives until I located the ones of the strange men turning quickly away from me. Taking those photos of what my instincts told me were dangerous men had been a crazed, unexplainable impulse, like sticking your hand in a fire.

"Only, you didn't get burned." I heard it as clearly as you rehear a line from a favorite television show, only I wasn't sure if the source was Aleese or myself. Trying to ignore it, I developed six of the images, and staring at so many sets of ominous eyes left my flesh crawling until I could take no more. I developed maybe twenty others—the children laughing on the duckie ride, people splashing in the water park. I was hanging the photos up to dry with clothespins on a wire that Henry had strung across the room. I had sent the first photos way down to the far end. The photos of the children and even the spectators in front of the convention center brought me around to a calmer state.

However, a knock at the door made me jump. I grabbed my chest, remembering the annoying truth about how the floors somehow didn't creak in this house.

"Yes?" I half hoped it was Henry having come over a bit early to show me the trails, though he would find it odd that I couldn't show him my work.

"Can I come in? I don't want to ruin your film."

It was Mr. Tiger. *Time to face the music.*

"Just a minute . . ." I stalled so I'd have time to think. *"Keep it simple,"* Scott had said a lot recently, since medications and circumstances made even simple decisions seem like climbing mountains. I simply went and opened the door and offered no speeches.

"Alan wants to talk to you upstairs, but there's no rush. He'll be here for a while."

"I'm just cleaning up. Come in."

He walked around, surveying my beginner techniques, and I felt dizzy, realizing what I had. Mr. Tiger was a nice man. Mr. Steckerman was nicer. I believed they were doing the best job they could, but the deaths of Shahzad and Tyler weighed against that, as did the love of my life lying in a bed upstairs with a mystery nosebleed. I supposed Mr. Tiger could simply take what photos he wanted, and I was prepared to give one- and two-word answers until I could hear from Scott.

He seemed neither surprised nor disapproving. I supposed these men had learned to let nothing surprise them, and they knew from the fax I'd handed to Mr. Steckerman the night before that I had somehow gotten deep into it. I took off my surgical gloves, washed my hands up to my elbows, and moved beside him again. I still had a mask on, which I hoped hid most of my blushing.

He stopped in front of the strolling man whom I had startled and looked at it for a long time. "Who's *that* guy?"

His words jolted me, though they weren't either judgmental or surprised. In fact, he sounded so casual that I doubted his sincerity.

"The first man who turned quickly away from my lens," I said. "There were maybe . . . six men who reacted that way when I put a camera to my face."

"Let's see if we can pick out all the ones who reacted so badly," he suggested nicely, like we were playing a game.

"I could do that better looking at the proof sheets," I said. "I was using a motor drive, which means the camera takes four photos in one-point-two seconds. I only developed one or two of each."

"Motor drive?" He sounded interested.

"Yes. We can see who turned away quickly by studying the four frames. Maybe we'll find ones I didn't see."

It was harder looking at the proof sheets, but I was able to point out six men who turned quickly from the camera. None of them were standing together. It would seem almost like they were posted in various points or were guarding something. Even with us taking turns using the magnifier, it hurt my eyes, and I was glad when I couldn't find any more.

"Mind if I take these?" He wanted the prints that matched up with the faces. I helped him pull down the right ones, and he circled the correct faces with a red Sharpie.

I put my hand on the counter to steady myself. Symptoms like chills and dizziness could come out of the dark, so my insides suddenly blasting with heat was nothing new. But for some reason, I didn't want him to think of me as weak.

"I hope, um . . ." I stammered. "I hope we didn't cause you any problems."

The tail end of it got lost in my trembling voice, and I wasn't sure he caught my meaning. He was staring into the magnifying cup and had been looking at one image for a long time. He finally straightened up and said, "No, you may have actually done us a favor. We didn't have clearance from Washington to get new agents in that city yesterday. We only have one agent down this way working undercover—in other words, who has not been ID'ed by ShadowStrike operatives—and that agent was detained with more pressing matters. Sending any of the agents they've already ID'ed would tip them off that we're on to them. We would have waited until tomorrow, probably, and who knows if they'd have been doing the same thing."

"What were they doing?" I asked.

I guess he noticed the trembling of my voice. He touched my arm and said, "Look, these people might not be anyone at all. They may be people who, coincidentally, turned away when you shot pictures. If you and Scott wanted to go for a walk in the sun, we had no reason to believe you shouldn't do that yesterday. Nothing is going to happen to you. I promise."

I let a laugh roll out of me. It wasn't that I was all so cynical about his pledges of security, I was simply amazed at my logic breaches. Owen had said once—and Scott told him to shut up and never say it again—that we could all be fine at noon and be on a slab in the morgue at four in the afternoon. Owen could strike into certain truths that Scott shied away from and that I did, too. But the concept backed up on me once in a while. I wondered what made me afraid of terrorists when my own health could put me on a slab in six hours.

"Can you get me the images you didn't print?" Mr. Tiger asked, obviously looking to direct my mind to a job as opposed to my fears.

"Sure."

"You're feeling up to it?"

"I think so. I have a friend, Henry, who—"

He put up a warning finger. "This is classified material. You absolutely, positively can tell no one outside this house. Can you do that?"

"Of course," I said, reeling from my error but feeling a tinge of regret. I would keep it from Henry, but I suddenly wanted to be with him—and away from all this dark talk.

My worsening weak spell wasn't getting past Mr. Tiger. He wrapped his fingers around my upper arm, holding a pile of photos in the other hand, and moved me toward the door.

"Well, maybe you should get away from these chemicals for a while. Though I'll take copies at your earliest convenience. We don't have a film guy anymore, what with doing everything digital, but I'm sure I can dig one up if you don't think you can—"

I considered these prints Scott's possessions as much as my own. "It'll give me something to do later this afternoon. It's fine."

He led me to the stairs. "We'll have to put some lights down here, outside of what's already been added for the darkroom, so you don't break your neck. I'll call an electrician right away."

"That would be nice, thanks." I climbed the stairs ahead of him, removing my mask, and enjoyed a blast of breeze that hit my face.

"Can you sit with me for a few minutes?" he asked, encouraging me toward the parlor. "I need to talk to you about something else."

I followed him and sat down on the couch. He sat down beside me. A moment of anxious silence passed before he finally said, "Scott, um, has had a recurring bloody nose all night."

I'd heard Marg mention a nosebleed, but I hadn't heard her say it went on all night.

"I just want you to know the truth. This might not be good."

I forced my thoughts back to how Rain had come to the emergency room with a bloody ear shortly before we were diagnosed in March. It turned out to be a localized ulcer, and I prayed it could be something like that. But his final words last night rang in my head until I held my ears: *"If I can't do that here? I'll wait for them in hell."* And then there had been my own poorly chosen words—

"*Damn* it!" My words sailed out like fireworks, directed mostly at Aleese, who I felt was aligned with Mrs. Kellerton behind me, or maybe it was Aleese cursing and she was inside me again. I could hear her all over the place. *"Pull a bitch routine, Cora. Now is the time."*

I simply couldn't. I took the words I wanted to scream out and found some miraculous means to deliver them in icy calmness. "If he dies, I will hold you and Mr. Steckerman personally responsible. Sometimes work helps people get better. Whatever secrets you hold so sacredly, I think you overestimate your own sense of importance."

To my amazement, he didn't back away, shake me, or holler defensively. He gently took hold of my arms, which were trembling violently over the shock of my words. "Listen. Some of the worst mistakes made in the history of mankind were made for what was perceived as the greater good. That's not an excuse. We're not making excuses. And I have no idea if we can save Scott Eberman's life at this point. But Tyler and Shahzad . . . that loss got under Alan's skin very much. He says he'll do anything—*anything*—to keep another kid from going down."

I could imagine he would feel that way but wasn't clear on what he was saying. I asked.

"We're going in there to talk to Scott right now."

"*Talk* to him?" I repeated. "I'm not sure I could accurately describe the amount of pain he is in. Voices, they're like cannons—"

"He's on that morphine drip," he reminded me, and I shut my eyes again. "The nurse approves. Alan wants to know if you would come and be there, too."

Such a rapid-fire exchange took place in my head that I had no time to think about its weirdness.

"Go!" Aleese said.

What if he slips away right in front of me?

"So, don't look. Go, and don't be a baby. When are you going to grow up?"

I love him.

"No, you don't. Get rid of the thought. I've got plans for you. Now, GO!"

"Look," Mr. Tiger said. "Maybe he'll still snap out of this, in spite of the lapse of time. Maybe it's just a nosebleed. If he's actually hemorrhaging, you'll see that bleeding out you saw in your mother—mouth, ears, etcetera. It would take about half an hour. You don't have to stay."

I got up, mostly because I was afraid Aleese would actually show herself and put one of the hiking boots she always wore in my backside. I floated to the bottom of the stairs, where Mr. Steckerman was standing and staring at us. I barely realized that Mr. Tiger still gripped my hand, and I pulled it from him and began climbing the mountain of steps.

THIRTY-TWO

SCOTT EBERMAN
SUNDAY, MAY 5, 2002
8:20 A.M.
HIS BEDROOM

OWEN AND I ARE IN TROUBLE AGAIN for jumping on the couch. He's just jumped on my head and is still laughing, despite that my skull plays like an accordion. And Mom's yelling, and as usual, it's at me. The oldest always takes the blame.

"Scott. Do. Not. Jump." She towers over me, holding her hands up in double-stop motion.

"Owen jumped on my head! Why don't you yell at him for once?"

"Do. Not. Jump," she repeats, the deaf mute as always when I defend myself.

This time weirdness erupts . . . blasts of smoke turn Mom from the 2D character of dreams into a 3D life form, with weird steam or white smoke or clouds roaming through her. She's more real, not less real. I can see both my new room at the Kellerton House and my old living room all at once, and she permeates both images, telling me something that made sense in both worlds.

"*Do. Not. Jump.*"

I gripped the clicker in my right hand. I'd been arguing with myself about it all night. I gave in finally, clicked the button for maybe only the tenth time, and the pressure in my head went *psssssssssssttttt* again. Hot air went out of the balloon.

I know she'll catch me if I jump. But she'll be disappointed.

Instead of jumping, I sort of free-fell. I was in a USIC meeting. The agents were watching me . . . whispering so low that I couldn't hear them . . . I could only see their lips moving in the morning light. Marg was standing there, opening one curtain, which is why I could see lips. It wasn't blinding.

"What is it?" I asked. "Speak up."

"You can tolerate low voices?" Alan asked.

I nodded, held up the clicker, and let my arm flop back down. It weighed a hundred pounds. "Morphed out . . ."

"We're about to do our dailies. That's what we call our morning meeting," Mike said. "You want to be counted in?"

Ah . . . some line of music I'd been waiting to hear. I let out a laugh, which made me cough, which would probably start my nose bleeding again, but what the hell. "Who's on drugs? Me or you?"

"You. We're quite sober and very serious. You wanna work for us?" Mike asked.

Someone was wiping my nose. I smelled Cora. I fumbled my clicker hand around her wrist and glanced up. She looked like she'd walked through an eggbeater. Too bad. I was in a good mood, a morphine mood.

I said, "Great exit line last night."

"Will you not go there, please . . ." She looked annoyed. Or like she might cry. "Do you want these men to be here?"

I nodded, taking the tissue from her and blinking at it. One drop. I wasn't nearly dead yet.

"We'll just talk to each other and you can listen," Mike suggested. "If you have any questions, just ask."

I still thought this might be a joke . . . or a bunch of unimportant truths, so I listened as well as I could for treachery.

Tiger: "Only two things I can share today. First, VaporStrike has been in New Jersey."

Steckerman: "Mm. Maybe we should have had this meeting in private. You're kidding."

Tiger: "Unfortunately not. Imperial says we have good people watching the borders carefully, but we don't have enough ID and the photos are grainy."

Steckerman: "How did USIC find this out?"

Tiger: "Apparently, one of the last things Tyler Ping and the Kid did before dying was send an e-mail to Hodji Montu. It said that VaporStrike was here."

The Kid was . . . sick or dead? Was I asleep or awake?

"Back it up," I slurred. They gave me the lowdown on the house fire. I hadn't let go of Cora's arm, I realized, and I let my hand slide down to find her fingers. Those e-mails had rolled around my head all night. She must be devastated. I felt my anger starting to mushroom, to the point where it would be dangerous if I let myself think about it. I tried to listen without smoldering.

Steckerman: "I only met the Kid that one time, at St. Ann's. I never met Tyler Ping, but it seems they were both devoted to the New York squad."

Tiger: "Ping and the Kid were either devoted to them or 'addicted' to them, as Montu used to joke. I hear Imperial allowed it to be released to the media as a suicide, but does this sound like a suicide to you, Alan?"

My eyes shot open and shut again quickly. Suicide. *The Kid and Tyler Ping committed suicide?* Impossible. The e-mails . . .

"USIC reported it as a suicide? That's vicious," I croaked. "God. Give 'em a hero's exit."

Steckerman: "The point is, Washington couldn't have been certain what happened by the time the TV crews showed up. Those boys were extremely ill, which means not in the best state of mind. When USIC isn't sure, our policy is to roll with what looks closest to the truth, and Tyler Ping's nickname with some of the agents had been 'Death Wish.' I'm just guessing here that it looked like a suicide, but there may have been another option—one that could jeopardize national security if it were known. It could have been an assassination. It's just not my or Mike's department. This happened on Long Island, and we're the Jersey guys. If the Long Island guys feel like we need to know for some reason, they'll tell us. They haven't yet."

Dead . . . dead. It didn't ring horribly with me. It's like Ping and the Kid had been standing to my left and suddenly they were standing to my right.

I remembered hearing the words "Beth Israel." Sickness? Suicide? Confusing. "What'd they have? They drink our water?"

"No . . . they were attacked. Ulceroglandular tularemia . . ." Some wild tale about being scratched in the face, and the stuff was under the guy's nails.

I groaned, pictures of tularemia pox floating through my head. Unpleasant. But not really killers. A few pox . . . it wasn't like smallpox or even chickenpox. I must have said something like that.

"This was a waterborne mutation. A dozen times more potent," Mr. Tiger said. "They looked like chickenpox victims. Only the doctors were experimenting . . . gave them too much steroid at first, which explains why they allegedly still looked like hell."

I let out a louder groan, an image forming in my head of skin closing over festering pustules.

"Sorry," Tiger whispered.

They'd have looked like a couple of beanbag chairs after that early screwup. I wondered what they'd looked like at the end. He brought the convo back to business, and he and Alan talked again like I wasn't there but could listen if I wanted to.

Tiger: "Alan, all that was said at the New York meeting is that they died of smoke inhalation, and Hodji Montu is taking a grief leave. You're only supposed to get that for family members, but he was ready to turn in his badge and walk away from the whole damn thing. Shahzad, the Kid, was like a son to him, so this morning they coughed up the grief leave rather than lose him for good. Hodji's got reason to be pissed. He suggested faking their deaths for security purposes. I was at that meeting. It went over like a lead balloon. No votes in favor, save Montu's. Not even mine."

"I think . . . I might have voted in favor," Mr. Steckerman said.

"Not if you knew these boys. The Kid we could help without any problems. Tyler Ping? He was very unstable. Son of a spy . . . he didn't exactly come from a background that teaches the virtue of loyalty. There were drug problems, credit card theft, one of the psychological illnesses—obsessive-compulsive disorder, I think. Hodji says it's probably all related to his mother, that Tyler was an ace until he was forced to live with her shenanigans, and then he started getting confused. But the cause is not the problem, if you know what I'm saying. The other agents felt we would have spent a fortune weed-whacking at policy, finding them a new place, and supporting them for months, and Ping would have announced whatever he felt like, wherever he felt like it. Besides, even if his mother is a complete pig, stunts like faking deaths have a way of working against you. If the media ever found out, how do you explain to every parent in America that you lied to a mother and told her that her minor son was dead? Even if she's in jail, that doesn't look good. In fact, it would give her a sympathy vote with the public that might eventually get her some parole—"

"What happened that made them think Tyler might not have done this?" Steckerman asked.

"Hodji was in the middle of a phone call with his son, Twain, when he started getting beep-ins from Tyler and Shahzad. It was like, you know, one of the only phone calls in the world he couldn't interrupt. If you can believe this, his son stayed pissed and finally hung up on him, after all that. Hodji was on one of those external runway delays when an emergency call arrived for him via the captain. Their nurse said the house was on fire. He had the pilots turn the plane around and drop him back at JFK. But by the time he got to where the kid was staying, the firemen, cops, and even the TV crew were already there."

"It's very coincidental timing for a suicide, I agree," Steckerman said. His sigh sounded far off. "I was correct last night. We've got blood on our hands."

"I don't think our actions—or lack thereof in the past few days—could have prevented this, Alan. There's still a chance it was Ping setting off that pong bomb in a dry, rickety old house. Some agents said they pegged him as suicidal. And again, there's still a chance it was an accident."

"Tragic loss . . . tragic, tragic loss to Intelligence." Alan was back to whispering. They were quiet for so long that I floated back into the center of it.

"Where's this VaporStrike now?" I asked, seeing what I could get away with. I hadn't detected any insincerity yet. In fact, it felt like information overload, considering how morphed-out I was.

"We don't know," Alan said. "We do know that Omar had a sizable lab in South Jersey somewhere. We haven't located it yet. But it's still active."

I knew that already. But still. This was like having won a shopping spree at Best Buy. I could pick out whatever I wanted.

"Omar might try to get to the lab?"

"Yes."

"What's he got in there?"

"A new strain of tularemia Omar was playing with back in March."

"Worse than what the Kid had?"

"About twenty times worse. Some dead animals turned up in Griffith's Landing last night that looked like experimental lab monkeys."

I flipped my eyes to him slowly. *Rain and the strange not-quite-a-snakebite.* I brought it up.

"We have no reason to feel it's related," Alan said, and added quickly, "though if we did—if let's say we realized Omar's lab was in this neck of the woods—we would move you kids in a heartbeat. They've no interest in you, but we wouldn't risk anything like you getting in the line of fire of any experiments they might dream up to try on animals."

I watched him and decided he was being very sincere.

"We believe Rain and Owen about the bones and the bell, and we think Owen just can't quite remember where it was. There *is* a goat missing, the Professor, as Mrs. Starn calls him, and there used to be as many as six, back when the school kids used to visit the place for field trips. But these goats have free rein. There's no fences, and it's not out of character for them to wander a mile or more before heading back. That's how the missing goat sparked the concept of the bells. He's a runner. We're thinking at this point that Rain sustained a bee sting. Godfrey's got her blood. Nothing weird is showing in it. He's far more worried about the antivenin and what it could do to her liver. He's watching that carefully. As for you? You did a great job, kid. You're worth your weight in gold around here."

I told myself it was a good thing it hadn't happened an hour or two later, when I was so desperate to get out of my pain that I was manipulating morphine out of people. Cora cleared her throat and I turned. She really did not look good. I reached my limp arm up until my hand found her face. Burning up.

"Go lie down," I told her.

"I'm fine, thanks."

But she wasn't fine. Even with my world rock-and-rolling, I could sense her tension, her overload of USIC business. She was part of this but wanted to spring out of here. Rock in a slingshot. She gripped the sleeve of my T-shirt and twisted, something she'd done compulsively at St. Ann's a few times that I never called her attention to.

"Go. Don't argue with me." I pushed her fingers away,

though some of the tension left her, like it could do when I was being Imposter Dad. Go figure.

I was glad she left. Because it got kind of smarmy in here, and I wasn't up for anyone else being here to witness it.

"Something for you," Alan said.

I felt a thump on my chest, and I put my fingers around something cold. It was a badge, obviously a USIC badge. I looked at it to make sure. Silver, with a USIC emblem in the center.

Okay...so these guys think I'm dying and are trying to save my life any way possible. You don't have to be off drugs to see some things. I'd hoped for something like this, though the badge was a touch I hadn't even dreamed of.

Mom's back. I'm jumping on the couch again, and 21 Jump Street *blares from the TV.*

"If you boys don't stop roughhousing, I'm turning off your favorite show!"

"Ma, I'm done. I'm sitting. See?"

I want to be Johnny Depp, the teenage cop with his crew of teenage cop friends. They go to high school but work undercover. I want a badge like they have. I want to be them—

Gripping the badge, I could feel one corner of my mouth roll upward. You can laugh at the strangest stuff. I read somewhere last year that Johnny Depp had always hated playing that role on *21 Jump Street.* He had trouble believing it himself. I understood. I knew I was getting something here that was damn near impossible, might have been completely impossible for a guy who hadn't signed a DNR form, with full assurance that Alan Steckerman would hear about it.

Alan was watching me, like, maybe with a tear in his eye. I

couldn't resist a wisecrack. "So. You gonna call me Nancy Drew when my back is turned?"

"Not on your life."

"Hardy Boys?"

He sighed. "Okay . . . You can give it back if you want."

He reached for the badge, only to realize he'd have to pry it out of my fingers with a crowbar.

THIRTY-THREE

CORA HOLMAN
SUNDAY, MAY 5, 2002
8:50 A.M.
HER BEDROOM

I DIDN'T WANT TO LEAVE SCOTT, but it was like being forced to leave someone in a burning building when your back is already on fire. I threw myself onto my bed but couldn't bang all the bad words out of my head even when covering it with four bed pillows. *VaporStrike, house fire, tularemia, funeral, hackers, terrorists, nosebleed, bleed out, Omar* . . . Shutting the light out only made the images grow stronger . . . Bloody tissues, morphine drips, hypodermic needles . . . I had trained myself to think at the age of fourteen that my life would be peaceful again if only I could get Aleese out of it. Peace, embedded in that dream of a condo down in the marshes of Trinity, was all I'd ever wanted.

But I was drowning in muck and growing compulsive about imagining her ghost. I pulled the cell phone Henry had given me out of my pocket and speed-dialed. I got his voice mail and, trying not to show my disappointment, left a message. Aleese was behind me, suddenly. *Good going. It'll take your mind off lover boy. Steer clear of him. You know what I mean . . .*

I shot straight up and yelled, "Marg!" loudly, though I knew it would startle Scott. Her footsteps came flying out of Rain's room, and I grabbed my lips and pulled as she stuck her head in my door, going, "*Shhh.* That's why we have buttons."

"I'm sorry." I shut my eyes, rubbing my forehead.

"What's wrong?"

"I want off a certain drug. Today."

"Which one?"

"I don't know. Scott knows. The one that keeps making me imagine I'm being haunted by my mother."

I lay back on my pillows, avoiding her gaze by keeping my eyes closed.

"The Nabilone can make patients foggy—"

"Yes. That's it."

She kept standing there, and I sensed a lecture coming. She didn't disappoint. "I can talk to Dr. Godfrey about switching you. But consider. You may continue to have whatever thoughts are disturbing you."

"What do you mean?"

"Just that generally speaking, medications don't conjure things that aren't there anyway. They just make those sensations stronger, or they make you confused about what's really going on. Maybe you need more closure. Maybe you should listen to that voice . . . so long as it's not aloud—I wouldn't like that."

"No, it's not aloud. It's just very annoying."

"Is there some problem with dwelling on your mom sometimes? Maybe . . . thinking of why you're, um, hearing what you're hearing?"

"Only the fact that I couldn't stand her, and when she died, I had great feelings of relief." I felt like a caterpillar who's supposed to become a butterfly, only I was becoming a bat. It was a horrible thing to say.

"What I mean, Cora, is that the voice you're attributing to your mother could be some part of yourself."

Just what I need to hear. I have a gremlin side, and, oh, I enjoy leading myself to make bad decisions. "And will you please close the door again on your way out?"

She hadn't said she was leaving. "I'll talk to Dr. Godfrey . . ."

I laid the cell phone on my nightstand so I could hear it if Henry returned my call, and I went to sleep.

No relief. I kept dreaming of Aleese or of Mrs. Kellerton rising out of the pond, sometimes the two of them. At times they were covered in muck. At times they shone like angels. In one, Jeanine Fitzpatrick was standing beside an RV camper, shouting, "Rise, rise!" In all the dreams, Aleese would reach her hand out and try to talk me into coming in swimming. She knew I couldn't swim and would break out in harsh cackles when I tried to run from her.

I awoke with a disgusted sigh, probably for the dozenth time, rolled over, and was just snuggling into the soft mattress and pillows yet again when Marg brought in a big arrangement of roses.

We hadn't gotten any flowers in over a month. I sat straight up and reached for the card, dizzily finding a smile.

"They were hand delivered," Marg said, setting them on the table beside me. "*Red* roses. I don't know about this . . . How old are you again?"

I glanced at her in confusion, opening the envelope. I didn't see the need to be a certain age to receive flowers. "I'll be eighteen September second."

"I didn't think I read that wrong in your file." She smiled, befuddled.

The card read,

Sorry you weren't feeling well enough to go walking today. I hope to see you soon. All the best, Henry

A tidal wave of relief poured out of me. Henry had done better than call. Life wasn't all bad.

"They're beautiful," I said, but pinched at my throat, which was starting to hurt.

"They're *red*," she said. Then she added in a singsongy voice, "Red is for romance."

My eyes flew to her sneaker, which was tapping with some sort of anxiety. And I was starting to think Marg's hands had a permanent home on her hips.

"You sound like Scott," I said dryly.

"He's not so very stupid about the ways of the world."

You should hear what he dreams about you. "How is he?"

"Better. Gave us a good scare. You should be able to see him in an hour or so."

I wanted to, so badly. And yet he was tied up with thoughts of medicine and symptoms and terrorists and USIC schemes. I just wanted to sleep. "Please tell him I'm glad he's all right."

"You don't want to tell him yourself, huh?"

I had no answer. Fortunately, she said it for me. "You're sick of sickness, aren't you? That's perfectly understandable. Let's bring

Henry up here and give you a few minutes of relief. Just keep in mind: Red roses mean romance. You didn't know that?"

I shook my head, embarrassed by my lack of working knowledge of all things romantic. "He'll be thirty soon. That's ... very old," I said dismissively. "And as an absent-minded, brilliant professor, he probably knows less about color schemes than I do. I'm sure he understands the situation with our health."

"He's not stupid, but he's probably an optimist. Your condition shouldn't last forever."

I turned my fiery cheeks from her gaze to glance at my clock. It was already after three. I'd been asleep for more than six hours. She pulled a thermometer from her pocket, stuck it in my mouth, and waited for the beep. I felt achy and feverish, but she merely shrugged as she read the results. We didn't worry about fevers under a hundred and one.

"Other symptoms?"

"Just throat," I said.

"I'll bring you a slushy, and I'll bring him, too." She sized up the red roses again in a wary way that made me realize, *She's serious. She's taking these red roses at face value.*

I knew better, but curious thoughts drifted through me that had a *Well, what if?* undercurrent to them. The only boy who'd ever shown any interest in me was Jon Dempsey, and as Jon's tastes were basically indiscriminate, I never paid any attention. The idea of somebody older being interested had never crossed my mind. I wasn't quite sure how I felt about it. But Henry was so completely unaffected by all that went on around us that I craved his company.

She disappeared, and I found myself groping in the nightstand for my hairbrush and running it through my hair so numbly that I didn't feel the smile forming on my face again. *Older men.* It was an entirely new concept for me in my denseness, but it was like the door to a whole new world had opened just a crack and a line of sun was trying to break in.

Marg arrived with Henry—and she put a slushy down on the table and left again.

I thanked him for the flowers, watching his face, which looked friendly, cheerful—not with that piercing stare Jon Dempsey could give, which left me feeling like he was looking through my clothes. I figured Marg had made too much of it.

"I won't stay long. I was concerned and wanted to see for myself that you were all right. Getting lost in the woods would have to be stressful to you."

I rolled my eyes. "That was the *easiest* part of the day," I said, before realizing I shouldn't tell him about Griffith's Landing or the scary staring men.

"You had worse adventures than getting lost in the woods?" He was taking off a summer windbreaker, mumbling about it being warm up here. All I could feel was the breeze, which was again making me cold.

I felt that biting annoyance that USIC could come between me and what could conceivably amount to my first romantic interest, however unlikely the odds.

"Well . . . Scott came down with the kind of headache that is really cause for concern," I said, avoiding our secrets with enough grace that I felt surprisingly proud.

"So I heard from Mrs. Starn. She was here this afternoon. But he's all right now?"

I nodded, sending off a prayer of gratitude, which I hoped would make up for my lack of interest in going back in that room. I was about to point out a chair on the far side of the huge bed, but he sat down on the bed beside me.

"I brought you something else." He was close enough that I could smell him, smell soap and fresh spring air, which left me feeling like I was perched on a swing. I lay nearly frozen as he pulled a sizable frame out of a large shopping bag he'd been carrying.

He turned the frame around, and it was an enlarged print of the picture he took of me yesterday. I've always hated pictures of myself, thinking my eyes were too dark and I looked stoned on some drug that dilated my pupils. But in this enchanted wooded setting, they fit. I looked mystified and yet somehow . . .

"Alluring," he said.

"Excuse me?"

"I may hang this in the gallery at school. You're supposed to give it a name. I can't think of one except . . . 'Alluring.'"

He didn't watch me or touch me or do anything to make me feel uncomfortable, but he sensed my discomfort, I think, because he went on about the *woods* being alluring, seeming to beckon people, and I was the Guardian of the Keep.

I thanked him again, and he set the picture by the side of the bed. "I went down to the basement today to leave you some organic chemicals in the darkroom. I thought they would be better for your health."

"Organic chemicals," I repeated. "I didn't even know there was such a thing."

"You can find organic just-about-anything these days if you're willing to pay. I've been using them this year. Of course, the ultimate answer is to give up film development and switch entirely to digital. But what fun is that?"

"No fun," I agreed, feeling my heart sinking over Tyler and Shahzad. Their needs and mine had been miles apart yesterday. Today, we were eternities apart. I forced myself to mumble a thank-you.

"You're welcome. The problem was, I couldn't get in. The door was locked." He chuckled. "I've been using that room for two years and didn't even know it had a key."

"I didn't either," I said in confusion, then remembered Mr. Tiger saying he would put electricity down there. I wondered if he'd moved that quickly, getting electricity and locking rooms where important prints were being kept.

This time, I almost sighed in aggravation. I said, "It's probably Rain's dad. He's . . . you know, the Mounted Police."

"Ah, Mr. Steckerman." He nodded in continued cheerfulness, being a sport. "Well. The house belongs to the State now. I suppose those with a vested interest can park themselves wherever they want and the rest must bow to the inevitable."

I said remorsefully, "Maybe we can find us a darkroom in one of the outbuildings."

"Good idea. I'll look around. And you should probably rest now." He grabbed both my hands in his, pulled them to his mouth, and kissed the backs of my fingers. I didn't know whether to dance or fly. He moved through the doorway.

"Henry?"

He turned. My normal ease with adults became twisted with the concept of him being attracted to me. My jaw bobbed. I'd only wanted to plan something with him for tomorrow. But I couldn't find the words. He smiled, looking relieved, surprisingly. I wondered if I could possibly have been making him nervous.

"I will call you," he said. "And if you're feeling better tomorrow, maybe you can help me find the perfect new darkroom on the property. I've got plenty of equipment."

That made me realize that all the equipment in the current darkroom, the one he could no longer enter, probably belonged to him. He was a nice person. USIC was putting on airs of superiority and assumption. Still, he left with a smile.

A thirty-year-old man. I lay there performing an exercise I'd heard other girls discuss when they thought a teacher was hot. They tried to decide what the teacher had looked like and acted like in high school. A chronic subject was Mr. Duran, the physics teacher, who had been in his second year of teaching last year. He was twenty-three.

"He teaches physics! Definitely, he was a dork," Merrillee Witherspoon had decided. "Math Club material."

"Nah, he looks more to me like the invisible student. Not dorky, not cool," Rachel Mathers replied. "But once people get through college, they're not dorks or cool. So it doesn't matter. He's *hot.*"

I tried to think about what Henry was like when he was in high school and came up with the same diagnosis as Rachel. He hadn't been a dork, just invisible. Like me. But I was not accustomed to looking even at Mr. Duran as *hot.* Henry was slender but not rail thin. He had dark wavy hair and blue eyes that ran close together over a straight nose, which gave his gaze intelligence and perception. *Thirty years old.*

People had done a special section on my mother's adventures across four continents, and I remembered the answer I had given when asked, "Do you want to follow in her footsteps?" I had said, "I've no desire to leave Trinity Falls. I'm going to Astor College, and after that, I just want to be normal." But to have a friend who was *thirty years old.* It cut into some adventurous side I wasn't even aware I had, almost making me forget about our health problems and how no easy answers were in sight.

I was like a hot-air balloon, rising, rising, until a strong hand clutched my door, and I heard voices in the corridor. I would know Scott Eberman's fingers anywhere, and they left me hovering but confused and anxious, like I was expected to jump from one hot-air balloon to another midflight.

"No, I'll talk to her," he was saying.

"Do you want me to come in, too?" Marg asked.

"No."

He pushed the door open and locked gazes with me as he walked to the foot of the bed. His eyes were still swollen, his expression flat. The lines under his eyes smacked of exhaustion, but he'd managed to come out of his bed in the past six hours while I had slept, and, just recently, to shower. His hair was half wet, half shiny and dry.

Scott had never knocked on our door at the hospital, assuming more a role of medic than fellow patient, but it felt a bit odd up here, like he was violating boundaries. Not that it mattered. His easy entrance smacked of entitlement.

His gaze was drawn away from mine only by the flowers, which caused him to fake a whiplash with his neck. I felt slightly horrified as he changed direction, grabbed the card, and read it. I had jumped hot-air balloons, I suppose, as I waited almost hopefully for some sign of jealousy. But he just gave me a slight pinch on the cheek that made me feel childish again, far more childish than having spent time with a thirty-year-old man had.

He passed slowly around the bed and dropped into the chair, staring at me. Staring and staring. I thought his sore throat may have returned.

"That was quite a show you put on last night and today," I said quietly, realizing it was a terribly backhanded remark— yet another that was more like Aleese, whom I suddenly imagined sitting square in the middle of my chest and staring at me. *"Don't you love him. Don't you dare."* She had been nowhere when Henry was here.

He brought a bottle of water to his mouth, I sensed, to cover a smile. "That's what you call my brush with death? Quite a show?"

His eyes lit with humor as he swallowed. He liked my gremlin side. But it wasn't me. It was some "possessed" me. I wanted to reach out, take his strong hand, and tell him if he ever died I'd have no option but to follow. But Aleese sat firmly on my chest and refused to budge. I had a dawning revelation.

"*Was* it really a brush with death?"

His eyebrows went up and down, and his face turned serious. "Obviously, it wasn't. But it really, really hurt."

"So . . . it was just a bad headache."

"Let's hope. My throat thing had moved up to my sinuses. That helped, too."

"It's just that . . . our talk yesterday . . . I thought you might be doing something to manipulate Mr. Steckerman into giving you a job."

"I told you men generally don't lie. On the Richter scale, that headache was a nine. I would not have let anyone shoot me full of morphine if I didn't need it."

"And signing the DNR form?"

"I hoped I hadn't signed my death warrant. I just knew Alan would catch wind of it."

He put the bottle to his lips again, looking totally serious, not like he expected me to laugh, which made me laugh. Men were forever confusing.

"So . . . how'd you do the bloody nose?"

"How do most people get a bloody nose?" he asked impatiently, like he was suddenly sick of the subject. "I picked my boogers."

I threw the spare pillow over my face, and he waited patiently until I pulled it away again. It was a sharp contrast—entertaining a neat as-a-pin professor, then a former quarterback donned in sweatpants and a sweatshirt with the sleeves cut out. Somehow, their age difference didn't show.

"We have news," he said finally, in a voice that was soft but not raspy.

"Good news?" I asked as the silence lingered.

He laughed. "I haven't decided yet. But . . . it's news, and we have to make a decision, so I think we should keep it simple. The medical team in Minneapolis—the one that designed the drug protocol we're on—they've come up with a cocktail."

I felt my eyebrows rise in surprise. A cocktail was a familiar word, something we'd all been hoping for, which meant that many of the drugs we were taking could be administered once daily, with time-released substances doing the work of a nurse.

It meant we could live a more normal life, perhaps go to school, or at least be free to take day trips.

"So soon?" I asked. "I thought you had said maybe in the fall."

"That's what the Tallahassee guys were telling Dr. Godfrey. The Minneapolis team says they've got it." He put his arms out and shrugged, looking less exuberant than I would have thought.

"So, what's wrong?"

"They . . . want *one* of us to try it."

I lay waiting, and it wasn't until a half minute into the silence that I realized how haunting a decision this might be.

"Is it dangerous?" I asked.

He kept staring at the floor, and I marveled at how he could tackle a problem like this six hours after a headache so severe he'd been put on morphine. He still had a Band-Aid on his tricep that did little to hide the silver-dollar-size bruise left from the drip.

"I haven't talked to them on the phone yet to run them through the third degree, but obviously they are not going to send something over to us that they don't believe could vastly improve our quality of life, maybe even send that person into remission. However, the idea that they're insisting on sending it for *one* of us, and not all, smacks of risk factors. It's experimental, of course. Generally speaking, with cocktails there are fewer side effects, but there's also less efficacy. Some of the drugs we need the most might not work as well, and Dr. Godfrey's been saying for weeks that it's the drugs that are keeping us alive. It's like we're four soldiers in a foxhole, and we're deciding if one of us should run for reinforcements."

"It's like Russian . . ." I stopped myself, but he got my drift.

"Roulette." He stood up, walked to the window, and turned around to walk back again. His eyes stopped on my roses like he was seeing them for the first time, and he shook his head in what appeared to me to be annoyance.

"At the same time, if it *does* work the way the Minneapolis team hopes, then that person gets better faster." He grinned, and the positive energy actually made it to his eyes. "That person might be moving about freely in a month. That person might be able to start college in the fall and begin to forget all of this ever happened. And since we have this saying among us right now—'Keep it simple'—let's not go round and round about who's going to take it. I'm thinking it should be you."

We exchanged stares as I waited for him to say more, but he didn't.

"Why me?" It seemed to me I had less of a life to get back to than any one of them. "Why not Owen? He's the biggest health risk. Maybe he would benefit."

"He's *too* big a health risk. Same with me."

"But . . . if it worked, your arteries would strengthen. You could get the surgery," I said. "I know how stir-crazy you are."

"Well, it looks like Alan is really serious, and I'm going to work for USIC. Don't worry about me right now. Besides, if something happened to me, Owen would have suffered a double loss. I honestly don't think he would live through that."

"What about Rain?" I asked.

"She's been taken off bed rest already, but they are trying to ignore questions that might not have great answers. You heard those guys this morning. She's out for the next thirty days. Let's say that she touched a WMD. They don't have an incubation period that's reliable, so they'll have to keep watching her. As for you, you've had addictions in your family. I'm concerned about you being on all these drugs for too long. The narcotics especially could be hot-wiring you for problems down the road."

I had tried so hard in life not to be like Aleese that I almost took offense. I could hear her laughing all over the place. I might have argued, except I thought of the flip side of this. If something were to happen to the person who took the new drug, I would be the least likely one to be missed. I glanced at my flowers, glanced at him, and found myself imagining any of those three having lost each other.

"I'll do it," I said.

He had been resting his forehead on his hand, and he continued to stare at the floor. *Such a brooder.* I turned sideways on the mattress, trying to position myself under his gaze, but he was still lower.

"Hel-lo? I said I'll do it. Be happy now."

He sat up, watching me half upside down, but without a sign of a smile yet. "If anything happens to you, I'll feel responsible. I'll never get over it."

"You're not responsible," I said, certain that all the implications had not hit me yet, but there was no point in worrying. I shut my eyes, waiting for one of his Perfect Ten head pats that never came. He got up and crossed the room, the flowers catching his gaze again.

He rolled his eyes and sighed. "Be careful," he said. "Mr. Professor. He's still a guy, and guys think only of one thing. Unless they're perverts who never came through the Oedipus stage of potty training."

"You're being silly again," I said. "And you're generalizing."

His eyes stopped on the framed photo, which had lain face inward against the side of the bed. He picked it up and looked at it. I bit my lip. I don't think he blinked or breathed for five seconds. Then he put it down again.

He stuck a finger out at me on his way out the door, but dropped it again with a sigh. "Just go back to sleep."

"Oh, for Pete's sake," I mumbled to myself after he closed the door. I was now straddling two hot-air balloons at four hundred feet up. But there was no point in getting out of bed to follow him, as I was certain he would find some USIC files to read before he burst with morbid curiosity.

THIRTY-FOUR

RAIN STECKERMAN
SUNDAY, MAY 5, 2002
3:30 P.M.
TV ROOM

IT WAS THE MOST BORING OF DAYS. I wasn't allowed outside to wander and overexert myself, and we weren't supposed to watch TV, according to Dad. I almost decided to read a book. Owen spent the morning in the TV room reading *Searching for Eternity: A Scientist's Spiritual Journey to Overcome Death Anxiety*, which sounded like a total downer. Marg had let me downstairs to lie on the couch in the TV room, and I ended up merely flipping through channels to shows that used to make me laugh and turning the channel if a commercial break looked like it could break into news.

After lunch, Owen and I were back in the TV room yet again. Neither of us had bothered to discuss yesterday's almost-a-kiss. I'd noticed him sending a few defensive glances my way in the morning when I got too close to him—like he wanted to make sure I wasn't going into attack mode. I looked at the bad ending yesterday with some superstition. You try something, and a minute later you get bit by an invisible snake—that means the gods are against you. And the antivenin had done what Dempsey promised. I was half seasick, very tired, and not the least interested in thinking about elephants today. I hoped yesterday was just an initial reaction to Miss Haley, and now I was back to normal.

Owen had made a trip upstairs right after lunch, sticking to some promise he'd made to Scott about trying to climb the stairs at least four times a day. Now he gripped a video and huffed, out of breath.

"Cora was sleeping. I just walked in and took this. Think she'll be mad?"

"Who knows? All I can gather is that she really doesn't want to look at them herself. She's still afraid she'll catch her mother tap-dancing on a bar, drunk out of her tree, and flashing people. Supposedly the woman taped everything, like it was some compulsive tic. I wouldn't be surprised if she taped her own sex life."

"My humble opinion? Cora's too paranoid about her mom." Owen turned on the VHS machine manually and stuck the tape in.

"What did you pick?" I asked. All the tapes had been carefully marked by the news station that transferred them from news format to VHS.

"I was afraid of waking her up. I just grabbed what was on top and charged out again. I don't really care. I think her mother was probably more trustworthy in her glory years than Cora is thinking. It would be hard to think clearly about a mother who was chronically wasted when she was around you."

With the tape inserted, IRAN-IRAQ WAR, JANUARY 1986

flashed up on the screen and went to sand again. I wished Owen wouldn't watch this stuff. He always had been prone to a morbid streak, but not every day, not even every week. It would hit him at the end of playoff seasons when he'd been pulled in too many directions by too many people. Now I felt like he lived in it.

We watched for half an hour as Jeremy Ireland filmed Aleese either running through battlegrounds or interviewing soldiers in languages we couldn't understand. It was nothing scandalous—a lot of corpses, a lot of soldiers, a lot of the sounds of bombs behind their voices. But the soldiers they interviewed were wearing very different uniforms and using different languages: I assumed she and Jeremy got the Iraqi and the Iranian take on things. Owen would sit forward every time she talked to the Kurds, whom you could tell by their dusty yet colorful, swirling headpieces. We'd seen a tape back in March where Aleese had filmed the Kurdish massacre. I wondered if all the Kurds she was talking to in this tape would end up being the dead ones on that other tape.

I wanted to watch something laughworthy and was just lying there staring at the screen and counting the minutes until it was my turn. The couch was long, and Owen was sitting maybe six inches past my head. As he'd seemed so alarmed this morning over the idea that I might even touch him, I was surprised when he suddenly took my chin in his hand and pulled it upward so I was staring at him. Even upside down, I could see he looked very concerned about something.

"Are you okay?" he asked.

"Fine."

"Sure?"

I looped my chin up and out of his grip. "Yeah, I'm just tired." He was still looking. I grew annoyed. "Why? Am I turning yellow or something?"

"No. You're just . . . not laughing or crying. You're sort of . . . unusually limp."

"You ought to be happy about that. Maybe I'm cutting you a break."

"Thanks. Just . . . let me see your eyes."

Godfrey had told us one sign that your liver is acting up is that the whites of your eyes take on a yellowish tinge. I didn't know what Owen expected—me to do a back bend or something. He moved over and looked down into my face.

"They yellow?" I asked.

"I can't tell."

I felt a little washed out, but not enough that I really had to think about whether I wanted to rouse myself to go look in the mirror. I decided if my eyeballs were yellow, I really didn't want to see it right now. And he was seeping with drama from the looks of him, though I couldn't have guessed the source of it.

"Those lines you told me yesterday from Godfrey kind of freaked me out," he finally admitted.

"The ones where he told the guy from the CDC that he felt he'd lose one of us?"

"Yeah. I've been thinking about it—how I would feel if it was me. Because I know that I'm the one people would suspect. But I just started thinking, what if it's you?"

"It's a statistic, that's all, Bubba. Doesn't mean anyone's lost. Don't go morbid on me. Or if you have to, turn this tape off. I'm being double-barreled."

"Any of us . . . it would be really bad. Even Cora. She's like that deaf-mute sister that you feel extra protective of. Besides, I think my brother's, like, falling in love with her."

I looked at him upside down again, watching his worried gaze. I giggled—couldn't help myself. "That could create some drama on the home front. Maybe I'm not used to thinking of Cora as attachable, to anyone. What makes you say that?"

"Just that he reads her like a book, gets her to talk, even makes her laugh. Since we've arrived here, she's replaced me as the person he's most likely to spend time with. I'm making a point here, about all of us, not just Cora. It's dangerous. We're in a game of rolling the dice. None of us should put it all out there and risk falling in love. Not until—"

"See, that's the difference between you and me," I snapped, fighting the urge to add *jerk face*. "This is when you *do* put it all out there. I haven't entirely stopped thinking of Miss Haley's speech, but today, instead of thinking about elephants, I'm thinking about how an outsider would view us."

"How is that?"

"Two brothers from Trinity Falls, in the prime of their lives before this came down, who happened to be sent away to live, kind of isolated, with two girls in the prime of their lives. We're supposed to pretend we're nine years old? Somebody's going to break down and start spreading germs around. And you know what I say? Leave your brother and her alone. Better to have loved and risked the loss."

"I disagree."

"Maybe you don't have any feelings." I sighed.

"Maybe I have the *most* feelings. Ever think of that?"

I let him gaze at the screen while I started to think about elephants again. I started to do a couch version of the Dreaded

Fifteen, to the point where I was imagining clothes flying and total skin against skin. Truth? He's got chronically wet and shiny lips that always drove me mad. I was thinking about how I might get my way when I realized he was staring intently at the screen, his jaw suddenly downward.

I turned. All I could see on the screen was a rock on the ground. It was like the camera had been turned over.

"What did I miss?" I asked.

He leaped up and hit the OFF button. Then he stumbled backwards and plopped down on the couch all agog.

"Who was it?" I asked. "Who was she with?"

He shook his head slowly about five times. He said, "Oh my god."

Because he generally thought "Oh my god" was a curse and not a good thing to say, I just sat there waiting. I waited what I thought was an eternity while he got up and walked to the win dow and stared out in horror.

"Who *was* it?" I asked, which snapped him into turning around and coming back to the couch, where he stared at the floor.

"Rain. If you never promise me anything else as long as I live, promise me you will never look at that tape. Then you can never tell Cora what's on it. Maybe she'll . . . never ask."

"Why would I tell?" I asked, ruffled.

"Because you tell everything."

I flipped around and stared at the blank screen, not know-ing whether to be upset. It seemed like I only had two talents people would find notable: crying and talking. I turned my thoughts to Cora and how she'd been through enough hard-ship. She didn't need more. But I kind of thought that Owen had either misinterpreted something or was overreacting. Whatever Cora's mom had done wouldn't shock me.

I almost said as much. But Owen had worded himself funny. The usual saying is, "If you never promise anything else as long as *you* live . . ." He had said "as long as *I* live."

Owen secretly thought he was going to be Godfrey's statistic. He might toy with the idea that I could be it, but that's not what he really thought. I didn't know what to do with that. I promised, grabbed for the remote, and put on Nickelodeon.

THIRTY-FIVE

The realities of agreeing to take the cocktail set in Monday morning when I sat at the breakfast table. We took what amounted to a handful of pills every morning—two a half hour before breakfast, one just before, one just after, and two an hour after. I was offered nothing until just after, and the one pill I took was not the cocktail. That would start Wednesday. In the interim, I was to take only a flushing agent that would get all the drugs out of my system quickly, so some of the new wouldn't react with the old.

"Promise you'll let us know if you feel weird," Rain said, watching me with concern. I felt like I was falling off a cliff. She laced her fingers through mine and kissed my hand.

"Don't worry about me," I said with my best smile, which I was determined to use for Scott's sake.

Scott told her to wipe the look of horror off her face and stop scaring me half to death. I hadn't expected her to be so understanding about my feelings toward USIC, but I supposed our game of "Russian roulette," as we decided to call our lives, was the final touch that got her to stop being mad. I smiled at Owen gratefully, but he avoided my gaze with his usual humility.

I turned to Scott. "What qualifies as weird?"

He swallowed a huge gulp of juice and laid his glass down. "Don't expect a cakewalk. Withdrawal symptoms? Let's see. Dizziness, sleeplessness, various forms of digestive-tract upset, headaches, anxiety—"

I wondered if I weren't better off not knowing, and interrupted him with fake cheeriness. "Sounds like everything we've been told to watch out for anyway!" My lips stuck to my gums.

"Dry mouth," Scott added. He didn't miss a trick. I scowled at him while sipping water. "There's only two symptoms that would be alarming, might mean we should slow down the process. One would be double vision, and, drumroll ... hallucinations."

"I thought drugs made you hallucinate, not withdrawal from drugs," Rain said, spinning her glass of orange juice round and round on the table.

After a moment, Scott added, "Learn something new every day," but it seemed mostly to break an awkward silence interrupted only by the *sh-sh-sh* of Rain's spinning glass on the tablecloth.

She finally said, "I could stand it when Owen and I were fighting. That's normal. But when I start fighting with you, Cora? That's abnormal. And I can't stand it."

"Well, I've just been abnormal since we arrived here." I pooh-poohed her guilt over attacking me last night for distrusting her father. "I'm looking forward to the absence of drugs returning me to ... to my former glory."

That made Owen and Rain smile, though I could have done without the sarcastic blast from behind Scott's smile. I made myself a firm promise that I wouldn't blurt out any more unbecoming remarks, and I bit my lip just in case, despite the absence of Aleese all morning. I was improving already. No imaginings today of Mommie Dearest.

"So you know, my dad is not mad at you. He told me you chose to talk to Hodji Montu instead of him, and he's cool with that. He says Hodji's coming here. He says you can talk to Hodji whenever you want instead of him, and he really doesn't care, so long as you're not . . ." She let go of my hand and held both of hers out like she had huge imaginary weights in them. ". . . you're not shouldering burdens too heavy for you. That's his main concern."

I nodded, trying to find words of gratitude, which simply got drowned in feelings of inadequacy. I wondered if I would ever, ever be close to people. I sensed myself coming out of a shell, being more open, more honest. But that was different from feeling a oneness with the human race—something I'd lost when Oma died and Aleese and I had been left alone. I had often blamed it on Aleese when I felt lonely. But the truth is, I hadn't felt lonely as often as most people would have. Maybe she had just ignited some part of me that had always been there—for whatever reason.

"I wish I were just . . . a huggy person, who could run out there and just . . . hug your father."

I must have looked awful, because in response I got three versions of, "You don't have to do that."

"Just know that he's there for you, too," Rain said.

I was glad when Owen changed the subject—he not being

the world's huggiest person either. I supposed he wanted to ease my suffering, though there was no easy subject to jump to.

"Before we get too bummed out, let's talk about Tyler and the Kid. Rain mentioned to her dad that we should go to their funeral. It's going to be on Thursday, according to the latest horrendous TV report. He said no way, no funerals. But I think we should try to get him to change his mind."

We all nodded.

"I think Daddy will change his mind if the New York office tells the media the truth about them," Rain said. "If we're going to the funeral of two guys who tried hard to help save Trinity Falls, that makes a lot of sense. If we're going to the funeral of two high school dropouts who had a suicide pact, the media will wonder why. They just *have* to release the truth. That newscast Saturday night was horrid."

"I'd almost like to go either way," Owen said. "We can wear bags over our heads. But there's another problem with Thursday."

"Which is?" Rain asked.

He stared at her in amazement. "Dude, for all the times you got pissed at me for forgetting your birthday, now you can't even remember your own?"

"Ohh . . ." She bumped the back of her head against the chair. ". . . god. Can I do a funeral on my birthday? How big a person am I becoming?"

Scott's eyes went to me and stayed there. "If we don't get permission, I'm scared Cora will hitchhike. She was e-mailing with them about half an hour before their house blew."

They all watched me, waiting for me to short-circuit and smolder, I supposed. I may have, except, enter Aleese: *Don't waste your energy on grief. Save it for—*

I got a sense of impending dread, knowing I would have to spend time in the darkroom today, enlarging those prints for Mr. Tiger. And unless there was some way around it, I would be expected to go to the USIC "daily meeting" that Scott was so hyped about. After all, I'd been at the last one by his bedside and I hadn't objected to being included.

"Well, we'll celebrate my birthday on Friday, which is better anyway," Rain said. "I'll start calling people. We'll turn this house into party central. It's almost a must that we have a bash. Our friends are starting to think we're losers. I've had a cracked rib before. Field hockey. It never got me down. Today? We'll go shopping, Cora. We need party attire, and all my jeans are too loose. Marg'll take us."

"You really think?" Owen asked. "I think she wants you to relax for a few days . . . to watch for anything else that might be wrong."

Rain refused to let him ruin the mood. "Shopping is as therapeutic as drugs. Come on. Enough with the bummer talk."

"Maybe you shouldn't go to this funeral Thursday if you've got all this going on today and Friday," Scott suggested.

"When you gotta, you gotta," she said, and added defensively, "Some people thrive on activity. You ought to understand that."

"I do," he said. "And you do. They don't."

He gestured at me and Owen. Owen said mildly, "I'll . . . go today. So long as we can park close to the door. I'm four-star for once. Maybe I shouldn't waste it."

"Just skip shopping, for Cora's sake," Scott said. "Order your clothes online."

"I hate computers," Rain said. "We'll deal with it! One step at a time. Okay? As you say, 'Keep it simple.'"

"Cora shouldn't have this much activity," Scott insisted, and something about it irritated me, despite him speaking the truth.

Rain rolled her eyes. "So, she can rest up this morning, and we'll go shopping this afternoon."

"Actually, she can't," he said. "I need her this morning. For something."

I almost sighed aloud, thinking of making those prints . . . close-ups of potential terrorists.

"You need Cora for something related to this new 'badge' I understand you have?" Rain asked.

"Yes, related," he said.

"That's so *21 Jump Street*. Wow."

"Don't start with me, Rain."

"Scott, we were talking Saturday, sitting out by the pond . . . and . . ." She flipped her fingers back and forth from me to her to Owen. "Some people are not cut out to be you. I'd say *most* people are not. Cora . . . is not."

I wished she had let me say it myself. But being honest, I wouldn't have. He nodded hard, staring down into his lap. I sensed he didn't look my way so I wouldn't have to see his disappointment. "I know."

"She did everything in her power when you were out of it yesterday to influence my dad. It worked. Leave it at that," Rain said. "Most people don't want to chase down their mother's murderers. It's a scary and violent world out there. That's why we have police."

"I totally understand. Problem is, she's kind of into it up to her ears right now. Photos to develop for Mike Tiger. Maybe she could just do that much."

His eyes rose to meet mine.

"I can . . . do that much," I stumbled. It had come out worse than I wanted it to.

"Pictures of what?" Rain demanded impatiently.

Close-ups of potentially dangerous Richard Awalis. I put my fingers to my forehead, and I think they were shaking.

"Cora, you don't have to," Rain said quickly. "You're seventeen. Who would expect you to get, um, up to your eyebrows in . . . all that?"

"Shahzad and Tyler."

We turned to stare at Owen, who was flipping his napkin with his thumbs, staring into the middle of the table. "I can't stop thinking about those two guys."

Always looking to provide comfort, Rain put an arm around him and rested her chin on his shoulder. "As you said, we're not rocket scientists and computer jocks."

"No, we're not," he said. "Who are we?"

"We're . . . normal people from Trinity Falls, New Jersey," she answered.

"No. That's who we *were.*"

Scott's eyes wandered to me, then fell into his lap, but I felt the stab of judgment. Little Miss Stuck in Neutral. *Who am I?* If I had any clue, I probably wouldn't be getting all trembly over developing a few prints. *I need to find my father. I need to get over my fear of watching my mother's tapes and simply watch the one Jeremy told me to. Then I'll know.*

Rain sighed, leaning away from Owen, saying hesitantly, "I really hope I'm not going to be the bad guy here because I'm excited about a party."

"No . . . no," the brothers chimed.

A vibrating sensation jarred me, and I fumbled into my pocket, almost dropping the cell phone before figuring out how to open it. But I could feel myself starting to smile. "Hello?"

A voice outside the intenseness at this table was like a pause in a bombing. It gave some sense of being something instead of nothing.

"Much better," I answered Henry's question. "Thank you."

"I'm finished teaching at noon. I thought perhaps if you weren't up for learning the trails or looking for that darkroom that I could at least bring you some of my homemade raspberry lemonade. It's very healthy. I make it for faculty who failed to get their flu shots. They say it'll kill anthrax."

I giggled. Scott rolled his eyes.

"We could just sit on the porch around one o'clock, and I could show you the rest of the prints from Saturday. If you're up for it, that is."

To sit on the porch with a normal man and listen to the normal birds chirp. I realized I might be defining my own type of heaven. Huge parties left me feeling naked and exposed. I didn't expect Rain to understand this.

"That sounds really wonderful," I stammered, having cleared my throat and put in a couple of "ums." "But—"

"Cora..."

My head snapped to Scott, who was staring up at the ceiling, his fingers laced across his forehead like he was cutting another aftershock. His voice was edgy. "Whatever it is, tell him *yes.*"

"Just a minute..." I covered the phone with my palm, staring at Scott. My brain wouldn't move.

I stammered to him, "Why?"

"Because I said to."

Generous as he was being, he'd just ordered me about. And he was speaking for me again, only this time over another man.

"Because . . . you deserve it," he rearranged his words in a milder tone, though his eyes didn't fall from the ceiling.

He was thinking of Tyler and Shahzad. No, maybe *I* was thinking of Tyler and Shahzad. Maybe Aleese wasn't really saying, *"Do it! Do it! Do it!"* Maybe it was all me and I really wanted to make a decision for myself.

"I have some photos to develop this morning for a friend, but after that would be fine."

As I hung up, Rain showed her disappointment by pressing her lips into her knuckles with her elbow on the table.

"I'm sorry," I said sincerely, looking for forgiveness in her eyes. I found it quickly after highlighting the conversation.

She laughed, however uneasily. "Cora. How many weird things have you heard me say in the past three months? If you want to sit on the porch with an old geezer as opposed to going to the mall . . ."

It was a merciful, funny moment. The smile only made it halfway across my face. Scott, who had just called all my shots, stood up and walked out of the room without saying anything.

THIRTY-SIX

SCOTT EBERMAN
MONDAY, MAY 6, 2002
9:17 A.M.
BASEMENT

Yᴇsᴛᴇʀᴅᴀʏ HAD BEEN TOO TOUGH, and I hadn't been able to add any more thoughts to it—such as Cora's flowers arriving from Mr. Almost-Doctorate. But today I was faced with how I'd feel if some other guy showed up interested in her. I was pretty stunned at the threatened heartburn working its way through me. I guess maybe I'd thought I had all the time in the world. Maybe I'd even been dumb enough to think she'd play the invisible-girl role forever.

Yet I'd seen this happen a dozen times in high school. Girls you'd never notice suddenly graduate and don't only become noticeable—they become some sort of radiant. They come into themselves. Successful older men who weren't in high school couldn't care less if invisible is what they *were*. It's not what they *are*.

I didn't do anything wrong. I reminded myself of that quickly to ward off creepy feelings of stupidity. I had never come on to Cora, which would have been ludicrous—confusing for her and downright agonizing for me. I was definitely beyond stealing a kiss and feeling like I'd accomplished something. I sighed, big-time, letting it out in a breeze that sailed over the trees. *So . . . what? The answer is to let some other guy come over here and flirt with her?*

I felt around in my instincts and knew I had done the right thing. It was a good move, the perfect move, something about giving a girl enough rope and she'll be sure to hang herself. If I was appalled by her thinking of some other guy, the last thing I should do was try to stop it. People always want what they're told they shouldn't have.

What is up with this guy? He was a professor, smart and responsible, who had written the grant for this place. He knew our condition, and he knew he couldn't have her, couldn't touch her. *Is he stupid?*

I suddenly wondered if *I* was stupid. For me with girls, the Final Conquest had involved only One Thing. Maybe some guys were better people. Maybe they were on Owen's higher plane of existence. *Maybe Henry simply likes Cora for Cora and is willing to take a risk that she'll recover properly.*

I had heard my mother say so often about that next husband she never found, "Scott, I just want a man to like me for me. Not because I'm a lawyer. Not because I do so many charity cases that my bills are over my head. I don't need an admirer, and I don't need another Savior! I want a friend."

I heard her just fine until freshman year, when Amanda Stahl, a junior who lived next door to us, climbed in my bedroom window early one Saturday morning, blitzed out of her tree. She taught me any number of things, and left me with this hickey the size of my foot. It was an advertisement around school that got me a reputation that worked out kind of well. Amanda moved away, but I'd been programmed to think there were a thousand other Amandas out there, and if I just kept shuffling the deck, I would flip one now and again. I came up with so many Amandas that I never had the nerve to confess to Owen. The estimated figure alone would probably kill him. If Henry was deprogrammed, or had somehow managed not to get programmed, I felt more defenseless against that kind of finesse than about the fact that he was ten years older and wiser than me.

I was on the verge of overthinking. Definitely not something I was comfortable with. I was glad when Mike Tiger showed up.

"How'd you get the electric company out here so fast?" I asked, after I followed him into the basement. I still carried the exhaustion of an HH, so walking around and examining the wall sockets, new computer, and fax line in one of the servants' rooms gave me energy. These guys were fast movers. I could be one, too.

"We say we're USIC and that we have an 'immediate need,'" Mr. Tiger said, toasting me with his coffee mug. "They got here around noon yesterday, finished at two. They'll get weekend overtime and a government bonus for signing our hush-hush statements."

I watched the faint glow of green from a computer screen. "We have laptops. Not that I've used mine yet, but what's up with the tower? Isn't that slightly antiquated?"

"Laptops are too easy to steal and their hard drives are easier to hack. We Jersey guys haven't succumbed to them. For one, we intelligence agents are trained to carry around a microchip in our heads. We don't need extra memory," he boasted. Then his face grew serious. "Only the field guys like Hodji Montu are allowed laptops, and Imperial sweats bullets even about that." He looked at his watch. "Alan just ran up to the halfway point on the Parkway to pick up Hodji. You're going to have a guest for a while."

"So we heard. How's he doing?"

"Not great. He's on a grief leave. Don't expect him to be Mr. Personality, but this is the type of person this house is set up for, eh?"

"Right," I said. "We'll take care of him."

"If you want him to warm up, you'd do best not to say you're working for us. He might not put it together, the way he is. He sent in his resignation. We refused it. It was actually his idea to come down here, hang out with you guys."

I went into full medic mode, trying to remember what all they'd told me already, but it was buried in a morphine blur. "What are his injuries? Neck? Spine? Is he walking?"

"He's walking. He's got a broken nose, broken cheekbone, concussion, couple of black eyes. He flipped credentials and pulled a citizen out of his vehicle at the airport, and the car had no air bags. Just be polite. We can't vouch for his moods."

I watched through a small window as the car pulled up, and I said, "Wow," as Mike came to stand beside me. Montu's injuries were nothing I hadn't seen before, but you couldn't recognize him except for the cowboy hat. He got out of the car slowly, and Alan tried to take his arm, which he pulled away with some strong syllables I couldn't make out. He insisted on getting his own bags out of the trunk while Alan looked on helplessly.

"He really thinks he's a cowboy," Mike noted. "The New York squad said he never told them about the car accident part until after he ID'ed the bodies. That was more important to him. Let him sleep it off for a while. He hasn't slept at all."

Alan eventually came down with the new fax machine and a smile he must have pulled out of some angel's pocket.

"And what do you think of our setup?" he asked, gesturing at the primitive inner office. A bunch of office supplies lay on the servant-bed mattress. "Nobody can know about this computer down here—not even Rain and Owen. We'll keep everything locked. Meeting here instead of in Trinity saves Mike twenty minutes of driving each way, and after seeing what Hodji's going through, we need to do what we can to preserve family time. Yet I'm still a target, if you get my drift."

He was referring to the conversation he'd had with Rain on the porch about why he couldn't be here all the time. Seemed like USIC was suddenly bending its rules all over the place, between my "briefings" and this satellite office being placed in a weird yet functional spot. It was a shame two kids had to die before it happened.

Alan went on. "Your job actually comes with permission from On High—from James Imperial, but with limitations that you'd expect. Imperial did some fast paperwork, adding into our budget a certain type of clerk called a CC. That's 'classified clerical,' one that gets to handle and hear certain classified materials. It's sort of like being an agent without firearms, the age restrictions, and the eight weeks of training."

"I'll take what I can get," I said.

"At some point you'll have to sign all the paperwork and take an oath of secrecy. Then, it becomes a crime to repeat classified information to anyone on the outside. If you breach, you wouldn't just be fired, you'd be prosecuted. You sure you're up for this? Be careful what you wish for. I think the hardest thing for our agents is trying to stay connected with the rest of the world when there's an obvious disconnect. We have secrets we can't share with wives, can't breathe in our sleep. That's too hard for some. It's why I chose never to remarry. We'll tell you bits and pieces that you'll need to know, and I'll explain all of this to Cora, too."

I tried to keep my face blank, not tip them off that she was not in love with the idea of being included. She hid her emotions so well at times . . . *Well, it isn't my job to speak for her. Let Henry speak for her from here on in.*

"First, let's give you some basics." Alan gestured at some rocking chairs, and we sat in them. "Two things to know if you're going to help out USIC. First, be patient. Everything takes longer than you think it's going to take. Second, don't ask a lot of questions. We don't ask questions unless we need to know something that affects our little circle of responsibilities. It's better that way, that the left hand doesn't know what the right hand is doing. Because if one of us got picked up by a ShadowStrike operative—God forbid, but they're close by somewhere—we can't reveal under duress what we don't know."

Griffith's Landing. Right across the water. I can almost smell them from here. That brought on a thousand questions, but I had no trouble holding on to them as a shadow appeared over my right shoulder. My insides jumped, but the agents had seen Cora coming. The house was like a steel ship. Nothing made a sound.

So, she had presented herself for this meeting, too. This is how "give a girl enough rope" works. My generosity about

Henry made her feel guilty, and this was her idea of penance due. Or maybe I wasn't cutting her enough of a break. Maybe she thought of Shahzad and Tyler.

"Did you lock the door at the top of the stairs?" Alan asked.

"I pulled it tight, yes," she said.

"The security code is three-one-seven-one-five," he said. "Can you both remember that?"

I nodded. Three odds, out of order, with ones in between.

"If you leave that door open more than ten seconds, you'll set off the alarm. The alarm will ring in the house, and it will ring to our cell phones, too. That door stays closed at all costs. For one, Rain and Owen are, well, different from you two."

Cora sat and looked like she had at her mom's funeral—no emotion showing.

"I don't want them walking into potentially upsetting information that they haven't asked to hear. And second, the historical society still has access to this building. Take it from us: You wouldn't believe how people gossip, even people with a good deal of education and a sense of charity."

My eyes rolled Cora's way, and this time I made sure she saw it. *No Henry down here, babes. My cave.* I sensed uneasiness wafting off her, though she was better than I would have thought at maintaining her cool on the outside. For someone who could get visibly shaken at St. Ann's by accidentally hurting someone's feelings, she was pretty good in hearing lines like "they're close by." She hadn't missed it.

"You saw Hodji, I take it," Mike said to her.

"Yes." I thought she might shudder, but her eyebrows bounced up and down once. "He just refused a tranquilizer. Hmm..."

Under stress, she could even make them laugh. I wanted to shake her, rattle her, tell her she'd make a perfect CC. Obviously, from the years of living with her mother-the-drug-addict she had developed nerves of steel for facing anxious situations.

"He's keyed up right now," Alan agreed. "He'll conk out on his own, and you won't even have to remember he's here until tomorrow."

I took it their car ride wasn't a joyful reunion.

Alan whipped out a small notebook and settled in to his seat. "The purpose of Mike's and my daily briefing is to catch up on any news since the day before. He goes to meetings in North Jersey, sometimes New York, and if I'm not there, he tells me what went on. I stick down here and report to him on anything new from Trinity Falls, and now Griffith's Landing is in my jurisdiction, too."

He turned from us to look at Mike. "Yesterday we told the local police to stand down and have our CDC guys contain the monkey corpses—just as 'a routine precaution' after Trinity Falls. We tried two different containment procedures before packing them in a steel drum. It was oozing something that ate through the garbage bags they were found in." He swallowed hard. I didn't dare look at Cora.

"When we got it to our guy from the CDC, who's still at St. Ann's, he opened the drum in the morgue, and guess what was in it?"

"Pudding?" Mike asked. Cora cleared her throat.

"Try smoking liquid. Smoking liquid and bones. Anyway, we're telling the Humane Society that it's an emerging infectious strain of tularemia, which is close to the truth. It is an *intentionally mutated* strain of tularemia, a WMD. The cops, the Humane Society, they don't need to know it's a designer germ, created with the intention of wiping out a convention."

Cora didn't move. I tried not to ball up my fists.

"The CDC said the germ is beyond our worst nightmares. In humans, the strain has an incubation period of only two days. The strain that infected Tyler and Shahzad had an incubation period of ten days. This new one is a killer, and in the worst of ways, which we can verify by what happened to the lab monkeys. Monkeys and humans have absorption and digestive commonalities. Hence, we could assume that people's skin would bubble, they'd lose hair, and they'd grow disoriented, all while their insides are festering. The strain Tyler and Shahzad had didn't affect the major organs. For one, they neither drank it nor sat immersed in it. This one, if drunk, as in tap water, or absorbed through the skin, as in a ten-minute shower or a visit to the water park, will basically cause people to . . . to burn to death from the inside out. That's the bad news."

Cora cleared her throat again, and it took all I had not to reach out and touch her.

"I've got the good news," Mike said. "We've alerted the top executives at Ryder Fitzgerald that their convention may perhaps be a target. Nobody from RF is going to get hurt. Same with the owner of the amusement park. He's Mafiosi. Supposedly. At any rate, he's good at keeping secrets."

Alan turned to Cora and me. "Ryder Fitzgerald is the aeronautical engineering firm that was planning to hold a convention Memorial Day weekend at the Griffith's Landing Convention Center. We're certain it's the target," he said. "We're just not saying that to the local jurisdiction. Hodji Montu was on his cell with Imperial before he even forced his way off the delayed flight. The Kid and Tyler had sent him a major script between Omar and VaporStrike about monkey corpses being buried in Colony Two. Along with some other captured chatter, it's a *bingo*."

Cora stared into the wall with a look of horror so subtle that I'm sure I was the only one to get it. But if she wasn't sharing her little agonies, I was done digging for them.

Mike carried on. "I got us some backup as of today. Two dozen extra USIC agents from North Jersey and New York will be in Griffith's Landing by noon. They're unknowns to Shadow-Strike. They can be planted in public around Griffith's Landing and carry hidden cameras."

Alan nodded like he had expected that. "So, here's the game for now. We go there and figure out where these hoods are hiding. The chatter Tyler and Shahzad scripted implied strongly that there are foot soldiers in Griffith's Landing looking to ID some of us as part of their intelligence. So we have to be careful while *we're* trying to ID *them*. Fortunately, Griffith's Landing is not huge, like Wildwood and Ocean City. What they call the 'summer district' is a likely area—crowded, slightly run-down, with buildings on top of buildings. Lots of nooks and one-bedroom places to hide in."

"How are we going to find them?" I asked.

Mike pressed the tips of his fingers together, then spread his arms. "There's no easy way. We have a half-dozen photos of the guys we *think* might be involved, based on previous intelligence reports. We have old photos that go with the few names we have. Our agents will simply be out strolling, but they're strapped with small video cams, the size of an orange pip, and wires so we can hear each other. They'll be watching CVS, Superfresh, places like that. Everybody eats and bathes. We'll watch who strolls past the convention center. We'll watch who comes out of houses in the summer district."

"Sounds like a crapshoot," I said.

"It is. We're not gods. This is how we operate. But we've got a couple of pretty solid IDs, we think."

He clicked open his briefcase and took out a couple black-and-white eight-by-ten photos. One was a profile shot of a guy walking down a busy city street. From the older buildings in the background, I got an idea it was taken in Germany. The other shot was a full face of the guy Cora had shot on the boardwalk on Saturday. He held them up side by side.

"For one, we think this is a match," Mike said.

I bent forward to study the pictures, trying like hell to ignore my guilty conscience. I had pushed Cora up so close to a terrorist that she could have reached out and touched his face. I turned slowly to stare at her.

She was sitting with one foot under her, her hands dangling over the ends of the rocking chair's armrests. But it was like she had turned to stone. She responded to my staring by glancing into my lap and away again.

"We think this is Abdul Khadisha, or one of his many aliases. Comes to us via Egypt, via Kuwait, via Jordan chronologically, going backwards . . . most of these charming gentlemen no longer claim a homeland. Online, he's been using the log-in Pasco."

Mike then stuck a pile of older photos in Cora's lap. She merely glanced down without touching them.

"I'd like your job for the afternoon to be looking through

these and trying to match them with any faces in the photos you took yesterday."

Mike watched her, noticing how she hadn't moved, and she finally picked them up and began leafing through them.

"We're only giving you guys safe jobs," Alan said. "Very safe. I'm not going anywhere near the convention center or the amusement pier, because my face has been all over the TV. All I'm doing is sitting in the video truck and watching the live feed from the undercover agents who will be up there in the neighborhoods. Scott, I'd like your good eye. I've known you since you were a kid, know you never miss a trick. Look through those photos yourself, then see who you can ident from the truck with me."

I nodded, and with that, Cora passed me the photos, stood up in a trancelike state, and moved down the corridor to her photo lab. I coughed loudly to cover for her—it looked weird. But when we heard her flipping through items, it occurred to me that maybe she wasn't just freaking out.

We found her looking through the film by holding it up to her red light. A couple of the early shots she had taken were of two men who had been on the boardwalk. Their faces came clear in the third frame. In all four frames, they were watching the convention center, while everyone else on the boardwalk was drawn to the amusement park.

She pointed. "I shot these before we went into the pier, so they weren't with the ones I showed Mr. Tiger yesterday. It could be nothing, but when I was developing these, I remembered how one of the bigger rides had just made that huge noise of air releasing as the ride sprung straight downward. It was loud. It caught the attention of everyone. Except these two were deeply engaged in conversation, probably to do with the convention center."

Touché.

Mr. Tiger brought his face close, his eyes wide. "Can you make us prints of these? The first shot is pretty clear. We have specialists who can sometimes get a computer to confirm matches, even if the subjects change their features significantly."

"Yes."

"You've got a lot to do, Cora. But don't overload yourself. As soon as you start to get tired, walk away from it," Mr. Tiger said, but he didn't mention having any guys on his crew who could still develop old-fashioned film.

"She's got other plans this afternoon," I said, so easily it was downright vindictive, and I saw her throat bob outward as she swallowed a bucket of guilt. I felt torn. I was pushing her hard. I had put her in harm's way unintentionally. But I was losing patience with her scared-puppy routine when I could see she had some talents—everything from keeping secrets to being good under pressure to taking photos—that could help catch the guys who did this to us.

So she had been attacked by a terrorist in the ICU of St. Ann's. So, *I* had been in the ICU unit, too, with the guy who tried to inject her. *I* had helped wrestle him away from her. *I* had the presence of mind to disconnect her from everything that dripped, and all she had to do was lie there. She ought to remember that. And if she was mad about me putting her in danger, well, *get a grip*. Our health was in danger anyhow.

"Scott, after whatever medication it is you take next, you

can be gone for how long?" Alan asked, and I looked at my watch.

"I've got something in twenty minutes, and then I can be gone for three hours," I said, which wasn't exactly true. I had a semiharmless dose of sulfadiazine, a simple antibiotic that prevents brain inflammation, two hours later, but I figured I could get Marg to slip it to me to take on the road. What the State didn't know wouldn't hurt it.

"We'll leave then."

Mike and Alan headed back up the stairs, and I made a show of studying prints, pulling some down as if they were of special interest. Really, I just wanted to watch Cora squirm.

THIRTY-SEVEN

CORA HOLMAN
MONDAY, MAY 6, 2002
10:02 A.M.
DARKROOM

I DIDN'T WANT TO BE A COWARD, and in my heart of hearts, I sensed it was something other than fear that made my stomach twist into knots over all the sights and sounds and phrasing of a meeting like that. My relationship with my mother had been virtually nonexistent, and yet I wondered if my aversion to a life of adventure wasn't some sort of teenage rebellion against her. That would be something so normal as to be almost ironic. But with Scott absorbed by these photos, I could only shuffle through my thoughts like a deck of cards in the middle of fifty-two pickup.

I stood there and tried not to seethe—at Scott for studying gross pictures so hungrily, and at myself for not feeling at least some of the same.

Granted, I could work mechanically, develop photos of violent men, watch the images come forth without allowing myself to look into the men's eyes. I could force myself not to wonder if they were more of our attempted killers. I could serve my country. He wasn't the only one.

But I couldn't forgive myself for grabbing hold of a delusion back in the dining room—that it was all right for me to rely on him to get filthy with danger while I sat around sipping tea with a normal other-man. As much as I yearned to hear normal talk of normal college classes and normal picture taking while drinking normal homemade American lemonade, my guilt overwhelmed me.

I was trying to put on my surgical gloves, but my hands were trembling and sweating so badly that they kept sticking. I finally tossed them on the table, laying a hand over my mouth. Scott Eberman had seen me do a lot of things. I threw up in his lap once when he answered my nurse's buzzer before the nurse could. He was adjusting my IV, never broke form, and merely muttered "oops" when it happened. But he hadn't seen me totally cry since the day I was first hospitalized. He was watching me now, frozen with a pile of prints in his hands, waiting for something entertaining to evolve.

Would you mind leaving, please? The words wouldn't form in my throat. I sensed some compassion in his sudden slump, which only made me feel worse. He put down the prints and patiently picked up one glove, blew into it until it looked like a five-fingered balloon, and let the air out again. He held it open, and my trembling fingers slid in easily.

"Even doctors get nervous and out of sorts," he said.

He blew up the other, and as my fingers slid in, my heart dissolved into a puddle. I cried loudly, and I pitched into him, grabbing him tightly around the waist and laying my head on his chest.

My Perfect Ten little head pats of the past diminished, as he wrapped me up in his arms, rubbed my back for comfort, and laid a kiss on the top of my head. I didn't deserve it, and again the picture flooded my mind of sitting idly on a porch with Henry, who suddenly had as much appeal as week-old birthday cake. Aleese cackled with joy off in the corner as I sniffed like a big baby. I merely wanted to restore my dignity, but efforts to speak charged out like a gunned engine. "Will you not touch me, please!"

He backed away with his hands in the air, like I was holding a gun, and fell back against the counter. "Women!" he whispered in awe. "I am never getting married."

"Me neither."

He put his hand down on the counter a little too hard. Now he was angry. I stood there and absorbed his lecture, a deserved payback.

"You know what, Cora? You might be right about yourself. I'll find somebody to put up with me when all of this is a spark in my memory. You? Underneath the sweetness routine, you've got this rigid pride thing going on . . . god forbid you should turn out even a drop like your mother. God forbid you get close to anybody. If you so much as let some guy touch you, you might go down like a sub like she did and drop a baby you don't want into this world."

A more together person might have smacked him. But I choked on it, hiccupping and feeling ludicrous. I had to wonder what Scott's life had been like—what there was about him or people in general I didn't understand—because he simply turned and banged prints together. Like hearing a girl sniff and snort and hiccup was *normal.*

After an endless minute he reached for a box of tissues I'd brought down here the first day and held one out to me with two fingers.

"I'm not a child," I said, and crossed my arms.

"I'm a medic! I hand out tissues. Get over yourself."

I reached past him for my own tissue and blew intensely until I had blown away the urge to keep crying.

He kicked the ground with the toe of his sneaker. "I dragged you into this USIC stuff. I know it's not you, and you're entitled to be how you are, Cora."

I tried to not ask the question. But it flew out anyway. "Do you think any of those men in the photo recognized us from *People* magazine?"

"Who, that Abdul Khadisha?"

Leave it to him to remember an unfamiliar name. I'd been fixated on the face. I nodded.

"Just shoot me." He leaned down guiltily with his elbows on the table.

"I don't want you to feel guilty. I just want to know."

"Why? Can we just keep it real? We could all be dead by August. How would you like to go out, Cora? With a bang, or in a mountain of snotty tissues?"

I didn't necessarily want to go out with a bang, if going out was what I faced. I supposed I wanted to go out on my own terms. These weren't mine. They were his. In some twisted way, they were Aleese's.

He came back over to me. "Finish these photos and then go off and enjoy yourself. You need it. God. Look at you shake." He lifted my fingers under his, and they were trembling. I would have written it off to crying. "It's the Nabilone withdrawal.

You'll lie down to sleep tonight and think you're on a vibrating bed. It won't hurt you, though. If that's the worst you get, consider yourself lucky."

He reached onto the table where my mask lay, offering me a lecture on not breathing the chemicals. He snapped the mask over my face. Playing father eased his conscience, so I simply let him.

"What really bad symptoms should I be looking for again?" I asked, feeling my eyes refilling. He was leaving. Whatever I'd felt for Henry was behind some gray mist.

He sighed, glancing at his watch. "Double vision and hallucinations. And I'll be back in three hours."

He pinched my cheeks affectionately and pulled his hands away again, as if expecting me to lash out. But I didn't. I reached for the sleeves of his T-shirt, twisting them in agony, and I suppose he was in the same vulnerable state. He wrapped his hands around my back again and appealed to the ceiling, saying, "I'm going to try to start being a better person, okay? Tomorrow."

His hands moved to my face and pulled it upward. He kissed me firmly on top of the mask until the fabric crumbled and I felt the pressure on my lips. The sudden desire to claw the thing away and dive into the realities beyond it was almost overwhelming. But the floor gave way, or so it seemed, and it was his arm holding me up by the small of my back that kept me from plummeting. He pulled his face away and stared, some victory smirk slowly working his lazy bottom lip as he set me on my feet. He let go of me when I was leaning firmly against the counter.

"You're horrible," I breathed, mortified at my knees for betraying me.

"No, *you're* horrible. You caused that." He backed away, staring at my hand on my thumping chest, which I balled into a fist so he wouldn't see it shaking. But he was silently laughing as he walked backwards through the door frame. I couldn't tell whether he was still congratulating himself or laughing in honest awe over the effect he could have on a girl who hadn't been kissed since some seventh grade closet game.

"Joking aside"—Scott's mature tone returned—"you'll be down here by yourself. You can't trip over anything. You can't fall. Do you want me to tell Hodji he has to come down here with you?"

"Do I look like I need a babysitter?"

I wished I'd put it as a statement instead of a question. He finally pulled the door shut after I studied the images he'd tossed on the counter for a good thirty seconds. I figured he laughed all the way upstairs.

THIRTY-EIGHT

OWEN EBERMAN
MONDAY, MAY 6, 2002
10:40 A.M.
RAIN'S BEDROOM

Rain went alone to the CVS with Marg, but even with that short a trip I parked myself on the sofa in the parlor and waited for the car to come back. Crazy, I know. But she had left in some giddy mood, and I knew it was mostly to ward off depressing thoughts of either her liver worries or the Kid and Tyler, or Cora starting a different drug already.

I realized it was the first time in months she had been more than fifty feet from me. And with my brother off the property and Cora in the basement behind a locked door, I felt anxious, like something awful was going to happen to one of them. And I kept to my resolve to do whatever Rain wanted today without fighting with her.

But even I have my limits. Ten minutes after she came back, I was parked on her bed, and she was filing my nails. No matter how much I prayed for strength to endure, I could feel no help whatsoever to get me through . . . a manicure. She was threatening to put this clear stuff on them that she swore would not show at all, though it came in a nail-polish bottle with one of those brushy things sticking straight down into it.

I bet I was standing in proxy for Cora. She owed me an apology, because at this point I was totally scared Rain would try to mascara my eyelashes next.

"Glad my hair's short right now," I noted. "No point in getting out the curling iron."

"Relax! Hands are a transgender thing right now! There's always guys in the nail salon these days."

"Yeah. And when these same guys get in car wrecks and Scott cuts their jeans off in the ambulance, they're wearing their mother's underwear."

"Don't be silly." She reached for the bottle.

"Naw!" I turned over, half on my stomach, hiding both hands under me.

"Yaw! Get up."

"Naw."

"I'll paint your toenails."

"I'll fart on your head."

She lay slowly backwards on the bed with a yawn, unwilling to wrestle for my arm. I looked. "Are you all right?"

She finished her yawn, watching me. "Stop asking me that."

I slowly leaned back on her pillows again, watching her eyelids relaxing, feeling slightly safe. She would either take a nap or think of something else quickly to amuse herself. I wondered what was on the tube. If I lay really still, she might nap out, and then I could leave without drawing attention to myself.

Her eyes snapped open, unfortunately. "I know. Something all guys do these days."

"Oh god . . ."

"We can whiten your teeth."

Please, God.

"Really. I was going to do it to myself, but we can do yours now and I'll get more tomorrow, which will give me another excuse to go to the store. We really should whiten our teeth, Owen. You know how medicine makes your teeth go dull? Well, it's starting to happen to us. I've been meaning to tell you."

I'm not a vain guy, but there's something about teeth. You don't want them grody. I got up and went to the mirror over her dresser, baring my teeth to my gums. I'd had this obsession when I was eleven. I thought my teeth were turning yellow. Every time I flashed my teeth in the mirror, they would be bright yellow.

"They're white," Mom would say. *"It's your imagination."*

And Scott would start in all "What's her name?" which you don't want to hear, so I quit mentioning it and eventually forgot about it. But every once in a while, I would see yellow teeth in the mirror.

"See?" Rain said. "They're going dull."

I hoped she was joking. But they looked kind of yellow. *Ohhhh god.* I collapsed back down on her bed. "What do I have to do?"

So, two minutes later I was staring at the wall while drooling behind some Colgate football mouthpiece, praying she wouldn't think of some other way to beautify me, because I couldn't very well tell her off like this.

She sat cross-legged beside me, just talking on and on, not caring that I couldn't answer. It was easy stuff. Jeanine this, calories that, field hockey this. She'd give it a pause until another thought struck her, not bothered by the silences.

"Can I ask you a personal question?" she asked.

I almost laughed. I *really had* farted on her head once, and not as long ago as you might hope. Sophomore year. She kept trying to do as much to me while I was watching the Cubs versus the Phillies, tie score, bottom of the eighth. She's a White Sox fan just to goad me. She kept grunting and moaning and carrying on, then saying nothing would come out. I'd thought, *I'll put "an end" to this.*

I nodded hard, wondering what between us was left to be personal.

"Are you acquainted with the five girlfriends on your right hand?"

I collapsed backwards on the pillows like I'd been shot.

"Seriously." She giggled. "I want to know."

I started shaking my head slowly back and forth and back and forth. This conversation would not happen.

"I *need* to know!"

And back and forth.

"I *know* you are."

So then, why are you asking? I stopped shaking my head, and she took that as the confession she needed to continue.

"Have you been acquainted with your five girlfriends since we came up here?"

"MMMtglemtlemmemmemem." I pulled the thing out of my mouth and drooled down the front of my T-shirt. "I wouldn't tell you if I had."

"Oh. So you *have.*"

"MMmmMM!" I could not believe she even thought that.

"It's just that yesterday afternoon and today, you're feeling pretty good, so . . ."

I took the thing out again, drooling ferociously in awe. "Rain! We've only been here three days."

"So? I thought boys did that at every available opportunity. Like every day."

"That's crazy. Well, maybe Dempsey does. We're all different, okay?"

"Put that back in your mouth. You're drowning my comforter."

I did, feeling eaten alive.

"So, like, what do you think about? Naked girls?" she asked.

"Mm-mm." End of discussion.

"Are they real girls? Or do you make them up, and that way you don't have to look somebody in the eye in the school corridors the next day?"

I took the thing out and tried not drooling so hard this time. "Rain, get to the punch line. Some things you just don't talk about, okay?"

"Don't be such a prude! Who else am I going to ask? Cora? Here's my problem. I tried my boyfriends on my right hand. Nothing happens. I'm doing something wrong."

I sat forward in case I laughed totally and gagged myself. I could see she was really needing to get a load off her chest, but I pounded the mattress, these laughs coming up all "Hmm hmm hmm."

I wanted to say I thought it was probably different for guys and girls, that maybe girls had to think harder or something. But I figured she would know that, and I didn't want to drool over a redundancy. And I didn't get what she wanted from me. I was not all that familiar with female anatomy. It's one thing to have "wandered downstairs" once or twice, and it's another to explain the fuse box. I felt that female anatomy was a lot like Dempsey's mom's new stovetop. It's flat and there's no huge buttons, so you can't tell where the heat is until you sit yourself up there and you realize the burner's on. (True story. Happened to Dobbins two days after Mrs. Dempsey bought that thing. I will never, ever, ever have one of those stoves in my house.) And it's not like I'd ever had a centerfold of some medical/sex journal shoved in my face detailing some girl's privates with everything numbered and labeled with those italic captions. *What is she thinking?*

And yet, she was right that she couldn't ask Cora. Cora might sympathize a moment before passing out in abject terror of a totally personal subject. It seems weird, but Jeanine probably didn't know squat. She could barely remember what happened the next day after each time she drank. Still, I probably would have told Rain to go pound sand, I was not discussing this, except this grand idea sort of went off in my head. It had to do with these new bathrooms they put in here. In my house, our bathroom had been really run-down, in need of new tiles and all this stuff. Our shower had been from the 1970s.

I glanced out into the corridor to make sure Mr. Montu wasn't waking up and standing there. But the hall was clear, and with Rain waiting for an answer without even breathing, I could hear him snoring softly on the floor above us.

I pulled the mouthpiece out. "Try that new thingermabob. The showerhead that's on the six-foot hose." I put it back in.

She looked at me like I was crazy and then collapsed over

sideways on the bed, laughing in fits. *It's only a riot when I get personal.*

"Mmm?" *Well?*

"But every time I get in the shower, you will wonder what's going on!"

Mouthpiece out. I couldn't resist. "Yeah, especially if you use up all the hot water while trying to figure yourself out." Mouthpiece in. Mouthpiece out. "When we hear Marg scream 'cuz there's a thousand-dollar water bill—"

"I cannot believe you are talking to me about the shower!"

I collapsed yet again, defeated. There was no winning in this situation.

"And what if it doesn't work?"

Mouthpiece out. I didn't like her tone. "We've been over this. Don't look at me to solve your problems." I hadn't told her about the lecture I'd gotten from Dan Hadley two days before Nurse Haley. *Do not touch her* had been the point. He was very, very big on the *do not touch* lectures to our whole Young Life group, about pregnancies ruining lives, abortions hiding emotional shocks that can jump out at you, like, twenty years later. He's yet another adult who had been worried about me and Rain up here.

He wasn't here to watch her face turn putrid.

"Pervert," she said. "I was strung out yesterday when I tried to kiss you. I'm not *that* desperate." Then she started moving back and forth like a pendulum, her eyes on my mouth. "Ohmygosh. Take that thing out again."

"Mmm-mmm."

She was totally staring. "No, take it out! Your teeth! You're not going to believe this."

I still had five minutes to go but went slowly to the bathroom, rinsed fifteen times, came back and shined my teeth in the mirror. They were totally white. Like, shining, searing *white*.

"They don't even look like teeth!" I said in horror.

"They look great! Ohmygosh. You'll have the bestest smile at my birthday. Why didn't we think to do this before *People* came?"

Like I needed even more of those crazy cavegirl get-well cards. I started to say to her, "Stand back, and don't get any dumb ideas." Not that she would.

I never said it. Some weird sound made me think a bell was ringing. Then I realized it was Cora, somewhere far off like the basement, screaming her fool head off.

THIRTY-NINE

I DROVE TO GRIFFITH'S LANDING WITH ALAN, wondering if my great feeling came from Cora pitching backwards when I first let go of her in the basement or from the notion that I was actually going to work. If yesterday was awful, today was fantastic. Life was like that. I'd enjoy today while it was today.

I lay my head on the headrest and put my energy in preservation mode. My throat was still bothering me, and I knew pacing myself would be a necessity. Alan drove to a supermarket parking lot, which was more blacktop than cars as the summer hadn't started yet, and parked near the street. We were dressed in jeans and polo shirts, and he put on a baseball cap and shades. I was already wearing my shades.

"Keep your head down, Mr. Famous, just in case," he said, "and follow me."

We headed across the parking lot to where a black van was parked, with a sign that read SUITOR'S PLUMBING on the door. It looked pretty banged up. When we ducked inside, the sight just about gave me whiplash. There were eight monitors on one wall—some on, some bleeping sand—and a thousand wires.

A guy who looked only about a few years older than me had been in the driver's seat reading the newspaper. Alan introduced him only as Nigel, a new agent from Washington.

"Sorry, no seat belts," Alan said, and he pulled a chair off a stack of four chairs in the far back corner and handed it to me. It was hard to get all four legs on the floor without hitting any cables, but as soon as we were sitting, Nigel took off.

Alan laid the pile of old pictures—suspected members of ShadowStrike—in my lap and said, "Start looking through these. Agents on the street already have them memorized. We'll be listening for our guys to make any idents and watching them tail anyone suspicious . . . and don't expect miracles."

The only new photo was Cora's, the close-up of one startled guy. Under it was written with a Sharpie pen in black, **Log-in: Pasco. Name: Unknown. Alias: Abdul Khadisha.** I was amazed at how typically American he looked—the biggest problem being there was no typical American look. But he could have been any little kid's granddad. I tried to memorize his features—circular face, curly hair, balding on top, graying on the sides, hazel eyes, thick bottom lip, thin top lip. While I did the same with the other eight photos, all of which had names and even some aliases scrawled beneath them, Alan began playing with the monitors and talking to agents he was hearing on headsets.

I glanced up once to see the Ferris wheel from the Icon Pier three or four blocks to our left. This was a primitive operation in enough ways to startle me. Alan had a roll of masking tape and a stack of index cards in his lap. He would say things into his headset like, "Mike, do a three-sixty . . . again . . . again," and he'd pick up the monitor that showed three complete circles from the view of someone walking on the street. He'd mark MIKE on the index card and say, "Mike, your number today is four." He'd tape the index card in front of the monitor marked 4 with "Mike" and "#4" scrawled onto it.

He did this with eight agents, some on the street, some on the boardwalk, one in front of the Superfresh where we'd just come from, and one in front of the CVS. Nigel had a laptop and clicked a few lines every time Alan would ident an agent. Gauging from the height shown in the monitors, I gathered these guys had the cameras hidden in their collars or in some button on their shirts. I didn't ask questions. But people strolled by them occasionally, and we were looking into their shoulders.

I began watching the monitors with Alan after every picture was stuck in my head and ignored a feeling of seasickness as their constant movement got behind my eyes. Alan would call them "Four" or "Six" and chatter with them, giving me the impression the agents were bored but used to it. Alan would laugh and send back what sounded like a punch line, though I couldn't hear the jokes. This went on for an hour and ten minutes. A preschool passed by Agent Six, two teachers bringing small children in a double line up to the boardwalk. A lot more women passed than men, and since none of the pictures I'd been shown were women, I let my eyes fall to those monitors where men passed. None of them had the facial features I'd memorized while trying to ignore hair, which could easily be changed.

"Seven, I'm alive, I'm alive," Alan finally said, and I watched the corresponding monitor as Agent Seven started to follow what I thought was a teenager at first. It was a little skinny guy in an oversize sweatshirt and baggy jeans. I could only see the back of his head at first. I watched him move farther down the street, until Agent Seven began following. The skinny guy stopped at a trash can and peeled a banana into it, finally glancing straight at the monitor. That's when I recognized his features as similar to one of my photos, a young suspect named Ibrahim Kansi. The agent passed him by and uttered something that made Alan say into the headset, "Six, pick up suspect Kansi on Ocean and Belmont."

Agent Seven kept going, and I watched Six's monitor as the agent turned a corner and caught the guy peeling the banana from the other side. He was far off. I wondered if the agents were sure it was the same guy as the one in the photos. Alan got his face within a foot of the monitor, slowly shaking his head back and forth, like he was doubtful.

I was, too. Just from the headshot, I would have put Ibrahim Kansi at about five-foot-nine, and this man was more like five-foot-two, and it made me respectful of the challenges intelligence had in making accurate idents.

As Agent Six strolled closer, Alan glanced at me. "What do you think?"

But the agent was on the far side of the street, and the suspect stood by the trash can down in the left corner of the monitor. As soon as I could focus in on the man's face, the agent bent down to tie his shoe, and I was faced with sidewalk and a sneaker toe. It almost made me pitch forward in the chair.

"All I could see is he's got the same nose," I said, and Alan, now standing, laid a hand on my shoulder.

"We'll see if he's meeting someone. That always helps. Seven, circle back around and get the banana peel. Can we fingerprint a banana peel?" Seven must have said something funny about DNA, because Alan laughed and replied, "If you find any bite marks, you get a bonus."

The suspect walked on down the street again, chewing and licking his fingers, a plethora of DNA and fingerprints and information that we couldn't touch. It was frustrating. Eventually the agent followed, and the guy turned into an apartment building, where he knocked instead of pulling out a key. It was impossible to see who let him in.

"Note address: seventeen fifty-one Belmont, bottom floor," Alan said, and Nigel's keypad clattered. We watched Agent Six sit somewhere, and a newspaper kept flying up into the bottom of the screen.

Another twenty minutes passed. I was starting to understand the level of patience these guys needed. The agents up on the boardwalk were getting no hits, and one look-alive at the CVS turned out not to be a match.

Agent Five had switched with Agent Six, I understood from Alan's chatter, and finally the door to the apartment opened on monitor five. The suspect came out with another man, whom I recognized immediately.

"That's Pasco," I said.

"Five, you might have another *bingo*," Alan said more calmly than I would have expected, and I watched as the two headed west on Belmont Avenue for a couple of blocks, talking away.

My desire to see them knocked to the concrete was eating me alive. "Are you going to arrest them today?"

"I hope we won't have to make any arrests until we're up to our necks in evidence. We may just be getting started. Our next step is to tap their phones, wire their premises. It'll be a couple of weeks, unless we see them folding up the op. We need evidence. Lots of it."

The shorter guy put his hands in his pockets at one point, which pulled up the back of his sweatshirt, and I noticed some sort of short club in his back pocket with something shiny on top.

I leaned into the monitor. "What is that?" I touched the image of the club with the Sharpie.

"Five, get closer," Alan said, which gave me some flinch-worthy sense of power, as I had only been curious. The agent sped up until he was maybe twenty feet behind. The shiny thing was a chain that ran from the top of this little billy club to a matching club that was down deeper in the guy's pocket.

"Looks like nunchucks," Alan said. "It's a martial arts weapon. A properly trained guy can flip those around and hit someone before they even know they're being attacked. Five, is that a set of nunchucks?"

The agent turned while the suspects crossed the street to the Superfresh, but Alan repeated for me, "Affirmative. Note that Ibrahim Kansi might have martial arts capabilities."

Nigel now sat sideways with the laptop on his legs. He clattered a note.

"Three, pick them up and follow them into the Superfresh," Alan said, and the scene on monitor three moved through an alley, then the parking lot, and picked up the two men. They passed by Alan's car and suddenly banged into each other.

Alan sighed. "Hmm. My car was just made."

I watched, intrigued, as the two stared at the license plate, took a step back almost simultaneously, and then headed into the store, looking over both shoulders just once.

"Isn't that bad?" I asked.

"Some of the chatter from the Kid implied that they were wise to us already. It doesn't mean they'll go into retreat. They'll just be extra careful. So will we. Three, go into the store ahead of them."

I guess it's normal to think of your own house as the center of the universe in a case like this, but I couldn't help thinking of how Alan's car had been parked outside the Kellerton House so often. Obviously, there were many ways to get an initial ident on his car, but I thought of him telling Rain that he was a target. I thought of dead animals turning up here, turning up six feet from our property.

I could feel my ire rise and start to smolder out my ears, though I kept telling myself I could be way off. And I watched the monitor as the agent passed these guys in the frozen-food aisle, loading something like a giant box of burritos into a pushcart. The agent picked out some frozen meatballs and passed the two again an aisle or two later while they dropped a tube of Colgate into their cart.

Alan had been speaking into the headset pretty steadily, and I realized suddenly that there were three agents in the Superfresh, and two outside. I looked at the different monitors to find the suspects on this one and then that one. It was like a poorly choreographed square dance, a do-si-do to make you dizzy if you let it. I walked in Cora's skin for a moment. There is just something over-the-top about seeing what terrorists eat and what they use to brush their teeth with. It's some shit you'd rather not see that makes them all too human.

Alan didn't seem awed by anything. He just choreographed the agents until another showed up outside, making the total at the Superfresh six.

His cell phone rang. He pulled it from his pocket and looked confused for a moment. "The alarm to the basement is going off at the Kellerton House. Let me make sure it's just a computer glitch."

He handed his headset over to Nigel, who switched places with him and watched the screens but said very little. Concerned about Cora being down there alone, I watched tensely as Alan speed-dialed the house. He got the voice mail and re-dialed three times before I flinched at a rap on the side of the van. It turned out to be Mike Tiger waving a cell phone in the passenger window.

Alan hit the UNLOCK button, and Mike jumped into the seat.

"I got Marg. Stop calling her now," he said to us, then, into the cell phone, "What's going on?" Mike listened for a long time. "Did you relock the door? . . . Already? Thanks."

He hung up. "Cora Holman had some sort of episode down in the basement. Hallucination, Marg said. She screamed and froze so nobody could get to her. She's got a boyfriend or something?"

"A . . . friend, Henry," I stammered. "Did she faint? Did she fall?"

"I don't know."

"So . . . what?" I asked, too loudly. "She's on enough blood thinner to make an elephant hemorrhage. She can't be falling—"

"Relax. That friend of hers had come over, and he heard her. Since the door was locked, he kicked it in and ran down to help. And Hodji, who had finally gone to sleep, heard the alarm and found a USIC security-code box by a kicked-in door. And when he discovered a stranger down there, he tackled the guy and got him in a body lock. It was a mess, but Marg said she's—"

I grabbed Mike's cell out of his hand and called Marg back.

"Did she fall?" I asked.

"No. She's confused and upset," Marg said, "but both men say she was standing straight up."

I heaved a sigh and glanced at my watch. I had to get back myself, but the idea of jumping to Alan's car when the suspects who saw it were about to walk out of the store gave me pause.

"She hallucinated?" I asked, trying to clear my head.

"Yes. Her mother and some pond creature. Her mother was telling her to come in the water even though she couldn't swim. She's shaken up."

It's normal to think your hallucinations are real, but that one sounded over-the-top. Most people hallucinate a chair moving a foot by itself or changing colors from red to blue. "Should we call the medication switch off?"

I still hadn't apologized for my outburst on Saturday. I put it on the top of my list of things to do as her levelheaded answer got me breathing slightly normally again. "I'd be more worried about white-cell counts and Q3 levels rebuilding than a withdrawal effect. Obviously, it's one we wish she didn't have, but it's not compromising her health."

Not unless she hallucinates me or Marg telling her to follow us out the window and fly.

Alan handed me the keys to his car. We'd already made arrangements for me to take his car back alone if I had to leave before him.

"You want me to go jump in your car after those guys just made it?" I said.

"They haven't even gotten to the checkout line yet. Just move quickly. The parking lot is crawling with agents. You're perfectly safe."

I looked at the monitors one more time, and it was like playing God, being able to know where your threat is every second. They were buying shredded wheat. My shades had been on the top of my head, and I lowered them. I still had Marg as I stepped out. Mike walked along beside me as I talked to her.

"Who's with her until I get there?"

"Henry," she said. "He and Hodji formed an instant friendship after their run-in. They're both accomplished chess players. Cora wants to learn to keep her mind occupied the next few days."

Games of the intelligentsia. I felt my problems deepening.

Mike had his fingers in my back, which meant to pick up speed; they were probably in the checkout line.

"Shit," I said, unable to think. "Just stay with her until I get there. *Don't* leave her alone. Not even with that guy."

"I've got a nineteen- and a twenty-year-old and both dislike me thoroughly, but that's because I was a good mother. I'll be ten feet away in the corridor, folding wash, darling."

"Hey, Marg?" I decided I shouldn't wait. "I'm really, really sorry about Saturday."

"You have nothing to apologize for. You deserve a medal. No harm done."

"If you say so." I snapped the phone shut and handed it to Mike with a grin. In spite of it all, *Marg likes me better than Henry.* Considering Henry was educated, talented, well-spoken, thoughtful, and now, as we could see, gallant, I couldn't guess why she felt that way. But it put a bounce in my step that I needed anyway.

I got to the parking lot, and between faces in cars reading newspapers, a female agent putting groceries in a trunk, a guy on a bicycle, and a guy holding the door of Alan's USIC car open and beckoning to me, I realized the place was indeed crawling. I got in and he slammed the door. I took off quickly without saying anything.

FORTY

CORA HOLMAN
MONDAY, MAY 6, 2002
12:55 P.M.
HER BEDROOM

I LAY IN BED, staring into the noon sunrays streaming in my window, trying to put the memory of the darkened basement behind me. Rain and Owen spent a few minutes making a fuss over me, asking all sorts of questions, and I just didn't have the answers to even the simplest ones. For example, Rain asked if I "felt okay." I felt outside of myself, airy, like I'd drifted up to the ceiling and was watching all of this. I didn't know how to make that sound plausible.

I felt so many things—confusion, embarrassment, exhaustion, dizziness from god knows what—but mostly embarrassment. I kept hearing Henry's yell of shock as he himself had been attacked from behind. And after one look at Mr. Montu's black and blue face in the red lighting of the darkroom, I had thought it was chapter two of my hallucination.

I needed to be alone to collect myself. And yet, I was afraid to be alone to face what god-awful imaginary thing I might experience next. Rain and Owen finally left, and Marg watched me as I sent her from the room, her hand on the doorknob in a pensive way.

"You might try crying," she said blandly. "It's perfectly all right."

"Thanks, I've had my jag for the day."

"You're switching medications. You're entitled," she insisted. Scott hadn't mentioned crying as a symptom of withdrawal. I couldn't simply cry on demand. I was struck with the image of trying to urinate in public. "Please. I really need to be alone now."

I suppose she wasn't stupid. She reappeared five minutes later with a cup of tea, telling me I could hold the breakable cup and hot liquid only if I agreed to have some company. When I said Henry could come up, he appeared from over her shoulder. I supposed he had been standing by the door frame, listening to make sure I was all right, the entire time Marg was making tea.

I put a hand over my eyes, feeling like a dimwit. The idea that he was even here ought to get him nominated for sainthood. He had a black and blue mark under his right eyebrow from Mr. Montu tackling him.

"Henry. I'm so sorry," I managed, though it clanged through my aching head in its emptiness.

"Please don't worry," he insisted. "It was not a big deal. As the saying goes, you ought to see the other guy."

Mr. Montu was behind him, and I found the grin in his black and blue face. My laugh was too loud, a testament to my nerves.

"Let me do the apologizing," he said. "It seems I can send in all the letters of resignation to USIC that I want, and somehow ... I'm still USIC."

His smile dimmed, and my heart went out. Marg had confided his situation before he arrived, so I didn't ask the wrong questions about him going through a terrible divorce.

"We're glad you're here, Mr. Montu," I said, wishing I could think of more creative words.

"Hodji. Please. Everyone ... called me Hodji."

He had said "called" and not "calls," which made me think of the Kid and Tyler.

"I hope you can go back to sleep," I said. I noticed he had his cell phone in his hand and a look in his swollen eyes that was alert and not very sleepy. Maybe "alert" was the wrong word. He looked agitated. It was just a spark in his eyes contrasting his otherwise calm demeanor.

"I might be able to ... if I can sleep on the couch downstairs. In Pakistan, I used to sleep on a straw mattress on the floor. I snore badly right now. Do you care?"

I remembered some things about hospice care I had heard when we first came here, when we thought at least a dozen other Stage Three Q3s might be coming with us. We had been warned that people who are sick have all different needs, and it would be good therapy for all of us to cater to the needs of the others.

"Scott and Owen both snore sometimes," I informed him. "Rain calls it a lullaby. Just be comfortable."

With that, his cell phone rang, and to my amazement, he almost jumped. The phone flew an inch out of his hand, and he caught it haphazardly and flipped it to his ear.

"What, Alicia?" he demanded, mechanically turning and

clomping down the stairs. "Why do you need the medicine cabinet cleaned out by tomorrow? I'm in New Jersey! I've been in a car accident, for Pete's sake . . . Then throw everything out! Where's Twain? . . . Why not?"

I dropped my arm over my face, primarily out of frustration for his words, and secondarily to put some heat on my pounding head. Heat could sometimes cut the onslaught of a Headache from Hell.

"I guess he was hoping that was his son," I muttered. I seemed to remember hearing that his name was Twain and he was a good student.

Henry was pouring tea into a cup for himself from the tray Marg had left at the foot of the bed. I could hear it, could smell it. I raised my arm to look at him, and the rays of sunlight were bathing him. A ring of light glowed off his wavy hair, making him appear angelic. This set my teeth on edge again. In spite of all that logic would dictate, I found myself wondering if I were dreaming him. *What if he disappears? Jumps into my closet, never to reappear? What if Marg comes in and tells me he left an hour ago?*

As he brought his cup closer, I reached out tenuously, touching his wrist with a sweaty hand. He wrapped his hand around mine, reassuringly.

"Please don't laugh. But for a moment, I thought you might be imaginary." I swallowed a mouthful of metallic saliva, generally a precursor to our headaches.

"It's me. The real thing. I'm right here . . ." He sat down on the bed. His voice was comforting, but not patronizing. "In fact, I can probably help you out with some information about hallucinations. When I was an undergrad, I was considering becoming a therapist. That was before I got so interested in physics. I actually worked in a rehab clinic and walked many a patient through the worst of withdrawal symptoms, including hallucinations."

I sipped the tea, hoping it would help my head. But it throbbed. Not in a Headache from Hell sort of way, but in a tension way.

"Did . . . people see ghosts?" I asked.

"Sure. It simply depends on the types of minds they have."

I had never thought of myself as morbid, but obviously it was true. And I had more questions.

"Did they hear things?"

"Absolutely. Audible hallucinations are very common." He stood at the side of the bed and said, "Face the window."

When I did, he took the cup from me, laid it on the night-stand, and started to massage my temples. It felt amazing. I dropped my hands, feeling embarrassed still, but also for-given—and comforted by his confidence in the things he was saying. I could hear Marg snapping sheets out in the corridor, just a few feet away, in case I "saw" anything else. I felt utterly safe—safe enough to examine what happened in the basement without losing it. *The hallucinations were so real.* I didn't know how to get over that.

"All the senses work in hallucinations," Henry said as he rubbed his thumbs at the base of my skull in a fantastic way. "What happens is, the part of the brain that you use in dream-ing overreacts to stimuli that it's become unaccustomed to. Sometimes, very real things will change shape or move slightly, so the resulting hallucination involves a combination of the real and the imagined. Other times, it can be the product of five or six dreams, such that you can barely recognize the outbreak as things you've had in your head all along. You have to let go of it. It's just ... a symptom. That's all."

It was everything I needed to hear. He used his thumbs to work the top of my scalp, and I felt my body going limp, though the slight throbbing persisted.

Aleese ... hissing, edging toward me, and she's got some side-kick who reminds me of The Exorcist. *They stink like muck, and Aleese hisses out, "You're not really seeing me! I'm just a dream," and then laughs in that awful way of hers.*

Scott had been concerned I would hallucinate because I'd already done so at St. Ann's. He'd said it showed that I was prone to them. He had not said anything about hallucinations containing a smell. Maybe he'd thought I wouldn't really have any.

Henry's head massage was beyond relaxing, and when he eventually stopped, he brought something out from under the tea tray. It was a children's book that looked slightly familiar, and I stared, intrigued. I recognized the artwork of Maurice Sendak, because Oma had read his stories to me over and over until I was at least seven. I had never seen this one before. *The Big Green Book* featured simple drawings of a couple, a dog, and a small boy.

I would recognize Sendak anywhere. I breathed, enchanted. "Where did you get this?"

"It belonged to Mrs. Starn's daughter when she was a little girl. It's pretty old. Early sixties. My parents read a lot of Maurice Sendak to me when I was little."

"My Oma read them to me, too." I took the book from him and leafed through the pages with it resting on my ribs. "I *love* Maurice Sendak. Loved ..."

"I just grabbed it on my way out of the house today. I was thinking..."

I turned to stare into his kind eyes and warm grin, wondering what on earth had inspired him.

He laughed awkwardly. "Gee. I don't know what I was thinking. If I'm telling the whole truth here, my brushes with womenfolk have revolved around work and research for many years now. I guess you could say I'm *all thumbs.*"

The pun worked well. He worked his thumbs into the base of my skull again, though I noticed for the first time a slight nervousness in him. More tension escaped me as the confession lingered in the air. *How charming.* It had never struck me before, but I saw no reason that "older" had to mean "very, very experienced," and therefore, "very, very intimidating." Any pictures I'd had of Henry pulling some fast older-man routine on me dissolved and was replaced with a firm trust.

"Your instincts are very good," I said dreamily. "I love children's stories. One thing I've considered, if I ever decide on a major, is to write them."

"I just imagined you would love some escape into another world. It's a sweet and innocent read for a sweet and innocent person."

Henry sat beside me on the bed, opened the book, and simply started reading. I could see Marg peering in from the corridor, but it didn't matter. We weren't doing anything or talking about anything I thought we should hide. I lay beside him and he read the title page. "...by Robert Graves. Artwork by Maurice Sendak." I smiled dreamily. Oma used to read all title pages.

The pictures brought to life a little boy named Jack, who'd found a book containing magic spells. He turned himself into an old man, then made himself disappear. Then, he turned the spells on his starchy aunt and uncle, triumphing over their rules and regulations. It made me feel powerful, like I could triumph over this world, however harsh and inconceivable it often seemed. At one point, I nodded off, Henry's hand still stroking my hair, while lulling me with his words. I awakened, still hearing his voice and not wanting to miss the end. But I never heard it.

FORTY-ONE

I RAN IN THE HOUSE and noted the basement door kicked in, and Alan's new security machine in three pieces on the floor. Like Mike said, Alan would not be thrilled to have to replace it so quickly. I made for the stairs, but a movement in the parlor caught my eye. Hodji Montu was sitting straight up on the couch, looking like hell. Without his famous cowboy hat and with his face rearranged, he was almost unrecognizable. He smiled and stood up.

"I've seen worse." I chuckled as he approached. "In the ICU."

He hugged me with three claps on the back—a lot, since I'd met him a total of four times, and the first time I was in a coma.

"It doesn't hurt much," he lied.

"Hodji, I'm sorry. I know how much you loved him."

He looked . . . angry. I could relate. But I couldn't imagine what would inspire him to want to quit USIC. The loss would have gunned my fight engine, but according to Rain, Owen, and Cora, I'm not normal. Plus, he had the other problems Mike told me about. He still had his cell phone in his hand. I gathered that meant his son, Twain, hadn't called yet.

"Listen, I'm here now, Hodji. Why don't you go get some sleep?"

He looked torn up. "If I drift off now, I'll never sleep tonight. That's my latest decision, though I'm back and forth like the wind. I was just enjoying sitting here with the breeze blowing in on my face."

"What happened?"

"I actually had been asleep. I heard a USIC security alarm far off, reacted like a USIC agent, and had Cora's photography teacher in a pop lock before I knew what happened."

If only you knew how good that makes me feel. Fortunately, I managed to bury my laughter in a cough.

"I was very embarrassed, apologetic. He's a great guy. Very understanding. Thinks he can beat me at chess. I've played while undercover as everything from a paper salesman to a chicken farmer. People tend to think I'm an easy mark. When I play money stakes, the truth comes out." He laughed, and I forced myself to do the same.

"There's only one person who has ever legitimately beat me," he said.

The Kid?

He walked to the window and stared out. I approached him hesitantly, not wanting to interrupt an obvious memorial moment.

I cleared my throat. "How is Cora? She seemed okay?"

"Yeah, she's up there with him."

"Did she fall? Hit her head? Get bruised in the ruckus? She's on a hefty dose of blood thinner."

"When I got down there, she was just standing in the darkroom screaming. I actually tackled Henry out in the corridor before he could get that far. She witnessed the whole thing, but we never came near her down there, and she never moved."

"Good, then."

"She's just shook up. The nurse told me she's switching medications?"

"Yeah. I told her she might be prone to hallucinations, but I didn't think she'd have a doozie like that. Sounds like a remake of *Creature from the Black Lagoon*."

"That's what the nurse said. She said most people hallucinate out of the corners of their eyes or through their sense of smell. Though she also said anything is possible. Your medication and dosages are highly experimental."

I was itching to question Cora, but I had my pride, too.

"Where's Marg now?"

"Sitting outside Cora's door, pretending to fold wash. She mentioned the huge age difference, and her motherly instincts are on full alert."

"Good for her."

He watched me, and I hoped my expression bore out nothing. But I was not going up there to play audience to their little drama. Still, that hallucination ate at me.

"Are you sure she didn't see *Henry*? And that's what made her hallucinate?"

"I don't . . . follow," he said. His mind was blotto right now, I assumed, though he probably wouldn't know about this stuff anyway.

"Generally, when people hallucinate something full-blown like that, it's not all hallucination. There's something there that they *did* see. For example, I have heard of people in withdrawal claiming to see spirits or even ghouls. But generally, there's someone standing there, and they make a transferal, add to it with their overloaded autosuggestion."

He watched me uncomfortably, to the point where I wondered if I'd alarmed him.

"She did not see Henry," he said. "Henry kicked the door open because she was already screaming."

So, that was no good. And true, the door had been locked. I'd given it a pull for good measure just before I took off with Alan.

"Maybe it's just one of those things," I said, but he moved toward the door and pulled it open, staring down in a way that made me edgy.

He sighed, banging his heel absently into the space above the top step. "God, I so do not want to play USIC right now."

I barely heard him, my heart revving up. "Hodji. Shadow-Strike would have no interest in the four of us, right? Alan assured me of that before I even agreed to the place. It's remote. We're wide open. The property is too big to fence in . . ."

He sighed more loudly. "What did I just say?"

"Sorry."

He pulled me out onto the porch, and the air seemed to revive him a little. I couldn't help it. Questions popped out of me as I followed him.

"You don't think they got down there somehow, do you?" I asked.

"Scott, all I can tell you is the common mindset of terrorists, which has worked throughout my entire career. They don't chase down individuals they missed the first time around."

"So, they would have no business in this house."

"None whatsoever. *Shhh*," he said, and a smile bloomed on his face. I looked over my shoulder to see Henry pulling on a light jacket.

"She is very sound asleep right now, and Marg is folding wash right outside her door. Please bid her adieu for me when she wakes up."

Oh, adieu? Adieu, and screw you.

"I will." I pulled a grin out of my ass. "And thanks."

"No problem at all."

"So, when's our first big chess game?" Hodji asked. "I thought you were staying for dinner."

"I wasn't invited."

I prayed really hard and bit my lip.

"Too bad," Hodji said.

"And I actually have papers to mark and a meeting at the college in about forty-five minutes."

"After dinner?" Hodji asked.

Henry laughed in disbelief. "You sure you want to take me on? I understand you're sleep deprived."

Please, God, no.

"Sometimes it's the more relaxed mind that takes the game. Why don't we make a scientific experiment of it? Your alert mind versus my concussion. Five bucks down. If you don't take it, Alicia's divorce lawyer will."

Henry looked at him in sympathy. "If it'll keep your mind off that. Sure."

I went through my sins of the day, trying to figure out where I'd gone so wrong. Maybe I could connive Marg into slipping Cora a sleeping pill so she wouldn't watch Henry beat Hodji's ass.

Hodji waved, his smile stuck on his face like plastic, but it dropped as soon as Henry was out of sight.

"Nice guy," he said. "But you don't tell him nuthin'. I'm sure Mike's been over that with you."

"Can I tell him to go to hell?" I blurted, at the end of my patience. I tried to cover it with a laugh but my face was on fire.

"Uh-oh," he said. He wasn't *that* asleep. "You're in love while she's got older-man syndrome."

"I'm not in love," I countered, but he ignored me.

"You'd better keep your mind occupied. I'll give you a job to do."

"Like what?"

"I don't know."

"I thought you weren't USIC anymore."

"I'm not. But if I didn't search that basement right now, I'd be half an idiot. I don't think there's anyone down there. But I'm going to pull my gun, so you stay out here right now. Don't let anyone onto the first floor. Where's your brother and the Steckerman girl?"

I listened for the TV and heard it. "TV room, probably crashed out."

"I'll be careful. Make sure no one else comes down here. God forbid, but if I should fire a weapon, it would probably go right through the floor. Listen for my holler."

He went through the foyer, and as he turned the corner I saw a flash of metal—his gun. He took so long that I almost went inside, but I wanted to do like he told me. After probably ten minutes he hollered my name loudly. *All clear.*

"I'm not done yet," he said as I came downstairs. "I just did the people search. I wasn't terribly concerned about finding 'somebody' down here, but rather, finding the evidence of somebody. That takes longer."

"What do you look for?" I asked.

"Microcams. Bugs. I've got a bug-and-cam detector in my bag. Wait here."

I guessed he was dead serious about being unable to untie himself from USIC. *A bug-and-cam detector in his bag.* I wondered if I would be so compulsive about this someday. I listened and stared all around, trying to pick up energy. I believed in energy. Having been a medic, I could wander into somebody's house and follow the sick energy without the homeowner showing me which room the person was in half the time. I had never opened a wrong door. If Cora had seen a ShadowStrike member, she would have sensed bad energy. She would have transposed this in her mind into something she could understand, or in her case, something she could more easily tolerate.

But my instincts were cluttered, and I merely wandered into her darkroom, noting that the carnation-talcum-powder smell of her was still here.

Hodji came back and started in with a humming machine, going up and down the walls of the outer room and most especially around the computer. It crackled pretty steadily but never bleeped.

"What do you think?" I asked as we stood in the hallway. "Is there any way someone could have broken the security code and gotten down here with her?"

"No," he said, sounding weary. I wanted to get him back upstairs, back into the sun and out of this dank basement, which was no good for a depressed and sleep-deprived person. But he wanted to check up the goddamn chimney flue, and while he was doing it, I noticed something stuck to the wall down near the baseboard that looked like mud. I ended up peeling away some mucky weed about eight inches long that smelled like pond scum. It was still wet.

"Um . . ." I held it up, not knowing quite what to say. "Didn't she say she saw creatures from the pond?"

He came over, studying it without touching it, and backed away before finding my eyes and staring into them.

He didn't have a chance to respond. We heard a beep from the computer. Nothing to make you jump, but under the circumstances we both went in there.

An icon had popped up that said "HodjiMontu22@yahoo: You've Got Mail."

He pushed me aside harder than he obviously meant to and plopped down in the seat, clicking the mouse.

"It's probably from Roger, annoying me, nagging me not to resign," he said. "He's called my cell phone twenty-five times, and since I'm waiting to hear from Twain, I can't even turn it off."

The computer loaded Internet Explorer slowly, and the longer it took, the more annoyed he got. He finally cursed and banged the mouse down. Mike told me to prepare for his outbursts, and I flew into medic mode.

"Look, you need sun. There's probably mold down here. Go upstairs and I'll bring you a hard copy, okay?"

But he refused to move. Eventually the screen finished its nonsense, and he clicked open an e-mail.

"No sender," he said, and added acridly, "I just can't wait . . ."

Not from Roger, I took it. The message made no sense to me, though I watched him closely to see if it made sense to him. It said, "And I will send a fire on Magog, and among them that dwell carelessly in the isles. Ezekiel 39:6."

Somebody had sent him a foreboding ancient message with a blank space in the sender line. I didn't even know that was possible.

And my thoughts landed on Alan this morning saying, essentially, anyone who drank FireFall in Griffith's Landing, which is a barrier island, will burn from the inside out. I wanted to get to Cora and make sure she hadn't been stolen out the window while Marg lay on the floor with her throat cut. I wanted to make sure Rain wasn't outside trying to kick people.

"Scott, don't worry," Hodji said quickly, and his eyes looked human and reflective for the first time since he came here. "This is not as bad as it seems."

"Hodji, I gotta know. If they were in this house, you have to tell me. I . . . we got kids upstairs."

He put a hand on my arm and looked me dead in the eye with all his purple flamboyance. "I said, *don't worry*. Shadow-Strike has no desire to hurt you or the rest of the Trinity Four. This e-mail . . . they're after me."

He rushed out and took the stairs. I was close on his heels.

"Why?" I asked. "I thought you weren't in USIC anymore."

But he wasn't listening. He was muttering under his breath and heading outside. The words he uttered scared me completely: ". . . let me catch sight of you, you morons . . ."

Alan called the ShadowStrike members hoods. Hodji called them morons. I guess all the curse words in the world lined up wouldn't do it, so the agents went for demeaning names. *He did think ShadowStrike was coming here.* Whether it was for him or for us, I couldn't relax. I wanted to put this house and him under some sort of lockdown. He seemed to want to search the grounds as he headed toward the outbuildings with stomps that rang of "Bring it on!"

I grabbed the house phone and wondered if it could be bugged, but I dialed Alan anyway. When he picked up, I said, "Forget what I told you earlier about stopping at the supermarket. Marg went. You can just *come straight back.*"

He said he would, so I guessed that wasn't too bad a cryptic message.

FORTY-TWO

CORA HOLMAN
MONDAY, MAY 6, 2002
11:45 P.M.
HER BEDROOM

My NIGHT PROVED NO LESS CONFUSING than my day. I had fallen asleep to Henry reading, and awakened to see Scott. He was sound asleep in my velvet chair, wearing a sweaty white polo shirt and jeans, one foot on the bed, the other on the floor. My arms had clutched *The Big Green Book*, so I knew I hadn't dreamed Henry, but I wondered if Scott was just one of my many dreams. I'd felt too tired to lift my head off the pillow, so rather than get up and risk waking Scott, I had fallen back asleep.

When I awoke again, it was dark, though the little light on my nightstand gave the room a warm, orange glow. My alarm read 11:45. I had vague memories of Marg coming in, taking vitals from me, and telling me I qualified as two-star, and she would bring me dinner when I was ready. But she was gone now. The house was very quiet, save for the sounds of Mr. Montu's rhythmic snoring from below.

When I rolled over, Scott was in the chair asleep again. Only this time he was in shorts, sweat socks, and his UPenn sweatshirt with the sleeves cut out. He was in the same exact posture as I had seen him in his polo shirt and jeans, with his head resting in the wing of the chair. So I was confused enough to reach out and touch his leg above his sock.

Definitely, he was flesh and not a mirage. His skin felt too warm, and there was a rush of red in his cheeks. He must have felt my cool hand, because his eyes opened, though his worn-out expression did not change.

"Why are you sleeping in the chair?" I asked.

His eyes shut again. "Don't ask."

I waited for more. His eyes were directed downward, but I saw him blink a few times, so I knew he hadn't fallen back asleep. During some of my headaches at St. Ann's, I'd come out of them to find him asleep on Rain's bed, which he said was due to my tossing and turning. Rain would not be able to tell if something had gone really wrong, and he could, so waking up to see him wasn't totally abnormal. But I felt little more than exhausted for no reason, so it couldn't have been that.

I tried again. "You're going to hurt your neck."

"Everything is fine," he mumbled, then added, "you're perfectly safe."

Perfectly safe? From whom? I laid the book on the pillow and was struck with a comical notion. I wondered if he had some thought that Henry had tried to rape me, or even make some sort of advances. *Henry, who read me a beautiful book and took all the terror out of the morning.* Scott's presence made no sense, and I was concerned, not only about whatever drama was playing out in his head, but with his flushed cheeks and warm skin. He ought to be in a bed.

I got up on the far side of the bed, stretching and moving toward the window. The full moon hung in the eastern sky, casting golden rays on the treetops and on the pond. All was still. The water was a mirror. Mr. Tiger's car sat parked in the grass, but Mr. Steckerman's was gone. If they went somewhere together, they often took one vehicle, and I supposed they were out taking care of business.

"Marg said she could only rifle three spoonfuls of egg salad into you," Scott said without moving. His voice sounded half dead. "You want your dinner?"

Marg forcing me to eat came back in minute flashes. I hadn't wanted to, but whatever I was taking required food. If I wanted dinner, I could call for her. Just moving took some of the cobwebs out of my head.

"Did *you* eat?" I asked.

"Yes."

"Can I bring you some iced tea? Or, Henry brought over some lemonade, I understand, though it never made its way up here—"

I realized my error when his eyes shot open. I was standing beside him, and he gazed at my left hip before slowly shutting them again.

He finally said, "The Kid and Tyler's funeral is going to be televised."

"Televised?"

"Yeah. USIC came clean to the media . . . told America all the heroic stuff those two had done. Anyway, they're going down as heroes. I think USIC told the truth to pacify Hodji. He's still on edge, but . . . NBC will be there with an exclusive. *Dateline*'s running it."

"That's wonderful," I said, sinking down on my bed in some relief.

"It is . . . wonderful," he said, and finally dragged his head off his arm and sat up straighter. "But I don't want us going."

"Why not?"

"TV crews and everything . . . I just don't."

We had already said yes to a *Dateline* interview, though Dr. Godfrey was keeping the producers at bay for now, knowing it would be an all-day session. Since we had already been in *People* and other magazines, it didn't seem to me he could be worried about the exposure. Rain and Owen had been set on going. My shudders over helping USIC were almost phobic, but phobic and selfish are two different things.

"I want to go," I said, and tried to repeat my thoughts, but he cut me off.

"Cora. Can we just leave it with, 'Don't ask'?"

Bossy. I couldn't pinpoint exactly when his speaking for me and dishing out orders had started to bother me. At St. Ann's, it had been comforting. I had been confused, and certainly nobody else was going to both walk in my shoes and lead the way. I didn't have any responses for him yet, but I had to compare him with Henry, who had shown up with flowers and gifts and kindness and only wished to carry me off to Magic Land. Scott? So far today, I'd been guilted at breakfast, made to cry in the basement, manhandled (I would certainly never have chosen my first kiss since seventh grade to be through a mask in a dank basement while crying), and left alone to make photos of potential killers by myself.

And who had heard my screams and saved me?

I was annoyed, but something broke inside me. For once, my throat didn't tense up with the thought of a confrontation. I didn't want to yell at him, but I didn't want to see him wake up with neck pain, for whatever reason he felt it would be necessary.

"Let's talk about it tomorrow," I said, pulling him by the arm to get up.

"You're not going," he insisted.

"You're dishing out orders," I said softly. *There. I did it without turning into Aleese.*

He groaned and pulled his arm out of my grip but followed me to his room.

"Get some decent sleep and you can tell me what's bothering you in the morning," I said, pulling up the comforter for him to drop under. He did, but jerked the blanket out of my hand, throwing it back on the bed.

"Please don't tuck me the fuck in."

"I wouldn't dream of it." I backed away.

I returned to my room, biting the smile off my lip.

Scott and Marg had both predicted I would be wide awake when I would normally feel sleepy, and vice versa, and I went back to bed, picking up *The Big Green Book.* Perfect for now. Maybe I could relive some of the sleepy peacefulness I'd gotten the first time. There wasn't a photo of Maurice Sendak on the jacket, but I supposed books didn't include photos of authors in the 1960s. Oma and I had always looked at the photos of authors and wondered what their lives were like. *I wonder what it would be like to do a photo book on Maurice Sendak's life,* I thought suddenly. I had been editor of our high school's literary magazine my junior year, but I had been asked because of my love of art and photography even more than for my writing. I hadn't given much thought to a major in college, but I suddenly wondered about photography. I had never felt like I could be particularly good at anything except studying, and now I wondered if I were being released from that, along with every other low-self-esteem curse Aleese had brought onto our house.

Do a photo book on Shahzad and Tyler. The thought struck darkly but deep at my core, in my conscience, in the center of my gratitude. I felt Aleese breathing all over me, and I suddenly came tumbling to a crossroads I knew I had to face. Maybe the drugs were leaving me very quickly, but I had a clear head, clear for one of the first times since she died. *If I don't forgive Aleese for her treatment of me, I will never inherit her conscience, which seemed to run so deeply for everybody else.* I could have a closed-off and safe life with so many feelings stuck in neutral, or I could have a caring and adventurous life, however long or short it might be.

But I have to forgive her first.

I sat there stunned, clutching the children's book and closing my eyes, feeling her draw very close. The hateful glint in her gaze roasted the backs of my eyelids—she had so loved to torture me, mock me, call me "Brat." How could I *ever* forget? And yet she surrounded me now, waiting, it seemed, for me to address her without my usual stiffness.

I hadn't been a stiff person before she came home. I'd been alive and a giggler and had a lot of friends. *I could have been Rain Steckerman.* But then Aleese showed up. My embarrassment had been profound, a lot of which had to do not so much with her drug habit but with *her*. I suppose I could have told my friends about a morphine addiction and still kept them. I simply could not bring myself to tell them that my mother shook my hand when she met me, called me Brat when she was high, and treated me with all the common courtesy of a roommate one secretly despises. *That's* what changed me.

How do I forgive that? It wasn't like crossing a bridge. It was like climbing a skyscraper. I pulled out my laptop and shot an e-mail off to Jeremy.

"I'm struggling," I said. "How do I ever forgive her? Thoughts, please."

As my first e-mail to him had been pages long and had left me bedridden for a day and a half, I hit SEND before I could argue with myself about creating a dissertation again.

I hadn't thought I would hear back so quickly, but after studying the Sendak artwork for only twenty or so minutes, "You've got mail" came from the laptop. He must have been on his computer anyway.

> *Cora: I'm glad you wrote. As your mother never mentioned me to you, I highly doubt she mentioned my father. He sat on British parliament for many years, which sounds slightly important, and perhaps it is. But more important is that for the past seven years he has been dying, and after I split from your mum, I finally had the time and nearness to pursue the kind of relationship with him that I'd always wanted. He finally made it across the precipice Saturday night, and I got word of it about the time I hit SEND to you.*

*While your mum and I traveled together, I often
promised her a portion of my inheritance, figuring she
had done so much for the world for free. Unfortunately,
she's not here to share it. Be advised I am putting seventy thousand pounds in an account for you. We can
talk more about that in a month or so. It will take as
long for the papers to be finalized.*

It was so unlike what I'd been expecting to hear that my eyes
bugged, and I read it twice. Seventy thousand pounds was a fortune, close to the same amount or more in dollars, though I was
otherwise clueless about currency conversion. I was speechless,
as I already had the amount to fulfill my dreams of college and a
condo from what I'd been left by Oma and the sale of our property. The figure hung in the air like the echo from a gong, and I
knew I would have to write him back and tell him I didn't need
it. He might have made a promise to Aleese, but I remembered
how she had begrudged me even her camera, and after she'd let it
sit in the closet for years. I simply couldn't accept.

I would tell him that while I was grateful, certainly he should
find some charity Aleese would have appreciated, like those that
helped the starving children she photographed. But that would
be for later. I was dizzy over the gesture and all it implied—and
all it didn't even touch upon.

I actually scanned the e-mail for signs that he had answered
my questions. He didn't mention the tape again, and maybe he
regretted telling me to watch it, when he was obviously distracted
by his father's death. And he didn't answer my question about
forgiving Aleese. But maybe he had. Maybe his feelings for her

so rang off the screen, rang in the very concept of leaving a huge inheritance to her child, that nothing else needed to be said.

I pushed the laptop away and lay back, dully staring at the ceiling, waiting for Aleese to swoop down on me, call to me from the pond, or find some way to imply how undeserving of Jeremy I was. I did feel something fill the room . . . if something not dark, then anxious . . . or maybe it was the echo of a voice outside, which made me sit straight up and forget everything for a moment. I hadn't heard a car. All voices entering this house, coming onto these grounds, were preceded by a car engine, and I listened through what now amounted to silence so deep outside that not even the crickets buzzed. The crickets could do that, whatever crickets were out here—be chirping madly and all of a sudden pause, in unison, as if some mystical force waved a magic wand over them.

I thought my head was playing tricks on me at first, but I couldn't resist standing slowly. I heard laughter—just one far-off echo that seemed to come from all directions at once. My gaze went to the corridor, to the closet, to the side of the bed, and rested on the moon outside. My last hallucination had started with a laugh, I suddenly recalled. And now it was back. If I called to Scott, I would wake everyone in the house.

I wondered at the enormousness of my stupidity in having sent him off to bed. *"You're perfectly safe,"* he had said. Perhaps it was just a poor choice of words, indicating that he was there to protect me from myself, my mind, my imagination that had run wild today.

Or had it? I had never completely believed that, and with almost autonomous calm, I floated slowly over to the window to stare at the pond. The moon shone on the surface, sending orange ripples across it though nothing else moved. It was picture perfect, except something looked off center that made me want to back away without reason. It was more an instinctive thing—the same instinct that had me shooting pictures of strange men and a water park in Griffith's Landing. I found myself moving closer to the glass, even putting my hand out to it, to stare without swaying. *Water doesn't move when there's no wind. When I last looked, it was mirrorlike—*

A round object broke the surface of the water. A pair of shoulders. I jumped back and threw a hand over my mouth. My next instinct was to keep from screaming again and disrupting the sleep of four sick people over a hallucination.

I saw an arm reach up off the phantom in the water, and I ripped myself away, running into the corridor. I stopped an inch from Scott's door, my chest cluttered with so many emotions that I could barely make out the doorknob. But the strongest impulse was suddenly not to bother him. He wasn't my father, and when we all stopped to remember it, he wasn't a nurse either. I was entirely my old self at the moment and could have dove under his blanket, my head in his chest, and refused to ever come out. But I fought it, blindly making my way to the stairs and taking them down with fumbling steps. If I didn't see what this was for myself, Aleese would sit on my chest all night tonight and taunt me.

I expected to find Mr. Montu on the couch, but he was gone. The front door was wide open. I stared into the pitch black of the dining room, knowing Marg lay two rooms beyond it, and to that spot in the parlor where I'd stood with Mrs. Starn, telling her that if I saw a ghost I would laugh at it. That had not turned out to be true, but with the door wide open and a missing Hodji—

"*. . . if one of us got picked up by a ShadowStrike operative—God forbid, but they're close by somewhere—*"

My fears of terrorists in this world grew worse than my fears of ghosts, and the question suddenly changed. *Are they drowning Mr. Montu in the pond?* I only took one step toward the dining room before I stopped again, staring into the darkness. *Is someone there?* I heard breathing . . . rustling. Marg? *Or have they carried her off, too?*

My instincts broke for the outside, like an animal's, where I could more easily get to an escape route, and I ran, for the first time in months, toward the trail to Henry's cabin, knowing all the while I would never make it that far in the dark of night.

I passed the little trail that forked off to the pond, but I'd only taken a step past the fork when I froze, hearing voices. Shadows of men in a huddle came up the trail. The moon illuminated similarities to some of the men on the boardwalk—dark hair, dark eyes. The whites of their eyes flashed in the moonlight. They had seen me.

My ICU scene flashed through me from when I couldn't move, couldn't run, couldn't even breathe on my own. I dropped into a dead faint on the ground, only I never passed out. I hoped to use one of the most basic instincts known to man—playing dead.

Footsteps approached, and I heard the ancient languages used by Aleese during her morphine madness. She was standing by my feet, plain as day, shaking her head and saying, "*You're such a rabbit. How is it you're mine? Get! Up!*"

But it was too late. A man approached dripping water, *cold, icy water drops . . . his face horrifying, even though his eyes are kind as he lifts my head.*

"Oh, Miss Cora! It is damp out here! Why you makes to come out from your bed?"

And then Mr. Montu's voice. "You sons of bitches. I'm beating both your asses."

"Don't listen to his filthy talk," the creature said, rubbing my hair like it was gold. He had trouble breathing. "He speaks dirty, like the American cowboy. You don't know who I am, do you?"

FORTY-THREE

THE SIGHT OF HODJI CARRYING CORA across the grass sent me flying off the front porch. I was not even sure I had heard her get up. I wasn't exactly awake until I was halfway down the stairs. The sight of the two guys who followed Hodji left me frozen at the bottom step, my brain in some godforsaken scramble mode.

"Cora's hallucination," Hodji spat out and moved quickly past with her. Marg was in her bathrobe, holding the door.

I'm slow. I thought two guys in Griffith's Landing had kissed the monkeys, by the looks of them. But then, no one who'd been infected from Griffith's Landing would be smiling. These two guys were laughing.

The first guy stopped in front of me. "You're Scott."

"Right."

"I'm Tyler." Before I could drop dead, his scabby face lit up with excitement. "We are in *so* much trouble." He giggled wickedly.

National lie. Historic lie. I could only imagine the incredible tale behind this.

The Kid was more sober. His huge eyes rolled down to my feet then back up to my eyes. "I speaks to you when you make the sleep. At St. Ann's. Um, hi, um . . . I get excited and my English not much very good."

I thought the better of shaking their crusty hands but couldn't help the rest. I threw my arms around their thick jackets and wet hair and hugged them like I'd known them my whole life.

"I'm dreaming this," I said, and my voice broke.

Hodji must have laid Cora on the couch, and I heard him say to Marg, "They're on the porch. Please make sure they're alive . . . *because I get to kill them later.*"

"Oh . . . no dream." Shahzad breathed, pulling back from me. "Nightmare."

I collared them both with a laugh that bounced off the moon and brought them inside. Marg kept telling everyone to hush, not to wake Rain and Owen.

She leaned over Cora, stethoscope in her ears, saying, ". . . only me in the dining room tying my robe. This house is perfectly safe, for the hundredth time—"

Hodji lowered himself onto the loveseat and threw his head back. He rubbed his bruised face until I nudged Marg, thinking maybe she should look at him and I could take Cora. But when he took his hand from his face, he looked surprisingly alert, and his report was alarmed but calm, considering.

"They went seventeen hours without eating. They've been sleeping in a car. And today they ate junk food. They went swimming in the pond to bathe village-style, only now they stink."

My overly keen sense of smell detected pond scum.

"What kind of junk food?" Marg asked, as the stethoscope flew back into her pocket. She ordered organic food for us. When no one answered, she left the room.

Tyler crept over to the chair out of Hodji's reach, but Shahzad didn't look so afraid of the guy. He plopped down beside him on the loveseat.

"Draw the drapes," Shahzad said at nobody. "And shut the door, so he can makes to yell." Tyler leaped up to shut the door.

"Just shut up! Give me some silence," Hodji said, and at the same time groped for the Kid's scabby hand and pulled it into his lap. He stared at the ceiling, huffing.

But his silence was interrupted by a knock at the door Tyler had just closed. I opened it. Rain stared in. "Who's yelling? Is Daddy okay?"

"He's not even back yet," I said, watching her eyes bug. "Go help Marg."

She wasn't as slow as I was. "Oh. My. God. The TV news thinks—aren't you dead? What's all over your skin?"

"Go. Carry some plates. They need food." I shut the door in her babble to get her moving.

With all the curtains drawn, Tyler edged up beside me. His eyes locked with Cora's and his grin spread slowly again.

"The famous, the photographed, the one-and-only Cora Holman. The goddess. Be still my heart." He laid a speckled hand across his chest, and considering he looked like hell and smelled worse, it was a riot. I kept from laughing, though, in deference to Hodji's heart attack in progress.

Tyler approached her cautiously, glancing back at me. "Can she see me now? She doesn't think I'm a spook, right? Hodji told us about the spook thing in the basement. Mostly in Punjabi, but I got the gist of it." He turned back to Cora. "I'm sorry we broke in on you today. We had to get to the computer we saw them bring in here. We needed printouts and an IP address. We were trying to be so quiet about our thieving. Problem? Everything dangerous that I do . . . *makes me laugh.*"

From yet another high-pitched giggle that exited him into the drapes, I knew the tularemia hadn't affected his vocal cords. Cora tried to sit up, and he fumbled with the pillows behind her, proposing matrimony, confessing to sleeping with her *Newsweek* photo under his pillow. I finally tugged his jacket, since she looked freaked out, and let my familiar face catch her eye.

I asked all the questions. Did you fall? Hit your head? Any bruises?

No, no, no. Her legs had just given way. She was fine.

"How'd you morons get the pass code to the basement?" Hodji asked the ceiling. "I can't wait to hear this one."

"It works on a computer chip. We're hackers." Tyler shrugged. "You want my secrets? Henceforth, they come with an invoice."

I finally decided to start with the obvious. "Uh, you guys. Your funeral is being televised. Can I ask . . . what's going on?"

"Don't!" Hodji held up a warning finger at Tyler's grin. "*I'll* tell."

He leaned forward, staring deadpan at the floor. Shahzad edged away from him, his eyes rolling in some sort of nervous horror.

"I knew you guys weren't dead the minute I got to the burning house. With my face in five pieces, I still thought to check the garage. Your mom's Audi." He jerked his head at Tyler.

Tyler brought the keys out of his jacket pocket, waggling them for me and Cora, but tensely, like he might have to jump back farther at any moment.

"Firemen must have thought the police impounded it when she was arrested. No one asked. I flipped my creds on the fire chief, telling him word had to go out that you were dead, in the name of national security. He did his duty, even brought out a couple of body bags on stretchers for the TV crew. I can't imagine what the hell was in them. Your mom's bone china, maybe?"

"You finally saw it my way," Tyler said.

"You forced my hand! My life is a shambles, thanks to the two of you," Hodji insisted. "I had to lie to my squad, say I had ID'ed the bodies—after I flashed creds on the coroner, too. The only way I would lie to my squad was if I resigned. They may accept that resignation yet. Wait until Alan gets back here and sees the likes of you."

"Hodji, VaporStrike was on his way to the house," Shahzad interjected, his English suddenly becoming clear as he unwound. "We had no choice."

"You could have contacted someone after you escaped the house!" Hodji insisted.

"On what? Our cell phones burned," Shahzad said.

"How about a phone booth?"

"Oh. And we would shock Americans with our most charming appearance. Tyler's car have the dark glass windows. My only option is to make for you today's e-mail." Shahzad inched away from him again. "Forgive us for waiting so long. We had no intelligence to offer until this afternoon. Plus, we were angry with you—"

"You had. No intelligence. To offer." Hodji slumped

backwards to stare at them incredulously. "I want you two to understand something. *You are not intelligence vats.* If you had any idea of the grief you laid on the New York squad . . . Mine wasn't the only resignation offered. I think there were four, total. Including Miss Susan—"

Shahzad flinched. Obviously, this agent was important to him.

"God knows they need every agent right now. I haven't slept, conjuring up all sorts of nightmares. The downstairs of the house didn't burn so badly. All your medication was right there on the counter, and your asthma canister was in the middle of the kitchen floor, Shahzad, black as pitch. As far as I knew, you had the clothes on your back, no money, no medicine—"

"We get more medication very quickly," Shahzad said, unlacing his fingers finally to pat Hodji's shoulder. "You should not worry about us."

Hodji's incredulous gaze turned to him. "What'd you do, hack into the CVS computer system and rewrite your own prescriptions?"

"Mm, not CVS. They have big, bad firewall . . . nasty firewall."

Hodji held up a hand like he didn't want to hear any more.

The door opened. Marg and Rain came in carrying plates. Rain must have woken Owen with this piece of juicy news, and he carried a pitcher of water, his eyes swollen but alert.

"Hi!" Tyler grinned at them, obviously loving this. "What's up?"

"'Sup?" my brother responded, and laughed in a way I hadn't heard him do in months.

Tyler took a plate Marg handed to him, dropped down to

sit on the floor, and landed the plate on the coffee table. He bit into a drumstick, rolling his eyes heavenward and staring at Rain while he chewed. "So. This is the famed 'yellow-haired female.' That is totally what my roommate calls you." He gestured with the drumstick. "I was just making a big deal of Cora before you came in here. See, Shahzad comes from a country where if you stare at a woman's ankle, your parents will smack you. And no girl has ever taken any interest in me, obviously. Let's just say" —he turned to me with a smirk and a cheek full of chicken meat—"we're infatuated with your womenfolk."

"Tyler, do you ever shut up?" Hodji asked. Shahzad was turning quickly to stone, which got me biting my lip. "I was in the middle of a lecture."

"Hodji, you won't be mad anymore. Honestly. When can we tell you what we got today?" Tyler giggled.

Hodji shot up straight. "Never, that's when. It all goes down the toilet, and I don't care what it is. You're two boys. You're not two computer chips."

"Boys, schmoys," Tyler griped back defensively. "Hamdani is not a boy. I'm not a boy. You want us to act our ages? Really? What's your pleasure? You want us to . . . snap each other with towels in some locker room and talk about what great movie we saw on Friday night? You want us to slip Scott, here, a few bills so he can get us a little buzz down at the liquor store? You want us to go out cruising in my mom's Audi? It's a convertible! Hey. Maybe we can get in a drag race and a fistfight. Maybe we can get laid in the back seat—"

"Oh . . . he makes to speak dirty before the women." Shahzad stuck his fingers in his ears and squinted his eyes totally shut, though he never stopped chewing his food.

Hodji drowned them out. "I want you to . . . read the classics! Go to Princeton!"

"Maybe we'll get around to it when we're done doing what we need to do now." Tyler gestured at Shahzad with his drumstick again. "We're graduates of the School of Double Dealings and Internet Hard Knocks. I feel good. For once. So lay off, maybe."

Hodji pulled his cell phone absently out of his pocket again, staring at it for calls missed, I supposed. His own son had not called, I took it, by the way he tossed the thing onto the couch. *Spoiled. Parents can wind up dead, and then you got nothing, and in the vast majority of cases, something is better than nothing.* I looked over at my brother, who was watching Tyler totally, like maybe he finally understood something.

Shahzad took his fingers out of his ears, and hearing nothing from Tyler, took another chomp from Marg's organic drumstick. They ate like I've never seen people eat. Marg went to get them seconds of macaroni and cheese.

I sat down beyond Cora's feet and asked a question. I couldn't help it. "That e-mail this afternoon was from you? About fires on an island?"

"Fires of Magog, yes," Shahzad said. "That message was an e-mail signature my father used to send off to Hodji in Karachi. If dangerous extremists come and we want more security before scripting them? That was one of several e-mails we make. I knew he would know it, would know we were close by."

"It sure fits the situation," I noted incredulously.

"Yeah. I thought of that. That's what made me laugh the first time." Tyler went off in high-pitched giggles again, looking apologetically at Cora.

Hodji tried one more time. "Scott. Tell these boys they need to go to college and put all this on hold, and . . . act normal."

Since my own history of "normal" was a lot like what Tyler had jokingly described, I finally said, "I think you love them. Hence, I think you're playing typical parent. But not much in this room right now is typical." I kicked Tyler in the back with my foot—not too hard, but to keep him from rolling out some inappropriate victory laugh. He didn't.

But he still took advantage. "Okay, Hodji. If you don't want to hear what we have, I'll just tell Scott. Okay?"

Apparently, he really wanted Hodji to hear, because he got up and left his food to pull me up again and look me in the eye. He put a hand on my shoulder. "Scott. Pulling the drapes was just a formality. VaporStrike is in Texas tonight. Omar sneaked across the border this morning, and VaporStrike is picking him up—in a blue Camry rental car in back of the Burger King in Amarillo, Texas, at 2 a.m. *Scott*. How do you like them apples?"

My eyes drifted to Hodji, whose jaw was somewhere low enough that I was afraid he'd drool. In one fluid movement he picked his cell phone off the couch and hit three numbers.

Rain piped up finally. "Who's Omar? Wait. Maybe I shouldn't ask."

"Yeah, maybe you shouldn't." Tyler giggled.

Hodji held out the cell phone like he himself didn't want any part of it. Tyler took the phone and walked out into the corridor. I could only hear, "James Imperial? Hey. It's a blast from your past," before he closed the door.

Hodji turned to Shahzad with a gesture of confusion. "You can go with him, too, talk to the big guns. I'm out of the game.

I don't want in. If something like this can happen to the two of you—thanks to bureaucratic nonsense—I'm not playing."

Shahzad looked alarmed. "Does James Imperial know that we're alive?"

"He does *now*."

Even I flinched, putting myself in Imperial's shoes. He'd probably spilled a massive obituary to *Dateline* today.

Shahzad breathed in awe. "Hodji. He will surely have your badge."

"I *gave* him my badge. I'm going to go work as a farm hand in Egypt. I don't even want to buy a farm. Too much responsibility. Do I look bothered right now? By James Imperial?" He actually looked pretty calm beneath his swelling.

Shahzad didn't. "Surely you will not leave me again."

"You had no trouble leaving me!"

"Farm hand . . . You were afraid of my mother's cow. She shakes her horns and you run like the big baby that you are!" They took off in Punjabi. We couldn't understand a word of it, but this whole thing was like a foreign film that is so suspenseful you can watch without reading the subtitles.

Tyler came back in holding the phone out for Hodji, looking only slightly less amused with himself. "He wants to talk to you."

Hodji shook his head.

"He's not mad. Honest."

Hodji kept shaking his head until Shahzad shoved his shoulder, muttering something in Punjabi that made Hodji reply in English, "When did you get such a fresh mouth? I don't remember this from Karachi. I'm calling your uncle. Tonight."

"You bluster. Take your phone call." And he finished with a Punjabi term, some breed of name-calling, as Hodji took the phone, left the room, and pulled the door shut again.

Tyler grinned at us. "Loose translation? 'Pudding face.' I'm getting used to Punjabi. The Pakistanis are a little more retiring than we are. It's their word for 'shit for brains.'" He giggled again, jerking his thumb between Hodji and the closed door. "They argue a *lot*."

My brother and Rain watched Tyler, warily and yet entranced. They were sitting on the floor by the door, and as he dropped down in front of his food again, their necks lowered automatically. They had never been mean kids, but they knew gleeps and nerds in only one context: such people had been invisible before. Owen talked sometimes about his dreams of mists and of misty beings circulating in them. He thought the beings had been Mom or angels. I wondered if they were Tyler.

"So, um, how did you guys fool everyone?" Rain asked.

"I don't think I'm at liberty to say." Except for Tyler's lips smacking, the silence resounded.

I realized all these exits with the phone need not happen if Rain and Owen and Cora weren't in here. As they were adding nothing, I reached down and tugged at Rain's arm. My head was so exploding with questions that I couldn't even be nice about it.

"Go. Cut some logs. They'll be here tomorrow, and you can chat it up then."

My brother stood too, looking torn, and if I was gauging it out right, a little humiliated. It was a strange moment, splitting a room of people exactly the same age in half, because some knew things that the others had chosen not to know.

"Are you *sure* they'll be here?" Rain asked.

Actually, I wasn't. They looked at each other, and Shahzad said quickly, "I have been so very happy to meet you and see all of you looking so well. But we . . ." He cast a glance at the closed drape, and I thought I heard Alan's car pulling in, finally. ". . . are not good to have around. But I shakes your hand again, Miss Rain. You give me much strength to go on. You do not know."

Marg came in with her medical bag as Rain stared down at Shahzad's hand clutching hers. He pulled away, but she and Owen didn't leave right then. Wise choice. Tyler and Shahzad removed their shirts, and Marg examined their skin. It was probably not as painful as it looked. If this new strain worked like chickenpox, I noticed their pustules were dry, no longer oozing, so they looked at their worst but probably had been there over a week ago. Still. I would be damned if they went anywhere else.

I could suddenly hear Alan's and Mike's voices rising with Hodji's. I gathered he was trying to tell them all of this while simultaneously telling Imperial.

"You're staying," I said, and I can't say I was totally surprised that my brother agreed with me immediately.

He hadn't said much, but he now said, "If you guys can't stay here, then trying to save us is a joke."

He looked shell-shocked and after some sleep would wake up with his complicated thoughts aligned better. He finally pulled at Rain's T-shirt, and they passed Alan and Mike in the doorway. Suddenly, this room was just how I wanted it—full of USIC, full of protection, full of questions for these kids that I would get to hear the answers to.

I barely noticed that Cora hadn't moved when Marg led Rain and Owen out.

"Want some help?" I reached out my hand to her.

"No, thank you."

I had no idea what she was thinking, but she could get up and leave anytime she wanted to.

FORTY-FOUR

CORA HOLMAN
TUESDAY, MAY 7, 2002
12:30 A.M.
PARLOR

I'D SAY IT WAS ALEESE MAKING ME STAY. I was nowhere close to forgiving her, but it was as if she had parked herself beside me, neither of us looking at the other, both of us looking around this room with interest. These agents were not musclemen, but their presences were somehow huge. Fortunately, the couch I sat on was removed from them, and it was more like watching a theater production than being an actor.

Mr. Steckerman and Mr. Tiger observed the skin outbreaks in silent reverence as Marg said, "Unless it's somewhere where we should retire before I look at it, I'd say you've got no localized infections."

She looked at the inside of their mouths with a light pen, making a bit of a face and saying, "*No* more junk food ... full of acid."

Shahzad looked warily at Mr. Steckerman. He was definitely being the shyer of the two, and I think he was very surprised when Mr. Steckerman said, "I want to hug you. How do I do that?"

"You forgive much," Shahzad said, after easing back into his shirt and letting both agents hug him. "We are sorry. Much big mess. We have to think fast the other night."

"Don't worry about that now. That's part of our job. We clean up messes. Just . . . tell us everything you know, and how you know it."

He turned and half pointed to me and then Scott, who sat on the arm of Tyler's chair three feet away. "These two are CCs. That's 'classified clericals.' You can speak at liberty."

Mr. Tiger leaned against the double doors, and Mr. Steckerman sat on the couch kitty-cornered to Shahzad and Hodji. I had to look past Scott's back to see much, which was fine with me.

"Who caused the fire?" Hodji asked.

Tyler raised his hand. "I used snap judgment. Well, bad judgment. Earlier that day it totally occurred to me to set off this pong bomb I had—after USIC couldn't find it in their paperwork trail to help us get out of my mom's house. I had a whole plan in mind of how to force their hands, but I have a conscience. It was all pissy daydreaming. I hope you believe that. Maybe thirty seconds after Shahzad sent you the text message that VaporStrike was nearby, one of their v-spies picked us up on Shahzad's terminal. It didn't have a patch. The IP address was in their laps, so we were sitting ducks."

It was a lot of French to me, but Hodji seemed to understand.

"So you blew up the house?" he asked. "I said I was done lecturing, but I can't help it. A pong bomb . . . you could have blown yourself and him into twenty pieces."

"We were e-mailing with Cora and waiting and pissing ourselves, and we heard the front door downstairs being jiggled. We called out to Miss Alexa, but she never answered. Scariest fuckin' five minutes of my life. Hamdani and I just stood there in the dark, not knowing what to do. VaporStrike is a trained assassin. He could probably do a lot worse to us than scratch us in the face."

The agents stayed quiet. Tyler threw his hands in the air with a very serious expression for once. "Excuse me for not being Rambo. I was scared, okay? On the spur of the moment, I figured if he was down there, maybe I could drop half my house on top of him and kill him. Or . . . maybe it would stun him enough to give us a better chance of getting out."

Hodji said, "Police report said they were suspicious a downstairs window had been broken from the outside before the explosion. They thought it was a neighborhood kid trying to vandalize the home of a spy. Nobody was around. They don't call them ShadowStrike for nothing." There was a long pause before he went on. "Alexa Vandecamp heard the explosion from her car two blocks away. Thank god she wasn't driving just a little bit faster. She might be a hostage at this point, or she might be dead from having the top floor of the house landing on her."

"And you were not going to lecture him?" Shahzad said, as Tyler's head pitched backwards and he sighed at the ceiling. "You know that he loves his nurse. And if you don't mind I should say so, *you* were on a delayed flight to check out intelligence we had fed you without being paid, without any protection, without telling us where you were going . . ." He reverted to Punjabi, and sympathy overwhelmed me. Keeping up with their conversation was difficult even before they reverted from

English. But no one needed to say that he was in a country he didn't know, halfway across the world, where he'd already been attacked by a terrible germ.

"What's Hodji saying?" Scott looked down on Tyler as Hodji's tone got even angrier.

Tyler shrugged and took what appeared to be a guess at a translation. "'Those fucking bureaucrats'?"

"Look, guys." Mr. Steckerman reached over and made a swiping motion between them. "Put it in neutral. What intelligence did you gather, and do you have scripts? James Imperial is coming tonight. You'll be asleep when he gets here. But this is your chance to get your ducks in a row."

Shahzad looked weary, slumping back beside Hodji, and Tyler began again. "Until this afternoon, it was an endless online comedy of them celebrating our deaths. They quote-unquote 'knew' they had caused two v-spies to squirt in their shorts and push the OFF button before they could behead us. To them, it was definitely a suicide and not an accident. In four different chat rooms they reveled in how badly they had scared us. Then this morning, they started to speculate about whether or not this was the Kid. I've got hard copies. You can see them. We got, like, six new log-in names for you. But if you've had any worries about us, the truth is, we spent the past twenty-four hours slapping our thighs and drooling with laughter onto the keypad."

The way Shahzad stared at his roommate, I think Tyler was being more courageous than accurate.

"*Write a book on these boys' lives.*" I knew Aleese was after me again, and for the first time in my life, I felt comforted by her presence instead of annoyed.

"Where are the hard copies?" Mr. Steckerman asked.

"Trunk of the Audi." Tyler reached into his pocket, brought out keys, mentioned which outbuilding they had hidden it in, and Mr. Steckerman went out and returned with a bulging laptop case.

The conversation continued in such a graphic tone that I was amazed to find myself drawn to it. I still felt numb, but not so numb that I wished to get away.

"What we sent Cora yesterday was just the start of it. It was an encryption program that we would need later—if we could hack into a certain hard drive. I e-mailed a copy to myself, and around four o'clock, the shit hit the fan on my laptop," Tyler said. "We got the big break."

He turned slowly in his chair and looked at me. I grew silently rigid under the weight of his grin. Everything was fine when energy was being thrust everywhere else in the room.

"You're awfully quiet," he noted, which shut my throat entirely.

"That's just Cora," Mr. Steckerman said. "All input, only the necessary output."

"She's okay to hear this? It's bad. It's scary."

"I'm fine," I said. I didn't know where on earth it came from, as the situation was suddenly so real that Aleese evaporated entirely.

"Okay. You know how dogs don't return to their vomit?"

Mr. Steckerman froze.

"Well, these dogs return to their vomit. I kept trying to think of ways these guys would be different from bomb makers and your basic terrorist mustard-gas thugs. The fact is, they're scientists. They want data. They want any records of success and failure they can get their hands on with how medicine works *against* what they've done. They've been in this house. They've been into the Trinity Four's medical files. Their entire drug protocol was on the hard drive. They had pictures . . ."

The eyes I saw through the bramble across the pond. My hand went to my heart.

Tyler took a photo out of the front pocket of the computer case and held it up to me.

"Do you know where this was taken?"

It was a far-off shot of Rain picking up the goat's bell on her pinkie. I nodded. "It's the trail in the woods on the other side of the pond. I saw somebody back there watching us earlier in the day. We thought it was a journalist or a local drunk."

The agents all reached for the photo, and it ended up with Mr. Steckerman.

"The site is right where Owen said it was," Mr. Tiger said, studying the picture closely. "They must have killed the goat, planted the corpse where the remaining she-goat would be sure to attract one of the kids' attention. Sonofabitch. They were hoping one of you guys would touch it . . ."

"It gets worse," Tyler said. "They've conducted a couple of experiments already, using you guys as guinea pigs. They were calling you 'swans,' and it was all highly coded, so we were just making guesses at what they were doing to you."

He handed a series of e-mails over to Mr. Tiger while Mr. Steckerman turned as red as I've ever seen him. He said nothing.

"Luckily, they weren't interested in killing anyone," Tyler went on, "though they wouldn't have cared much if they had. We found an e-mail address for the log-in Chancellor, and we were able to break into Chancellor's hard drive. It's the first hard-drive break we've ever gotten on any of these guys. He had pictures and data," Tyler said, pulling out a set of hard copies. Mr. Steckerman took them but passed them to Hodji, apparently unable to do much more without losing all control.

"Consider, this could be a woman," Tyler went on. "It's Shahzad's little theory that just as men's and women's voices sound different in real life, they sound different in writing, too. He says he can tell the difference, especially in the Middle Eastern languages, and he says this voice sounds gender neutral. There were a lot of files saved by dates, simple Word 6.0 files."

"Marg?" Scott muttered, his head down and turned. I may have been the only one to hear it. I thought of her out on the grass, talking on her cell phone right at the same time a Shadow-Strike operative was destroying the evidence of having planted an infected animal for Rain to touch. It was hard to conceive of another ShadowStrike member getting so insanely close to us. But Scott's instincts had never told him something was wrong when it wasn't, as long as I'd known him. My chest turned to hot liquid as I thought of how many meals she had served to us.

Tyler read: "'The four victims are responding all too well to the antiretroviral, but that can be rectified. If we commit our next mutation to three degrees hotter, culminating at a hundred and one degrees instead of ninety-eight degrees, the antiretroviral will lose fifty percent of its efficacy. We can finish what we started without modern-day medicine prevailing.'"

Mr. Tiger all but snatched the hard copy, then remained silent. I felt certain the agents were taking this news as personally as I was, but Aleese was suddenly alive and well again, holding my hand away from my throat, where it loved to be lately. She wasn't laughing at me yet, but I felt exposed.

"Oh. Chancellor took some pictures as well," Tyler noted. "Cora. Did you see anybody around when this was shot, or did they sneak it when you thought you were alone?"

He'd spun it to the room first, probably from having their attention so well, but he flipped his fingers automatically and it faced me. It was the very picture Henry took of me out in the woods, the one he had framed for me.

Not Marg. I felt Scott looking over his shoulder, and he suddenly stopped, his head down, facing thc floor. It was up to me to speak for myself this time, while every last crumb of strength just left my body. Aleese said nothing.

FORTY-FIVE

CORA HOLMAN
TUESDAY, MAY 7, 2002
1:00 A.M.
HER ROOM

I LET DOWN MY "PROFESSIONAL GUARD" UTTERLY,
giving the agents a taste of what Scott, Rain, Owen, and friends
had put up with daily—only it was worse. I sounded like a three-
year-old choking on a green bean, sending the guttural echoes
of my stupidity, of having betrayed every person in this room,
out in some great seizure. Everyone in this important meeting
suddenly knew "Cora's boyfriend" was the betrayer. I wanted
to make a mad dash for the door, but the room was shifting
sideways.

It must have looked slightly less serious than it was, because
Mr. Tiger stood up, too calmly, and said, "Cora, maybe this is
too much for you."

I'm being kicked out. Scott still had his back to me, staring at the floor, obviously embarrassed for me, by me, and he
had every right to feel that. He had sensed there was something
wrong around here. The fact that he pegged Marg instead of

Henry seemed small in comparison to what I'd allowed myself to think and feel for the man. When I shot past Scott, the swelter in his feelings of betrayal washed over me.

"I'm done . . ." Tyler stood up quickly. "Shahzad, finish."

I stumbled for the stairs, and Tyler suddenly had my arm over his shoulders, serving as a second railing, and he helped me up to the second floor. He'd either guessed about Henry and me or somebody'd muttered it so that I couldn't hear, like gossip in school corridors.

"Listen," he whispered as the door downstairs closed again. "One time my junior year, this totally hot girl called me every night for a week. We went out twice, and then I realized she was on a hundred-buck bet from four of her friends."

Okay, but had his interest jeopardized national security? Or the lives of great friends? I just kept crying. He tried again.

"Cora, I bet he zeroed in on you because you're the sweetest and the most innocent."

That surely didn't help.

"And because, even with the paleness thing going on with you guys, you're absolutely stunning . . . perfecto."

Oh, bullshit.

The only thing I could manage to do to show my gratitude was wipe my eyes on his shoulder and leave snot there in the process. He didn't seem to notice.

"Hey. Haven't you ever heard the rape victims being told loudly, *'This isn't your fault'*?"

But it *was* my fault. Because if it wasn't, *where was Scott?* I listened intently behind me for that door to open again, to hear the tread of his footsteps coming to me. All was quiet.

I threw myself on the bed, and all I could think to say was,

"Damn you, Aleese! Go back to your little hell and quit trying to stew me also!"

"Who's Aleese?" Tyler sat down facing me.

"My mother."

"That's right. She died?"

I could argue that. "She's hateful. She's worse now than when she was alive."

And as that would make no sense to him, I could barely believe it when his hand came down to pet my hair instead of him bolting out of here to join the sane-and-normal club downstairs.

"You wanna swap mom horror stories?" he asked enthusiastically. "My mom's in jail for treason. She stole secrets from her office in North Jersey and sold them to the North Koreans. For cold cash."

With that, I stopped. He seemed to like when I rolled to my side to stare, and he stroked my hair less hesitantly. His face was so scabby. And yet he was smiling. Or trying to. The smile wandered around his face and trembled worse when he added, "I turned her in."

I had forgotten about his mom.

I reached for his hand, though mine was a shaky, snotty mess, and I sent all my sympathies into lacing my fingers awkwardly through his. He squeezed my hand, his scabs leaving sandpapery feelings on my palm and between some fingers.

"Your turn," he said.

"I . . . she . . ." If it was hard to talk about her under normal circumstances, this was impossible. I finally managed, "Morphine addict."

"Ouch."

"She hated me."

"I bet not."

"No, she did. You've no idea. And now she's haunting me."

He nodded, trying, I think, not to look blown away. He rattled our hands a little and said casually, "Is she in here right now?"

I looked over to the other side of the bed. I didn't dare answer that. Or I thought I didn't, until he shrugged. "Sometimes in the middle of the night, I hear my mom wailing at me, screaming in these fits of betrayal. Her voice just rolls into the wind from federal prison and finds me, forty miles away, across a river and a harbor. Nobody would believe me, but it wakes me up."

I'd almost forgotten who he was, how important he was, how talented and incredibly brave he had been. He was so honest, so ready to be humble. But it was hard to look at his sore face and forget for more than a moment. I wanted some control over my answer so I wouldn't appall him, but I couldn't find any, and the truth just splattered out.

"Yes, she's in here."

"Where?"

"She's lying on the bed beside me, crying into my pillow." I didn't dare look. I knew she was there. "She does everything I would not expect, and right now, she's got the audacity to try to make me feel sorry for her, when she has spent weeks playing these horrid tricks—"

I stopped, but only because I'd gotten really loud. I heard Scott's sneaker tread on the stairs, finally, and I was such a combination of relieved and mortified that I jammed my face into the pillow and let my sobs be buried there. With one blurring eye, I saw him standing in the doorway, Marg's bag dangling from his fingers loosely while he talked easily to Tyler. I was wigging out, and Mr. Never Shakes had asked to bear witness and assess the damage.

Tyler stood and said something in a mutter.

"She's switching medications," Scott said in a low voice, circling his fingers around one ear to imply I was half drug withdrawal, half silly school girl crazy enough to think the teacher actually had the hots for me. He added, "Thanks, Tyler."

Scott had often taken our vitals for the nurses as part of his stay-busy routine at St. Ann's. And he chatted in his softest and kindest tone while finding my pulse, taking my blood pressure. I held my nose with my opposite hand, thinking it would keep me from crying, but it just turned me into a pressure cooker while he pretended to ignore it.

"Look. I had some serious, big, bad names in high school, of which Heartbreak was one I am not proud of. Still, I've been on the receiving end a couple of times. It doesn't feel great. I know."

What the bloody hell. My heartbreak had only to do with betraying *him,* but if I let go of my nose at this point, he'd be struck with a T-shirt full of snot, and I held on for dear life.

"If it's any consolation to you, that guy's life is basically over tomorrow. They're downstairs organizing a raid right now. He will rot in jail until he dies, cut off from his money, cut off from everything good in life that his massive brain could have gotten him. That ought to do something for you. Most people who break hearts simply get to move on and break the next heart that—"

He stopped and rolled his eyes, as he now had the thermometer halfway to my mouth, and my nose holding was creating a roadblock. He handed me a tissue with the free hand.

I managed to catch the explosion without tainting him, but it was my first stellar movement all night.

He read the thermometer, shrugged, and hit the nurse's button. "You want some synthetic lights-out? You've got an allowance for a sedative, in case the drug withdrawal is causing too much sleep loss."

To sleep and forget all of this for a while sounded like a great escape. Aleese poked me in the back, still sounding weepy. *"You want to do like I always used to do?"*

"No. Thanks . . ."

Marg appeared. "I was coming anyway. Tyler just knocked on my door and said your mother is giving you problems again."

I liked the way he'd put it. Scott stood up, talked to her quietly about my vitals being good, considering, and stopped in the doorway, looking helpless.

"Hey. I'm right next door," he said, and when I didn't respond, added, "I mean it."

I was too ripped up to know what he meant and only imagined myself diving under his blankets so he could protect me from the heartbreak of another man. Something was wrong with that picture. And with what Marg said next.

"Yesterday afternoon, I encouraged you to listen to that voice of your mother."

"You said you thought it was *my* voice," I corrected her.

"Well, let's find out. I'll sit here with you. I'll put my arms around you. You just listen to the voice."

And so I tried. Marg's arms at first felt invasive, but as minutes passed I warmed to them—I felt disoriented but not threatened. And it seemed all Aleese wanted to do was cry at first, which was so out of character. And then she spoke.

"You are my daughter. You need to forgive me."

I can't.

"You need to forgive me—for what it will do for you. Not for me. For the greater good."

Greater good of what? And why don't you ever apologize for my years of enduring you?

She didn't answer. At least not those questions. She picked up my hand. My hand remained on the bed, yet I could see only a shadowy image of my hand laced with hers. And I could feel it.

She asked, *"Do you want to love me?"*

She didn't say that she loved me. But it was something I could suddenly sense, that filled me like a warm white flame spreading outward from my center. It felt strange, and yet, somehow, very familiar.

You're my mother. What do you think?

"I'm asking you, then, to do one more thing. It won't be easy. Just be totally certain you are ready . . ."

FORTY-SIX

OWEN EBERMAN
TUESDAY, MAY 7, 2002
1:05 A.M.
TV ROOM

A WHILE AFTER WE LEFT THE PARLOR for the TV room, we heard the door slam and Cora take off up the stairs crying. I stood up in alarm, already feeling awful about having been kicked out of there—too awful to sleep. It had kind of made me realize I had more in common with my brother than I'd been realizing. He'd been saying he needed a job. I'd been saying I needed a calling. I just couldn't hack violence. I guessed Cora couldn't either.

"Don't," Rain said, lifting her head up off the couch, where she'd been lying on her stomach. "There's somebody with her... one of the secret guys. Maybe they're still telling secrets."

"Why aren't you all stirred up?" I asked, dropping back down. "You got kicked out of that room, too."

"Because I want to be a gym teacher. I want to be a mom. I don't need to be a hero."

"Rain." I couldn't help myself. "That sounds so ... dull."

She eyed me defensively. I don't think she exactly liked being kicked out of there either, so her response was harsh. "How are you going to spend your life? Striking matches?"

Ouch. She was talking about the candles I lit at St. Ann's, an old habit of Mom's. After she died, I took it up. It had been hard, trying to put myself in terrorists' shoes and think that maybe they had a rotten home life or something. It was not a journey that I could describe to anyone, even Dan Hadley, who had cleared his throat and shifted around in his seat when I told him I lit candles for them, too. He had said, "Maybe you should just forgive them in your mind and not leave the evidence down in St. Ann's chapel for everyone else to have to deal with."

Maybe he was right. So, when I came here, I kept my thoughts but didn't strike matches to them. I hardly ever doubted I had done the right thing.

"That is so not nice, Rain."

"I'm sorry. It's just that, you being the nicest guy I know—that's not something that's very helpful to everyone right now." She waved her hand everywhere, to imply all the people suddenly staying in this house. We'd passed Marg on our way in here, taking Mr. Steckerman's and Mr. Tiger's overnight bags from the foyer to the third floor in the elevator.

"Do you know how hard it is to be the nicest guy you know and take more flack for it than any guy you know?"

"You don't take that much flack," she said.

"If I were totally saying everything I think, I would take a lot more than I do. I wish for an apocalypse. I want to erase this world and start all over again. Yeah, I don't care if I'm dead in this world, so long as I'm alive in the next one. I don't want to chase down these guys. I don't want to have anything to do with them. I don't care. They're not my problem. God keeps good records."

She laid her cheek on the back of the couch. I got under her skin every time I said I didn't care how long I lived. I turned the volume up and the show came back on, but she hadn't moved. I turned my aching back so I could face her and plopped my cheek on the backrest, too. A smile was spreading across her mouth that she was fighting. I sensed a session coming with pseudopsychologist.

The laugh squirted out her nose. "Your teeth are *so* white."

Oh . . . God. I hid them under my lips and ran my tongue over them, trying to wear them down. The ornery grin stayed plastered across her face. In her mind, it would now be her job to get me to smile. I straightened out and looked back at the TV but bit my lips just in case she struck on something. I didn't think it was possible. It was late.

"I ever tell you about the time Dempsey let one rip in the music room?"

Not nearly good enough. Dempsey farted constantly.

"Leddie Wiley was in there. You know, Little Miss Concert Choir?"

Headie Leddie. Weedy Wiley. Wiley the Pot Smokin' Smiley. Leddie had a slew of names. I'd always wondered what Leddie stood for. The girl could sing rock opera.

"Mm-hm."

"She has perfect pitch. She told him what note he just farted, and when nobody believed her, she struck it on the piano, and it was the exact note. I was in there."

"Mm."

"It was something weird like . . . F-sharp below middle C."

"Mm."

I grinned but didn't spread my lips. I hoped that meant we both won. But she didn't see it that way. She kept on me, "Oh yeah. When I washed my hair this afternoon, I took your shower-hose suggestion."

I grabbed my lips quickly and held on.

"I can't believe you even inspired me to try that, you dumb-wad. I sneaked it out of the handle, and the pressure was way strong, and first thing I got was my sore pinkie. So, I went, 'Yyy-ow!' and let go, and it went wild. Like a runaway snake. I got the walls, ceiling, toilet roll, medicine cabinet, box of tissues, every snot rag in the wastebasket, and out the window. Hodji was down there on the grass. He got hit. You could hear him clear to Trinity Falls. 'Marg! Something's leaking in the upstairs girls' bathroom!'"

I slid off the couch and onto the floor so I would be in front of her when I flashed my pearls of whiteness into the carpet. "You're making this up!"

"All true, I swear. She knocked on the door, and I was just getting in my towel, so I opened it. 'Is there a problem?' she asked. 'No, I'm . . . good.' But she was staring behind me, and when I turned around, it was, like, raining. The ceiling looked like a thundershower—"

Rain's dad came in to kiss her good night and quiz her on her health, and he found us both rolling around on the floor and laughing our sides off. I guessed their secret meeting had ended. I'm sure it did his heart good to find us like that. He said very little except that there would be a lot of people sleeping here tonight, but not to worry ourselves about it. I didn't. I said to her, "You talking about your five boyfriends, you made me laugh so hard this afternoon that I think I actually burned calories. I ate my biggest meal in weeks."

We both climbed back up on the couch. Slowly.

"Too bad you couldn't stay asleep tonight," she said. "It's always something."

And it *is* always something. Twenty minutes later, Cora appeared in the doorway, almost making me jump. She looked worse than last night. Marg was with her, looking all too calm, considering the question Cora asked.

"Did you guys take a tape from my room?"

"Um . . . yeah," I confessed, and she seemed more tense than mad.

"Cora, what's up?" Rain asked. "Maybe you shouldn't be in those meetings if they—"

"May I have it back, please?" Maybe she was mad.

"Look, I'm sorry," I stammered. "It's just that yesterday Rain's dad told us not to watch any TV, and I . . . just grabbed the one on top because . . . I thought your mom's other video that we watched in March, the one shot after the Kurdish massacre, was, you know, cool . . ." I trailed off, because she didn't seem to hear me, which was good. I'd never referred to her mother as cool within her hearing distance.

Marg held her hand out to me. Her other hand was laced through Cora's. "Owen, the tape that was in the VHS today. I stuck it behind the couch. Get it for us, please."

I felt around until I felt it where she pointed and handed it over. My head was shaking back and forth and back and forth. Rain saw this.

"Why don't we all watch it together?" Rain suggested.

Marg shook her head. "I already saw it this afternoon when

I was cleaning in here. I know what's on it. She needs a private viewing with a trained professional. I'm sure you understand."

They left. I sat straight up, staring helplessly at nothing. After a while, Rain rubbed my back and brushed her thumb across my face, which made me realize I had a tear running down.

"I shouldn't have given it to them," I said. "I should have destroyed it. She's gonna jump out the window."

"What's on it?"

"You really need to hear that from Cora," I said, shutting my eyes, unable to keep the thing from rolling through my head. Aleese had been filming, and Jeremy was talking to a group of soldiers in late afternoon . . . Iraqi, Iranian . . . I couldn't tell the difference. She tripped or something, and the camera showed the ground. A rock took up half the screen with a plant growing out from underneath it. Every so often the camera would bump, and after five minutes, it *really* started to bump. We hadn't even had the volume up. I couldn't imagine what these rowdy soldiers must have sounded like. As if that wasn't enough, one of the perverts actually picked up the camera so he could pan, like, the whole thing. You could barely find Aleese in the middle of all these arms and heads.

The thing was filmed New Year's Day 1986, and Cora's birthday was in early September. It wasn't too hard to figure out where she had come from. I supposed Cora had a right to know. And I supposed watching it was somehow better than hearing the words, like maybe they would never stop echoing through your head. *Gang rape gang rape gang rape.* I hoped Marg knew how to counsel.

I wouldn't know where to start. I had been thinking of asking for a session with Hollis, just from having seen it. I turned onto my back, staring at the ceiling and stating my case strongly. "When she does tell you what's on it, Rain, you will understand why I'd like to see this world erased, and we could start over. I am *sick* of this place. Obviously, that is not an exaggeration. And I am sick of being tortured for my views, by my brother, by you, by our friends in sports who love to call me a fundamentalist simply because I go to Young Life meetings and I believe in an apocalypse and a better place after. You're all a pain, and . . . I don't want to be here. I want to be with Mom."

"No, you don't," she argued in a whisper that was somehow right in my face. "It is still a good world, Bubba. I swear it is. I promise it is."

I was sort of back to where I was on the porch the other morning, wondering how to choose between my love of locker-room humor and my future in the seminary. It seemed like I hung in some cosmic balance between choosing Rain and her love of life versus giving up on this world and simply moving on. The nurses at St. Ann's had confessed we could do that. Attitude is everything, they said. This world can be weak and dirty, and yet, some people were so great and strong. I knew Rain had her points, somehow, that she was seeing things that I wasn't, because her strength was all over me, and I was absorbing it slowly and coming out of my spiral while she kissed tears off my face. She was lying square on top of me.

I thought it would kill my hips, but it felt really good. I whispered, "Um. We're swapping bodily fluids."

She sighed impatiently and whispered, "Screw it." That kiss that skid and took off again Saturday totally landed. And felt awesome.

I just relaxed.

FORTY-SEVEN

SCOTT EBERMAN
TUESDAY, MAY 7, 2002
6:46 A.M.
DINING ROOM

I HEARD HODJI TRYING TO BE QUIET on his way down from the third floor around six forty-five, heard Shahzad's mild voice and Hodji shushing him, and that got me into the shower quickly.

Heading downstairs, I noticed no cars outside in the parking area where Mike and Alan always parked, but heard more than a couple of voices floating out of the dining room. When I went in, fourteen people were there, all the familiar faces from Trinity Falls and some others. They'd hidden their cars, maybe feeling the place might be watched.

Roger O'Hare greeted me, then Angela Bonterri, an agent who had been especially nice to us during our first week at St. Ann's. The agents were drinking coffee all around, and I took a mug, though I hadn't quite become an addict in paramedic school. James Imperial was beside the coffee urn talking to Shahzad and an agent he addressed as Susan, and I gathered that this was Shahzad's Miss Susan, an agent he had worked with on Long Island.

"Can I apologize to you now, or are you never speaking to me again?" Susan said to Shahzad while I reached for a mug.

"Please, you mustn't remember firing me. You mustn't remember any of that from March," Shahzad said uneasily. "I speak to you . . . much."

I had thrown on a T-shirt and jeans, not expecting this crowd, and I looked more like Shahzad than like the agents. I noted Tyler over in the corner, in some gangsta T-shirt to his knees, telling another agent, "I'm *giving* USIC my CellScan program. No charge. Just . . . watch my ass henceforth. That's all I ask." And the agent grimaced, hand over his eyes.

It seemed apologies were running all over the place for things I wasn't privy to, but I gathered some of these agents had been stony toward them over being minors.

Mr. Steckerman asked Marg to take trays up to Rain and Owen, because it was a highly unusual day and they wanted to meet in the dining room with this many people. No one mentioned Cora. I actually sneaked up there while Marg took trays to Rain and Owen, and for once it was me standing outside her door feeling silly. I couldn't hear a sound, and when Marg came to deliver her breakfast, too, she asked me not to come in with her. She didn't say why, and there was a lot going on downstairs. I just headed down again.

The agents found chairs on some invisible cue that I realized was James Imperial taking a seat at the head of the table. All sixteen seats were taken.

"Good news to report all around," Imperial said, holding up his coffee cup.

"First, VaporStrike is in custody. Captured last night at a rest stop two miles outside Amarillo, Texas, in a blue Camry rental car."

He turned his mug slowly to Tyler as the agents applauded. Tyler made something akin to a Buddhist bow.

"That is a big load off our minds," Imperial continued. "The bad news? Omar never showed. He must have smelled trouble. We're hoping someone in this room can find him."

He looked warily at Shahzad, who shrugged nervously at Hodji. I got the feeling he didn't like being the focal point of a roomful of important people.

"As for Henry Calloway, his real name is Ovid Contescu. Born in Romania, raised primarily in a Russian orphanage, educated in Hamburg, then the University of Pennsylvania. Three years of his life between Hamburg and Penn are utterly missing, which means he was probably trained as a terrorist, and his money comes from backers in Kuwait. This is the worst kind of terrorist, our absolute worst nightmare. Because he's been here awhile, he has managed to infiltrate upstanding American institutions the way anyone else would. As an active member of the historical society for two years, biding his time, he was able to write the grant for this place, knowing that it would give him easy access to medical records that would help them in the back end. Alan? Report?"

Mr. Steckerman said, "Mike and I, and Hodji, quote, 'took a walk' past his cabin last night, but we didn't infiltrate or act interested, as it could be hot-wired. It could be Omar's lab. We want to do an ASAP raid but have no idea when he'll be there. He's not at the college or at home or the cabin right now. We'll nail him, no fears."

Imperial nodded. "He's a spy; he's not a thug. At least not in the essential sense of the word. But we need to consider him extremely dangerous, especially given the nature of what he was up to. The four patients in this house were 'swans,' in accordance with some code words he dreamed up for discussing his research. From Shahzad and Tyler's chatter and Marg's input, we believe he gave orders to Ibrahim Kansi to plant the corpse of the infected goat somewhere the kids might touch it. They wanted to see what their new strain of tularemia would do if a human made a flesh contact, and since they were watching the kids anyway, it fit their, um, fun and games. Unfortunately, they never got to find out. The point of impact was sucked completely clean by a snake kit."

I realized he was nodding at me. I shuffled in the chair, much like Shahzad had wanted to. I didn't need applause; I needed their asses caught.

"And earlier that morning Contescu, under the auspices of a visit to meet Cora Holman, laced Owen's orange juice with a clotting drug used primarily for hemophiliacs that brought on a severe headache."

Chairs moved back and forth defensively around the table, and I swallowed swill, wondering what I'd gotten myself into. It required so much self-control that my opinion of Alan catapulted into the stratosphere. All I could picture was Contescu's stones served up to him in an orange juice glass.

Imperial went on quickly. "And then, the very idea that he would try to befriend an innocent teenage girl, right under Alan's nose, reflects that he is long of nerve. We need him caught. Today."

Helpless to do much for Cora, I turned my wrath to Hodji, staring at him across the table. He had the guy in the house until ten thirty last night, losing three rounds of chess, while I sat by Cora, scared someone would walk up our nonsqueaking stairs and . . . who knows? Attempt a kidnapping? I'd just felt like it was the place I should be. I thought my instincts had been dead-on, and maybe they were. But Hodji must have noted the look of challenge in my eyes. He sent a challenging look back at me before cutting a smile.

"Didn't you ever hear the expression 'Keep your friends close and your enemies closer'?"

"Oh," I said, for lack of anything better.

"I suspect everyone, especially when they show up with vats of liquid beverages to serve to people who drank poisoned water. Something about that didn't sit well with me, shell of a man that I am."

I shot up straight in the chair remembering something about lemonade.

"Don't worry," Marg put in. "I told him she'd already had her daily allotment of citrus and that I'd give it to her tomorrow. It's with the CDC. We'll see what's in it."

I hadn't noticed Marg here before.

"Are you . . ." I paused before realizing everyone at the table was looking at me.

She reached in her jacket pocket and flashed me creds and a second license. "Firearms," she said. "I'm one of the two agents not photographed by the media in these parts, so I had to keep my creds hushed, even from you guys. It was killing me Saturday. I actually ran out of the house because I got a good view of some movement out behind the pond from a second-story window. I'm sure now it was a ShadowStrike operative waiting to photograph it if Owen or Rain touched the corpse of the Professor. I couldn't find the guy, couldn't find the site where Rain got hurt, though I'd heard her scream . . . Very frustrating. Anyway. I've been CIA for twelve years."

I kissed two of my fingers lightly and flipped them at her. She grabbed her cheek like it had landed, apology accepted. *Nurses needed in Intelligence.* I wondered if maybe I wouldn't have to forget about going to medical school if I became an agent. I would always love medicine, and at the moment, I wanted to design a cocktail specifically for Ovid "Henry" Contescu.

"And finally," Imperial said, standing up again, "there's the business of our two young v-spies and how sorry we all are that things had to reach such a state of desperation before something could be done about it. My father owned a grocery store in Des Moines for fifty-three years. He saved every last nickel so that I could go to college, and when that degree got me a government job, he said he was sorry—he never wanted me working for a place with more than two dozen employees. He said it would wear me down. He said policies begin to take precedence over people, common sense drifts away to the wind because it has to, and human dignity falls by the wayside. These were all things I didn't exactly comprehend. I'd thought he would have been proud, and I guess I always held it against him that he wasn't. Until this weekend. I had to draft a new policy amendment for our manual for classified clericals. I was up all Saturday night doing it. I made sure it was forty-some pages long, and with all the convoluted, bureaucratic speak and worthless nonsense I threw in there, the paper pushers passed it on through yesterday, failing to realize I never included an age limitation."

There was so much snickering that he added quickly, "And that is classified to this table, Level Nine." Alan had told me that classified in USIC goes no higher than Level Four.

"Any opposed?"

The room was silent.

"All in favor?" Every hand went up.

"So, let's go find Contescu and friends before it's too late."

FORTY-EIGHT

SCOTT EBERMAN
TUESDAY, MAY 7, 2002
11:30 A.M.
KELLERTON HOUSE

I KNEW ALAN SAID I wouldn't get top billing on any job, but it was a little hard to watch all the agents taking off to Griffith's Landing to look for hoods or to Astor College to look for Henry while I got stuck waiting with Hodji for a security crew to show up and hot-wire the Kellerton House like the president was staying here. It was especially hard because I had access to the basement and could hear the two other CCs typing away and talking to each other in the inner office.

"Anything interesting?" I gave my back a rest and sat in with them at one point.

Tyler shook his head. "Omar probably figured out that VaporStrike is in custody, and he's a chickenshit when it comes to his own safety. He's probably hiding out in the stall of some bathroom, like the Amarillo, Texas, Burger King, with his feet up on the toilet, afraid to move. Hey." He nudged Shahzad at a terminal beside him. "IM Amarillo. Tell them to check the stalls of all fast-food restaurants, and get down on their knees."

Shahzad searched his face. "You wants me to do this?"

Tyler cackled and looked at me with triumph. "Do you see what I have to endure? He can't tell a joke from a jelly jar. Hey, but it's not such a bad idea."

While tormenting Shahzad, he clattered out the IM he'd just spoken of, probably to some agent he was connected to in Amarillo. He had those fast fingers of hackers, so that he could type as fast as he spoke and tell a different joke at the same time.

"Was that meant to be funny?" I asked.

"I'm not sure yet. I'm bored. And very keyed up." He drummed his fingers on the keypad and cast a glance at Shahzad. "So. How's Cora?"

"She's down. That's our word for bedridden. She had some howler around four thirty this morning—that's our word for nightmare. We all have them. I charged in there to shake her, and Marg was sleeping on the cot in her room, though she swears it's not medicinal. I dunno. Cora's either whipping herself totally, or she is heartbroken over the guy. Marg wouldn't let me stick around to see. Cora is, let's say, an ocean of secrets. We're working on it."

Tyler drummed his speckled fingers on the edge of the keypad. "We call your womenfolk the princesses."

I laughed. "Rain's just a good old, down-home girl." I stopped. "Cora, though . . . You're probably not far from the truth there."

Tyler wasn't stupid. "Okay. So, you're in love with her. Aren't you, um, kind of in a rough spot?" He spat out a couple of bars from a hip-hop song, "U Can't Touch This."

He wasn't demure either.

"I'm not in love with her," I argued. "But it's taking all I have to steer clear."

"Why not go? Offer some, ya know, words of wisdom and comfort."

"Because I'm the wrong person," I said. "I'm . . . that 'other guy with feelings for her.' Anything I say lacks credibility. I tried really hard last night, but she'll think I'm gloating. She's got self-esteem issues, big-time. We're working on that, too."

"She probably feels like a fool," Tyler said, having gotten a joking reply from the agent in Amarillo, something about how they already have video cams in every fast-food toilet in Amarillo. He sent the reply, "Ew," and went on. "Which is ridiculous. The guy's a very charming cutthroat who's probably got her IQ times two. How's she supposed to resist him? I know what she's going through, though."

He told the classic story of being on the receiving end of mean girls placing bets just to hurt him. At least the guy could laugh at himself.

"Maybe *you* should go talk to her," I said. "She warmed to you. Honestly. When I walked in and saw her gripping your hand like that . . . she's not real easy to touch. Once in a while she'll melt down for Rain or Owen. Other than that it's been me and nobody else."

"Except Henry."

"Sonofabitch . . ." I wished Tyler hadn't said his name. The guy had been in her room, which in my book was kind of a sacred shrine, and sat his perverted ass on her bed.

Tyler showed the same twitches I had. "No, maybe *you* should go talk to her. She might think I'm a spook again."

Cora's medication switch. She needed me, no matter how awkward it was. I'd hit Marg up for info and then head up there, I decided.

I looked at my watch. It was a little past noon. "We eat in twenty minutes. It's really good food."

Shahzad stood up slowly, rubbing his stomach. "Miss Marg won't let us make to the McDonald's. Now I wish we had not been caught."

They followed me up the stairs to the dining room, and I got out the silverware container, the smell of hot roast beef floating through the air. The chairs were all pushed out of place from this morning, and Tyler went around straightening them as I put the stuff on the buffet.

"Sorry," he said. "I could not sit in a room that looked like this. You know what obsessive-compulsive disorder is?"

"Sure," I said.

"You don't want to live in a car with a man who has this atrocious thing," Shahzad said, pouring himself a glass of water. He shuddered. "Go and see for yourself. You would think it is brand new, not the residence for two hackers for a day and night."

Marg came out of the kitchen, carrying a pitcher of juice.

"You need some help around here," I said. "You're an RN who shoots. *Jeezus.* That's enough talent for one person."

"Until Omar's lab is found and they know it's not near here, they won't let anyone work on this property who isn't actually USIC. I'll get by somehow. I always do."

I felt very soothed over and genuinely guilty. "Can I help you out with Cora now?"

She opened a drawer, pulled out a stack of paper napkins, and laid them on the buffet. "Very primitive, our setup right now. I've no background in, uh, banquet facilitating."

"Well?" I didn't like her pause.

"She's under sedation. I was up there twenty minutes ago. She was out like a light."

I flopped back down in the chair, not liking that either. "She didn't want to be sedated last night. What changed?"

Marg said nothing. And I really didn't like that.

"I'm going up there." I moved toward the door.

"I just told you, she's out."

"I've seen her awake, and I've seen her asleep. What's the—"

She turned around, looking at me with what I perceived to be sympathy. "It's more than having been betrayed by someone she liked. It's more than realizing a second terrorist had sidled up to her and could have killed her. There's another issue having to do with her mother that surfaced on one of her tapes early this morning. She'll have to tell you about that if she ever wants to—I can't. Trust me on this. She needed a sedative, and right now, she needs to sleep."

I backed toward the door, swapping gazes with her. "Call me when the security crew shows up," I said, and turned to run up there. I could at least park myself between her and the window in case she hallucinated again. Problem was, I nearly banged into Cora, who was coming through the door, looking like some kind of a zombie.

FORTY-NINE

TYLER PING
TUESDAY, MAY 7, 2002
12:01 P.M.
DINING ROOM

MY BELOVED CORA HOLMAN had raccoon eyes—with such deep lines under them that you'd think she'd been hit in the nose with a Frisbee. She had a blank look that overly medicated people can get. I'd seen my share while in the psych ward of Beth Israel when I was turning my mom in.

Scott pulled the chair out for her, and she slid into it, didn't say thank you—didn't say anything—just put her camera case on the table and stared past it. She'd been behind me when I did most of my talking in last night's meeting. So it turned even my big mouth to stone to watch her look so disheveled yet sit so straight, like a ballerina might, or a princess. She had the air of a queen, without saying anything and without looking anywhere except the dead center of the place mat, in front of her camera case.

Scott pulled the chair to the left up beside her, sat down, and started slowly rubbing her back. I don't think she noticed at first. After an eternity, his obviously experienced Don Juan hands went to her neck. He massaged, and her eyelids drooped a little.

Then he shook her shoulder and said, "Spit it out. Or do you want these guys to leave?"

She raised her eyebrows to help open her eyelids all the way again. "No, they can stay, I . . . may I have a Kleenex, please?"

Scott chuckled, like a private joke was passing between them, and Marg handed him the box from the buffet. He laid it in front of her.

"Voilà," he said, and after she pulled one out and mopped her forehead with it, he said, "Talk to me. Come on."

She said nothing. Scott simply waited, like this was some normal thing coming down around here—Cora not speaking when spoken to.

His eyes glanced down to Marg's shoe and flipped back, and he said so innocently you would never have guessed he'd been prompted, "If you're this tongue-tied, it's got to have something to do with your mother. What'd that she-devil do now?"

"You mustn't call her that."

"Okay . . ." The sarcasm came through slightly.

"I . . . something just happened . . . and I had to think quickly. And I hope . . . that I can help USIC to catch Henry," she said.

Scott flopped back in the chair. "You are not helping to catch Henry," he said. "No penance is due. Don't be stupid."

"It's already done." She pulled a cell phone out of her sweater pocket, laid it in one palm on the table and kept flipping it to the other, studying it.

"I failed to ask yesterday, all things considered, where you got that," Scott said.

"It's his. He gave it to me. He called just now . . . asked me to meet him. I said I would."

Scott's face flushed and he swapped gazes with Marg. He looked back at the phone again and only then started shaking his head. All he said was, "Whoa."

Shahzad reached past me, took the cell phone, and opened it. He made some passes through, obviously looking for the phone number Henry had called from.

"Well?" I said.

He laid it in front of me. "Blocked. Name only."

"Where's Hodji?" Scott said. He had Cora suddenly gripped by the arm, like she might try to get up and walk out of the house in her zombie state.

"I'll find him," Marg said, and left the room.

I picked up the phone and looked through some of its lesser-known subfiles. "I can find out the number to this phone and the number he called from. I can find out approximately how far he was from here when he made that call. Problem: There's a tracer on this phone. He'll know as soon as I do it."

"Can you do it from some other phone?" Scott asked. "Or your computer?"

"If I hack. It could take a few hours, and I'd say time is an issue," I said.

Scott turned to Cora. "What time did you tell him you would meet him?"

"In fifteen minutes."

He slumped backwards again and came forward in one motion.

"Where?"

"In the woods. Right where the main path meets with the

trail off to his cabin. He was going to spot-paint the tree trunks for me the other day so I couldn't get lost again. He wants me to come out so he can show me the markings. He's obviously not aware of how much USIC knows."

"So, you told him you would *come?*" Scott asked.

"I thought I would lead USIC agents to him. Maybe I wouldn't even have to see him."

Scott slumped back again. "Problem: They're spread out across Griffith's Landing and Astor College. That's a twenty-minute drive in either case, not including the time they'll need to sprint to their cars. Here, it's Hodji and Marg with firearms."

Hodji's footsteps came trudging up the basement stairs after Marg called for him. Scott told him the dilemma. He looked focused but not like any bundle of raw nerves. I should have guessed.

He said, "Obviously, we're not sending Cora out there. We can wait the extra ten minutes and get USIC to nab him."

I got restless over the thought. "Ten minutes late? It could make him suspicious enough to take off."

"Or, worse, it could draw him to the house to come look for her," Scott put in. "I don't want the guy anywhere near the house."

"I can get the local police that fast," Hodji said, taking out his cell phone. He dialed Mr. Steckerman, and they only talked maybe a minute before he hung up.

"He's getting four local Port Republic cops to meet us at the water hole. They know the trails. They can be here in five minutes in an unmarked car. I'll just keep them belly down until he comes into sight."

He was wearing a gun in a shoulder holster and went to the

hall to put on a jacket. I didn't feel comfortable. What if Henry had more guys with him?

He didn't seem concerned. "Marg, guard the keep. Don't draw arms with all these kids in the house unless you hear shots," Hodji said. "And Scott, you lock the door behind me. Both of you, go around now and make sure all the doors are locked, just in case. And don't, under any circumstances, let anybody in unless it's the USIC faces you know."

Scott went around checking windows and doors on the first floor after locking the door behind Hodji. Marg disappeared into her room and then went quickly down to the basement to do the same. I watched from the middle of the parlor as Hodji darted across the grass and disappeared down the trail to the pond. Shahzad had come up beside me. He was too quiet.

"I don't like this . . ." he said quietly.

"Why not? USIC will be here fast, and it'll be five to one until then."

"Where is Miss Rain?" he asked suddenly. We hadn't thought of that. I ran back to the TV room and whispered "whew." She was dozing on one end of the couch, and Owen was dozing on the other.

"Maybe they won't even have to know of this," Shahzad said, and we headed back to the dining room, where Scott was pacing around and Cora sat, still flipping the little phone from hand to hand. It rang suddenly. She jumped a foot, and Shahzad grabbed it from her, hit the speakerphone button, and set it in front of her. He nudged her.

"Hello?" she said. I thought she might turn to pudding, considering how bad she looked. But her voice didn't even falter, to my amazement.

"Hi. I'm a little early," the voice came through.

"Okay. I'll try to hurry."

"Don't bother. I'm here."

We all froze. We were watching the porch. The floor never creaked, but when the door from the basement swung open, we realized Henry wasn't on the porch. A tall man and a really short guy came into the hall, shutting the door behind them, which would prevent the alarm from sounding.

The tall one snapped his cell phone shut, looked at the four of us, and said, "*That* was easy . . ."

FIFTY

SCOTT EBERMAN
TUESDAY, MAY 7, 2002
12:13 P.M.
DINING ROOM

I DIDN'T KNOW whether Marg was alive or dead, and the thought would have to wait if I were going to keep my sanity. I got calm beyond what would be conceivably possible, watching Henry and Ibrahim Kansi come through the dining room.

I must have looked worse than I realized because he said, "Don't worry. I'm not carrying a gun." He closed the double doors and leaned against them. "I'm not a violent man." Then he laughed. "Well, put it this way. I don't like guns."

His little monkey friend walked around to me and simply said, "Excuse me," and I let him pass to the far end of the table. He had a gun sticking out the back of his jeans. I could have pulled it. *Nervy guy.* He was banking that we were stupid? He could have separated my face from my body before I figured out how to undo the safety lock. He stood looking at us with his arms folded across his chest, his nunchucks folded in the middle of them somehow.

"For me to have a gun would be redundant. I have him." Henry nodded down the table. "Because our dear friend Ibrahim could cause any one of the Trinity Four to hemorrhage in thirty seconds, and truth be told, we only need one of you to get hurt. Where's Cora?"

My heart didn't even lurch, though I knew it was all this weird defense mechanism my ambulance squad called CBS (calm before the storm). We'd get the calmest calls from spouses of people in coronary arrest. It's usually gone by the time we get there.

She was really calm, too. She raised her hand. The backrest of the velvet chairs came six inches above her head, and he poked his face around. "Hi there."

"Whatever drama you're creating, Henry, please just finish it before you disgust me too thoroughly and I ralph all over this table and horrify my friends."

It was her sweet voice but not her words. He sighed in fake frustration. "You cut me to the quick! I'm a man who loves beauty—under a microscope or in the world at large." He pulled something out of his pocket, and I quickly realized it was a handful of syringes. He kept pulling off red caps and tossing them in front of her on the table, but she refused to take her eyes off the pitcher of water Shahzad had left.

He put his hand on her shoulder, and that's when I stopped breathing. The needles were inches from her face. She finally turned her eyes to the side and looked away again.

"Henry. You're trying to scare people about dying when they're growing used to the idea."

"Well, you could be dead tomorrow. Scott could be dead tomorrow. I know who these other young men are, and, well, come to think of it, they could both be dead by tomorrow, too. But that's not what we want."

Tyler and Shahzad just sat there, as blank as I felt and Cora looked. Maybe there's a time you need to react that just doesn't work well in movies. Nobody seemed ready to scream. Maybe we'd been drugged for too long.

Henry stood up straight, took one of the needles in his right hand, and pushed the plunger slightly. Dots of liquid flashed in the air. "Watch this," he said in quiet awe. Three drops hit the table, and after a long minute, they started to sizzle. In another three seconds, the finish turned green, then white, and then the drops started to eat into the wood itself.

"You'll be able to see straight through to the floor in half an hour, and yet it won't eat through a latex hypo. It's a shame most of it's going to go to waste. I understand the USIC went ahead and made arrests today. Anyway, I don't necessarily want to waste what I have. Let me tell you why I'm here. It's not to be entertaining. Pass me a chair, please."

I passed him the one closest to me, and he set it down in front of the now-closed double doors. "I know USIC will be here in ten minutes. I also understand that they will do anything these days to prevent kids from dying. USIC has something we need desperately."

"Which is?" I found my tongue in the silence. I supposed he wanted me to.

"A friend of ours, arrested in Amarillo, Texas, last night. We need him back."

Shahzad spoke up. "American Intelligence does not make trades."

"I'm becoming a bit of a media expert. I get research grants and use the media to get more research grants. I know the media. USIC wouldn't make swaps to save anyone . . . except perhaps its 'minor children.' They wouldn't want the bad press if we start sticking you with hypos and throwing you out the door. Cora's going to take pictures. For the media."

Cora's eyes moved to her camera, then back to the pitcher. She looked so out of it. I knew she was fighting the sedative Marg gave her, but added to that seemed the idea that she really didn't care. It was the first jolt of fear I felt. If he couldn't get a rise out of her, I was afraid he'd lose all his charm.

"The bad news is that for USIC to know we're serious, we need to throw somebody out the door. Somebody's got to be sacrificed. And it's our order of business, because it needs to be done anyway. Which one of you is the Kid?"

Tyler and Shahzad looked at Henry. My heart turned to sludge. Your CBS only lasts for so long, and then you start losing it.

Tyler slowly raised his hand and said, "I am."

FIFTY-ONE

SCOTT EBERMAN
TUESDAY, MAY 7, 2002
12:18 P.M.
DINING ROOM

I SHOOK MY HEAD ever so slightly as Shahzad watched me, afraid if he confessed, the two men would get angrier. It felt like walking on a thread to keep them amused.

"Good," Henry said. "You're not going to waste our time. I like that."

"Where's Marg?" I couldn't help asking.

"I didn't shoot her full of FireFall, if that's what you're thinking. Though I don't know why not. She never liked me. She liked you more. Mr. Don Juan. Seems to me you'd be every parent's nightmare." He shot a glance at the back of Cora's chair and smiled. "I know all about the Trinity Four. And it's more than just your daily vitals, blood counts, and medications. After I wrote the grant, I went all out. I got curious. Did you know that on Sandy Copeland's blog, she writes that when she found out she was number nineteen, she got disgusted and broke up with you? What were you up to before we put you out of commission two years later?"

I'd never known why Sandy broke up with me. It was sudden. "We've all got our issues," I mumbled, then couldn't help looking him up and down with his fistful of hypos and adding, "don't we?"

He exchanged glances with Kansi, who looked suddenly more tense, and Henry shook his head. I brought one of my hands up to my lip and pinched it, knowing not to push my luck one hair farther. I thought of the goat and monkey corpses.

"In our strict culture, Mr. Eberman, you would be considered some sort of a freak. A miscreant, tainted and unfit for marriage."

I wondered if I was supposed to feel bad about that. I noticed that the doors behind Henry didn't quite meet up and that a tiny ray of sun shone through the slit. I was off to the side and figured Kansi had a better view than I did, but I watched it helplessly, thinking if USIC came back and was sneaking around, I would see breaks in the sunlight. It was all I could think to do. That, and focus on something Alan had told me back in March after the raid and the arrests. He said, "It's nothing like James Bond. They're more human than you think. They make mistakes. They *always* make mistakes."

"It's okay," Henry said. "Honestly, I found my situation with Cora close to unbearable. I just hated sitting on the bed with her, touching her hair, smelling her sweet smell. It made her seem almost human. And she's not, you know."

Cora's eyes closed, but she didn't move otherwise.

"A bunch of my friends and I, in college in Hamburg, we

knew a woman like you, Cora. Obviously, we never touched her. We called her the *Vergewaltigung*."

Shahzad's eyes rose to her and widened. He knew a lot of languages . . .

Henry went on, "Cora's e-mails indicate she's trying to figure out who her father is. Maybe one of these days she can narrow it down to one of sixteen or so Iraqi soldiers. Terrible, isn't it? To have a gang rape for a father? Isn't that rather like being an incest baby? My god. How can you walk about with your head so high? How is it you put on so many airs, Cora? What do you have to be so proud of?"

"My mother," she muttered, and watched the air like maybe she was hearing things again. She sat up and said in a nervy, loud voice not her own, "I haven't heard you say where *you* really come from, Henry. Maybe you'd care to share with everyone whatever . . . glorious lineage you're referring to."

Gang rape baby? For later. Now I wanted to stuff my fist in her mouth. I had gone quickly from thinking she should try to get a rise out of him to thinking maybe she should keep quiet because she would piss him off. But he merely smiled and waved down Kansi, who tensed, dying to strike.

"I'm exempt," he said. "I am sent from the Father Above."

I didn't consider myself a religious person, but there is something paralyzing about hearing a line like that from a guy like this. I swallowed metallic spit as my soul collided with my brother's.

Shahzad swallowed likewise and muttered into the table, "*Das ist Amerika, wo Sie sind willkommen, auch wenn Ihr Vater ist ein hippo.*"

436

Henry turned to them and spat out in a taunting whisper, "*Ja. Deshalb nennen wir es der Hund Haus. Die Grube der Mischlinge.*" Then he looked at his watch. "I had forgotten about you two. You're not nearly as interesting, are you? You're a write-off, a failed experiment of Omar's before he decided to listen to me. Scott, go get your brother and the Steckerman girl."

He must have sensed the "go to hell" wafting off of me.

"We only need one body, but we need everyone in one place. Sick kids fall asleep, sick kids wake up. I don't need them running around the house screaming in panic while I'm trying to kill people. Go. Don't make me angry."

I moved through the kitchen and felt Kansi following me, leaving Tyler, Shahzad, and Cora with one guy who held six syringes and maybe had a gun under his jacket. It was humiliating. I went into the TV room and found the window was wide open, the screen punched out. The room was empty. The remotes lay in the middle of the couch. Kansi checked behind the couches and the drapes.

"They must have heard you and taken off," I said. *Not as stupid as you thought, you little ape.*

He touched my arm to pull me back, and that sent me into a deeper level of calm, equal to how bad I should have wanted to kill him. I didn't try anything.

"They're outside," Kansi said as we returned.

"Ah. Our guys in the brush need hostages, too. That works well."

They're hostages. My brother will never live through this. Think of it later.

He pulled a flat-bottomed beaker out of his pocket and

with the hand holding the hypos, used his fingers to get the top off. Too much self-control. He set it in front of Tyler. "FireFall is a terrible way to go. This is not. Drink it."

Shahzad gazed at me again and I shook my head, looking to the floor. What Tyler had done was noble, but what was done was done. We needed to keep Henry seated. If the beaker got anywhere close to Tyler's mouth, I was diving for Henry.

Tyler's CBS was still with him for some reason. I glanced over my shoulder for something to hurl—not that we had a chance. The swinging door to the kitchen was still open, and I could see a carton of a dozen or so cans of organic tomato paste, but we'd all be dead by the time I reached and heaved even one. And I hadn't pitched in baseball since I was twelve.

Tyler stuck his head down to the beaker and smelled it. *Ballsy, ballsy.* "Smells lousy. What is it?"

"Just drink it."

"What if I don't want to?"

"You will. If you don't, I'll stick Cora with one of these."

Henry didn't even move to Cora, didn't hold it to her throat. His confidence stunned me more than his threats did. We couldn't rush him, not considering he was holding something more lethal than a gun. Kansi swung his nunchuks once, which I supposed meant he'd come after me as well, and then they disappeared into his crossed arms again. The *whir-spit-whir* sound caught Tyler's attention. He looked at me, then at the beaker, and I could see the terror written all over his face.

"Don't waste our time. You're supposed to be dead anyway." Henry was leaning back in his chair, the top still caught up under the door handles, not looking the least bit nervous. "I'm counting backwards for you. Ten. Nine. Eight."

Tyler pulled his sense of humor out of his ass. "Can I say grace?"

"You may not. Seven. Six."

"That's a terrible thing. Maybe you're not the only religious guy in this room."

"Five. Four."

"Thanks, God. Amen . . ."

"Three—"

The rest happened so fast, yet it left an eternity of flash images in my mind. A *bang!* drew my eyes to Kansi, who dropped his nunchucks and gripped his chest as blood poured through it. Tyler and Shahzad flew under the table, yanking Cora down with them, and Kansi staggered toward Henry, reaching him at the same time my brother did. I dove for Kansi and took him to the floor. I didn't have to hold him down for more than a few seconds. He went limp and was, I presumed, dead, leaving me to stare at my brother, frozen with horror.

Owen held Marg's smoking gun in his hands and had it pointed square in the middle of Henry's forehead. Henry had his fistful of hypos stuck up to my brother's neck. If either of them moved . . .

"Careful, Owen," I whispered in the most even voice I could find.

Henry smiled, though I noticed his Adam's apple bob deep into his throat as he swallowed. "Well. It appears we're at cross-purposes. I'll put mine down if you'll put yours down first."

Owen laughed once without smiling. His hands shook badly, even with one gripping the other. "What did you say a few minutes back? You're sent from *where?*"

"From the Father Above," Henry repeated without wavering.

My brother's exhale was so sickened, I expected his last meal to follow. I'm sure he was picturing Mom and thinking about the concept of guys sent from the Father Above sending her on.

Owen's whole face was shaking now too, even his eyelids. But he said, "I got a great idea. Let's both go there . . . and find out who stays."

The trigger made one little click. He would face off, in spite of his terror, I just knew it.

I think Henry got the idea he was serious. He didn't move, but tension rattled in his laugh. "I thought you were the non-violent one."

"I am," Owen managed to say. "I don't have to like it. But I will split your head open and put your soul into orbit. We can see where it lands. Shall we?"

"You don't want to die this way," Henry said. "It's slow."

Owen's shaking was ridiculous, yet the butt end was an inch from Henry's forehead, and Owen looked ready to squeeze the trigger. "So? We'll be dead a *long* time. I'm ready. Are you?"

Owen, just shut up and pop him. It's fast. Take a risk. The electric silence that followed could have killed the rest of us. Henry wasn't shaking—it could have proved fatal if he had been, what with a hand full of hypos—but I noticed his face was shiny wet. A line of sweat trailed in front of his ear. I got a flash thought that the only edge my brother had on this rocket scientist was that he'd had lots of time to think about this particular thing. My brother was born to think about stuff like death.

Rain's feet floated past me. I hadn't seen her come in. She stopped so her feet were beside theirs, square in the middle.

"What do you want, little Miss USIC?" Henry asked. "You come to watch your boyfriend sign off?"

"I just had an idea," Rain said. Her voice was really quivering. "Wouldn't you rather pick on me than him? Considering who my dad is?"

Her legs started to glisten. She was pissing herself. I almost dove for Henry, just because I couldn't stand it. But his voice rose.

"Frankly, I would. But I'm afraid to move," Henry said. "Do you have any persuasion with this man?"

Rain would not put herself in the death seat. I just knew it—not that she didn't have the nerve. She just didn't have the faith. I didn't either. Hence, what my brother was doing was so inconceivable that I could only watch.

"Oh. So you *are* afraid. What are you afraid of?" my brother yelled. I think Rain had confused him, had confused Henry, making them both panic, both more likely to screw this up. And she did about the stupidest thing you could do, only somehow it worked out. She shoved Henry's arm outward, and glistening threads shot into the air as he hit the plungers. My brother shot Henry square in the face, and he toppled to the ground. Owen's hand relaxed, and the gun dropped immediately.

"Don't move! Don't step!" I hollered, dropping to my knees and pulling Owen toward me, since most of the hypos had fallen to the side and behind him.

He collapsed onto his butt, and I shook him to clear out the stupor.

"Did any of that stuff hit you?" I demanded.

He never answered. A fist reached out of nowhere with yet another hypo. It wasn't a ghost. Kansi hadn't been completely dead. He drove the thing into my brother's back and hit the plunger. Another *bang!* resounded as Rain shot him with the gun Owen had dropped.

Owen gasped, went wide-eyed, and then came down like a ton of bricks into my lap.

FIFTY-TWO

SCOTT EBERMAN
TUESDAY, MAY 7, 2002
12:28 P.M.
BASEMENT

T YLER AND SHAHZAD had become shadows that now were jerking me to my feet.

"They didn't come alone!" Shahzad said. "Outside, they heard those shots!"

Hodji flew in from the porch and kicked the door shut with his foot. I thought a shot fired outside, but I was fixated on Owen. Uncharacteristically, my hands were trembling. I couldn't find a pulse.

"Basement," Hodji hollered. "Now!"

He moved into the dining room, gun in both hands, then kicked the door shut behind us as Tyler and I carried my brother downstairs. I yelled at Owen's lifeless form just because there was nothing better to do. Rain and I did CPR on him for three minutes straight. I did the mouth-to-mouth, having to fight her for it briefly, as we realized there was a chance he'd been injected with something that could poison the breather. I didn't want to think about it. Finally, a shaky hand reached for his neck, and then my chin, and Marg squatted beside me, looking half dead.

"Stop." She held up a hand and continued groggily, "He's breathing on his own."

We were in the little inner office. Only the computer screen lit the room. I'd been aware of the door opening and closing once. Now Shahzad said, "I found Miss Marg on the floor of the darkroom. They cut the window glass and created an ambush."

She rolled her neck around, grimacing. ". . . never saw it coming. I just felt it . . . jab to the shoulder. My last thought was of my gun, which I'd left unlocked on the nightstand before running down here. Hoped one of you guys would—"

"On three," I said, and Tyler, Shahzad, Rain, and I lifted Owen onto the old servant's bed. Marg was shaking her head every few seconds, trying to bring herself out from under the spell of the knockout drug, but it would take a while. I found Owen's pulse, which was only about thirty beats a minute, but strong. I couldn't let myself think about what might be coursing through him.

I turned my attention to this roomful of people who were either barefoot or wearing only socks. "Did anyone step on one of those syringes while leaving the dining room?"

I flipped my eyelids shut, prayed, and opened them to see Cora holding her fist out. She had her fingers wrapped around all of them. "I was afraid for the squad . . ." She trailed off.

The small needles could have penetrated a shoe . . . any agent could have carelessly picked one up, pricked a finger before stopping to think. I tried to say "nice going" but couldn't ignore how badly her hand was shaking.

"Just don't move." I tried to say it calmly and edged toward her, holding a hand out blindly toward Rain, who was behind me. "Gimme your sweat sock."

She put it in my hand, and I stretched it open and slid it up to the bottoms of the hypos sticking out of Cora's hand. I said, "Some will stick to your skin. Just open very slowly and let them drop off."

Her hand was less sweaty than I would have imagined, and only one stuck. Her trembling dislodged it after only a second. I put the sock gingerly in the drawer of the nightstand and started looking around to see who else was injured.

"I killed a guy." Rain's voice, having obviously flipped back out of serial-killer mode. "Oh my god."

"Hold on to it." I crawled over to Tyler, who sat with Shahzad against the wall opposite the bed. In the dim light of the screen, I could see the knot on Tyler's jawbone from where he took a flailing swat with nunchucks from a dying Ibrahim Kansi.

I felt around it, my heart bottoming out over him saying he was the Kid. "You ever pull a stunt like that again . . ."

He managed a smile and spoke without moving his jaw. "I'd love to say it was heroics. Truth is, when my mouth isn't running, I'm deadly uncomfortable. Just don't know why I didn't say I'm *not* him . . . Roll of the dice?"

It was bullshit. Tyler had covered for his best friend, Cora had yelled at Henry and carried WMDs downstairs in her bare hands to keep the USIC agents from stepping on them. Rain and my brother had killed two guys. Hodji was still upstairs with the madmen. I felt like a wuss for once. We'd have a lot to tell. But before anyone started announcing heroics, we had to get out of here. I hadn't heard any shots fired since we came down, but we were buffered.

"Broke your jaw," I said, pulling my fingers away. "Hope you're good with pain. You don't have much choice—"

"I thought two years ago I couldn't possibly get any uglier. Amazing, eh?"

"Relax. Don't talk," I said.

I moved to Shahzad. "Any injuries?"

"No." He looked at Cora. She was now sitting with her arms wrapped around her knees, her forehead on them. He moved over to her and knelt, looking down at her neck until he put a hand on her hair and patted.

"Miss Cora, we have a belief in our village that you can absorb words the same way as you can absorb oxygen. Or food. You must not do that. You must not let the words of bad men enter your spirit. It is a gift from God."

She nodded without raising her head. He had said something in German upstairs to Henry in her defense. I asked him about it.

"*Das ist Amerika, wo Sie sind willkommen, auch wenn Ihr Vater ist ein hippo*? I had said, 'This is America, where *all* are welcome, even if one's father is a hippopotamus.'"

She laughed once into her knees, but when her head didn't go up, Tyler crawled over on the other side of her, ignoring my edict not to talk. "You wanna compare dad stories? I didn't know mine. I never did. But I know he slept with my mom, which makes him pukeworthy by default. You're not your dad, okay?" he said. "Am I my mom?"

In the dim light of the monitor I was able to see my brother's eyes flicker, then fly open. I went to him. He covered his face with his hands and let out a telltale groan.

"Your head?" I asked.

"Yeah. What happened?"

I didn't like the foreboding headache but heaved a huge sigh, deciding that Ibrahim must have injected him with the same stuff he'd injected Marg with.

"Forget about that. Just gimme a number," I said. "Richter scale."

"Uh . . . six," he said. Six wasn't bad, but he could be lying. I was afraid to touch my brother, afraid not to. I put a hand on his forehead. He was burning. "Owen, man. You did a great thing. Take a look around at these people. Some of them are important to national security. Some are important to us because we love them and they're good people. They could be dead right now, but some of them may get to see their ninetieth birthdays because of you."

I didn't want him feeling guilty of murder or something else dumb. He shook his head like he might argue with me. He said, "Someday, every person in this room will be vital to national security . . . or something even bigger." I don't believe in people being prophetic. I took it as just great babble, and I loved the look of victory that crossed his face.

Rain didn't. She gasped in some horror I didn't get and contradicted me. "Owen, don't even go there! You did *not* do anything that great!"

She climbed up on the bed, lay half on her stomach, half on him. She kissed the side of his face, and they started swapping spit like crazy, to the point where, when the nosebleed started, I couldn't tell at first whether it was hers or his.

FIFTY-THREE

CORA HOLMAN
WEDNESDAY, MAY 8, 2002
1:20 P.M.
BASEMENT

Wɪᴛʜ ᴛɪᴍᴇ ᴍᴏᴠɪɴɢ ꜱᴏ ᴘᴀɪɴꜰᴜʟʟʏ ꜱʟᴏᴡʟʏ while we waited for USIC, I knew Scott was losing his mind, going back and forth from holding his brother's hand to breathing like a pregnant woman in the ninth hour of labor.

It was almost an hour before we heard a voice.

"Scott? Rain?" Mr. Steckerman.

Scott stood and opened the door. Both Mr. Steckerman and Hodji were there.

"Everybody all right?" he asked.

"Tyler's got a broken jaw and my brother's bl— My brother has a nosebleed."

Mr. Steckerman looked over at Marg, who shook her head to imply, I think, "It's out of our hands."

"Anybody get shot?" Tyler asked through his clenched jaw.

"Two of their guys, none of ours. There's at least two more

of them. We've got a SWAT team forming out there to clear out these woods. You have to stay put."

Marg asked to be released to get a shot of morphine for Owen, and Mr. Steckerman accompanied her upstairs. We could barely hear them crawling on the floor above us.

"We'll be right outside this door," he said when they returned, and he shut it.

Hardly anyone said anything. I drifted off, came to, came to again, and only one time in the next few hours did I think I heard a gunshot. They might have fallen back to Henry's cabin for all that it was so quiet. Then things got beyond quiet. There was a point, several hours into it, where everything froze. Time, the people around me . . . I sensed it, and when I drew my head up from my legs, I saw them dozing, or praying, heads down, not moving. There was something reverent in the air, as if questions could radiate and answers could glow, if not be spoken aloud. I sensed a strong source of that glow to my right. Aleese was sitting and watching me, her arms around her legs, her chin on her knees, her back to the door two feet away from me.

She kept staring until I thought she was about to say something profound. She reached her hand up and ran her finger down my cheek. "Got blood on your face," she whispered.

I knew to hold the silence, to not expect answers to complicated questions, to not even ask. I can't say why. Maybe the dead speak a higher language with their higher thoughts, and we can only hear when they use the simplest of their terms. Perhaps, when it appears the spiritual realm is not answering us, the answer is over our heads, and we're the sluggish ones—not them.

I could see a bit of sense in why Aleese might have drawn me in to Henry while warning me so brazenly about Scott. It had nothing to do with her liking one man better than the other. It had to do with practicality, what would serve us all best in the long run. If Henry hadn't had a "lure" into the house, he might have ended up—someday, if not today—in a cross-fire between USIC and ShadowStrike and would not have fallen into the hands of people whom he assumed he could toy with. He had drastically underestimated us. Oma used to say that adults can remember their childhoods better than their teenage years, when awkwardness is ruled out as acceptable behavior, yet continues to rule so much of life. Under the bad memories of so much intimidation, adults, she said, forget how sharp and fearless they actually were.

An unhappy child had become an unhappier teenager. Henry had forgotten *a lot*. Enough to get himself killed.

I still didn't understand why she seemed leery of my feelings for Scott. My eyes rose again to Aleese. She watched me and, after a moment, started shaking her head slowly back and forth.

I love him.

"*Later,*" Aleese said. "*I promise. But much later.*"

How much later is much later? Seven years?

I thought of telling her either to please leave or to tell me something bearable once in a while. But how could I do that— with all that came clear in last night's tears and tossing.

I could see that I would have been a simple pregnancy ter-mination at the nearest hospital in nine hundred and ninety-nine cases. To have delivered me and sent me home to a woman desperate for ten children who weren't meant to be—that was the best that Aleese could do. That she went back out into the field to get nearly slaughtered in Mogadishu five years later was beyond commendable. That she had given me her own mother at the expense of ever visiting her childhood home was more so. That she might end up living with me, having to look at me every day, was surely not something she foresaw. She owed me nothing—less than nothing.

And yet here she sat. I was certain of it, regardless of how the memory fogged over later, regardless of how I tried to reinterpret it once my strong sedative wore off. I wanted Scott Eberman, and I wanted her to tell me it was all right. All I could get from her was, "*later . . . much later.*"

I felt a shadow fall over the room, a darkness with density. Aleese's eyes went sideways to Owen and came back again, troubled.

Don't take him, Aleese. You can't.

Her eyes radiated sympathy. For me, I realized. She had no foreboding thought for Owen.

Please. Not on this day. Think of Scott. I know you don't like him, but—

Her eyebrows raised as her head lowered slightly, though her gaze never left my eyes.

"*Rethink, Cora.*"

But I wasn't otherworldly. I still fought for the comforts of lower logic, which didn't include thoughts of life versus death, still so magnanimous that I covered my ears to keep out Owen's sniffing and focused on Scott. It took a while. But I focused on that soapy-alcohol smell of him wafting over my way until I could sort it out from everyone else's. It had always made me feel safe, and I felt safe enough to proceed.

Logic: If your mother likes the boy, your mother approves of the relationship. I had a mother who loved the boy yet resisted the relationship, and who wanted another man wiped off the face of the earth badly enough to thrust me to him. What kind of a mother would do that? I hunted my soul for some answer other than that I was turning into a paranoid schizophrenic given to strange imaginings. One answer seemed to be that I had a mother who didn't fear death and who understood the future . . . a higher form of mother instead of the usual, the lower form. Maybe, for once, I was the most fortunate person in Trinity Falls.

Life had been a gift from her, a gift that most others would not have been willing to give. I couldn't conceive how to repay her. At the same time, it was my life, and I felt pushed, exhausted by the tug-of-war games I put myself through. Or she put me through.

You're not here. You're a figment of my imagination.

"*That so?*"

You're a sedative I accepted at the wrong time.

A hand gripped my wrist and pulled. "Are you all right, Miss Cora?" Shahzad's voice whispered from the other side of me.

"Yes. Why?"

"Your fingers are in your ears, and there is no sound. And you are mumbling to yourself."

I glanced over at the bed. Owen was sleep breathing, no longer thrashing, no longer sniffing. Rain lay beside him, staring up at the ceiling. Scott sat with his back to the bed, a bloody tissue in his hand, staring at the floor. I couldn't say when the last time was that he wiped his brother's nose. It may have been a while ago, because he turned his head and watched me without seeming distracted.

"Sedatives." I sighed, patting Shahzad's knee. "Sorry."

I studied Scott so long and so hard that I didn't realize he was studying me back.

"Don't, Cora."

Oh, leave me alone.

I crawled across the floor, slid under his arm, and leaned into his body heat. He rubbed my arm, and I listened to his heartbeat, rhythmic and strong for now. What we had was too mysterious to predict. Learning to live in the now was not an option.

"Cold?" he asked.

"No."

He froze in a moment of confusion . . . but only a moment.

"Dumb, stupid teenagers . . ."

A few minutes later I sensed Aleese drift away. I felt released from her higher-thought obscurity, though I sensed strongly she would be back. But that would be then, and this was now. He stroked my arm, played with my elbow, and at one point when everyone's head was down, lifted my four fingers on his index finger and kissed them.

Mr. Steckerman found us in these positions an hour later. One man on the SWAT team had been wounded. Three more ShadowStrike members had been killed, six were under arrest, and every square inch of woods had been combed. We were safe to come out. Owen was still alive.

FIFTY-FOUR

CORA HOLMAN
SUMMER 2002
KELLERTON ESTATE

Owen DIDN'T DIE THAT NIGHT. But a change occurred in him, appearing first as a small shadow then extending slowly outward over what would otherwise have been a glorious summer.

Two white baby goats were delivered to the property by a Hammonton farmer who had read the news accounts, which had detailed our losing the Professor and Owen's fondness for sharing his thoughts with the goats. Owen named one Cow, and the other Champ, despite it being a girl. He took to feeding them and Sheep, and on the days he wasn't four-star, we would sneak them into his room until Marg realized their *baa*-ing was coming from within these walls.

Tyler's and Shahzad's skin cleared up by June—as much as it might ever clear. They still had white dots, a dozen on their faces and several hundred on their bodies, and their permanency remained a question. They didn't care. They spent much of each day in the basement, trying to find their enemy, Omar, turning to other international terror plots when he failed to show up every day. They scripted plans of a bombing in Britain and didn't fail to thrive.

I suggested to them once, "Why don't you come outside and get some sunshine? Maybe a tan will change things with your 'dottage.'" Tyler had dreamed up the term "our dottage."

I suggested it down in the basement, while they were poring over some new programming element they were adding to one of their famed search engines. Tyler said, "Maybe if we stay here, we'll get pale enough that our nondottage will turn white."

They seemed happy enough, so I never pushed them. Scott worked down there every morning, making USIC phone calls, typing notes, and filing papers. And if everything was done, he would sit and watch Tyler and Shahzad, understanding nothing of what they were doing but saying little.

USIC bought me a computer, and I started getting training in the program that declares matches of old and new photos. I wasn't a very fast learner, and though I eventually got the hang of it, I was not asked to use it all summer. I felt relieved USIC didn't need me.

The four of us came up for lunch and often stayed upstairs together to play cards in the parlor in the afternoon, though Tyler and Shahzad refused to watch television or even enter the TV room.

"Images without html support leave me feeling ungrounded and dizzy," Shahzad confessed once, and Tyler, I supposed, only enjoyed dramas of his own creation. Scott and I usually chose their company over the TV. For one, Owen watched a lot of TV and read less these days, his headaches being the excuse, which came no less frequently than when we first arrived. Scott spent some time with his brother every day. But, thinking of his own health, he made the tough choice not to be around a situation all day and night over which he had no control.

Tyler and Shahzad were sympathetic to every sad situation and helped Rain a lot, who still passed through periods of despondency. Having an image in her head of killing a man—even a violent man—took her down dark mental tunnels where I simply could not follow and Owen did not travel. He refused to think about it, he said, and since he felt he had nothing on his conscience, any discussions would be pointless. We respected that. Rain was still not allowed in the basement, but sometimes when we would come upstairs, we would find her sitting against the wall, waiting for us. Tyler made her laugh. Shahzad listened to her with all due respect, saying little. But when he did speak, it was gold.

One boring afternoon in July, she paced and blathered in the parlor. We were all in there, except Owen. Her topic was her friends, how they'd "stopped coming." Her May birthday had drawn a couple of hundred people out here, and I argued that they hadn't stopped. But it was nearly two months later, and we hadn't seen Dempsey, Dobbins, Tannis, or Jeanine in maybe two weeks. Rain was wondering aloud how long it might take them to call her.

"So, why not call them?" Tyler said. "I can't remember too much about having friends, but it seems to me that calling is an option."

"We bum them out," she said. "I felt removed from them when I was still in St. Ann's. Having killed a guy? That changed things, somehow. I don't feel, like, young anymore. And then there's the fact that a part of me enjoyed it. I don't know how I'll ever feel normal."

She started her sniffing routine, and we were thirty conversations past assuring her that her actions had been beyond heroic. Shahzad put in his rarity. "The CIA actually trains snipers, Miss Rain. Did you know that?"

"And?"

"Food for thought, as you say in America."

She spun, horrified. "I want to go to college, have two-point-five kids, and a house in the 'burbs . . . When are you suggesting I shoot people? Between feedings? I can't get over having killed a very, very bad guy. Are you nuts?"

"Perhaps. As I recall, a strong conscience is the CIA's top criterion."

We all thought he was only looking for a good way to distract her, but he found it. He had her outside five minutes later, having brought out a gift from his Uncle Ahmer, who showed up here three hours after Shahzad and Tyler's televised funeral and stayed a few days. It was six knives in a little black bag, and Shahzad was showing her how to wing them at the trunk of an oak tree. Having played at this since age nine or something, Shahzad could actually flip one by the blade, catch it with the handle, wing it, and stick it in a tree thirty feet off.

Hodji stood behind Shahzad, arguing in Punjabi, probably about the inappropriateness of certain village games here on American soil, but Rain went gaga over it.

She smiled back at Scott and me after hitting the tree once out of her two tries. "This appeals to that awful side of me . . ." She hit the tree trunk with two of the remaining four.

"If it would keep her from crying, I'd order her a crate

of grenades," Scott said, and we walked back to the house together.

We turned the corner, safely out of view, and I jumped in his arms, wrapping all my limbs around him, and kissing him over and over. We'd just decided to risk swapping germs, and what Marg didn't know wouldn't hurt her. After all, Rain had swapped spit with Owen in the middle of a nosebleed, and no stray germs had passed between them. Scott reasoned that carrying me around for a minute or two at a time was his only exercise outside of climbing the stairs. "Us" was a highly guarded secret that probably fooled no one, especially Marg. But the truth was, after rushing for our first private moment once we left that basement, I had probably spent more time kissing Scott than not kissing him.

Affection, toward him only, had become my drug of choice, the only thing that numbed the horrifying sensations that came with the knowledge of my roots. I wore the vest of rape child, no matter how often or how hard I tried to tear it off. It could grip me and itch and smolder, making me wonder about genetics and children of violence and the feeling I'd had since puberty of never quite belonging anywhere.

I had yet to do things like sneak into Scott's room in the middle of the night, or vice versa, as his aneurysm scared both of us into stellar behavior. But kissing him was a dream, a great escape. His lazy, loping bottom lip still drove me crazy. And he had this maddening way of planting his lips on mine and then saying something.

"How are you feeling?"

"Divine." I devoured his bottom lip, and then both at once.

"How long?"

"Twenty-one days, same as this morning."

He kissed my nose, let me slide down, and leaned back onto the house while rubbing my back. "Every hour counts. I want that cocktail soon. We *all* need that cocktail," he said, implying things about his brother, though there was nothing really to say.

The Q3 in Owen's bone marrow wreaked such havoc in his hips that he could only stand for a few minutes at a time. We had ordered him a wheelchair, which hadn't arrived yet. With him spending more and more time in bed, I often wondered if he would ever have gotten up if it weren't for Scott's insistence.

While Owen showed no evidence of false guilt about what happened that day in May, it had been a great catalyst in his downward spiral, and I was never sure whether it was brought on by the physical energy he had to exert or if the world simply became too ugly a place for him after that.

That Owen simply "wanted out" was a thought I stumbled on in private, though Rain confirmed it one day when he was too sick to feed the goats, and we'd walked across the lawn to their trough to do it.

"I know he loves me," she said. "He loves me . . . as much as Owen can love anybody."

I'd never thought Owen lacked in the heart department and asked her what she meant.

"He's just not in love with this world. He's in love with . . . some other world I can't begin to see. He thinks he's going to see his mom, see his favorite saints, and become, like, some super-hero that, like, helps people out during disasters. Like, from the other side. I go back and forth. Sometimes I think it's pathetic. I mean, I do believe in heaven. But I think of people sitting up there like stars. Like, twinkling or something. Other times? I can't forget how even his voice was when he held that gun to Henry's head. You have to believe what you're saying to not buckle at a moment like that. At any rate. Whether he's right or he's wrong, he's going, Cora. I can't stop this anymore."

Scott couldn't accept the concept at all. He drummed on my hips.

"What would I do without you?" he asked.

He raised the question often, and it was beginning to make me uneasy. I had not sensed Aleese again, at least not close up. But as his question hung in the air, I felt afraid to look around. It wasn't exactly a new fear. I had thought lately that I would see her out my window at night or while gazing from the edge of the forest at a time like this. She was a shadow that could cloud my sunny moments. There were other shadows, too, that were like her—little summer storms that passed as quickly as they came.

We jumped apart and began innocently walking along, three feet between us, as footsteps approached quickly. Tyler and Shahzad ran past us.

"Visitor at gate," Shahzad said, and they leaped onto the porch then disappeared into the house.

We weren't expecting anyone, and the fifteen USIC agents who sometimes worked out of the basement were allowed to know about the two of them. So we watched the long driveway, hearing the crackling voice of the security officer down at the new gate via Hodji's walkie-talkie.

He and Rain caught up with us next, and he said, "It's my son."

"Twain?" Scott asked. "I thought he wasn't speaking to you."

"I thought so, too. I'm relieved as hell, though this isn't exactly the place I would like for him to see me."

I didn't see how it mattered—here, there, anywhere. I was simply relieved for Hodji, figuring his broken heart could now start to heal, and I wanted to be as nice to his son as was humanly possible. He was our age, having just graduated from a private prep school in Manhattan.

Twain parked his car out in front of the porch steps.

A beaming Hodji opened the driver-side door, and when his son got out I could see a slight family resemblance. Scott took hold of my upper arm. "Maybe we should disappear."

"Why?" Rain asked. "Maybe he'll want to hang out with us."

I agreed with her but got my first inkling of what Scott was thinking when Twain merely shook his dad's hand and didn't return the hug. Then I remembered how Shahzad had told us once that in March, Hodji had asked Mrs. Montu if a kid from Pakistan could stay with them while he was ill. I believe she was only told that Shahzad was very quiet and had done some computer work for USIC in the past. Mrs. Montu had declined quickly after hearing the symptoms, saying nothing had prepared Twain for sharing a household with someone covered in scabs.

Twain was taller and better looking than his father and had that ornery yet unscathed prep school look that lots of girls adore. And while we all looked fairly healthy, save Owen, I wondered what he would think of us.

Scott hauled us inside, which I thought was rude, but I said nothing. When the two of them finally came in, we were sitting in the parlor, where Marg was distributing meds to Rain and Scott with glasses of her homemade iced tea. Twain stood in the doorway and stared, first at Scott beside me, then Rain, who was lying on the floor. Hodji introduced us, and he said "hi," then simply leaned against the door frame.

"Do you want some iced tea?" Marg asked him without an introduction, something she must have sensed was right.

"No, thanks." He watched us like Shahzad's speckles had jumped from his face to ours, and multiplied. He said to his dad with noticeable acrimony, "So . . . these people are your new job?"

"Yes. I'll be the training supervisor to all Washington's classified clericals," he responded before the awkwardness of it could set in. "That would be Cora and Scott for now . . . There will probably be more in the fall." He gestured to the two of us on the couch, then pointed to Rain. "Rain is the daughter of the South Jersey supervisor."

He didn't even nod at Rain. "And where's *him?*"

There was no denying the hostility this time, and Hodji didn't try to jump in quickly to cover it. He stayed quiet for a minute.

"I told you in my first e-mail. He died. In a house fire."

"Oh." Twain finally came into the room, ignoring us but studying the portrait of Mrs. Kellerton and looking at some of the books on the shelves.

Hodji attempted a joke. "If you don't read my e-mails, don't you at least read the news? It was all over the papers. Even *Dateline* covered it."

"Dad, I'm out of school. Why in hell would I read the news?" He stuck his head in the library and then turned back. "Nice digs."

"Let me show you the outside," Hodji said, almost shooting toward the hallway.

Twain followed him to the doorway and stood there, I suppose realizing that to not say *something* to us would be ridiculous.

"So . . . you're also the guys who drank the water, right?"

"Right," we chimed, and I went after an itch on my ankle attentively as my heart went out. He was jealous of our time with his father, though I couldn't begin to see how to mend it.

"Oh. Sorry."

Right, see ya, bye.

"*Wow*, what a fucking brat," Scott said in awe after he left.

Rain pulled Shahzad's bag of knives out from under the chair. "I was afraid he might use one on us if I let him know I had them."

Nobody stated the obvious, that there were only two parents among the six of us, and one was in jail. I said that if Twain could become grateful and supportive, maybe he could end up a CC and have more exciting time with his dad than he ever dreamed of.

Scott stared after him, shaking his head. "If that kid doesn't sell weed, then he hasn't worked a day in his life. I don't think it would have dawned on him."

The whole thing had lasted only a couple minutes, but I call it one of those shadows thrown over our summer because it served as a milestone. Trinity was an upper-middle-class community with its own population of pink-cheeked, well-dressed, car-owning, depressed people our age. I'd always shrugged before and assumed it was normal. Now it was another reminder of how far we were drifting away from our roots, though where we were going remained a mystery.

Aleese came back to me the first week of August. She appeared in a dream the day after one great thing happened and one terrible thing happened.

The great thing: I was declared to be in full remission. The cocktail had worked even better than the Minneapolis team anticipated. I could be released from the Kellerton House in a month and take up my life any way I wanted to.

The bad thing: That same afternoon, Owen failed to wake up after a Headache from Hell and was declared comatose shortly after dinner. As he had signed his DNR form a month earlier, there was nothing for us to do but sit in his room and await the inevitable.

His friends and teammates came quickly, filling his room, the corridor outside, and at one point, the entire stairway. Not wanting to risk my own newly declared remission, I finally poured myself into bed after a twenty-four-hour vigil that ended around seven o'clock in the evening.

Aleese sat on the footboard, her hiking boots on the bed, her fingers laced between her knees, while she nodded. *"Now we've got a real mess, don't we?"*

Scott and me, she meant. I told her to go away.

I've heard it said before that comatose patients often come to for one last goodbye before they die, and it was that way with Owen. He awoke several days after falling comatose, he opened a few cards, laughed at a few punch lines, and listened to Dempsey play the guitar—Jon played poorly, but the song he had written about friends was beautiful.

464

Owen kissed Rain, told her he loved her, then said, "I'll see you." A half hour later, he was gone.

The service was bigger than his mother's. Scott dissolved in a heap at his passing and again getting out of the limo at the church, though he gave a beautiful eulogy about courage and hope and the afterlife, which told me that Owen had left the most important part of himself in his brother's heart.

The aftershocks were something I anticipated, but their harshness was totally unexpected. Scott barely ate the following week, went back to bed several days in a row after doing his morning work for USIC, and was little comfort to Rain and me, though he tried. I measured his and Rain's agonies against my own, which were extreme. I couldn't stop seeing Owen talking to the goats. I'd overheard enough to make those conversations among my favorite memories.

"See that butterfly?" Owen asked.

"Baa-aa."

"That used to be an ugly ole hairy caterpillar."

"Baa-aa."

"That's me. I'm an ugly caterpillar. But guess what?"

I would go into Scott's bed, and he would want to sleep with his arms around me, his face in my hair, but he didn't speak much. Tyler and Shahzad succumbed to watching TV—in Scott's room, so we could all hang out together—and Marg said she was praying this phase would pass. I was praying for a miracle. It came in the strangest of ways.

I was writing in my journal on the eleventh afternoon past the service when I heard Rain crying. I didn't run to her quickly, as this still happened two or three times daily. Scott noticed before I did that there was an echo to it—she was in our bathroom, which meant it could be a medical emergency. He stomped out of bed and down the hall, and knocked on the door.

She refused to answer, which alarmed me deeply. Back in March, one new drug had created ulcers on our intestines, and we passed blood for a week. Their graphic three-way conversations describing this phenomenon left me pulverized but thinking there was nothing we couldn't discuss.

"Rain. Open the door or I'm breaking it down," Scott said. She let him in, and by the time he reopened it thirty seconds later, Shahzad was at the top of the stairs with Tyler behind him, and Marg was at the door. Scott closed the door behind him and slid down the wall.

"Oh, Jesus," he said. "We got a pink stick."

Apparently, Rain and Owen had been withholding bigger secrets than Scott and I have. I wished it had been Marg who went in to her first instead of Scott. She entered with that compassionate and nonpanicking nurse's tone, but the argument had started. And I was more scared at that moment than I was weeks later, after the doctors had scoured her condition for the passages through this pregnancy that wouldn't kill her. The arguments she presented were so typically teenager-ish, and she would so need to start acting like an adult.

"It was his idea!"

"Now, why don't I quite believe that?" Scott shouted.

"Okay, it was nobody's idea! It just happened! Damn that Miss Haley—she started it. We did it less than ten times!"

Shahzad was simply gone, down the stairs in a whoosh of too-much-information, and Tyler and I finally moved to stifle Scott's mouth. "Is Miss Haley so stupid after all, Rain? *Why* didn't I see this coming? Are you trying to kill yourself?"

Tyler tried to pull him up. "Either get up and get dressed, or go back to bed, but you can't sit here and terrify her."

Scott got up. And he only had two two-star afternoons in the weeks that followed that kept him down. They say routine is healing, and his was etched in stone. He spent mornings doing clerical tasks for USIC. He spent afternoons waiting hand and foot on this vessel that was carrying his brother's offspring. We all did. Evenings he spent with me.

Come September, I felt like Scott had escaped death-by-Q3 twice. Once USIC saved him, and now Rain had. With a twenty to forty percent chance of the baby being born with the virus, the situation was still scary enough for him to feel needed, which had always been his greatest therapy.

He and Rain began the cocktail September 2, my birthday, and a better present I could not have had. Scott was in a contented, hopeful mood that night as we walked to the bay, where we'd been swimming a couple of nights a week. Shahzad had talked him into believing that Jersey bays had some sort of healing powers. Often they came out and swam with us at night, when the amusement pier was lit up at Griffith's Landing, an icon of American innocence that had come so close to being tarnished. We watched that Ferris wheel turn, all lit up with lights. This time they decided not to join us.

Out of view of the house, Scott patted his chest and I jumped on and let him kiss my neck and my chin.

"Don't fall," I said.

"I'm careful. Besides . . ." He kissed me twice, the second one endless. ". . . if I fell I could now use you for a cushion."

"I think I'll get down now."

"Stay. You give me strength." He meant it both ways, and I

knew I could not go a minute more without confessing my sins. I'd had them planned out, starting only a week ago. I'd never thought of myself as a fast mover, nor as a nervy person. But Jeremy Ireland called *me*, his plans already in forward motion. Everything he'd wanted fell into place like some rock of ages falling from the heavens and landing at my feet. The confession had gone off very well in my head, in spite of Aleese showing up in two more dreams to tell me, *Now we've got a mess.*

"Say it," I began.

"No, *you* say it. I'm always saying it."

"I love you."

My reward was a bumpy kiss while he walked and a lecture with his mouth on my lips. "That was good, Cora. You didn't even stammer over the *L*."

"Scott . . . um."

"Spit it out," he said.

"Would you ever consider marrying me?"

He stopped dead in his tracks, looking into my eyes in confusion. "Funny thing. As soon as I started kissing you I stopped being able to read your mind. *What?*"

"I'm asking you a simple question."

"Are you *proposing matrimony* to me?"

"Well," I said. "I'm just saying. I'm a girl, I'm in love, and I think of it."

"Cora, I'm certainly not marrying anybody else."

"So, like, when? How many years?"

He started walking us toward the water again, though slowly. "Okay . . . I'll be twenty in December, but it's an old twenty. And you're an old eighteen on this most auspicious day." He kissed me swiftly. "However, we don't live in Indiana. I'd say three. Three years. Why? What's the rush?"

"I'm not in any rush," I said. "I was thinking four years. Four years feels right for me."

He stopped again.

"Am I getting heavy?"

"No, you're getting weird. Maybe I can't read your mind anymore, but I could name a hundred girls who would bring up the M-word to their boyfriends. You are not one of them. What's up? This conversation stinks like some that went on in the break room in the hospital. A couple of guys' numbers came up to go to Afghanistan, and they got engaged really—"

We exchanged stares a long time, my heart slamming through my chest so strongly I was sure he felt it. "Oh . . . no . . ." he breathed. "You wouldn't do that to me. Not after Owen . . ."

I stumbled for words about chronically wearing the yoke of rape child, of feeling the need to embrace my mother in order to get past my father, and Jeremy Ireland having offered me the perfect opportunity. But my thoughts had been too intense to be driven out in just a few sentences. I said some of it, and, "It's the perfect job. It's less than three years. But I'll come back every time there's a break on airfare—"

He dropped me fast and intentionally. I barely got my legs under myself in time.

FIFTY-FIVE

SCOTT EBERMAN
SEPTEMBER 15, 2002
KELLERTON HOUSE

CORA DID TRY TO EXPLAIN, even after my arms gave way. Jeremy Ireland had gotten a contract with PBS to produce some ongoing documentary series about female war correspondents, of which her mother would be episodes one and two. Cora blathered on about needing to be one of Jeremy's four assistant producers—to get to know her mother's life. Then more on the psychology of being a rape child.

Rape child would obviously be an uncomfortable identity—I could understand that totally, but not what she considered therapy: They would shoot three months in London and three months in Paris, where the international journalists hung and where Jeremy and Aleese got to know each other. And if Cora's blood stayed clean for those six months, she would be pronounced officially "cured." Then they would start chasing around Third World toilets, shooting Aleese's former battlegrounds and those of other female war correspondents.

With the words "Ethiopia, Rwanda, and Somalia" pouring out of her mouth, I got more angry than I'd ever been. She started to hyperventilate, sensitive to my energy, and I just stalked off. *Great. I start out thinking she wants a wedding date. I find out I can have it if she first goes to places where people get decapitated on the Internet. Am I supposed to love this? Do I need a third urn of ashes?*

And I kept telling myself I was not being selfish—she was being *totally* selfish.

I had just lost a mother and a brother, and her losses were not even close. And yet I had totally been there for her. Now I had to make it through January before Godfrey would consider the surgery to remove the aneurysm from my brain, and that was only if I went into remission as quickly as she had. Rain had to deliver a baby in February without it killing her or my niece/nephew. Cora had her health, and suddenly she wouldn't be around for either tense moment.

I got further bugged remembering how in June she penned out all these thank-you notes to the nurses on our floor at St. Ann's, because the truth was, *I* beat them to her room half the time when her nurse's buzzer went off. *I* had nursed her back to health more than any single person, and my thanks was that she was taking off with her she-devil mother's best friend.

If hell hath no fury like a woman scorned, there's got to be some counterpart for guys. I couldn't risk yelling and blowing a fuse, but I was an expert manipulator going way back, and she was a lamb led to slaughter.

I made an announcement at the breakfast table the following morning, instead of telling her my great news in private first.

"When Godfrey was here earlier, we were talking about my 4.0 in paramedic school. He told me that experience will cancel certain facts, like that I was thirty-sixth in my class at Trinity instead of valedictorian. He said that just from name recognition of being one of the Trinity Four, I could probably get a full ride in any premed program in the country. He said he'll write in his recs that not only was I *one* of the Trinity Four, I was *proactive in the care of* the Trinity Four. With Cora's remission, he's more famous in his medical circles than we are. There is some justice in the universe. At one time, I had only the grades. Now I've got the funding, it looks like."

I turned to Alan, who was so focused on Rain lately that he was clueless about me and Cora. "You use nurses in USIC. Do you use doctors, too?"

He reminded me of their relationship with the CDC. They had six on their payroll.

Everyone applauded, Cora the loudest, bouncing in her seat and making a few highly supportive comments. I grunted. I ignored her while I filled out applications like crazy—Harvard, Penn, Georgetown, Stanford. Then she began realizing *I* might end up in some far corner of the country, and she'd start acting worried, all "Where will you be?" *It's only funny when you take off,* I wanted to say but held on to it. I made sure to accidentally leave every application on the dining room table. She asked more concerned questions. I grunted.

Whereas I'd generally spent my evenings with her, I suddenly got interested in the newspaper. I read, out on the porch, all of Hodji's five daily papers, because she'd sit beside me at that point and cry and beg me to pay attention to her. It was fun, passing her tissues, just so she'd throw them down and storm off to cry in her bed pillows.

After five nights of this, Marg told me I was being an ass. Rain felt the baby kick but said she wouldn't let me feel it until I quit my pity party. Hodji even made some comparison between me and his douche-bag ex-wife, which hurt to my core. I was risking losing Cora for good, he said, and I needed to grow up. And it irked me to no end that they could all see her side of it more than mine. Still, Hodji's words humbled me enough to be civil, at least through one conversation that first week.

It started with her versus me and the *New York Times* out on the porch.

"Scott?"

"Hmm."

"Uncle Jeremy says of course I can come back for your surgery. I can take as long as I want. I just spoke to him . . ."

Uncle Jeremy. That was rich. "Oh. Well. That's something. That's an expensive ticket, I know. Tell him I said thanks."

"I will. I wish you knew him better."

That made one of us.

"I actually set aside enough of my inheritance before donating it to the project to come back both summers for three weeks."

I already knew their production schedule went from October of 2002 through May of 2005. "Three weeks. We could do a lot in three weeks," I said sarcastically.

"He said the whole production crew could take off the entire month of June, both years. That's three whole weeks, given travel days."

Guess it's a lot of flight hours to get back to a Third World potty. "June. Not bad. It's too early to go to the beach yet—here, where the beach is everything. I'm sure we can find something to do, though."

"We could go to New York . . . see some Broadway shows."

I sighed, trying not to get all worked up, but my fury just wouldn't back down. "Sounds good. I'll just spend Christmases with Rain and Alan. Or maybe I'll just stay at school and take two winter-break crash courses. Maybe I won't miss Mom and Owen so much if I pretend the whole holiday thing isn't happening."

Dead silence.

Duh-uh-uh. When all of Cora's schoolwork had been graded, even with the Q3 virus giving her hell, her class rank had only slipped from eleventh to twelfth out of over six hundred. *Twelfth.* And yet *I* had to think of details like Christmas. She hadn't even landed one of those pristine brain cells on Scott's First Christmas without Mom and Owen.

After a worthy silence, she was crying again. Guilt is good, I reasoned.

She made a tearful recovery attempt. "Scott, you know how I babble when I'm nervous, but this is really important . . ."

I had to listen really carefully through her jabber and fill in some holes. The gist: After sponsors bought into their PBS series, their initial investment would double back, and that money could be used for one of her mom's big dreams: To get these women out of northern Iraq who had been jailed for committing adultery—and their kids were in jail with them.

I was all *Fuckin' A, would you just shut up? I* suddenly felt manipulated. Kids being in jail because their mothers were there . . . the concept was so inconceivable that I wondered if

474

she'd been lied to. And something else was bothering me, but in this cyclone of business-slash-charity speak and tears, I couldn't have found my own face in a bucket. I couldn't pinpoint my problem.

"I don't quite get the big picture, either," she cried on, and grabbed a Kleenex from the box she had in her lap. She'd been carrying the box around since I refused to touch her. "But Uncle Jeremy is very smart, not just about journalism but about international laws and immigration policies, and even raising bribe money. He says you can get anybody out of jail in Iraq if—"

She stopped. I was totally staring by this point, my confused heart melting a little.

"Anyway," she went on. "I hope you can forgive me for not thinking of Christmas. That was stupid. I'm really sorry. It's just that . . . I forgot what it was like on Christmas to do something besides read a book in bed. I haven't had one in four years . . ."

My world turned sideways. *How could I have not seen that?*

Cora's five years of heartache were working *for* her instead of against her, I realized. She could have been a drug addict, a pity party, a dropout, a suicide. She was one of those people making lemonade out of lemons. But how could she be equipped to chase around the globe, raising money for causes that would make my mother rejoice, but she couldn't remember something far simpler, like Christmas with your boyfriend who just lost his family?

I didn't have any answers. I pulled her into my lap, kissed her all over her face, cried, and apologized my ass off. She didn't hear any of it; she was simply happy to be back where we both wanted her.

Only thing was, my forgiveness didn't stick. In the middle

of the night, I started to zero in on what I couldn't pinpoint that bothered me. *"He says you can get anybody out of jail in Iraq if—"*

I walked across the hall, opened her door, and sat down on her mattress. She was curled up in a ball facing me, and I shook her, though I didn't have to. She woke up easily. Her radio alarm showed 4:10.

"You haven't been reading the newspapers," I said.

She cleared the sleep from her throat. "I figured you'd been reading enough for both of us."

Very funny. "Just please tell me that adventure-crazed uncle of yours isn't planning to take you into Iraq. We might be going to war with Iraq."

"Oh . . . no. We haven't talked about going inside Iraq at all." She put a hand on my arm, stroking it for reassurance. Her warm touch did bad things to me. I still had an aneurysm in my head, and I stood up, reminding myself of why, when I was four-star, I never sat on her bed or let her sit on mine. *Someday, if there is a God in heaven . . .*

I kissed her swiftly on the forehead and walked out again. But I stopped dead in the hall, scratching my sleep-clogged head, and did an about-face. This time I stood in the doorway.

"What do you mean, you haven't 'talked about' it? Don't you think you ought to 'talk about' it? How's he supposed to get a million bucks in bribe money into Iraq? FedEx?"

"No . . . specialists carry in bribe money. I know nothing about them and don't want to. I can assure you; a trip into Iraq is not on the production schedule."

She was saying the right things . . . it just felt *wrong.* I decided maybe it was a general alarm bell going off, and I didn't need

Iraq to make it specific. *All* these places were fucking dangerous. And they were germy. Had we nursed her back to health from a WMD so she could go off and catch some local plague in Africa or the Middle East? She might have book smarts, but she was an airhead at times, off in her own little world. She'd be walking down the street, bang into some warlord, forget to say "excuse me," and get herself executed online. *What the fuck, Cora?*

I started in again the next morning as she was helping Marg with the breakfast dishes, only this time I wasn't ignoring her. I was on a nag-rant fest. "Such charming places for the girl who never wanted to leave Trinity."

"I *do* just want to be normal, Scott. I just need to do this first. I swear. I'm still me," she argued tiredly. I wondered if she'd gone back to sleep after I woke her up. I hadn't. "I *don't* want to turn into my mother. I just would like to relate to her a little more. Really. Who else do I have?"

This was an indirect reference to her father being a face in a gang rape. I wasn't meaning to be glib, but it seemed so obvious. I took her hands, put them on my face. "Touch," I said, pressing them to my cheeks. "I'm flesh and blood." I laced all my fingers through all of hers and squeezed. "I'm *here*. Your mother's *dead*."

She wiggled her fingers away. "Weren't you the one always pushing me to be stronger? To send away my own demons? I have a chance here to get a lot stronger. Why can't you be happy about it?"

"Can't you be stronger without wandering around the world's unflushed toilets for two, almost three, years?"

"So you only want me to be stronger if *you* reap the

benefits," she said with this cold and upright tone she'd developed recently. "Like your pushing me to do work for USIC ... because *you* are in USIC."

I wasn't used to thinking of myself as a selfish person. If I didn't think I could withstand another loss so soon, did that make me selfish? No, I decided. This wasn't about me. If she'd hit me up with California or Alaska, I'd have felt betrayed but would have bitten my tongue.

"You know what I think? I don't think you will be back. I think you're gonna get in some big, damn trouble. I think you're *looking* for trouble. Penance due for having a mystery dad, or some damn thing—"

She left the tea towel and retreated to the dining room to look out the window. *Ba da bing,* I made her cry again. And so soon, too. Justice is sweet.

"Don't forget to iron your burqa." I stumbled past her and paced into the parlor, where Hodji lowered his newspaper to watch me. I shouted in to her, "I hear that's all the rage in Somalia. You can get arrested there for going outside without your head covered."

"Some people need to watch their blood pressure," Hodji muttered in a singsongy voice, which I didn't want to hear, so I paced back to the dining room.

"I'll keep my head covered." She wiped a tear, and I shoved the whole box of tissues across the dining room table just because.

"And don't forget Afghanistan," I shouted over my shoulder, taking up her job beside Marg.

"Scott, honestly," Marg whispered.

"She's in remission. Let her sweat some bullets. It's good for the pores."

"I am definitely not going to Afghanistan," she hollered in, which was supposed to soothe me over, but it only said to me that the truth was, she hadn't made up her mind about Iraq— where Saddam Hufuckingssein had George Bush Senior's face tiled into the floor of his favorite hotel, so Iraqi dignitaries could wipe their shoes on him every day.

The very word *Iraq* left a punch in my gut. I went with my instincts.

"Listen to me." I moved to the doorway and spoke with a tremor in my voice that I was pretty sure only I could hear. "If you go into Iraq? Do not ever call me."

She spun to look at me, never a good liar. "It's the place where I was conceived, Scott."

Alas, the truth: She wanted to go. She was hoping we wouldn't go to war, so she could tread on in there with Uncle Adventure some week when the workload was extra light.

"I was conceived in a cheap one-bedroom condo in Las Vegas!" I yelled. "Has that turned me into a fucking weekend gambler?"

"*Shhh!*" she and Marg implored me. It was the kind of outburst I'd had to learn how to resist.

I took three deep breaths, and Cora approached me in her calmest voice. "This is *temporary*. Why can't I make you understand? I'm *incomplete*. I can never really be there for you if I don't work on myself. This is as much for *you* as it is for *me*."

"Oh, bullshit," I said. She actually meant it, I was sure. She just didn't know what she was talking about. Relationships can't withstand this kind of wear and tear. All my friends went off to college with girlfriends at home, and none made it to spring break without biting some forbidden fruit.

"All right!" She moved toward the door, holding her head like ghosts of Headaches from Hell were after her. "I won't go! I'll call Uncle Jeremy this morning, tell him you wanted me to choose between him and you, and I've chosen you. I'm half a person right now, Scott. But if you're happy with half, I guess I owe you that much."

She started to leave the room for the phone. *How did I end up being the prick?*

"No, stop! For god's sake!"

She cried into the door frame. I'd never been afraid before that a person would get dehydrated from crying so much. For someone who didn't used to cry, she'd done a huge turnaround this week. I dropped down into a chair, stared at the table, and let Marg tiptoe up behind me and rub the stress out of my neck. I didn't want Cora to stay with me—I wanted her *to want to* stay with me, or something that would sound equally stupid.

All that came out was, "This is a *mess*. A gigantic, major, fucking *mess*. *Why* did you break down that day in the basement and all but jump my bones? I hadn't let myself love you. I had everything under control ..."

Her eyes went wide with some horror I wasn't privy to, and she simply stormed off to her room. I clomped up to mine and fell onto my bed in exhaustion. All my weirdest dreams up to that point had been sex-driven, and I'd had this recurring one that was my big secret. I'd dream I was with Cora, and the lights would change, and some rum-ridden babe from my partying past would suddenly be underneath me. I'd flip awake, wanting to hurl. Sometimes I'd still be smelling rum.

The switch to the cocktail hadn't taken away that whacked, oversensitive sense of smell. Hence, I wasn't surprised when cigarettes hit me—I decided I was dreaming again, but I was too tired to wake myself up. Cigarette smoke is a smell I hate, and I never let any girl smoke in my car or around me. So my memories of stale cigarettes are few and far between—enough that I remembered the last time I'd smelled that. It was the last day in February, after my squad got a call that we possibly had a death at the Holman residence.

The image of Aleese's dead body had always stuck in my mind—not because I hadn't seen a dozen DOAs before. But because I could see right away that this dead addict on the couch had caused some major hells for the sweet little thing who had called us, who sat in the chair beside her. Aleese had been waxy, skin-and-bones, and full of Q3, though I didn't know that last thing at the time. Cora, with her perfect posture, yet tormented, feverish eyes, did not belong in the same room with this emaciated figure, the empty hypo Phil found in the couch, or the strong smell of cigarette smoke wafting off a half-full ashtray.

Now it was like someone took that ashtray and waved it under my nose while I slept. I knew I was sleeping, knew weird things happened in my drug dreams, and my reaction lately was to be all *Okay, maybe I'll get laid*.

The cigarette belonged to a woman who came in and sat on the footboard of my bed with her feet on the mattress. My first thought was, *Definitely not a sex dream*, though how I knew that wasn't clear. My second thought was, *Whew. Whoever she is, at least this won't be a dream about Aleese Holman.* I'd always dreaded one. The strange woman looked only ten years older than me, tops, with shoulder-length, dark fluffy hair that flounced. Some other news lady . . .

It was a tomboy squat, and she had good muscles in the arms she rested on her knees. She flicked her cigarette into the middle of the bed, and I was all *Set me on fire, why don't you?*

That made her eyes rise, though her head was still down, and she had this ornery grin that worked mostly on one side. She was really stunning in a tough-girl way. I recognized her not from the laughing eyes or from the thin lips, but from an overall aura that made me realize all features were the same, except that Cora's lips were thick and pulpy. And I was suddenly all *Shit. This is Aleese Holman.* She just looked nothing like the corpse.

I started in right away. *You can get the fuck out of my head. I was there to pick up your dead body, remember? So Cora's off to make a documentary about your life? I've done more for her in the past seven months than you did in eighteen years. I'm not asking to see my name in lights.*

She blew smoke over my head in a thoughtful way, and then her eyes came back to me. Her ornery smile dimmed some, but not entirely. Thus began the strangest fight I'd had yet in any drug-induced dream. She started it.

"*You know what? You whack off too much.*"

That's rich. Mother of the Year. You talked to Cora like that? I bet.

"*And you got a lot to learn about real charity, Mr. I'm-Such-a-Giver. Grow up some before you think you're going to touch my daughter. You've no concept of what you've laid hold of.*"

I know her better than you ever did.

"You ain't so pretty when you cry, so stop. You'll get her back."

Oh really? Odds are against it.

She laughed, pointing the two fingers pinching the cigarette back at herself. *"You're talking to me about odds? Are you forgetting something? I'm dead. I know what's coming."*

I decided I should throw myself forward, one way I could always get out of dream company that freaked me out. But she got me on that line that I'd get Cora back. I lay watching.

"It's not that I dislike you, kid. You're okay in my book. Just understand that you're a pigeon with a peacock. You wanna be a doctor? Fine. Be a surgeon. Scratch your own itch. But you better learn how to play second fiddle—"

If I'm a pigeon, what are you? A turkey buzzard?

"She's going to outshine you in every conceivable way. Get used to it. 'Cuz I'm bringing her back. To you. So watch your mouth."

I couldn't control her stinky stale smoke, but I'd learned to control when annoying dreams ended. I shot up to a sitting position, and the room cleared of cigarettes and mouthy comments.

I screamed so it banged off the walls, "Marg! I want off this Nabilone now!"

Marg trudged up and reminded me I was now on the cocktail and hadn't had Nabilone in a while. I smelled Cora out in the corridor, so when Marg asked what I dreamed, I had no problem telling her slightly loudly, "I just dreamed Cora's butch-ass mother was in here. Can you imagine a worse nightmare than that?"

I was being a horse's ass. But it was a mess. I'd had this six-month crash course in being everything from the best medic out there to the best big brother to the best labor-and-delivery counselor to the best non-sex-crazed boyfriend. Add Cora leaving me, and I was beyond my lessons.

But we had no choice except to go on like the whole blowout never happened. It surely had accomplished nothing except prove to me that looking after people—the thing I do best—was not the thing needed by the girl I loved most.

We watched every sunset together like we did before. We walked, talked, hugged, kissed, played with the goats, took pictures of all the nature around here, and I applauded her images as we developed them. We avoided the immediate future at all costs. We could talk easily about what our kids might look like, being she was dark and I was blond, but we never touched on two weeks from now. We'd grown so accustomed to living in the now that it was possible to keep the future dim.

Our best moments were watching the sunsets from the porch. Cora is petite enough to fit in my lap with her feet on my knees, her arms on top of mine, and her head tucked into my neck. I figured I had grown up a little since that night Hodji and Marg let me know I was being an ass. We were sitting like that, and I could smell that faint carnation scent in her hair. I kissed her ear and took my thanks in her fingertips squeezing into my palms, as her fingers were laced through mine from on top. The sunset was red and gold and pink, and the air was perfect. There was enough breeze so that the bugs were not around. The goats kicked up grass at each other in the foreground. I let that be enough.

"Right now. Right this very minute." I searched through myself, forcing the past, the future, and any grief therein to the shadows. "I am happy."

She wasn't so easy to please. She didn't look out at those woods, like I did, and see nature's reminders that God was in charge and we would make it through our lives. She still saw ShadowStrike, I think.

I don't know if she'd ever see those woods as cleaned out and terror free. She'd been attacked twice—both times with USIC agents surrounding her. I wondered if she wasn't actually leaving because of Omar and whatever ShadowStrike operatives remained at large. I wondered if she thought she could escape her fear of them only by running as far away as was conceivably possible, burying herself in the masses of far-off lands. If so, her gut reaction defied common sense. How much easier would it be to pluck her out of a marketplace in Rwanda than it had been to get at her while surrounded by USIC?

But of course I didn't say that. I had no reason to believe we would ever turn into assassination targets. We'd just been kids in the wrong place at the wrong time. She wasn't any less safe than anyone else.

"You're happy?" She turned her head, kissed my temple, and smiled. "I'm so glad."

The statement kind of throbbed with the notion that moments of complete contentment still eluded her.

It seemed to help her to say, "I'll be back. I promise. The one thing that means more to me than anything else is making sure Scott Eberman gets his happily-ever-after."

I could not understand how anyone choosing to go as far away as possible could be sincere about coming back. I ignored the chill that swept down me as a gust blew in our faces. *She will come back. We'll grow old together.* We'd learned this year to walk through mine fields and not flinch when the ground rumbled. I let her presence be enough as the sun sank slowly behind the trees.

CAROL PLUM-UCCI'S novels have been highly praised for their suspense, complexity, and relevance to teens. Her first novel, *The Body of Christopher Creed*, was a Michael L. Printz Award Honor Book, an ALA Best Book for Young Adults, an IRA-CBC Children's Choice, and a finalist for the Edgar Allan Poe Award for Best Young Adult Mystery. Her subsequent books—*What Happened to Lani Garver, The She, The Night My Sister Went Missing,* and *Streams of Babel*—have all earned much critical acclaim and many awards.

Carol Plum-Ucci grew up on a barrier island off the East Coast and now lives in a seaside community in New Jersey. Visit her online at WWW.CAROLPLUMUCCI.COM.